# MEDICAL

## Life and love in the world of modern medicine.

### Paediatrician's Unexpected Second Chance
Kate Hardy

### Nurse's Twin Baby Surprise
Colette Cooper

## MILLS & BOON

PAEDIATRICIAN'S UNEXPECTED SECOND CHANCE
© 2024 by Pamela Brooks
Philippine Copyright 2024
Australian Copyright 2024
New Zealand Copyright 2024

First Published 2024
First Australian Paperback Edition 2024
ISBN 978 1 038 93896 1

NURSE'S TWIN BABY SURPRISE
© 2024 by Colette Cooper
Philippine Copyright 2024
Australian Copyright 2024
New Zealand Copyright 2024

First Published 2024
First Australian Paperback Edition 2024
ISBN 978 1 038 93896 1

MIX
Paper | Supporting
responsible forestry
FSC® C001695

Published by
Harlequin Mills & Boon
An imprint of Harlequin Enterprises (Australia) Pty Limited
(ABN 47 001 180 918), a subsidiary of HarperCollins
Publishers Australia Pty Limited
(ABN 36 009 913 517)
Level 19, 201 Elizabeth Street
SYDNEY NSW 2000 AUSTRALIA

Cover art used by arrangement with Harlequin Books S.A.. All rights reserved.

Printed and bound in Australia by McPherson's Printing Group

# Paediatrician's Unexpected Second Chance

## Kate Hardy

MILLS & BOON

**Kate Hardy** has always loved books, and could read before she went to school. She discovered Mills & Boon books when she was twelve and decided that this was what she wanted to do. When she isn't writing Kate enjoys reading, cinema, ballroom dancing and the gym. You can contact her via her website: katehardy.com.

For all the readers who've been on this journey
with me for nearly half a lifetime—
thank you for your support. xx

# CHAPTER ONE

'MUM? WHAT HAVE you done to your eye?'

Mandy stifled a groan. If her bloodshot eye was visible to her daughter on a small phone screen, then it was going to be *really* obvious in real life. Just what she didn't need on her first day in her new job. 'I'm fine,' she said. 'I must've sneezed in my sleep, or something, and burst a blood vessel in my eye. It'll go away by itself in three or four days. And, no, it doesn't hurt. Stop fussing.'

'I'm nearly seven months pregnant. I'm *allowed* to fuss,' Gemma said with a grin. 'I'm not going to hold you up. I just wanted to wish you good luck on your first day.' Her grin broadened. 'Mind you, if you go in with a pirate's eye patch, it'll fascinate all the kids. The ones who are crying will stop and ask if you're Captain Hook's sister, and the ones who aren't crying will perk up and ask if you've got a ticking crocodile following you. Or perhaps a parrot for your shoulder.' She squawked meaningfully. 'You could always pretty up an eye patch. Stick on some sequins and some lace. Actually, no—that can be my class's task this morning, to design you an eye patch. The prettier, the better.'

'If I turn up wearing an eye patch covered in sequins, then my new job-share's going to think the hospital's hired someone who either won't take the job seriously, or is trying a bit too hard to get featured on his TV show,' Mandy said drily.

'Ah, yes. Dr Sexy.' Gemma laughed. 'Do you know how many of my colleagues have asked me if you'll give him their phone number?'

Daniel Monroe—Mandy's fellow joint Head of Paediatrics—was also the star of *London Victoria Children's Ward*, a documentary that showed life in the Paediatric Department and the sheer bravery of their young patients. He was the epitome of tall, dark—well, with a fair sprinkling of grey in his hair—and handsome. Add twinkling brown eyes behind his glasses, a slight scruffiness to his haircut that made women want to fuss over him, and the kind of smile that made female pulses beat a lot faster, and it was no wonder that most of the press referred to him as 'the thinking woman's crumpet'.

Every single female of Mandy's acquaintance had given an envious sigh when they found out who was going to be her job-share.

Not that she'd actually met him yet, because Daniel had been laid low by a virus the day before she'd gone for her interview so he'd had to drop out of the interview panel. But the senior nurse who'd taken her round the ward afterwards had told her that Daniel was even nicer to work with than he seemed on the TV. Calm, capable and kind. He respected the nursing team, and he gave junior doctors a chance to blossom.

In short, Daniel Monroe was a dream doctor.

And this was a dream job. Mandy would spend two days a week in charge of training, while Daniel headed up the department; two days a week heading up the department, while Daniel filmed his documentary; and the other day working with Daniel on admin and strategy. Though their separate roles would also have a fair amount of crossover.

She shook herself. 'He's probably very happily married.'

'Nope. He's definitely single,' Gemma corrected. 'Angelica at work checked him out on social media. And I'm under instructions that I'm not to go on maternity leave next month without getting at least one person's telephone number to him.'

'Tell them your mother's difficult and you daren't ask her,' Mandy said.

'Too late. They've met you. They already know you're perfect.'

'Perfect?' Mandy couldn't help laughing. 'Thank you for the compliment, darling, but I'm far from that. I'll settle for being OK.'

'You're more than OK, Mum. You're going to be a brilliant head of department.'

'*Joint* head,' Mandy reminded her.

'Still brilliant,' Gemma insisted. 'I'm proud of you. So's Dev—' her husband '—and so's The Bump.'

Her first grandchild. When had she suddenly become old enough to be a grandmother? She still felt as if she were twenty-five. 'I'm proud of you all, too,' Mandy said.

'Have a fabulous first day, Mum. Dev's cooking a special dinner so you can tell us all about it tonight. Spiced paneer tikka with baby spinach, lemon dhal, and parathas.'

'You know I'm only coming for Dev's dhal, and not to see you or the bump,' Mandy said, her face deadpan.

Gemma gave a rich chuckle. 'Dev's dhal is responsible for the bump.'

Which served her right for teasing. 'TMI!' Mandy said, making exaggerated gestures of horror. 'It's supposed to be my generation making yours cringe, you know, not the other way round.'

'Bring it on,' Gemma said, her eyes sparkling. 'Right, your challenge is to date someone. For the first time in about—well, you'd need a whole library of calendars to calculate how many years it's been since *you* last dated someone.' Worry bubbled up from behind her daughter's teasing. 'Mum. I really hate to think of you being lonely.'

'Of course I'm not lonely,' Mandy said. 'I have you, Dev, the bump-to-be, Aunty Jen, Gran and Linda. I have book club on the first Monday of the month, ballet class on Fridays, and dance aerobics on Tuesday and Thursday. I'll be your permanent babysitter on Wednesdays so you and Dev get a date night every week, and I'm just about to start a new job. Between my family, my social life and work, I don't have *time* to be lonely.'

'That's not what I...' Gemma stopped herself and sighed. 'Love you, Mum.'

'Love you, too,' Mandy said. 'I'll see you tonight.'

'We're eating at seven. Come whenever you like. And have a brilliant, brilliant day.'

Wearing glasses instead of contact lenses meant that Mandy could get away without wearing eye make-up, and hopefully the tortoiseshell frames of her narrow glasses hid some of the redness in her right eye. Thankfully her skin wasn't having a bad menopause day, so a tinted moisturiser and a neutral lip colour were enough to make her look professional.

Her mum and her sister Jen both texted.

Good luck on your first day!

Her best friend Linda sent a picture of a cute spaniel puppy with the message:

You'll be pawsome!

And even the weather was on her side; although it was grey and a bit on the chilly side, a typical October London day, it wasn't raining. She caught the Tube from King's Cross to Victoria, and walking briskly to the hospital meant she didn't feel the cold.

Mandy had to check the hospital map in the reception area to remind herself where the children's ward was. Hopefully it wouldn't take too long before these corridors felt as familiar as those of Muswell Hill, the hospital where she'd worked for the last fifteen years, she thought as she headed down the corridor.

Before she had the chance to start feeling nervous, she pressed the intercom button on the wall outside the ward.

'Good morning. How can I help?' a voice crackled through the grille.

'Good morning. It's Amanda Cooke. I'm starting work here today, so I don't have my staff card yet and I need someone to let me in,' she said.

'Great—we're expecting you. I'll buzz you in. I'm Khaj, one of the nurses. You'll see me as soon as you walk in. I'm updating the whiteboard.'

The door buzzed, and Mandy made sure she closed it again behind her without anyone following her in; security in vulnerable wards was important. She glanced over towards the reception desk and saw a cheerful-looking nurse in scrubs writing names on a whiteboard, which showed which team members were looking after the patients in each bay.

'Welcome to the London Victoria, Ms Cooke,' the nurse said with a smile.

Mandy smiled back. 'Nice to meet you, Khaj. And please call me Mandy.'

'Mandy.' Khaj looked concerned. 'What happened to your eye?'

Oh. So her glasses really weren't enough to hide the redness. It looked as if she was going to be explaining this all day, then. 'Subconjunctival haemorrhage. I woke up with it this morning so I must've sneezed in my sleep,' Mandy said ruefully.

'Poor you,' Khaj said sympathetically.

'My daughter said I should wear an eye patch,' Mandy said. 'I have the nastiest feeling she's going to get her class to design one today. And a five-year-old's idea of an eye patch means I'm definitely going to regret buying that pack of offcuts in the fabric shop for her class's craft box.'

'You sew? Oh, you're definitely going to go down well here,' Khaj said, looking pleased. 'There's a teenager I need to introduce you to later. Now, let's get you loaded up with coffee before I take you through to Daniel.'

'Thank you.' Mandy indicated the bag she was carrying, containing a plastic tub, a box and a bag of apples. 'I brought goodies to say hello to the team. Can I leave them in the staff kitchen?'

'You most certainly can,' Khaj said. 'By the way, your

ID card isn't here yet, but I'll get someone to chase that up for you. In the meantime, just buzz the intercom when you need to be let back in on the ward.'

'Cheers,' Mandy said.

While Khaj made two mugs of coffee—one of which was bright orange and emblazoned with the words 'Dr TWC', which told Mandy that Daniel's colleagues ribbed him mercilessly about his reputation as the Thinking Woman's Crumpet in the media—Mandy put the tub of home-made brownies on the worktop so anyone who walked into the staff kitchen would see them, along with a couple of packets of individually wrapped gluten-free lemon cakes, and some apples for anyone who didn't eat cake. Hopefully she'd covered all dietary requirements and not left anyone out. She left a note on top of the tub:

*Look forward to meeting everyone on the ward. Brownies are egg-free and dairy-free; lemon cakes are GF. Cheers, Mandy*

'Do you know if Mr Monroe would prefer brownies or lemon cake?' she asked.

Khaj laughed. 'Daniel likes anything sweet. He really deserves to be thirty pounds heavier than he is. We'd hate him for being able to scoff cake with impunity, except he's one of the good guys.'

Brownies, Mandy decided, and wrapped one in a piece of paper towel. And it was good to have reassurance that her new job-share partner was well liked.

She followed Khaj down the corridor, and the nurse rapped on an open door. 'Good morning, Dan. Here's your first appointment of the day. Don't dump all your filing on her.'

'As if I'd do something so underhand,' Daniel drawled, looking up from his desk.

Daniel Monroe on screen was a heartthrob; Daniel Monroe in the flesh was utterly gorgeous. And Mandy really hoped her face didn't look as red as her eye, because it certainly felt hot enough.

'You must be Amanda Cooke. Lovely to meet you at last.' His eyes narrowed. 'What did you—?'

'—do to my eye?' she finished wryly. 'I woke up with it this morning. It could've been a cough, a sneeze, carrying a heavy bag—anything.'

'Subconjunctival haemorrhage,' he said with a grimace. 'Sorry. You've probably had to explain it to half a dozen people already.'

'Yes, and no doubt I'll have to do it for the rest of the day. Still, it's a way of breaking the ice. Have a home-made brownie,' Mandy said, and gave him the paper towel containing the cake. 'I made them last night to say hello to the department.'

'You brought in home-made cake on your first day? Oh, I like you already,' he said with a grin. 'Welcome to the department. I think she's a keeper, Khaj,' he added in a stage whisper.

'Don't badger her into doing your filing,' Khaj repeated sternly. 'I'll leave you with him, Mandy.'

'Of course I won't expect you to do my filing,' Daniel said, rolling his eyes when Khaj had left. 'Though I admit I need nagging to do it. I'd rather clean up projectile vomit, poonami diarrhoea or a pus-filled wound than... Well.' He indicated his very full in-tray.

'We all have bits of the job we hate,' Mandy said lightly.

'Welcome to the London Victoria. We use first names

rather than formality here, so may I call you Amanda?'
He stood up and held his hand out.

'Mandy,' she said, taking his hand and shaking it. His
handshake was firm and dry, but his smile disconcerted
her because it really did make her heart feel as if it had
just throbbed. She hadn't felt a pull of attraction like this
to someone in years, and she was going to have to get
a firm grip on that reaction. He was her new colleague,
and—even though she knew he was single—she wasn't
looking for any relationship other than a professional one.
She'd learned the hard way that charm was usually part-
nered with unreliability, and she wasn't going to forget it.

Oh, help. Amanda Cooke's handshake was firm and professional, but her skin was warm and soft—and it made
Dan feel all quivery. The kind of quiver he hadn't felt towards anyone in a very long time, because he always kept
his relationships light and fluffy and very, very short.
And that meant not dating anyone he worked with.

This woman could be seriously dangerous to his peace
of mind.

He shook himself mentally. Talk about an inappropriate reaction—and it was bad timing as well.

*Focus*, he told himself. *She's your new job-share.
You've just met her. You don't want her to think you're
a total numpty.*

'Everyone calls me Dan,' he said. 'Sorry I didn't meet
you at your interview.'

'I completely understand. They told me you'd gone
down with a virus,' she said.

'The usual occupational hazard of working in Paediatrics,' he said with a rueful smile. 'I probably could have

dosed myself up and dragged myself in, but I didn't want everyone who'd been in the same room as me to feel grim as I did, the next morning.'

'That's considerate,' she said. 'Thank you.'

He looked at her. 'I thought we'd take today to settle you in and plan workloads. I've been muddling along for a while; it's going to be so much better for the team having you here. Obviously the ward needs one of us in charge while the other one's teaching or filming, and we need a day together to make sure we iron out any issues that crop up and deal with the suits, plus share the on-call rota at weekends. I normally film on Thursday and Friday when we're working on a series—the new one starts next week—but we can move things round if that doesn't work with your teaching commitments. And I thought we could alternate weekends on call; we can always swap if one of us has something special on.'

She looked surprised, as if she'd expected him to dictate the schedule to her. 'That all works fine for me,' she said.

'Good. And please don't feel awkward about the TV stuff. If you've got an interesting case, I'd be delighted to look at including it on the show; but if you'd rather avoid the cameras completely, that's also fine.' He indicated the orange mug with a sigh. 'As you can see, the team won't let me get away with trying to be a luvvie. That was last year's Secret Santa present. I still can't work out who got it for me; I think they were all in cahoots because they all *really* enjoyed watching me open it.' He grinned. 'But I'll forgive them for teasing, because they also filled it with caramel chocolates.'

'Chocolate's the way to your heart? I'll remember that.'

Daniel really hoped that he didn't look as red and flustered as he felt. Because the glint in her lovely brown eyes made him imagine lying against a pillow while she fed him squares of caramel-filled chocolate, teasing him by rubbing it along his lower lip and then holding it just out of reach and demanding a kiss before she handed over the chocolate...

Oh, for pity's sake. He was fifty-five, not fifteen. Fantasies like that shouldn't be filling his head, particularly in work hours. Despite her red eye, Mandy looked completely cool, calm and professional: which was what he needed to be, too. Preferably right now.

'Let me introduce you to the team,' he said. 'Then we'll grab something to drink—the canteen here does decent coffee—and we can talk about your teaching, training plans for the staff here, and work out our schedules.'

'Sounds good to me,' she said.

Daniel was as good as his word, introducing Mandy to the whole team—from the most junior health care assistant up to the senior consultants. Not only was he on first-name terms with everyone, it was clear from the way he talked that he actually knew all the staff and what mattered to them. They all seemed to bloom in his presence. The patients, too, all had a smile for Dr Dan, whether they were an out-of-sorts toddler or a grumpy teenager.

Perhaps she'd been unfair to him, assuming that his charm meant he was like all the other charming but shallow men she'd met; maybe there really was depth underneath Daniel's surface allure.

Finally, they went into the Paediatric Intensive Care Unit. 'Mo, this is Amanda Cooke, who's sharing the Head of Department role with me,' he said, introducing her to the consultant on the unit. 'Mandy, this is Mohammed Singh, our paediatric intensive care specialist.'

'Nice to meet you—and please call me Mandy,' she said, shaking Mo's hand. 'I'd like to have a meeting with you at some point in the week to discuss training, whenever works for you, to talk about the new intake of students at the university and what we can offer them here. Plus I'd like to know what your team's needs are so I can make sure they're covered.'

'That sounds good,' he said. 'Nice to meet you, too, Mandy.' He looked at Daniel. 'I'm glad you're here, Dan, because I've got a potential case for your show. Though it's a tricky one and I haven't got a firm diagnosis at the moment.'

'That's unusual for you. Want to pick our brains?' Daniel asked.

'Definitely,' Mo said. 'I'll give you the background: the Emergency Department sent eight-month-old Noah Carmichael up to us this morning. His parents took him to the walk-in centre yesterday because he seemed lethargic, was a bit constipated and wasn't feeding well. His mum also thought his cry sounded funny and a bit weaker than normal. The GP told them to keep a close eye on him and bring him to the Emergency Department here if he got any worse. They didn't sleep much last night, worrying about him, and about five o'clock this morning the mum went in to check on him and discovered he was floppy. They rushed him straight here.'

From years of experience, Mandy knew that very young children could become very unwell, very quickly, and a floppy baby usually meant the little one was really poorly. 'Good call,' she said. 'Does he have any other symptoms?'

'That's where it gets weird,' Mo said. 'He's drooling, his eyelids are droopy and his pupils are a bit sluggish. I was thinking it might be some kind of cerebral virus, except he hasn't got even a hint of a fever.'

'So it's unlikely to be one of the usual viruses, then,' Daniel said, frowning.

'There are signs of bulbar palsies,' Mo added. Bulbar palsies were a set of clinical conditions that occurred when the lower cranial nerves were damaged, possibly by a stroke or a tumour. 'There's also moderate hypotonia.'

Muscle weakness, Mandy thought. The baby was constipated, drooling, not feeding, and had droopy eyelids. No fever. Mo was right; it was an odd set of symptoms. With a virus, she would've expected a fever. But something rang a bell in the back of her head.

'We've intubated him and put him in an induced coma while we run some more tests,' Mo said. 'Starting with a CT scan to see if there's anything obvious causing the bulbar palsies. That's where he is at the moment. He's due back on the ward any minute now.'

'Were there any complications with the birth?' Daniel asked.

'No. Labour and birth were both as standard as it gets, and he's been between the fiftieth and sixtieth centile on all the development charts all the way along,' Mo said. 'His parents didn't have a thing to worry about until yesterday.'

'You mentioned hypotonia. Is there any evidence of paralysis, especially if it's symmetrical and heading downwards?' Mandy asked. 'And do his facial features look flattened at all?'

'His face does look a bit flat, yes,' Mo said. 'Paralysis... obviously he's in an induced coma at the moment, but that's a good point.'

'What are you thinking, Mandy?' Daniel asked.

'It's something a friend came across when she did a couple of years on a job-swap in America,' Mandy said. 'It's really rare here in England, but I think we might be talking about infant botulism.'

'That's so rare I've only ever read about it in medical journals,' Daniel said. 'I've never actually seen a case.'

'Me neither,' Mo said. 'And I've been qualified for twenty years.'

'I haven't seen one myself, either,' Mandy said. 'But this sounds really like the case my friend told me about. If someone's given Noah some honey, he might have swallowed *Clostridium botulinum* spores.'

'In an adult or a baby over the age of one, those spores would go through the digestive system too quickly to cause a problem. But Noah's digestive system is still immature, so the spores would've had time to colonise his large intestine and produce botulinum neurotoxin,' Daniel said thoughtfully.

'Which affect the nerve endings—and that would account for the hypotonia and bulbar palsies,' Mandy agreed.

'Given the other differential diagnoses, I'm not sure if that makes me feel more or less worried,' Mo said. 'The Carmichaels seem pretty switched on, the sort who read every parenting book and magazine going. I can't imagine they would've allowed anyone to give their infant son honey, not when all the health visitors and GPs are so clear with the message about not giving honey to babies under the age of one.'

'They might not have been the ones to give it to him. If a well-meaning older friend or relative took the view that they'd had honey as a baby and it hadn't hurt them, so it wouldn't hurt Noah…' Daniel spread his hands. 'Then his parents wouldn't have known anything about it until it was too late.'

'We need to get a stool sample to the lab,' Mandy said. 'And, if I'm right, we'll need to start treating him with antitoxin.' She grimaced. 'The only thing is, because infant botulism is so rare over here, it's unlikely that any of the hospitals in this country has a stock of infant antitoxin. We certainly didn't have any at Muswell Hill.'

'Where's likely to have it?' Mo asked.

'The head of Pharmacy will know—or at least know where to check,' Daniel said.

'Worst-case scenario, we'll have to ask the pharmacy to talk to the public health department in California, and have the antitoxin couriered here and expedited through Customs,' Mandy said. 'What I do know is that it could take a few days to get the lab results back, and we can't wait for them. The quicker we can start the treatment, the quicker Noah will recover.'

'Including from the paralysis?' Mo asked.

'Yes, but it could take a while, depending on how long it takes for his nerve endings to grow again,' Mandy warned. 'Can we talk to his parents?'

'Of course. They're waiting in the relatives' room while Noah's having his scan,' Mo said. 'I'll introduce you.'

As Mo introduced them to Lucy and Rob Carmichael,

Mandy thought Noah's parents both looked worn out with worry, their faces pallid with dark shadows smudged beneath their eyes. And what she was about to tell them was a parent's worst nightmare.

'Hang on—aren't you the doctor off that telly programme?' Rob asked, looking at Daniel.

'Yes, but I'm also a qualified senior doctor who works here, so please don't worry about the TV presenter stuff,' Daniel said. He gave them both a reassuring smile. 'Mo's told us about your son, and you did absolutely the right thing bringing Noah here when you were concerned.'

Rob looked miserable. 'He's so poorly. Dr Singh had to put him in a coma, and nobody seems to know what's making Noah sick.'

'We're running tests to rule some things out, and the CT scan will hopefully give us a better idea of what might be causing Noah's symptoms,' Daniel said gently. 'The three of us have been talking about his symptoms, and my colleague Mandy might have worked out what the problem is.'

'It's a strange question, but is there any chance that someone might have given Noah honey or any kind of preserved food in the last couple of days?' Mandy asked.

'Honey?' Lucy looked shocked. 'Of course not. You're not supposed to give a baby honey because it might make them ill.'

Exactly what Mo had suggested Noah's mum's response would be. But Daniel had also had a suggestion about where the honey might have come from. 'We were wondering, could someone else have given him anything with honey in it? A cookie or a piece of cake, maybe?' Mandy asked. 'Something that somebody made at home, perhaps, or maybe from a toddler group bake sale? And Mo said it was yesterday he started being ill, so maybe he ate something on Friday or Saturday that started affecting him yesterday?'

'He was with us on Saturday,' Lucy said. 'But on Fridays, we both work and my mum has him for the day. She takes him to a baby music class and they both love it because a few other grannies go, too.' Her eyes widened in horror. 'If one of them brought in some home-made snacks and sweetened them with honey instead of sugar, thinking it was healthier...'

'Your mum dotes on Noah,' Rob said. 'You know she'd never willingly let anything happen to him.'

'I'll call her now,' Lucy said. 'Do I need to go into the corridor to use my phone? You know, so it doesn't interfere with any of the equipment?'

'You're fine in here,' Mo said. 'We'll give you both some space.'

Ten minutes later, Lucy came out of the relatives' room with Rob holding her hand and tears running down her cheeks. 'Mum says she went to her friend's for lunch after the class, and Noah ate half a cookie there. It never occurred to her to ask what was in it—Mum didn't eat one because she's on a diet—but it's the only thing she can think of that might've had honey in it. She rang her friend to ask her, and Mum just called me back to say yes, there was honey instead of sugar in the cookies.' She dragged in a breath. 'What's in honey that's made Noah ill like this?'

'Not *all* honey,' Mandy said, 'but some raw honey has been shown to contain botulin spores.'

*'Botulin?'* Rob looked horrified. 'But that kills people, doesn't it? Are you telling us that Noah's going to die?'

'No. He should make a full recovery, over the next couple of months,' Daniel said. 'A century ago, you're right, the outcome wouldn't have been so good; but thankfully medicine has advanced in this area. We can get some special infant antitoxin for him. We're going to talk to the pharmacy now, because we think it'll have to be shipped here from abroad.'

Lucy's eyes widened. 'Why isn't there any of this antitoxin stuff in a London hospital?'

'It's not a stock item because infant botulism is really rare in this country. It's less rare in America, so we'll contact the public health team in California that produces the antitoxin,' Mandy explained. 'We're going to test Noah's stools for the bacteria, but the lab results might take a few days. We won't wait for the results before we start treating him. The clinical diagnosis makes a lot of sense where his symptoms are concerned. Basically, the toxin stops the nerve endings telling the muscles to contract, so the first symptoms of the illness will be the baby finding it hard to suck or swallow, and being a bit constipated—which is what you reported.'

'Plus it doesn't cause a fever,' Mo said.

'This thing with the nerve endings—is that why Noah's floppy?' Lucy asked.

'Yes, and it's also why he might have trouble breathing,' Daniel said. 'We'll keep him in the coma for now, to keep him comfortable and support his breathing. It'll take him a little while to recover, because the nerve endings need to regrow before they can send the right signals to his muscles; we'll need to give him support for breathing and feeding until he can do it himself, but over the next few weeks he'll get better.'

'And it won't affect him…the way he develops?' Rob asked.

'The toxin doesn't go into his brain or anything like that. He'll develop completely normally,' Mandy said. 'The only thing that will need to be delayed a bit are his immunisations, until six months after we've treated him, because the antitoxin would interfere with the live virus vaccinations—that's the MMR and varicella. We'll make sure your GP and health visitor know.'

'So he's going to be all right?' Lucy asked.

'He's going to be all right,' Mo confirmed.

'Thank God,' Lucy whispered. 'But right now I don't think I want Mum to look after him ever again.'

'It wasn't done deliberately, and your mum wasn't to know,' Daniel said gently. 'Remember, you're *her* baby, and my guess is she'll be in bits at the idea of being responsible for something that hurt your baby and therefore hurt you. Don't be too hard on her.'

'But if Dr Cooke here hadn't realised what it was, Noah might've become too ill to be treated,' Rob said. 'He might have…' He shook his head, clearly unable or unwilling to voice his deepest fears.

'I'm going to be a grannie in a few weeks' time,' Mandy said, 'and Dr Monroe's absolutely right in what he said. If I inadvertently do anything that hurts my daughter's baby, I'll never forgive myself for that—or for the pain and worry I caused my daughter. Your mum will be hugely upset about this, Lucy.'

'I don't have children,' Daniel added, 'but I have nieces and nephews, and I feel the same way about them.'

Something in his expression, quickly hidden, made Mandy wonder what he wasn't saying. Had it been his choice not to have children? Not that it was any of her business.

'You'll see Noah recover a little bit more every day,' Mo said. 'He'll need to be in hospital for a few weeks yet, but you can have as much involvement as you like in his care. The nurses will help you set up a routine. You'll be able to give him baths, feed him and cuddle him. Though for the next three months or so you'll need to be super-strict about handwashing after you've changed his nappy, because the toxins will come out in his faeces. If you've got an open cut on your hands, I'd wear gloves when you change him, to make sure the bacteria doesn't spread to you.'

'So we could catch it from Noah?' Rob asked.

'With an open wound, yes. But it won't affect you in the same way,' Mo said.

Once the Carmichaels were reassured that Noah would still be poorly for a little while but was going to make a good recovery, Daniel took Mandy to meet the pharmacy team.

'Baby botulism antitoxin? We'll definitely have to talk to California for that,' Navreen, the head of Pharmacy, said. 'Actually, this'll be good training for my team, because we haven't got well-established processes for getting something like this from abroad. We'll need to coordinate authorisation and Customs.'

'But you can definitely do it?' Mandy asked.

'We've done it a couple of times in the past. The systems have probably changed since the last time we did it; but don't worry, we'll get it sorted.' Navreen glanced at Daniel. 'Is this case going on your show?'

'Maybe,' Daniel said. 'I need to talk to the baby's mum and dad about it, but I think they could do with a bit of time to come to terms with what's happening before I ask their permission.'

Navreen nodded. 'If they say yes, we're happy for you to film here, too.'

'Great. Thank you.' He smiled at her. 'It'd be good to showcase other bits of the hospital, so the audience realises how wide our team is.' He gave her a hammy wink. 'Not just Dr Charming showing off and hogging the screen.'

Navreen laughed. 'Dan, we all know you're not like that.' She checked something on her computer. 'I was about to say the bad news is, we're eight hours ahead of California and we'll have to wait to get hold of them; but the good news is that their helpline is twenty-four-seven and we can call them now.' She glanced back at her screen. 'Though it looks as if you'll have to talk to their doctors about your clinical findings before they'll agree to let us have the antitoxin.'

'We can do that. Let's make the call,' Daniel said.

# CHAPTER TWO

'WELL, THAT WAS a baptism of fire,' Daniel said, two hours later, finding them a quiet table in the hospital canteen and sliding the tray of their sandwiches and coffee onto it.

'At least now there's a procedure in place, if we ever get another patient with those symptoms,' Mandy said, 'even if it ends up needing to be tweaked in the future. The lab's extracting the toxins and culturing the faeces so we can isolate the bacteria, the public health authority is sending us the antitoxin, and we've got all the legal permissions in place to get it through Customs quickly.'

'And we can start treating baby Noah later today.' He took a sip of his coffee and closed his eyes briefly. 'Ahh. Just what I needed.' He opened his eyes again and looked at her. 'You said earlier that you're going to be a grandmother?'

'I don't really feel old enough,' she said. 'But, when I look at it logically, Gemma's almost the same age I was when I had her.'

'Are you and your partner looking forward to the baby?' Oh, way to go, Daniel, he thought. Why not make it obvious that you're fishing? He blew out a breath. 'Sorry. That was intrusive and it's none of my business.'

'It's fine. Actually, there's just me,' she said.

Did that mean she was a widow? Divorced? Was Gemma's father not involved in her life at all? Not that he could ask. He'd already been pushy enough. And why was he so intrigued by her, in any case? He pushed the thought aside.

'And, yes, I'm looking forward to the baby arriving. Ten weeks, if he or she is on time.' Mandy raised an eyebrow. 'But you and I both know from experience that babies arrive when they're ready, and not when a calendar says they're supposed to.'

'Don't they just?' He couldn't help smiling at her. 'I remember my sister being furious when she went overdue with her first, and she got crosser by the day. In the end, she had to be induced. And even at the age of twenty-five my nephew's still very laid-back.'

'Have you got many nieces and nephews?' she asked.

'Four—my brother and sister both had one of each,' he said.

'You weren't tempted?' And then her face turned bright pink. 'Sorry. That was nosey. I apologise.'

He'd wanted children, all right. But he hadn't wanted to risk them turning out like him.

*Like his father.*

Not that he was going to tell Mandy any of that. He hadn't told anyone about those feelings, not even his mum and his siblings. 'You and I have only just met. How are we going to know anything about each other, unless we ask?' And if she asked him questions, he could ask her, too…

'That's true,' she said. 'Although I could say I know you from your TV show.'

'Tricky,' he said. 'If I say I'm just like I am on TV, that sounds a bit vain—and I can assure you, I'm not vain. The production team are forever waving a comb at me.' Though his sister teased him that having messy hair just attracted women who wanted to mother him. 'On the other hand, if I say I'm nothing like I am on TV, that makes me someone who can put on a false persona at will—which also isn't true.'

'The truth is that, like most people, you're somewhere in between,' she said. 'I admit, I assumed you were charming, like you are on the TV—and my mum's very fond of saying that charming is as charming does.'

Interestingly, Mandy's face went a little bit tight as she quoted her mum. So did she agree? Had she been hurt by someone charming—the father of her daughter, perhaps? 'We work in an area,' Daniel said, 'where the parents of our patients can get very, very anxious, very, very quickly. We need to be charming so we can put them at their ease and stop the panic spiralling enough for them to be able to breathe, think and listen to us. Then they can make an informed decision about their child's treatment, and let us get on with doing our job and making their child better.' He spread his hands. 'What's the use of a doctor who can't make eye contact, mumbles and sits with his back to the patient or their parents, tapping notes into a computer?'

'Much better to listen to the patients and their parents and look at them, so you can assess what kind of approach works best for them,' she said. 'That's not being charming. It's using your skills to do the best by your patient and showing them they can trust you.'

'I think they're one and the same,' he said. 'Is your

definition of charming something that's surface and has no substance?'

'Yes,' she said.

He grinned. 'That's my definition of a politician.'

'You'll get no arguments from me, there,' she said.

Had her ex been a politician? he wondered. 'Well, I'm not a politician. In fact, you might have to kick me under my desk before a meeting with the suits and remind me that I have to play nice.'

'When really you're dying to ask why they need an antique desk instead of a perfectly serviceable flatpack desk, and point out that the price difference could go towards equipment to help our patients,' she said. 'If I kick you for that, you'll have to kick me as well.'

'A woman after my own heart—as well as being a bringer of brownies. We're going to get on fine as job-shares,' he said.

'Even if I turn up wearing an eye patch with sequins tomorrow?'

'Like a pirate?' He couldn't help laughing. '"Dr Cooke" rhymes with "Captain Hook", you know.'

She groaned. 'I walked straight into that one, didn't I?'

'You're seriously going to have a sequinned eye patch tomorrow?'

'Gemma's planning to do it as the craft session at school today—at least, that's what she threatened, this morning. She teaches Reception class,' Mandy explained with a smile.

Clearly they had a close relationship, and he pushed down the little twinge of envy. He'd made his decision, years ago, and he knew it had been the right one. Even if he did feel sometimes that he'd missed out.

'So what else did you want to ask me?' she asked.

'We could always start with the one everyone uses at conferences—what made you pick your specialty?'

'Paediatrics was my favourite rotation. I like how quickly children respond to treatment and start getting better,' she said promptly. 'You?'

'Same,' he said. 'I nearly stayed with obstetrics, because that moment when a new life comes into the world is so special. But generally the jokes from our patients are more on my level.' He raised his eyebrows at her. 'Why did the bicycle lean against the wall?'

'Do your worst, Dr Monroe,' she said, putting her hands on her hips and fixing him with an amused stare.

'Because it was two-tyred.' He mimed playing drums and crashing a cymbal.

She groaned and then laughed, and Daniel realised just how pretty she was. It felt as if she'd just lit up the room, and it caused another of those weird swoopy feelings in his stomach.

'Can I pass that one on to Gemma for her class?' she asked.

'Be my guest. And I'm all ears if you have a secret stash of bad jokes,' he added.

'The cheesier, the "grater"?' she asked.

He grinned. That terrible pun made him like her even more. 'It'd Brie rude not to share,' he said back.

Her eyes crinkled at the corners. 'I suppose it's Feta to let you have the last word.'

'That'd be really Gouda,' he said, unable to help himself.

This was work. They were meant to be talking about

serious things. But everything about Amanda Cooke made him want to smile and have fun.

'I think we've done enough cheese jokes,' she said, though he rather thought she sounded rueful instead of bossy. 'What made you become a TV doctor?'

'I fell into it pretty much by accident,' he admitted. 'A friend volunteered me to help another friend with the pitch she was writing for the series—telling her about the kind of cases we treat here. She got a slot for the pitch and asked me to go to the studio with her to answer questions on the medical side. At the end of the pitch, the producer said I had a good voice for TV. The next thing I knew, I was talking to the CEO of the London Victoria about whether we'd be prepared to film the show here, and if I could fit filming round my job.'

'Clearly the answer was yes, as it's been running for five years now,' she said.

'I've been lucky,' he said. 'I never expected to enjoy it so much. And the best bit for me is getting letters from viewers—when someone's been really struggling to get a diagnosis for their child, sees a similar case on the show, and then puts it all together and finally manages to get the help they need. Hearing that the show's been able to make a real difference to a child's health is just brilliant.'

'Is that why you showcase case studies with common conditions as well as the rarer ones?' she asked.

'Definitely. We always have a bronchiolitis case in every series. I remember my first winter as a junior doctor in Paediatrics; I walked in one morning to see a whole bay of poorly babies all on oxygen therapy, with a laminated note on their door warning "RSV+"—it really shocked me, especially when the nurses told me I needed to use extra protective clothing before I went in to check them on my ward round, so I didn't spread the virus to the rest of the ward. That hadn't even occurred to me. And seeing them all struggling...' He grimaced. 'It's always harder for the tinier ones.'

'Because their airways are so small, they get gummed up more quickly and they're also more likely to develop pneumonia,' Mandy agreed. 'And it's really scary for the parents when their baby's too tired to feed and they need feeding through a nasogastric tube.'

'I've had letters from people who were sure their baby had more than just a bad cold, but at the same time they didn't want to bother the doctor with something trivial. Thanks to the show, they could see what intercostal recession actually looked like, and it prompted them to take the baby to their family doctors and get the right help,' he said. 'And it's also comforting to parents who are worried sick about their baby being on oxygen therapy and fed through a nasogastric tube; the show reassures them that it's standard treatment, loads of babies get the virus every year, and they really will get better.'

'I'm all for reassurance,' she said.

He'd already gathered that. It was another one of the things he really liked about his new colleague. He'd never felt so in tune with anyone in his life.

Daniel opened his mouth to ask her if maybe she'd like to have dinner with him, and thankfully stopped himself just in time. Was he insane? They'd only just met. Asking her to dinner would send completely the wrong message. He didn't believe in relationships and it really wouldn't be a good idea to have a fling with his new job-share.

The last thing they needed was things to become awkward between them, which of course they would when the fling was over.

He'd simply have to keep his usual pleasant, professional distance from her and damp down that flare of attraction he felt, because it couldn't go anywhere.

Instead, he switched the conversation back to a safe topic: work, and her training plans. 'So how did you end up teaching?'

'Pure accident. I stepped in for a colleague who was off sick and hated the training aspect of the job in any case because he didn't have much patience with students. I discovered I loved it—I enjoyed their energy and enthusiasm, and they all liked the way I worked with them. They asked me quietly if there was any chance I could keep teaching them when my colleague came back. I had a chat with my colleague and he agreed. It worked for all of us.'

Daniel wasn't surprised her students had responded to her in that way. Just from seeing the way she'd interacted with the team in the intensive care unit and the pharmacy, he'd realised she was supportive and enabling. 'That's so good when that happens,' Daniel said. 'I love the energy and enthusiasm of students, too. And I never mind questions, either; we've all been in a place where we don't have a clue. And I'd much rather someone asked me the same question ten times than panicked, guessed and got it wrong.' He glanced at his watch. 'We need to get back. And hopefully by now the estates team have put another desk and computer in our office, which was supposed to happen last week, and your staff card's turned up.'

\* \* \*

Mandy left the hospital after her shift with a smile on her face. She liked her new colleagues and the way the team worked together.

The only thing that worried her was her reaction to Daniel Monroe. She'd found herself instantly connecting with him—they shared similar values and a similar sense of humour. She'd liked the way he'd reassured the Carmichaels, supported Mo and clearly had a good working relationship with the pharmacy team. He was a dream colleague.

*But.*

She'd also found herself reacting to him as a woman. Responding to his warmth and charm. Even though she'd learned the hard way from her marriage that charm was the flip side of unreliability and selfishness, her libido had practically sat up and begged at the first smile from Dr TWC.

And that made him dangerous.

Her smile faded.

Even if he was interested—and by no means was she going to assume that the attraction she felt towards him was mutual—she didn't have room in her life for a relationship. When Gemma was small, Mandy had been too busy to date, unable to find the time between the demands of parenting and the crazy hours of a junior doctor. By the time Gemma was a teenager, Mandy had learned how to deflect the question before it was even asked, and made it clear to any seemingly interested male that the only relationship she was interested in was friendship. But now…?

Now, she'd just need to make sure those defences stayed in place whenever she was around Daniel.

On the way to Gemma's, she texted her mum, her sister and her best friend to confirm that her first day had been fabulous and she'd got on well with all her new colleagues.

Her sister texted back.

What about the sexy TV doctor?

Mandy replied firmly.

Nice guy and will be a good colleague.

She answered her mum's and best friend's questions in the same vein.

And then it was time to face Gemma.

'Mum, your eye looks so *sore*.' Gemma hugged her.

'I'm fine,' Mandy said lightly. 'Something smells delicious, Dev.'

Her son-in-law smiled. 'Perfect timing. Dinner's ready in five minutes.'

'Something for you, Mum.' Gemma gave her a small parcel wrapped in tissue paper.

Mandy groaned, pretty sure she knew what was in it: and, just as she suspected, when she opened it she found a pink eye patch covered with silver sequins and bordered with lace.

'My class wants a picture of you in your white coat, wearing it,' Gemma said.

'I don't wear a white coat,' Mandy said. 'But all right,

I'll take it to work tomorrow and take a selfie with this and my stethoscope.'

'Atta-Mum,' Gemma said. 'Seriously, tell me all about your day.'

'Wait for me!' Dev called from the kitchen. 'I'm dishing up now.'

Over dinner, Mandy told them about her day.

'Does this mean you might end up on TV, too?' Dev asked.

'Possibly,' Mandy said.

'That's cool,' Devi said.

'And what's Dr Monroe like in the flesh?' Gemma asked.

'Calm, capable and kind,' Mandy said.

Gemma raised an eyebrow. 'You're blushing.'

'Don't be ridiculous,' Mandy said, even though she could feel the colour seeping into her face.

'So he's as gorgeous in real life as he is on the screen?'

'Like a lot of actors are,' Mandy said. 'Except Dan's a proper doctor.'

Gemma eyed her thoughtfully. 'You know, if he's a nice guy and he's single, you think he's attractive and he likes you too—and of course he'll like you, because you're the loveliest person I know—there's no reason why you can't date him.'

'I can tell you one, straight off: he's my colleague,' Mandy said.

'Plenty of people meet at work,' Dev said. 'It's not a barrier.'

'I don't have time,' Mandy said.

'Maybe you need to make time, Mum,' Gemma said gently.

'I'm happy with the family and friends I already have. I don't need a relationship,' Mandy protested.

Yet the idea lodged in her head, and despite trying to ignore it she found herself thinking about Daniel all the way home.

Even if he was as attracted to her as she was to him, dating him wouldn't be sensible.

But she'd spent a lifetime being sensible. And, even though she'd refused to admit it to Gemma, she did have moments where she felt lonely. Moments when she wished she had someone to share her life with. Even if it was only for a little while.

She'd see how things went, this week. And then maybe...

By the end of the week, Mandy felt as if she'd been working at the London Victoria for ever. Baby Noah was still in Intensive Care and still needed support for his breathing, but the antitoxin had arrived safely from America and his treatment had started. Khaj had introduced her to Hayley, the teenager with cystic fibrosis who loved sewing, and Mandy had brought in a complicated embroidery pattern for Hayley and taught her the stiches during her lunchbreak. She was really enjoying working with her students—and with Daniel. He was more than just the charming doctor he seemed to be on the television; he really did care about their patients. So maybe he was the exception: a charming man who was actually reliable.

'Are you doing anything nice tonight?' he asked on Friday afternoon, when they were both finalising the last bits of paperwork towards the end of their shift.

'Yes—it's my ballet class on Fridays,' she said with a smile. 'It's the highlight of my week.'

He tipped his head to one side. 'Thinking about it, you

do move like a dancer. Graceful,' he said. 'I can just see you in a—not a tutu, but one of those floaty long skirts.'

Mandy felt tell-tale heat flood into her cheeks. 'Thank you. The class is for older adult beginners; I've been doing it for four years, now. Having to remember the choreography's really good for my synapses.'

'It's good for flexibility and balance, too,' Daniel said. 'Plus mental health—if you're concentrating on the movement, you don't have headspace to think about anything else and you can switch off.'

'I always feel lighter of spirit, afterwards,' she admitted. 'The way you just talked about it, it sounds as if you do ballet classes, too?'

'No. I count reps in the gym, which does the same sort of thing for my mental health,' he said. 'Obviously the music I use in the gym's a bit faster, but I listen to ballet music when I want to chill out. And I've been known to accompany someone to the ballet.'

Of course he had. Probably a prima ballerina, she thought. Someone as gorgeous as Daniel would always have a beautiful companion.

It must've been written in her expression, because he said, 'My youngest niece, for her sixth birthday,' he said. 'I took Daisy and my sister to see a matinee of *The Nutcracker*. She was spellbound—I wasn't sure what I enjoyed watching most, the show or the sheer joy on her face.'

Yet again he'd wrongfooted her. This wasn't about him being a celebrity dating another celebrity; it was about family. 'That's a lovely thing to do.'

'I take my duties as an uncle very seriously. I want to be part of their lives and spend proper time with them, doing things they love,' he said. 'Whether it's an afternoon at the park, pushing them on a swing, reading a gazillion stories, making cupcakes with glitter sprinkles or a big birthday treat like going to the ballet. Or sitting drinking a glass of wine with them, now they're older.'

The fact he'd enjoyed spending time with the children in his family really struck a chord with her: it was just as she'd done with Gemma. 'Making memories is important,' she said. 'How old are they now?'

'Daisy's twenty-two; she started off studying medicine, but she really hated it and she switched to train in music therapy, which suits her a lot better. Her brother James is twenty-five; he's an archaeologist and still likes dragging me mudlarking on a Sunday morning, if the tide's right,' he said, smiling fondly. 'Milo, my brother's son, is also twenty-five; he's in software development and loves gadgets, and his elder sister Hannah is twenty-eight and has just qualified as a GP.'

He sounded as proud of them as if they were his own children; to her secret delight, he took out his phone and scrolled through some snaps before handing it to her. 'That's them after Daisy's graduation.'

The photograph was of four young adults, all dressed up and with their arms around each other, with a background of a flower wall. 'That's lovely.'

'We had dinner with them; then they all went off clubbing with Daisy's mates while we went back to Ally's—Daisy's mum's—for champagne and cheese.'

'That sounds like what we did for Gemma's graduation. A family meal out to celebrate, then sending her off for cocktails and clubbing with her friends.' She smiled. 'Are you doing anything special, this weekend?'

'Supper and a grilling at my parents' place, tomorrow night, with the whole family,' he said cheerfully. 'They'll want to know all about my new job-share, and if she might be suitable for sharing more than my job.'

Mandy's eyes widened. 'Seriously?'

'I'm very tempted to tease them and tell them you're a goddess and I've begged you on my bended knees to date me, but you're utterly heartless and won't take pity on me.' He grinned. 'But I'll resist the temptation, because I know that'd blow up in my face. My sister and my sister-in-law would make an excuse to drop in and grill you as to exactly what you think's wrong with me and why you haven't accepted a date with me. So I'll just tell them the truth. It feels as if you've always been part of the team, you brought in home-made cake on your first day and I'm rather hoping that's going to be a Monday morning thing in the future, and you're absolutely not in the market for hanging around with a reprobate like me.'

She wasn't quite sure how to react to that. Being single, did he get the same worried inquisition that she did from her own family about when she was going to settle down, and he was making light of it? Was he teasing about wanting to maybe date her? Or had he secretly been thinking the same thing that she had—that her new colleague was very easy on the eye, made the day feel brighter, and over this last week she'd discovered that she really looked forward to coming into work and seeing him?

'Don't forget to tell them that I have a better stock of terrible jokes than you do,' she said, deciding to take it all as teasing.

'That's rampant cheating, because your daughter teaches Reception class and that gives you an unfair advantage,' he retorted. 'But I suppose you have a point. What about you—are you seeing your family at the weekend?'

'My best friend goes to ballet class with me, and I'm seeing my mum and my sister tomorrow for dinner,' she said. 'They'll all want to know if you're the same in real life as you are on TV. I'll tell them that you're probably better, because you always listen to the nurses and you've got time for the patients and their parents.'

'That's nice,' he said. 'Better than I am on TV. I like that.' His eyes glittered. 'Seems that we have quite a mutual admiration society going on here.'

They did. But it wasn't going anywhere further than friendship.

'Well, have a lovely weekend, Ms Cooke,' he said.

'You, too, Mr Monroe.' She sketched him a bow.

# CHAPTER THREE

'DAN, ARE YOU ever going to settle down?' his sister asked, pushing a dish of apple crumble in his direction and indicating to him to add his own custard.

'I'm already settled, Ally,' he said, giving her his sweetest smile. 'If I went any higher at the hospital, I'd be stuck in a suit's job doing nothing but meetings and never seeing a patient, which isn't why I became a doctor. I love my job just as it is. Plus I've lived in the same house for ten years. I don't think I can get more settled than that.'

She narrowed her eyes at him. 'You know what I mean. It's half a lifetime since you split up with Roxy.'

'I'm too busy to date, between the hospital and the TV show and spending time with my favourite people—which, strangely enough, is you lot, despite all the nagging,' he said lightly.

'What about your new colleague? Is she nice?' Sasha, his sister-in-law, put in.

'You mean, is she available?' He rolled his eyes. 'I knew you'd all start. I told Mandy exactly what you'd say—and I'll tell you what I told her. It feels as if she's always been part of the team, she brought in home-made chocolate cake on her first day to introduce herself to everyone, and even if I was in the market for a relation-ship, she's not.'

'She's married, then.' His mother looked disappointed.

Not any more, but they didn't need to know that. He looked at his brother and brother-in-law. 'Um, a little male solidarity, here, please, guys? Call them off?'

'You're on your own, mate,' Jake, his brother-in-law, said.

'It's more than my life's worth,' Colin, his brother, added.

'Scandalous,' Daniel said, sighing, and poured custard over his apple crumble. 'Now, let's talk about something more interesting than my love life. Which, as I've been telling you for a very long time, isn't going to change any time soon.'

Though he had to acknowledge later that night that the idea had lodged in his head.

Amanda Cooke.

He liked her. A lot. She had a warmth people couldn't help responding to, a sense of humour that was similar to his own, and he'd caught her taking a selfie in her of-fice for her daughter's class, wearing her stethoscope and the pink sequin and lace eye patch they'd made for her. She was a woman who noticed the little things, and she'd learned the names of everyone on the ward within two days, regardless of their role on the team.

And there was no denying that she was attractive. He wished he hadn't thought about her wearing a floaty chif-fon ballet skirt, because he couldn't get that picture out of his head: a graceful pirouette towards him with her skirt swishing round, and then he'd catch her round the waist and…

Oh, for pity's sake. She'd made it clear she wasn't interested in him other than as a colleague. He had no intention of ruining their professional relationship; he'd learned a very hard lesson when his marriage had disintegrated. So he'd just have to stuff these little flutters of awareness back into their box and ignore them.

On Monday, Mandy left home-made cookies on Daniel's desk, wrapped in greaseproof paper and with a note.

*Happy Monday, dear Job-share* ☺

But her bright mood disappeared fast when she did the ward round with her students and came to three-week-old baby Aarya, who'd been admitted with scarlet fever caused by Group A Streptococcus.

'Group A Strep's quite common,' she said. 'Usually it causes a sore throat and a fever, but not a runny nose or a cough. You might see white spots on the back of the baby's throat and they'll be poorly for a few days. Can anyone tell me what it sometimes leads to?'

'Scarlet fever?' one of the students suggested.

'Yes,' Mandy said. 'What can you tell me about scarlet fever?'

'It makes a child's tongue and lips go red, and they get a red pinprick rash all over their bodies,' another said.

'Starting where?' Mandy asked.

'The trunk, and then it spreads to the arms and legs,' another said.

'Can you see a rash on baby Aarya?' Mandy asked.

'No,' one of the others said.

'It's harder to see the rash on brown skin. So how else can you check?' Mandy asked.

'The skin feels like sandpaper?' one of the students asked.

She nodded. 'What would you recommend for treatment?'

'Antibiotics for the bacterial infection, and liquid paracetamol for the fever,' one of the students said.

'Good. Anything else you'd suggest?'

'Keep the baby home for the first twenty-four hours, to stop it spreading?' another student said.

'Yes. Scarlet fever's a notifiable disease,' she said, 'so you also need to let the local health protection team know; and give the mum penicillin as well, as a precaution. And remember to check for penicillin allergy before you prescribe the antibiotics.'

She got them to talk through how scarlet fever spread, the incubation period and how long an affected child would be infectious, the possible complications, and which groups were most at risk. Most of them knew that most cases occurred in the under-tens, and the most common age for children to get it was four.

What worried her was that Aarya was in a really high-risk group because of her age.

'Most babies with GAS throat infection recovery quickly with antibiotics,' she said, 'but rare cases turn into iGAS—invasive Group A Strep. The virus decreases the baby's ability to fight off the infection, which spreads through the bloodstream and releases toxins into the body, and that can lead to organ failure and, in the worst-case scenario, the baby doesn't make it. Hopefully that's not going to be the case here.' But the baby's notes told her that the GP had already given antibiotics, two days before, and Aarya's temperature was still sky-high.

She led the students through the rest of the ward round, assessing their knowledge, but between ward rounds and clinic she popped back to see the baby.

A woman who looked to be in her early thirties was sitting next to the baby's tiny cot, holding her hand.

'You must be Aarya's mum,' Mandy said.

'Yes. Neelam Chakrabarti,' the younger woman confirmed.

'Hello, Neelam. I'm Mandy Cooke, one of the ward doctors,' Mandy said. 'I saw Aarya when I did ward rounds earlier—thank you, by the way, for agreeing to let my students see her, too. How are you doing?'

'Not great,' Neelam admitted. 'Nish, her dad, was called into work, or he'd be here as well.'

'It's tough when your little one's in hospital,' Mandy said. 'Is there anyone else I can call for you who can give you some support?'

'No.' A tear trickled down her face, and she wiped it away. 'I just wish I could take this from Aarya.'

Mandy, who'd felt the same over the years when her own daughter had been ill, reached over to squeeze her hand. 'She's in the right place. How long has she had the rash?'

'Three days. I didn't think she was well last week, because she was fussy and refusing to feed and had a runny nose. I thought it was a cold. Then her temperature went up, and I couldn't get it down. The GP said it might be a streptococcus infection, because it was doing the rounds, and he gave her antibiotics. When the rash started, the doctors here said it was scarlet fever.'

'Strep A can cause scarlet fever,' Mandy said. 'Did the doctor give you antibiotics as well?'

'When I went back to see him, after the rash started and I still couldn't get her temperature down, he said I should take the antibiotics too and see how Aarya's doing in a couple of days.' She bit her lip. 'I know the hospital's busy and you don't need the extra patients fussing, but...'

'You did exactly the right thing, bringing her in,' Mandy reassured her. 'Babies can become so ill, so quickly. I never mind seeing a baby who's got something really minor and I can reassure the parents it's nothing to worry about. I know it's scary, being in hospital, but it means we can keep an eye on her and treat her quickly if anything changes.'

'I know where it started. My friend's little boy had a bit of a cold,' Neelam said, brushing away another tear. 'She wanted to come and see the baby. It was only for a few minutes, on the way home from the childminder. She feels terrible that he might have given her this.'

'If you give me her details,' Mandy said, 'I'll give her a quick call and ask her to get him checked over by her GP in case he develops scarlet fever, too, and let her childminder know to tell her other clients, just to be on the safe side.'

'All right,' Neelam said. 'Her number's in my phone.'

'Whenever you've got a moment,' Mandy said. 'Is there anything you want to ask me?'

'How long will it take until her temperature comes down?'

'A fever's a sign that her body's fighting an infection,' Mandy said. 'Usually a fever will break on the fourth or fifth day. The main thing is to keep her comfortable and well hydrated. Right now she's too tired to feed and struggling a bit with breathing, which is why she's on a nasogastric tube and oxygen therapy.'

'I'm expressing milk for her,' Neelam said.

'Which is great, plus you're here with her—she can hear your voice and feel you holding her hand. That'll help to comfort and calm her,' Mandy said. 'But you also need to look after yourself, Neelam. If you're tired and need a break, please take some time. We'll keep a close eye on her here.'

'I just want to be with her,' Neelam said.

'I understand that,' Mandy said gently. 'My daughter's due to have her first baby in a couple of months and it's very hard not to call her all the time, just to check on her.'

'So you never stop worrying, as a mum?'

Mandy gave a wry smile. 'No. Your worries just change. But the love makes up for it.' She checked the baby's charts. 'Someone in the team will be popping in very regularly to see how she's doing, but please come and find one of us if you're worried about anything at all. That's what we're here for.'

'I will,' Neelam promised.

Mandy dropped in to the office she shared with Daniel and was relieved to see him there at his desk.

'Good morning, Mandy, and thank you for the cookies,' he said. 'I was teasing—I really don't expect you to bake every Sunday and bring me goodies every Monday morning—but thank you. They were appreciated.'

'Pleasure,' she said. 'I know you're busy, but there's a case I really think we need to keep an eye on.' She gave him a quick rundown on baby Aarya. 'Especially as she's so young, I'm worried about that GAS infection.'

'Good call,' he said. 'I'll keep a check. How are the students?'

'I think they enjoyed ward rounds. There's one of them I think will make an exceptional doctor. Anyway, I've got them paired off for clinic next—including one with me, so I'll get going.'

'I'll keep you up to date with the baby,' he said.

'Thank you. I appreciate it,' she said.

'And remember,' he said quietly, 'it's rare.'

He'd clearly picked up on her secret worry: that something might happen to Gemma and Dev's baby. 'I know,' she said, hoping that the wobble didn't show in her voice.

Even though she was busy with clinic, she was half expecting to be called out during it. It overran slightly, so at lunchtime she had just enough time to gulp down a sandwich and a coffee and to see Aarya, who appeared to be holding her own.

But then, late afternoon, she was called to a crash team. Baby Aarya's blood pressure had dropped rapidly, due to the infection, her oxygen saturations had also dropped, and she'd gone into arrest.

Daniel was already there, managing the neonate's airway. Neelam and a man Mandy guessed was her husband Nish were also present; another of the nurses was clearly explaining what was going on and making sure that they didn't distract the resuscitation team.

'I've just given Aarya the adrenaline,' Daniel said.

Mandy's training kicked in, ignoring the fact that this was a three-week-old baby in trouble. The important thing now was to get that heart beating again. 'I'll bag,' she said. Daniel held the mask in place while she gave the baby twenty-five breaths per minute. In the meantime, Khaj had put the ECG leads in place.

'Asystole,' Khaj said, glancing at the monitor.

Daniel and Mandy exchanged a glance. The baby's heart still wasn't beating, and they could only shock the heart if it was a case of pulseless ventricular tachycardia or ventricular fibrillation. Any other rhythm wasn't shockable.

'Khaj, hold the mask in place for me, please,' Daniel said. 'Mandy, keep bagging. I'll start the compressions.'

He pushed down on the baby's chest, counting out loud.

'Two minutes—swap,' Mandy said, and continued the fast compressions, counting them while Daniel took over bagging.

Still no response.

'Come on, Aarya. You can do it,' he whispered fiercely.

At the end of the two-minute cycle, Mandy administered adrenaline again.

'Still asystole,' Khaj said.

'Swap,' Mandy said, and did the bagging while Daniel did the compressions.

Two more cycles, another bolus of adrenaline, and still nothing.

'Keep going,' Daniel said.

Two more cycles of CPR, more adrenaline, and still nothing.

They worked for twenty more minutes.

Finally, Daniel shook his head. 'I'm sorry, everyone. She's not responding. I'm going to call it, now. I'm so sorry.'

Neelam wailed in grief and clutched at her husband.

Mandy knew that having the parents there while a child was being resuscitated was painful, but at the same time it would be comforting later because they could see for themselves that the team had done everything they could.

Gently, she stroked the baby's face. 'I'm so sorry, little one,' she whispered. She walked over to the Chakrabartis and hugged them both. 'I'm so very, very sorry.'

'She can't be gone. She *can't* be!' Nish said, his voice cracking with tension.

'I'm sorry.' Mandy knew how inadequate the words were.

'It happened so fast—one second she was fine, and the next there were alarms going off and...' Neelam shook her head. 'I can't...' Her words faded and she just looked numb.

'Group A Strep infections can be nasty,' Mandy said. 'Because she's so young, Aarya had fewer defences against it.'

'It caused her blood pressure to drop,' Daniel said, joining them, 'and some of her organs went into failure, including her heart. We tried our best, but we couldn't get her back.'

'Why didn't you do that thing everyone sees on the TV? Why didn't you shock her heart?' Nish asked.

'We can only shock a heart that's in a certain type of rhythm,' Daniel explained. 'Asystole is where the heart muscle doesn't contract, there's no electrical activity in the heart, and no blood flow to the rest of the body. Giving adrenaline, chest compressions and breathing for her, like we did, can sometimes restart the heart and get a different rhythm going, so then we'd be able to shock the heart, but it doesn't always work. I'm sorry. We tried our hardest.'

'It was only a cold,' Neelam whispered. 'She's not supposed to die from a *cold*.'

'I'm so sorry,' Mandy said yet again, knowing how inadequate it was but unable to find any other words to say.

Khaj came over to them. 'Would you like me to bring Aarya over to you so you can sit with her for a while?' she asked. 'We can clear the room so you have time with your daughter on your own.'

'Our little girl,' Nish said. 'We loved her so much. She was only three weeks old.' His eyes filled with tears. 'This doesn't seem possible. Why her? Why now?'

There weren't any answers to his questions. Just a wall of sadness and grief.

'Come and sit with Aarya,' Khaj said. 'It'll help you to be with her. We can contact the hospital chaplain to come in and say a prayer with you, if you'd like that.'

'I...' Neelam shook her head, looking dazed and as if she couldn't process anything.

'You don't have to decide anything now,' Mandy said gently. 'You've got all the time you need. If you want us to call someone for you, just tell us and we'll do it.'

'Anything you need, just tell us,' Daniel said.

'I think, right now, we just want to be on our own with our daughter,' Nish said.

The rest of Mandy's clinic felt like a blur. At the end of her shift, she went into her office. Daniel was there, looking grim.

'Are you OK?' he asked, glancing up at her.

'No,' she said. 'And you don't look OK, either.'

'I'm very far from OK,' he said. 'Losing any patient is hard. But a three-week-old baby, and the way we lost her...' He blew out a breath. 'Khaj contacted the chaplain to come and see them, and I've given the Chakrabartis details of a bereavement counsellor and a support group. Though it doesn't feel like doing anything near enough.'

She knew exactly what he meant. She felt the same way. 'We tried our best. We all wanted a good outcome. But invasive Group A Strep can be a seriously nasty thing. Overwhelming. Intellectually, I know there was nothing more we could've done. But it still feels s—' She cut the word off, slumped into her chair and closed her eyes for a moment. 'I can't face going to my book group tonight. I'm not fit for anyone's company. I'm going to cancel.'

'I can't face people tonight, either,' Daniel said. 'Look, do you want to go for a walk with me? We don't have to talk—just put one foot in front of the other and keep each other company, on the grounds that it might help to decompress with someone else who's just been through what happened today.'

She thought about it. If she went home on her own, she'd brood. If Gemma rang her, she'd pick up on the fact Mandy wasn't her normal self. And Mandy absolutely couldn't tell her heavily pregnant daughter what had upset her so much. 'All right. That'd be good.'

'Give me twenty minutes to finish my paperwork?'

'Sure,' she said. 'Cup of tea?'

'You're an angel,' he said gratefully. 'Yes, please.'

While Mandy was waiting for the kettle to boil, she messaged her book club with an anodyne excuse; she managed to find some biscuits in the staff room, and came back with the spoils.

'Thank you,' Daniel said, though the strain around his eyes was obvious.

And although they both slogged through their paperwork, Mandy knew that neither of them was finding it easy. She was pretty sure that Daniel was thinking the same as she was: of the Chakrabatis, and how the light had gone out of their world. How their team had tried so very hard to save little Aarya, but they hadn't been able to start her heart again because the bacterial infection had been just too much for her tiny body to fight off.

Eventually, Daniel sighed. 'I think I'm going to come in early tomorrow to finish this lot. Right now, I can't concentrate.'

'Same here,' she admitted. 'Shall we just *go*?'

'Yes,' he said. 'After you went back to your clinic, I made sure the others weren't going to be on their own when they went home tonight. I'm going to do a proper debrief tomorrow, when we've all had a chance to get some rest and it doesn't feel quite as raw as it does now. Logically, I know we did everything we could. Just, in my heart, I keep wondering, what if we'd tried for another five minutes?' His face twisted.

'She wouldn't have survived. Her brain had already been too starved of oxygen. But I know what you mean. Me, too,' she said. 'Come on. We need those endorphins. Let's have that walk.'

# CHAPTER FOUR

IT WASN'T QUITE dark when they left the hospital, but it was a grey and chilly autumn evening, and Mandy was glad of her coat.

'Shall we head for the river?' Daniel asked.

'Good idea,' she agreed.

Although they didn't speak as they trudged through the streets, it wasn't an awkward silence: more that neither of them could quite bear anything resembling a normal conversation just yet, and they took quiet comfort from each other's presence. A couple of times, their hands accidentally brushed; the third time it happened, Daniel took her hand.

It wasn't a clumsy attempt at a pass; she knew that he was simply offering her the comfort that she really needed, right then. He clearly needed that same comfort, so she walked hand in hand with him rather than pulling away. Funny how the warmth of his skin against hers made everything hurt just a little bit less. She hoped it was working for him, too.

When they reached the River Thames, they stood watching the traffic move over Chelsea Bridge for a while; the lights on the suspension bridge were reflected in the darkening water of the river.

'It's pretty in summer,' Daniel said. 'I usually walk to work this way.'

'You live in Chelsea?' Mandy asked.

'Round the corner from the Physic Garden. Which is always a lovely place to go,' he said. 'Where are you based?'

'I have a flat in King's Cross,' she said. 'In a gorgeous Georgian building.'

'Snap—well, mine's a townhouse. I had the chance of buying a modern flat overlooking the river,' he said, 'but I much prefer old buildings. They've got so much more character.'

Another area where they chimed, Mandy thought. She was starting to feel really in tune with Daniel—more than she had with anyone else she'd ever met. Which was unexpected, and also slightly unsettling.

'Shall we keep walking?' he asked.

She nodded, and they strolled alongside the river.

'Chelsea Hospital gardens are over there,' he said, indicating the other side of the road. 'That's my route home during summer, because it's open until sunset—well, obviously it's closed during the Chelsea Flower Show, too. But it's nice to have a green space so close.'

'I know what you mean,' she said. 'There are lots of pockets of little gardens near me, too, or I can walk down to the canal and the park at Camley Street. As you say, it's nice to walk through green spaces in summer.'

Still holding hands, they walked by the river down to the Albert Bridge and leaned against the embankment wall under one of the streetlamps, looking across the Thames.

'Did you know, apart from Tower Bridge, this is the

only bridge in central London that's never been replaced?' he asked. 'And it's the only one with its original tollbooths—as well as a sign telling troops to break step when they walk over it. Apparently, if the men had marched in step, there's a chance the bridge would've collapsed.'

'It's that fragile?' she asked.

'Yes, but it gets patched up every so often,' he said. 'I like this bit of London. Henry VIII's old manor house gardens are just round the corner, with mulberry trees allegedly planted by Elizabeth I, and there are all the statues and monuments tucked along the embankment. Not to mention all the wisteria in the spring, and the gorgeous tree full of blossom outside St Luke's—where Dickens got married.'

Clearly he was distracting himself by dredging up facts and figures; though it was helping to distract her, too. 'There's so much of London I haven't explored,' she said. 'I really must make the effort.'

'In a job like ours, there isn't time to do much outside seeing your family,' he said. 'Especially in the early years.'

'Yes.' She bit her lip. 'When Gemma was born, I used to worry so much about her. Every sniffle took me back to being a second-year medical student, convinced that I'd developed the symptoms of whichever disease we'd covered that week—except this time I was convinced *she* was the one who'd developed those diseases.'

He gave her a wry smile. 'I remember being like that as a student, too. I think we were all hypochondriacs, those first couple of years.'

'Weren't we just? As a parent, I worried myself sick.

As a grandparent, I think I'll be as bad,' she said. 'But what happened today…that's made it feel a hundred times worse. What if I go to see Gemma and the baby, and I don't even realise I've picked up a virus?' The idea almost made her hyperventilate with terror. 'What if I pass RSV to the baby, or Group A Strep, when she's still so tiny it'll overwhelm her system?'

'RSV's very possible, even if you use the extra PPE,' he said. 'But you already know we can do a lot for that particular virus, and anyway you won't go to see the baby if you've got what feels like a super-heavy cold because you're experienced enough to know what it is. And you're really not very likely to pick up Group A Str—oh, come *here*.' He wrapped his arms round her and held her close, resting his cheek against her hair. 'It's going to be OK, Mandy. Today was horrific, but how often does this happen?'

'It's rare,' she admitted. 'But it still feels horrible.'

'I know. But know also you did everything you could. We all did.'

It was a long, long time since a man had wrapped his arms round her, offering her comfort, Mandy thought. Not since her dad had died, five years ago. And if she didn't include her dad it had been even longer. Laurence, her ex, had never comforted her like this when she came home from a tough shift, tired and out of sorts; usually he'd been grumbling about having to miss a social event with his friends or colleagues because she was at work. Until he'd started going to them on his own…

She ought to pull away from Daniel. Now. For the sake of her own sanity. She wasn't going to let herself rely on a man, ever again.

Yet the bleakness in Daniel's expression when he'd called the time of death on the baby made her think that he, too, needed the comfort of a cuddle. He'd made her feel better; she should do the same for him. So, instead of extracting herself with a feeble excuse, she wrapped her own arms around him. Held him close.

They stood there for a long, long moment, saying nothing, just holding each other.

Then she tipped her head back.

Whatever she'd been about to say was lost to the London evening, because his eyes were oh, so dark and all the words went out of her head. His mouth was very slightly parted. She could see the beginnings of a beard on his face; and, unable to stop herself, she reached up to glide her fingertips across his skin, feeling the catch of stubble.

Daniel sucked in a breath.

And then he twisted his head so his mouth brushed her palm. His lips were warm and soft, and she ached to feel them against hers.

Crazy, crazy, crazy.

This shouldn't be happening.

But now it had started, she couldn't stop it. Didn't *want* to stop it.

She wasn't sure which of them moved first, but the next thing she knew her arms were round his neck, his arms had tightened around her waist, and he was kissing her, his mouth sweet and gentle, offering temptation as well as comfort.

How could she resist letting him deepen the kiss?

Desire and need swept through her, pushing away the last vestiges of her common sense. The only thing that made her stop kissing him back was when an impatient car driver leaned on their horn, and the harsh sound crashed into her head.

She pulled back and stared at him.

What the hell had she just done?

Colour slashed across his face. 'I'm sorry, Mandy. I shouldn't have done that.'

It was noble of him to take responsibility, but it wasn't fair. She was just as much to blame. 'It wasn't just you,' she said. She'd been with him all the way. It was the first time she'd been kissed since she didn't know when, and it had put her into a total spin.

'I—look, I don't do relationships,' he said. 'It's complicated. But I don't. And that's not me trying to tell you in a nice way that I don't find you attractive, because actually I do. But that's exactly why I can't…' He closed his eyes briefly. 'Listen to me. Incoherence city. Sorry. I'm not usually this hopeless, this inarticulate. I don't kiss women at random. I…' He stared at her, as if he couldn't find the words to explain.

The words were jumbled in her head, too, but she made the effort. 'Me, neither. I don't kiss men at random, I mean.'

'Mandy. I like you. A lot,' he emphasised. 'But all I can offer you is friendship.'

'Snap,' she said. 'I don't have time in my life for dating.' She didn't try to tell him that it wasn't her way of saying no gently, because it wasn't: and she was all too aware of how easy it would be to say that it didn't matter—that they were both middle-aged and single and they *could* do this, if they wanted. How easy it would be to slide her hands into his hair again and draw his head back down to hers. To touch her lips to his, offering and teasing and cajoling. To forget the world around them, the traffic and the people and the noise, and let herself drown in his kiss.

Though the sensible side of her knew that doing that would make life way too complicated. Daniel was her new job-share. She'd been working at the London Victoria for a week. It would be utterly insane to let anything more than friendship happen between them and risk making things awkward on the ward or in their shared office.

'So we're all right, you and me?' he checked.

She nodded. 'What happened just now was purely for comfort. For both of us. And it...' It was her turn to close her eyes for a moment. 'I'm shutting my mouth now, before I dig myself into a deeper hole.'

'I think we've both had the worst shift in months and we're feeling a bit wobbly right now,' he said. 'My recommendation for fixing that is—'

*Another kiss*, her libido supplied.

'—a good dose of carbs,' he said, and she was really glad that the words in her head hadn't burst out.

'My place is about ten minutes from here,' he continued. 'Or, since I don't have a clue what's in my fridge right now, we could walk up to King's Road—I know a good Italian trattoria there that does the most fabulous gnocchi.'

Even though a very big part of her was intrigued to see where Daniel lived, Mandy knew it would be a bad idea. They'd just agreed to be friends, but she had a nasty feeling that they were both still so wobbly that if they were alone it would be all too easy to start kissing again—and who knew where that might lead?

It would be much more sensible to stay in a public

place. Talk themselves down from the edge of doing something risky.

'Gnocchi sounds fabulous,' she said. 'And we'll split the bill.'

'Fine by me,' he said. 'Because I like to think we'll become friends as well as colleagues.'

'I hope so, too,' she said. She liked what she'd seen of this man. The way he was with junior colleagues at work appealed to her; there was no boasting or trying to make himself look superior. He listened; he got them to talk and work things out for themselves but made it clear that he was there if they needed him. He was good with patients and with parents. And it was always good to have a friend.

They walked up to the restaurant. La Roma was pretty outside, with fairy lights and foliage decorating the enormous windows; inside, the floors were wooden and the pale terracotta walls were hung with photographs of iconic spots of Rome, from the Colosseum and the Pantheon to the Trevi Fountain. The small tables were covered with red-and-white-checked linen tablecloths; each had a small terracotta pot of herbs and a red candle set in an old raffia-covered Chianti bottle in the centre. And the scents from the kitchen were divine.

'What do you recommend?' she asked Daniel when the waiter had shown them to their seats, given them the menu, talked them through the specials on the chalkboard and brought them a jug of water when they admitted that neither of them was in the mood for a glass of wine.

'Everything I've ever eaten here has been excellent,' he said. 'But I'm having the gnocchi with gorgonzola sauce. Normally I try and have something different, but tonight I want the comfort of an old favourite.'

She scanned the menu. 'I'm tempted to join you, but then there's the mushroom risotto on the specials board. And I *love* risotto.' She blew out a breath. 'Though it feels *wrong*, enjoying choosing dinner after what happened today.'

He wrinkled his nose. 'I know what you mean—but today for me was a reminder that we never know what's going to happen in life. We should enjoy the little moments of joy when we can.'

'That's a good point,' she admitted.

Once they'd ordered, the waiter brought them a sharing board of olives, tiny arancini, marinated artichoke hearts and a creamy burrata along with some focaccia.

'The simple stuff's the best,' Daniel said. 'And they do it so well, here.'

'Do you come here often?' she asked.

'I normally bring the film crew here for dinner once a month, to say thank you,' he said. 'They're really good and make sure they don't intrude on the families or get in the way of the medics, so showing my appreciation is the least I can do. And I've brought my family here a few times.'

She noticed that he didn't mention girlfriends. Not that she should be noticing that. Nothing was going to happen between them, and that flare of attraction she felt towards him needed to be buried. Pronto.

'What about you?' he asked. 'Do you eat out often?'

'With my best friend, after ballet class; sometimes with my mum and my sister; and I have dinner once a week with my daughter and son-in-law,' she said. 'Though more recently that's been at their place. Dev is an amazing cook. He's taught me a lot about Indian cuisine, and it's very far from chicken tikka masala.'

'It's nice that you're close to your family,' he said.

'I've been really lucky,' she said. 'When Gemma was small, I could never have managed without Mum and Dad and my big sister, Jen. You know what it's like as a junior doctor.'

'Long hours, being on call and never having enough sleep,' Daniel agreed. 'Your ex didn't help?'

She might as well tell him the truth. Particularly as it would be a useful barrier between them. 'My ex has never been part of Gemma's life,' she said. 'I didn't find out I was pregnant until after I'd filed for divorce. I did tell him about her existence, because I felt it would've been wrong not to tell him, but he made it clear he wasn't interested in being a dad, so if I kept her I'd be on my own. And that's how it's been ever since.' She sighed. 'Sometimes I feel guilty and think I should've found someone who would've made a good dad for Gemma. But I couldn't face dating again.'

Because she'd loved her ex that much? Daniel wondered. Then again, she'd just said she'd been the one to file for divorce. Not that he was going to ask her why; it was none of his business, and he didn't want to trample over old scars. 'I'm not sure that potentially being a good dad is enough of a reason to marry someone,' he said instead. 'I think you should marry someone because you want to spend your life with them.'

'That's what I thought I'd done,' she said. 'Laurence was charming, good company and I thought he was perfect. I met him at a party, fell for him like a ton of bricks, and six months later we were married. And I really thought everything was fine—until I came home sick from a night shift to find someone else in our bed with him.'

He winced. 'I'm sorry. That must've been a shock.'

She nodded. 'And then I found out she wasn't the first.' She shrugged. 'I guess not everyone can cope with a junior doctor's shifts. He got fed up with me not wanting to go to a party with him because I was on call or on nights, or being too tired to do anything after a long shift, or the fact I was still studying as well as working.'

'Plus, if you're not a medic, if you go to any social event you'll feel left out because everyone's talking about the hospital or gossiping about people you've never met,' Daniel said.

'That,' she said, 'sounds personal.'

'Yeah. My marriage didn't survive my houseman years—and it was my fault. I let the gap grow between us.' Which was only part of the truth. The rest of it was much more shameful.

'It takes two to break a marriage,' she said. 'In my case, Laurence decided to fill the gap with someone else.'

'I'm sorry he hurt you,' Daniel said. 'He was an idiot.' And now he knew he had to tell her the truth about his own marriage. OK, so it risked souring things between them, but at least it would remove some of the temptation if she knew the worst of him. Because, right now, he was looking at the curve of her mouth, remembering how well that curve had fitted to his own mouth, and wondering when he could kiss her again...

He took a deep breath. 'And I can say that because I made the same mistake.'

'Your ex cheated on you?'

He shook his head. 'I'm ashamed to say that I was the one who cheated. Things were getting rocky between us. We were both working long hours and getting snappy with each other—and then I met someone at work. Leila was three or four years older than me. Bright, sparkly, enormous fun. Everything I wanted—and I fell head over heels for her.' Exactly the same excuse his own father had used when Daniel, aged fifteen, had asked him why he'd cheated on Daniel's mother. Keith Monroe had blustered that he'd simply fallen head over heels in love with someone else. But then it had happened again. And again. When Daniel learned that the first affair he'd known about had been very far from the first one, he'd realised that his father was a serial cheat and a pathological liar, and he couldn't forgive Keith for it.

Daniel been so determined not to behave like his father did, especially as everyone said he was Keith's mini-me. He resembled his father in looks, and there wasn't much he could do about that; but he didn't want to be like his father in any other way. Maybe it was part of the reason he'd married Roxy so young; he'd wanted to prove to himself that he could offer his partner stability. That he could have a long-lasting, happy marriage.

Except it turned out that he really was a carbon copy of his father, letting himself fall for someone else when he was supposed to be committed to his wife. And that had horrified him. He didn't want to be 'all boys together' with his father, focusing on the thrill of the chase and not caring how he hurt his partner.

The night he'd split up with Roxy and Leila had responded by dumping him, he'd vowed to keep all relationships light, in future. Never again would he take the risk of repeating his mistake and hurting somebody else.

'I left my wife for Leila,' he said. 'It was the most stupid thing I'd ever done.' He'd been shocked to discover that Leila was a player; she'd seen her fling with him as nothing more than a bit of fun, and had been horrified to find out that his own intentions were serious. He'd wrecked his marriage for nothing, devastating both Roxy and himself—and it wasn't fixable. 'I bitterly regret the hurt I caused my ex.'

'You had an affair,' she said, her voice cool.

The collar on Daniel's shirt suddenly felt too tight. He'd wanted to put a barrier between them, show Mandy that he was the worst possible person she could think of falling for—she'd been cheated on, and he was a proven cheat. Unreliable. Though, at the same time, he didn't want her to despise him. Because he *wasn't* his father. 'I was very, very stupid and very, very wrong.' He sighed. 'There are no excuses. Roxy and I met in the first week of university; we were inseparable as students and we got married the week after I graduated.' Maybe because he'd been so desperate to prove to himself that he could have a good, stable marriage. 'Looking back, we were probably too young to settle down, and we definitely didn't realise what kind of strain a junior doctor's hours can put on a relationship. But none of it was Roxy's fault.'

Mandy was silent for so long that Daniel started to wonder if she was going to get up and leave.

Then she looked at him. 'At least you're shouldering the blame instead of trying to dump it on your wife.'

'Of course I'm not going to try to blame her. She didn't do anything wrong. I regret what I did. *Not* because I got caught,' he emphasised, 'but because I hurt her and she didn't deserve that.'

'And you didn't stay with the woman you had the affair with?'

That stung, but he knew he deserved the question. 'I planned to, but she dumped me. It turned out that half my attraction for her was that I was involved with someone else—which made me forbidden fruit. As soon as I left Roxy and asked Leila to make it serious, she broke up with me.'

'So she didn't actually care about you?'

'No.' He grimaced. 'And I was young and naive enough not to see it in the first place. I got burned. But I know I hurt Roxy even more, so I'm not looking for sympathy. It was my own fault.'

Her brown eyes narrowed as she assessed him. 'That's honest,' she said.

'And I've been honest ever since,' he said. 'It's why I don't do serious relationships. I make it clear to anyone who dates me that it's going to be just for fun, just for now, and I'm not looking for forever.'

'I don't do relationships, either,' she said. 'Not because I'm still in love with Laurence, because I'm not. I just don't have the time or the space in my life for anything else.' She took a deep breath and gave him a wry smile. 'And, if I'm being honest, I guess it's a little hard to trust again after that...'

Which told Daniel exactly where he stood with her; and he definitely needed to damp down the attraction he felt towards her, because it most certainly wasn't going to be reciprocated. Once bitten, definitely twice shy.

'Did you try to get back together with Roxy, when it all went sour with Leila?' she asked.

'No. I could hardly go running back to her and tell her I'd made a mistake. I decided to give us both a bit of time to get over the bitterness, and then see if there was a way we could move forward. But I left it too long, because when we talked she told me she'd met someone else at work,' he said. 'She said she thought we'd got together too young and we'd started growing apart. She probably had a point. But that still doesn't excuse what I did. I'd made a commitment, and I should've just pushed through the difficult stuff and stuck by her. Instead, I let myself get distracted by Leila. I took the easy option—and it was wrong.'

'Thank you for being open with me,' she said. 'And I'd like to assure you that I won't be gossiping about anything you just told me.'

'Thank you. I won't be gossiping about you, either,' he said. 'And I'd like to assure you that my past idiocy in my private life doesn't apply to my work. Ever.'

'I've already seen that for myself,' she said. 'I'm pretty sure we'll rub along OK together in the job.'

He didn't dare ask her about whether they'd still become friends, now. He'd probably derailed that, too, with his confession. And he was seriously relieved when their food arrived. If he filled his mouth with carbs, maybe it would stop him saying something else he'd regret later.

In some ways, Mandy wasn't surprised by what Daniel had just confessed. He was even more charming than

Laurence, and she'd learned the hard way that charming men were unreliable.

In other ways, she was shocked. The kind, caring man she'd been working with at the hospital had too big a heart to be unfaithful, surely?

Then again, his affair had happened half a lifetime ago. She wasn't the same now as she'd been in her twenties; doubtless Daniel had changed over the years, too. And it sounded as if he'd been vulnerable at the time, struggling with his marriage and his job, and he'd fallen for someone who'd treated him just as badly as Laurence had treated her. He'd told her that he didn't date; clearly the fallout from his marriage ending had made him avoid relationships as much as she had.

Daniel was probably the worst person she could ever let herself fall for.

It would be much more sensible for them to stick to being colleagues, maybe friends.

'Is your risotto all right?' he asked.

'Lovely, thank you.' She winced, hearing how stilted her words sounded. It wasn't her place to judge his past. 'It's actually delicious. Would you like to try some?'

Colour rose in his face again. Not surprising, because sharing a taste of your meal was something you'd do with a lover. She should've chosen her words more carefully, or picked some anodyne topic of conversation. The weather, holidays, work... Where was easy small talk, when you needed it?

'Thanks for the offer, but I'm happy to stick with my pasta. Which you're welcome to try,' he added hastily.

'You're finding this as awkward as I am, aren't you?' she asked.

'Yes.' He sighed. 'This evening was meant to be a walk to clear my head and having dinner with a colleague who'd shared my rough day. A chance to decompress a bit. And what do I do? I kiss you stupid, I'm nosey about your ex, and I tell you I'm basically your worst nightmare.'

'Agreed. Though, actually, I think I might've kissed you, first,' she said. 'And I was the one who brought up my ex.'

'So where do we go from here?' he asked.

'I think,' she said, 'we muddle through and try to be kind to each other. And maybe avoid being in a situation where we might end up…well, too close to each other,' she added.

'Work's fine. We're not going to do anything stupid in our office or on the ward, not when we both know what a hospital grapevine can be like,' Daniel said. 'But outside—agreed. Only public places. If we go for a walk together, we'll make sure there are no secluded bits.'

'Technically, the Chelsea embankment doesn't count as secluded,' she pointed out. And still they'd ended up kissing, in full view of anyone passing by.

'True.' He raised an eyebrow. 'I guess we just have to keep reminding each other to be sensible.'

'Works for me,' she said, raising her glass of water. 'Friends.'

'Friends,' he said, chinking his glass against hers.

They managed to split the dessert sharing board of orange polenta cake, tiramisu and an amazing apple tart served with cinnamon cream without their fingers accidentally brushing.

'It's probably not a good idea to invite you back for coffee,' he said.

'Definitely,' she agreed.

'Can I call you a cab? The nearest Tube is Sloane Square, and that's a ten-minute walk. In the rain.'

'My coat has a hood,' she said. 'I'm fine getting the Tube—I don't even have to change lines from Sloane Square to get to King's Cross. And you don't need to walk me to the station, either.'

'My mother would say otherwise—and so would yours, I bet,' he said.

'Our mothers are from a different generation,' she retorted. 'If you walk me to the station, I'll be tempted to give you a hug goodbye. And you know what our last hug led to.'

'That was before we agreed to keep things platonic,' he argued.

'Even so,' she said firmly. 'We're splitting the bill, walking in separate directions, and we'll see each other tomorrow at the hospital.'

'And now I know,' he said, 'you're not going to be a pushover as joint Head of Paediatrics. You'll give the suits as good as you get.'

'Better,' she said, 'because nobody's getting away with being a cheapskate with our ward.'

They split the bill, said goodbye in the middle of the restaurant, and after he held the door for her they walked in opposite directions.

Part of Mandy liked the fact Daniel had wanted to walk her to the station. But she knew they'd made the right decision. If he'd walked with her, it would've been too easy for their hands to brush, then cling together—

and this time it wouldn't have been merely for comfort. Both of them would've thought about that kiss. Both of them would've acted on that kiss. And it would all end up in an awkward, difficult mess.

All she had to do now was wipe that kiss from her memory.

Though her mouth would have to stop tingling, first...

# CHAPTER FIVE

DANIEL COULDN'T GET that kiss out of his head. The softness of Mandy's mouth. The way it had fitted so perfectly against his. The feel of her hands tangling in his hair.

A cold shower didn't help much.

Neither did counting backwards from five hundred in seventeens.

Or the cryptic crossword.

Or a run before work, on Tuesday morning.

Or the triple-strength coffee he made in the staff kitchen on the way to his desk.

All he could think about was her. What the hell was he going to do about this?

He'd read an article about wearing an elastic band around your wrist and pinging it when you needed to distract yourself from thinking something. Maybe that would work. Except of course there wasn't an elastic band to be found anywhere in his desk.

*Focus, Daniel*, he told himself grimly.

This was a work environment, not a place to let his mind roam free. He was going to concentrate on the paperwork he'd come in early to finish. And he managed it. He even filed some of it.

But then Mandy turned up. Bringing coffee—and an almond croissant.

'Peace offering,' she said. 'And because you're doing the debrief this morning. You need carbs before that.'

'That's kind,' he said, touched. 'I appreciate this. Very much.'

'You're welcome.' She lifted one shoulder in a shrug. 'There's a nice bakery between my flat and the station, and they open early.'

And she'd thought of him. Thought of the horrible morning he had ahead, and bought something to bolster him. It warmed him all the way through.

Maybe they could be friends, after all. Just as long as he managed to stop himself thinking about kissing her again.

He wished he'd thought of buying biscuits for the team at the debrief. As it was, the best he could do was be open with his team. 'We all did our best, yesterday. Nobody could've done more for little Aarya, and nobody's to blame for her death,' he said. 'How are you all doing, this morning?'

'Grim,' Khaj said. 'We don't have many deaths on this ward. And they hurt.'

'I know they do,' he said gently. 'We wouldn't be any good as medics if we didn't feel the losses. But I don't want you to feel you have to carry on as if nothing had happened, see your next patient and smile.'

'To be fair, we *do* have to see our next patients and smile,' Ginny, one of the junior doctors, said. 'We can't stop treating people.'

'But we don't have to carry on as if nothing had happened. It's all right to take a moment. To acknowledge how you're feeling,' he said. 'I don't want any of you to feel you're burning out. So if you need to talk to someone after we lose a patient—whether it's me, Mandy or a counsellor—that's fine. It's a sign of strength, not weakness, to recognise you need help and to ask for it.'

'The palliative care team at my old hospital used to hold weekly meetings, and someone would read a poem or a multi-faith prayer,' Mandy said. 'They said it helped. We were going to start trialling that with my team.'

'It's an interesting idea,' Daniel said. 'Can you all have a think about whether you'd like to do something like that? We could probably manage it on Wednesday mornings when Mandy isn't up to her neck in students and I'm not filming.'

'Actually, if we do this, it'd be good to include the students,' Mandy said. 'We should teach them about self-care and show them how to cope with the rough bits of the job.'

'Agreed,' Khaj said. 'And maybe we can take it in turns to bring in cake or what have you.'

Daniel chuckled. 'No arguments from me on that one.' He paused. 'While we're here, I'd like to review our procedures for infant cardiac arrests and check we're all on the same page. And if anyone has any questions, I'm listening.'

After the debrief, Daniel checked in on baby Noah. Lucy Carmichael was sitting with him, reading him a story.

'How are you doing?' he asked.

'Getting there,' she said. 'Everyone's been so kind. And we're starting to see improvements. Mo says we can try taking him off assisted breathing, at the end of the week.'

'That's good,' Daniel said. 'Though if it turns out he's not ready for it yet, try not to worry. These things take time, and we can't always predict them.'

'All right,' she said.

'Given that he's improving,' Daniel said, 'would you and Rob consider letting Noah be one of our case studies on the *London Victoria Children's Ward* documentary?'

Her eyes widened. 'He'd be on TV?'

'Only with your permission, and there's absolutely no pressure. It won't make any difference to the care he receives whether you say yes or no. Talk it over with Rob.'

'I guess it'd be a warning about what could happen if a baby's given honey,' Lucy said. 'And it might get the message across to people who haven't thought about it before—or those who take the attitude that it didn't hurt them or their own kids.'

'It might,' Daniel agreed. 'And it'd be nice to show other parts of the hospital working as a team, bits that patients and visitors never really see. I'd love the chance to bring in the pharmacy team. But, as I said, there's no pressure. Talk to Rob, and if you're both interested then come and ask me any questions you might have. I can also put you in touch with other parents who've been part of the series, to give you a better idea about what to expect.'

'I will,' Lucy said.

On Wednesday afternoon, Daniel caught up with Mandy. 'Now Noah's recovering, the Carmichaels have given me permission to use him as a case study on the show. As you're the one who worked out what was wrong, would you like to be part of it?'

She looked surprised. 'Me, on TV?'

'If you'd rather not be on camera,' he said, 'I'll still make sure you get the credit you deserve and I'll explain how you worked it out. Have a think about it. If you'd like to see how we film a case, I've got Matthew Field in tomorrow—he's ten and he's in for his last surgery for Shone's syndrome.'

'Shone's—that's where the heart structures don't form properly on the left, isn't it?' Mandy asked.

'Yes—three out of the eight possible problems, in Matty's case. He's had quite a few surgeries over the years. We're filming him and his mum in the morning. If you sit in on it, you can meet the crew and see how we work. Matty's mum, Theresa, is getting to be quite an old hand at this now.'

'Do I need to keep out of the office on Thursdays and Fridays when you're filming?' she asked.

'Not very much,' he said. 'Most of what we do is a fly-on-the-wall approach, so we'll be in the consulting rooms, operating theatres and on the ward. If we do need to use the office, I'll stick a note on the door saying how long we'll be.'

'This is all really interesting,' Mandy said. 'I've spoken to journalists before, back at Muswell Hill, but I've never done anything with TV broadcasting.'

'It's not as glamorous as you might think,' he warned. 'We're a small team, and there's a lot of repetition to make sure we get the footage we need. Some of the time Shalmi will film me nodding my head, so if we have to cut bits we have some visuals to help with continuity.'

'OK. What time do you need me in?'

'We start filming at ten,' he said. 'So, after ward rounds works for me.'

'Got it,' she said.

On Thursday morning, after she'd finished ward rounds, Mandy went into the office to meet Daniel's film crew.

'Everyone, this is Mandy, who's the joint Head of Paediatrics with me,' Daniel said. 'Mandy, this is Shalmi, our camerawoman; Carey, who's in charge of light and sound; and Keisha, our producer.'

'Otherwise known as the person who sorts the schedules, trouble-shoots and drives everyone mad bossing them about,' Keisha said with a smile. 'Dan tells me you've agreed to be filmed as part of Noah's story—you're the one who worked out what was wrong with him.'

'It was a hunch,' Mandy said.

'A good one, and you're the only one who suggested it,' Daniel reminded her. 'Mandy, this is Theresa Field, Matthew's mum; and Matty, who's having his final surgery later this morning. We'd hoped to do it before he started high school, but now he gets to miss half a term of football.'

'I don't mind,' Matty said with a grin. 'Cricket's way better than football anyway, and I'll be well again before the cricket season starts.'

'Nice to meet you, Theresa and Matty,' Mandy said, shaking their hands in turn. 'I'm one of the doctors on the ward, so I'll probably see you on ward rounds. I teach students on Mondays and Tuesdays. Thank you for letting me sit in on your interview.'

'No problem,' Theresa said. 'We're quite used to talking to the cameras, now.'

'As last year, we'll be cutting your story with the photographs you lent us and some footage of similar operations,' Keisha said, 'to show Matty's journey so far.'

Shalmi took some test shots, Carey adjusted the lighting and then Daniel started talking to Theresa, who explained her son's story.

'When Matty was born, he struggled with breathing, and the doctor told us he had critical aortic stenosis— that meant his blood couldn't flow properly through his heart. The next day, they gave him keyhole surgery and put a balloon into the valve so they could open it. He recovered well, but then he went into heart failure. He was taken to Intensive Care and put on life support.' Theresa swallowed hard. 'Even now, remembering how tiny he was, how sick he was and how scared we were makes me well up. But the staff were brilliant. They saved his life. Matty had open heart surgery to repair the valve, and five months later they created a new circuit in his heart so it could pump enough blood around his body.'

'I was in hospital quite a lot over the next few years,' Matty said, 'but Mum and Dad could stay in a flat just round the corner so they could be with me, and I did a lot of my lessons here. Later today I'm going to have open heart surgery again, which will help my circulation, and we hope it'll be the last big operation I need. I know I'm never going to be able to play really fast sports or climb a mountain, because I get out of puff, but I've joined my local cricket team.' His smile broadened. 'One day, I want to play for England as a really ace bowler, but for now I'm happy to play for the village.'

'And I'm looking forward to cheering our Matty as he takes out all the opposition's wickets,' Daniel added.

Keisha reviewed the footage and got Theresa and Matty to repeat a couple of bits, and add in some different information, and then it was done.

'Well done, Team Field,' Daniel said. 'Khaj is going to settle you in on the ward, Matty, and the surgeon will be along to see you shortly.'

'Good,' Matty said, and his stomach growled. 'I'm *starving*. The worst bit of having an operation is not being allowed to have breakfast!'

'Oh, wait—I want that,' Keisha said.

'Don't tell me—smile and repeat it?' Matty teased, clearly used to the filming routine.

'If you can make your stomach growl again, that would be cool,' Keisha said, 'but a smile will do.'

Matty duly repeated his comment for the camera.

'Do either of you have any questions for me?' Daniel asked Theresa and Matty.

'No—I think my last questions are for the surgeon,' Theresa said.

'Which I'll be filming,' Shalmi said.

Once Khaj had collected Matty, it was Mandy's turn to speak to camera, explaining how baby Noah's symptoms hadn't made any sense until she remembered a case her friend had come across on secondment in America, and they'd realised that the baby had infant botulism.

'That was good,' Keisha said. 'I'm going to make you redo all that from a slightly different angle—not because you got anything wrong, but because I want to cover several angles. And I might need you again later, depending on how it looks when we cut everything together.'

'Sure,' Mandy said.

She was busy on the ward and in the office for the rest of the day, and on Friday morning she was filmed in their shared office for a few last tweaks.

'Thank you for all your help,' Daniel said. 'I think our viewers are going to find this all really interesting.'

'I agree,' she said. 'And it's really good to see how things have changed for Matty's family—from all the worry of his first couple of days through to the well-balanced pre-teen he is now.'

Later that afternoon, Mandy was just finishing her last bit of admin when Daniel came back into the office and smiled at her. 'Have fun at ballet tonight.'

'Thank you. I will.'

She noticed a tide of colour sweep into his face and wondered what had caused it. She knew she ought to act as if she hadn't noticed, but the question burst out of her anyway. 'Dan? What is it?'

He groaned. 'God. I'm blushing, aren't I? My face feels hot.'

She nodded, and he closed his eyes. 'Sorry. Just pretend I look normal.'

But he didn't. And, even though part of her knew this would be dangerous, she wanted to know what was in his head. 'Dan,' she said softly. 'Talk to me.'

He opened his eyes again and looked at her. 'You want the truth? All right. I can't get you out of my head, Mandy. I haven't been able to stop thinking about you since Monday night. And I shouldn't have mentioned ballet, because right now I'm imagining you in a sparkly leotard and a tutu, pirouetting towards me at the end of the Sugar Plum Fairy solo, and ending up in my arms.'

And now the picture was in her head, too. Along with the music.

'I'm not a proper ballerina, Dan. I don't wear pointe shoes, just normal soft ballet shoes. It's a beginner class for older adults and the most we do is demi-pointe—tiptoes,' she said.

'That doesn't help,' he said. 'Actually, if anything, you've just made it worse. Because now in my head you're barefoot on the sand, dancing towards me in a swishy skirt. Still to the Sugar Plum Fairy music, because that's my favourite bit of the entire ballet.' He dragged in a breath. 'Ignore me. I'll get my common sense back. I'll have lots of cold showers and keep my distance.'

'What if you didn't have to?' The words came out before she could stop them, and suddenly there wasn't any air in the room.

He took his glasses off and sat down at his desk, opposite hers. His gaze was intense. 'I don't do relationships, Mandy.'

'And you've been honest about the reason for that. So I know you're not going to cheat on me,' she said.

'I'm really not a good bet. Mercurial, my mother calls me, but it's not...' He gave an odd smile. 'Mercutio, maybe. The annoying friend who's always the joker, always lightening the mood, shallow as a puddle. We've all got one in our lives. Except I think I'm the Mercutio in everyone's life. Ballet Mercutio, that is, not Shakespeare Mercutio. I'm about fun, not fighting.'

'That's a good life skill,' she said softly, 'being able to lighten someone's mood. Talk them out of a dark space. Not many people are good at it. Don't do yourself down.'

'I never, ever let myself feel like this,' he said. 'Not about anyone. But I can't stop thinking about you.'

'Same here,' she said. 'I don't have time in my life for a relationship. I don't want to date anyone. But when we kissed...' She bit her lip. 'Dan, we can't talk about this here. Not when someone might walk in and hear us.'

'How about tonight?' he asked. 'After your class?'

'I'm having dinner with Linda, then,' she said. 'Though I could ask her to cancel.' Her best friend would understand. More than understand. Linda would probably tell her to skip the class, dance for him instead, and have a mad, crazy fling—that it would do her good.

'You have a busy life. A life you love,' he said softly. 'I'm not going to disrupt that.'

Though she had the nasty feeling that he really could. If she let him close, Daniel could disrupt *everything*.

She could make herself resist the temptation. Eventually the attraction would die down.

Except...

Since that kiss, she didn't want to resist any more. Which was exhilarating and terrifying in equal measures.

'How about tomorrow?' he suggested. 'We'll do this the practical way. Talk. Over lunch.'

'In a public place,' she said. Where they'd have to contain themselves.

'That would be prudent,' he said. 'Except I don't want to be sensible. If I'm going to have lunch with you, I want to cook for you.' He gave another of those odd, self-deprecating smiles. 'That's Dan the show-off talking. TV Dan. Shallow. Dr TWC.'

'I don't think you're shallow,' she said. 'I think you

like everyone to believe you are, but you're not. You just don't let people close enough to see who you really are.'

'You,' he said, 'are terrifying.'

'So,' she whispered, 'are you.'

'I'm not scary. Not in the slightest,' he protested. 'Mercutio Dan, that's me. Dan of the terrible jokes.'

Daniel whose kiss made her feel as if the world had melted away. Not that she was going to say that out loud. Not here, at least, because the last thing either of them needed was to be the hottest gossip on the hospital grapevine. 'Tomorrow,' she said. 'Text me your address. And I'll bring pudding.'

At ballet class, as always, Mandy had to concentrate on what her arms and legs were doing, and there wasn't space to think about Daniel and wonder if she'd temporarily taken leave of her senses.

Afterwards, she went for dinner with her best friend at a little bistro round the corner from the dance school, and confessed all. 'The thing is, Lin,' she said, 'I can't get him out of my head, and he can't get me out of his. I've agreed to have lunch with him tomorrow. We're going to talk it through.'

'Which sounds perfectly rational,' Linda said.

Mandy wrinkled her nose. 'It would be, if we were going to be in a public place. But he's cooking for me. At his house. And...' She shook her head. 'Maybe I was temporarily insane to agree to it. We kissed in the middle of the street. What's going to happen in a private space?' She bit her lip. 'Would I be wiser to call the whole thing off?'

'If you call it off,' Linda pointed out, 'you're going to spend the entire weekend brooding about it and wishing you'd been braver.'

'If I go... What if something happens?'

Linda sang a snatch of The Clash's 'Should I Stay or Should I Go' and spread her hands.

'That's just it,' Mandy said ruefully. 'I think we're both scared of what could happen. Neither of us wants a serious relationship.'

'Not every guy's a Laurence,' Linda reminded her. 'There are good men out there who don't cheat.'

Mandy sighed. 'I'm not gossiping about him, because you're my best friend and I know you won't say a word to anyone else about this, but his marriage broke up because he was the one who cheated.'

Linda frowned. 'Hang on. I thought he was single?'

'He is. This all happened half a lifetime ago,' Mandy said. 'He's had a three-dates-and-it's-over policy since then, because he doesn't want to risk hurting anyone again.'

'I'm not making excuses for him, but half a lifetime ago we were all still very young and we didn't always make good choices,' Linda said. 'But if he's stuck to keeping every relationship short and sweet, since then—that's the opposite of what Laurence would do. Laurence is the sort who strings every relationship along until he thinks he can get a better offer.'

'I think Daniel's never been able to forgive himself for what he did,' Mandy said.

'In which case, he's definitely not going to hurt you. If he's got a three-date rule, you could have a three-date fling with him,' Linda suggested.

'I could,' Mandy said. 'But what if we get to the end of date three and that's still not enough?'

'You're breaking your rules to have a fling with him

in the first place, so he can meet you halfway and break his own rules to have a longer fling with you,' Linda said.

'Maybe. But what i—?'

'Mand, I love you dearly, but you're overthinking this,' Linda interrupted gently. 'You're both in your fifties. You're both perfectly capable of keeping your private life and your professional life separate. So just *do* it. Have the fling. Get it out of your systems. And then you can stay on friendly terms and it'll be fine at work.'

'It's that simple?' Mandy asked.

'It's that simple,' Linda said firmly.

Mandy's phone beeped in her bag.

'Check it,' Linda advised, 'or you'll be worrying it's Gemma and she's gone into labour really early.'

'She'd call me, not text, if there was a problem,' Mandy said.

'I know we normally try to avoid tech at the table, but I think you should at least look and see who it's from,' Linda said.

Mandy did so, and felt the colour flood into her face. 'It's Daniel. Giving me his address. Checking if there's anything I don't eat.' She smiled. 'He says he's making me *mezze*.'

'Let me get this straight. He's gorgeous, he respects the nursing team, he's good with the patients and their parents, he tells the kind of jokes you like *and* he can cook? Why on earth are you dithering about this?' Linda shook her head. 'Actually, I think you should've cancelled dinner with me tonight and gone to see him straight after class.'

'He likes ballet, too. He took his niece to see *The Nutcracker* when she was six.' Mandy thought of what he'd said in the office with the door shut, about her pirouetting towards him, and her skin heated even more.

'He sounds like a man worth breaking your rules for,' Linda said. 'Give yourself permission to have that fling, Mand. Because I think you'll really regret it if you don't.'

# CHAPTER SIX

HE AND MANDY were simply having lunch. Talking it through—no, talking themselves down from having a fling, Daniel reminded himself. Being sensible. So why did this feel like a date? And not like the 'have fun but keep them at an emotional distance' date he specialised in, but a proper 'let's take a chance and see where this takes us' kind of date?

He forced himself to focus on cooking. Mandy had texted him back last night to say that she ate practically anything but preferred to avoid red meat, so he'd put together a menu he hoped she'd like, given that she'd enjoyed their sharing board. He'd made a smoky aubergine dip, which was on the table along with a crisp green salad, a bowl of hummus, a bowl of large green Kalamata olives and a bowl of heritage tomatoes. In the oven, he had spinach and feta borek cooking, along with chicken mini fillets that he'd rubbed with sumac, pomegranate molasses and chilli flakes, and spiced roasted cauliflower. The tahini dip for the cauliflower was ready, along with a bowl of pomegranate seeds to sprinkle over it. The flatbread dough was proving and ready to cook on the griddle pan; and the house was tidy. There wasn't anything else he could do.

Mandy wasn't the sort who'd just not turn up at the last minute; he was pretty sure that if she'd changed her mind she would've texted him earlier. But Daniel still found himself feeling nervous, pacing the room and picking things up for no reason and putting them down.

Oh, for pity's sake. This was *lunch*.

But it felt like something else. Like the start of something that could change everything...

Mandy walked from Sloane Square Tube station, heading towards the Chelsea Physic Garden and checking on her phone app that she was going in the right direction. Finally, she turned onto Daniel's street and checked the house numbers as she walked along. The road had several blocks of three-storey Georgian townhouses with a white stucco ground floor and yellow London brick for the upper storeys; the houses all had beautiful big sash windows and tall chimney pots in a row. The doors were painted a glossy black and had a brass door knocker, letter box and doorknob; there was an old-fashioned bell press at the side of the door, with an old-fashioned lantern light above it which matched the equally old-fashioned lantern-style streetlights.

Most of the townhouses had a small square front garden with wrought iron railings, which was laid to stone flags and contained lots of terracotta pots filled with pruned rose bushes and shrubs. There wasn't much colour at this time of year, but no doubt the street looked incredibly pretty in summer.

At last she came to Daniel's front door and took a deep breath. This was it. Her heart was beating a mad tattoo; it felt like being a teenager on a first date with a boy she'd liked from afar all year.

Her best friend's words echoed in her head: *'He sounds like a man worth breaking your rules for. Give yourself permission to have that fling, Mand. Because I think you'll really regret it if you don't.'*

Maybe.

Maybe not.

But there was only one way to find out.

She took a deep breath, raised the knocker—this was it, no going back—and rapped three times.

A few moments later, Daniel arrived at the door. He was dressed casually in faded jeans and a plain white shirt, and looked ridiculously sexy.

'Hi.' He smiled at her and her heart felt as if it had done an anatomically impossible backflip.

'Hi. You said you were doing *mezze*, so I thought about cheating massively and bringing a pot of Greek yogurt and fresh fruit for pudding,' she said, 'but I know you're a cake fiend. So I hope you like this.' She handed him the tote bag containing a cake tin.

'Thank you,' he said. 'I'm sure I will.'

'It's *karythopita*—a Greek spiced walnut cake. I made one for my sister and my mum, too.' And now she was gabbling.

*Shut up, Mandy*, she told herself silently.

'May I?' He opened the lid of the cake tin, took a sniff and grinned. 'That smells glorious. I'm tempted to skip the entire main course and just scoff this.'

His enthusiasm made her smile. 'You're an adult,' she said. 'You can do whatever you choose. Pudding instead of mains, cake for breakfast...'

'I like the way you're thinking, but my sister and my mum would tell you not to encourage me,' he said with a smile. 'Come in. Let me take your coat and get you a drink.'

'I'm on call,' she reminded him, 'so I need to stick to soft drinks.'

'I thought you might say that,' he said, 'so I made a jug of alcohol-free pomegranate mojito—it's my sister-in-law Sasha's recipe.' He closed the door behind them, took her coat and hung it on the bentwood stand in the entrance hall. 'Righty. Come through. The loo's there, under the stairs, if you need it.'

'Should I take my shoes off?' she asked.

'No, you're fine,' he said with a smile.

The whole of the ground floor seemed to be one large reception room; the flooring was all beautiful light parquet, and the walls were painted a pale sage green that went with the Georgian high ceilings and made the room feel light. There was a comfortable-looking chesterfield-style sofa upholstered in sage green, with two armchairs opposite it, and a coffee table on the Persian rug in between them. The TV was set above the fireplace; there were shelves of books that she itched to browse through, wondering what kind of thing he read.

Once past the stairs and the cloakroom, the room opened out further with the kitchen running along one wall; the cabinets and worktops were cream and of a plain design that complemented the style of the house. There was a dining table big enough for eight on the other side of the room set underneath a glass roof, leading to French doors that looked out onto a small and very neat courtyard garden. Next to the door were a standard lamp shaped like a globe, and a zinc tub containing a large, variegated rubber plant. It was incredibly stylish, yet at the same time it felt warm and welcoming.

Daniel took a jug from the fridge and poured them both a glass of pomegranate mojito. 'The stuff in the oven is almost ready; I just need to cook the flatbreads on the griddle pan, which will take about two minutes.'

'Is there anything I can do to help?' she asked.

'Sit and chat to me.' He indicated the table, which had an array of delicious-looking mezze set out on it, and two places were set opposite each other at the end nearest the garden.

'This is delicious,' she said after a sip of her mojito. 'Refreshing and not too sweet.'

'Perfect for summer barbecues,' he said. 'But it's also nice in winter. It reminds me of the sunshine.'

'Your house is lovely,' she said.

'Thank you. It's the light that made me fall in love with it.' He smiled. 'The previous owner used some of the garden to make the kitchen wider, adding the glass roof and the glass wall, so this end is a kind of a kitchen-cum-conservatory-cum-garden-room, and it's all full of light. I love it when the family comes over and we all sit round the table and talk; then after dinner we can just leave everything where it is and go and collapse on the sofas and carry on talking.'

A sound system somewhere was playing piano music.

'Is this OK or would you prefer me to change it?' he asked.

'It's lovely—Einaudi, isn't it?'

'Yes. I find it good to chill to.' He raised his eyebrows. 'Though I do have a fairly broad taste. Everything from my big brother's old punk rock records through to Abba from when Daisy was a tot and insisted on playing "Dancing Queen" on repeat. And by "repeat", I mean for a good ten or eleven times in a row, until we could talk her into letting us play something else.'

He sounded like a completely devoted uncle; he would've made a good father, too, Mandy thought. Very unlike Gemma's own father.

She watched him deftly cook the flatbreads and transfer them from the griddle pan to a serving dish; then he served up the rest of the meal.

'I admit to buying the hummus. Whatever I do, I can never get the texture right, and there's a good deli round the corner—the olives come from there, too,' he said. 'But I made everything else.'

'It all looks fabulous,' she said. When she'd helped herself to a little of everything and tried it, she added, 'And it tastes even better.'

'Thank you. I enjoy cooking,' he said.

'Me, too,' she said.

They kept the conversation light until they'd finished lunch, he'd eaten two slices of cake and he'd made coffee.

'Can I at least wash up?' Mandy asked.

'That's what the dishwasher is for,' he said.

'No more excuses for avoiding *that* conversation, then,' she said.

'No. And you're right—we need to face it head on instead of skirting around it.' He looked at her. 'I still can't stop thinking about you.'

'Snap.' She paused. 'I hope you don't mind—I talked about the situation with my best friend, last night. Linda's known me since our first day at uni, and I trust her completely. She won't gossip or run to the tabloids about you.'

'I envy you,' he said. 'I can talk to my best friend about work and money and practical stuff, but neither of us would know where to start about emotional stuff. We'd both be squirming.'

'That's pretty standard for our generation,' she said. 'I think the next one down from us has more of a clue.'

'I hope so.' He paused. 'What's her verdict?'

'I have a no-date rule. You have a three-date rule. Linda thinks we're old enough to be able to separate work and...other stuff.'

'So we break the rules and see what happens?'

Her mouth was too dry to let her speak, so she nodded.

'Interesting,' he said. 'I assume, since you knew her from your student days, she knew your ex.'

'She was one of my bridesmaids. And she never liked Laurence,' Mandy admitted. 'She said he was vain.'

Daniel gave a bark of laughter. 'And a TV doc isn't vain, by definition?'

'You're not vain,' Mandy said. 'Not with that hair.'

'Believe me, I'm vain. I changed my outfit twice before you got here,' he confessed. 'Jeans and a T-shirt looked too casual and I didn't want you thinking I couldn't be bothered to make an effort. A proper shirt and trousers looked too much like a work outfit and as if I was trying to keep you at a professional distance.' He indicated his jeans and shirt. 'This was a compromise.'

He'd changed twice, for her? She couldn't help smiling. 'You know what? Me, too. A dress felt like overkill, not a relaxed Saturday lunch between friends. My black trousers are smart, but I looked as if I was about to go into work—as you say, putting a professional distance between us.' She indicated her top. 'This made my trousers feel a bit less formal. But, as you say, still making a bit of an effort.'

'That floaty top is really pretty,' he said. 'It suits you.'

'Thank you. And you look sexy as hell.' She closed her eyes. 'Uh. What is it about you that makes me blurt out whatever's in my head instead of filtering it like a sensible person would?'

'The same thing about you that makes me blush all the time, I think,' Daniel said. 'So what do we do now? Follow your best friend's advice?'

'A fling. We don't put an end date on it before it starts, but we keep it fun,' she said. 'So neither of us gets hurt.'

'That works for me,' he said.

'At work,' she said, 'we're colleagues. Friendly, but colleagues. Professional. And it stays that way when our fling ends.'

'Agreed,' he said. 'And outside work...'

*They'd be lovers.* A shiver went down her spine.

'It's been a long time, for me,' she whispered. 'I have no idea any more what you're supposed to do on a date.'

'I don't date anywhere near as much as the media likes to make out,' he said. 'And right at this moment I feel as clueless as a teenager.'

'Like standing on the edge of a cliff, knowing you're supposed to jump in but not sure if you can remember how to swim,' she said.

He pushed his chair back, walked round the table to her, and held out his hand. 'Then let's jump. Together.'

She took his hand and let him draw her to her feet.

The butterflies in her stomach were doing what felt like a stampede.

'Now what?' she asked shakily.

'Dance with me?' he asked. 'I'll change the music.'

He instructed the smart speaker to play 'Something' by George Harrison.

The perfect song, she thought.

'A pedant would point out that it's actually by The Beatles,' she said.

'Bring it on. I've got George Harrison's *Best Of* on vinyl upstairs, and this is the first track,' he retorted.

She laughed. 'I want to look through your vinyl. And your bookshelves.'

'Any time you like,' he said. 'But right now I want five minutes just to hold you in my arms and dance with you.'

Slow dancing on a Saturday afternoon in late autumn, when it was grey outside yet warm inside, felt perfect. Dancing cheek to cheek, because he'd stooped slightly to accommodate the fact she was shorter than he was, even with her shoes on. His hands settled round her waist, and hers were looped round his neck.

She closed her eyes, enjoying his nearness. And slowly, as they swayed together, their faces turned slightly, so the corners of their mouths were touching. Turning further, so his lips were brushing against hers, making every nerve-end tingle. And then they were really kissing, holding each other close, lost in the magic of a kiss.

When he finally broke the kiss, she felt dazed. And no music at all was playing—the song had clearly ended and the sound system had paused.

'Um...' He stroked her face. 'Sorry.'

'No need to apologise. I think we're both on the same page,' she said lightly.

He gave her a wry smile. 'I might just have turned into a troglodyte, wanting to carry you up the stairs to my lair.'

She laughed. 'You don't need to carry me.' She paused. This was where she could leave—or she could stay. Adrenaline pulsed through her, and she decided to take the risk. 'You could always just show me where your lair is.'

'One problem,' he said, his expression suddenly serious. 'Unless you have a condom in your bag... I don't have any.'

She appreciated his concern—and the fact he'd been honest with her. So she could be honest, too. 'Do we need one?' she asked. 'I'm through the menopause so I can't get pregnant, and I haven't slept with someone for a long time.'

'I've always been careful when I've slept with someone—and there are a lot fewer notches on my bedpost than rumour would have it,' Daniel said. 'Though it's your call.'

He was giving her the choice. Offering, not demanding. 'I'm happy to manage without,' she said.

He brushed his mouth briefly against hers. 'Then let me give you a guided tour of the house. You've already seen the living areas.'

And all of a sudden, she wasn't quite ready. She needed a little more time to strengthen her nerve. 'Though I've not browsed your bookshelves or looked at the photos on your mantelpiece,' she said.

As if understanding why she was suddenly backtracking, and wanting to reassure her that everything was fine and he wasn't going to pressure her, he said, 'Come through and look your fill.' He took her hand and led her through to the section with the sofas and the built-in bookshelves.

'Medical textbooks. Classic science fiction. Oh, and what's this?' She looked at the title of the book. '*Uncle Dan—This Is Your Life.*'

He smiled. 'The kids made it for me for my fiftieth birthday. With a bit of help from Mum, Ally and Colin, so they had access to the really embarrassing photos with me wearing terrible nineteen-seventies clothes.'

'May I?'

'Sure.'

She leafed through. There were photographs of Daniel as a baby and a toddler, and as a young child; his nieces and nephews had clearly had huge fun with the captions, mocking his fashion choices. Daniel as a scowling teenager with a terrible haircut. Daniel on the day he passed his driving test, the day he graduated and his first day as a junior doctor. Daniel clearly as the favourite uncle with his nieces and nephews, pushing them on the swings and helping them make sandcastles and chasing them with a garden hose in what she presumed was his parents' garden. Daniel with each of them on their graduation day, and what looked like their eighteenth and twenty-first birthdays as well, clearly taking them out for beer or cocktails. Daniel with smiling brides and grooms. And each page was filled with stories—filled with love.

The last page said it all.

*May your half-century birthday be as golden as
you are.
We love you, Uncle Dan.
Hannah, Milo, James and Daisy*

'They obviously adore you,' Mandy said.

'It's absolutely mutual,' Daniel said.

There was a slight crack in his voice, and again she
wondered if maybe he regretted not having children of
his own. Not that she intended to hurt him by asking; if
he wanted her to know, he'd tell her.

'That's lovely,' she said. She went over to the mantelpiece, which was crowded with photos of graduations
and weddings. 'Clearly you're as close to your family as
I am to mine.'

'Yes,' he said. 'I'm the baby, so obviously I was hugely
annoying to Ally and Colin when I was little. But if I
don't see them during any particular week we'll talk on
the phone. We text each other all the time. And they know
they can always stay here if they're coming up to London
for an exhibition or a performance, or even just meeting
friends and they want a bed for the night. Mum lives with
Colin and Sasha by the sea in Sussex, and Ally and Jake
live in a pretty village just outside Cambridge—Jake's
just about ready to retire from teaching history.'

She noticed that Daniel didn't mention his dad. Had
he, like her, been bereaved? Maybe he found it too hard
to talk about. Now wasn't the time to ask.

'It's nice that you're close now,' she said.

'It is,' he said. 'Righty. Tour. We'll start at the top of
the house—though I think we'll leave the roof terrace
for today, because it's started lashing down with rain.'

'You've got a roof terrace?'

'It's a lovely place to sit on a summer evening. I've got a few pots of flowers up there, thanks mainly to Ally—she's the gardening guru of the family, and she's fixed me up with stuff I can more or less neglect and it'll still thrive,' he said. He ushered her up the two narrow flights of stairs to the top floor. 'This is the boxroom, really—it's where I keep my vinyl. I can't quite bear to get rid of it. But there's a sofa-bed there too, for guests.'

There was a cabinet with a turntable and amplifier on top; the shelves were filled with albums, and there were a couple of smaller boxes that looked as if they contained seven-inch singles. Another, much narrower, shelving unit contained CDs; and there were a couple of framed tour posters on the walls for bands from the nineties.

'Just remembering what I said downstairs,' he said, and quickly found the George Harrison's *Best Of* album. 'The first track. "Something". So it counts as George.'

'Raise you *Abbey Road*,' she said, with a grin. 'We could argue this until the cows come home.' She browsed through his albums. 'Oh, Dire Straits—I *loved* this album. I played mine to death.' She sang a snatch of 'Romeo and Juliet'. 'And you've got the older Fleetwood Mac stuff, not just the Lindsey and Stevie years. I approve.'

'Are you telling me we've got a similar music taste, too?' he asked.

'I think so. Led Zeppelin and Pink Floyd—Jen's three years older than me, and she got into them when her best friend's older brother played the classic tracks to her. And I wanted to do everything that Jen did, so I listened to them as well.'

'The more I get to know about you, Dr Cooke, the

more I like you,' he said. He led her through to the other room, which held a wooden-framed bed and a matching pale wood chest of drawers; there were built-in storage cabinets, and a couple of beautiful watercolour landscapes. 'The guest bedroom,' he said.

On the next floor down was the bathroom, with a bath and separate shower; again, the room was beautifully light and very tidy.

He stood outside the last door. 'My room,' he said softly.

'Your space,' she said, equally softly. 'Your decision.'

For a moment, she thought he was going to lead her downstairs again, but then he opened the door.

The walls were painted the same pale sage green as the rest of the house, again with watercolour landscapes on the walls. The floor was parquet, and there was a red Persian rug on the floor next to the bed. His sleigh bed was wide and looked incredibly comfortable, with deep pillows; there was a bedside cabinet next to the bed with a reading lamp, a book and a smart speaker. As with the other bedrooms, the storage was built in.

'Your house is lovely. And incredibly tidy, given how terrible you are about paperwork at the hospital.'

'I just hate paperwork,' he said. 'Everything here's tidy, because it makes my life easy. Though I do admit to having a cleaner. I want to spend my free time with my family and friends, not slogging through chores.'

'I'm not judging. My family and friends are important to me, too,' she said.

He took her hand and dropped a kiss into her palm, then folded her fingers over it. The sweetness of the gesture made her heart skip a beat.

'Whatever's going through your head right now, hold that thought,' he said quietly, and went over to the beside cabinet. A couple of moments later, the first notes of 'Romeo and Juliet' filtered into the room, making her smile. He switched on the bedside lamp, closed the Roman blind, then walked back over to her. Drawing her into his arms, he swayed with her to the first three lines of the verse, then crooned the fourth line into her ear.

It felt as if he meant it.

'Yes,' she said.

# CHAPTER SEVEN

MANDY WOKE THE next morning, warm and comfortable, her head pillowed on Daniel's shoulder and her hand holding his against his chest.

'Good morning,' he said.

'Morning.' She pressed a kiss against his shoulder. 'What's the time?'

'Nearly nine,' he said.

'Then I,' she said, 'need to get home, shower and change. I'm due at my sister's for lunch.' Her hand tightened briefly round his. 'You're very welcome to join us, but I should warn you that my mum, my sister and my daughter will all grill you mercilessly.'

'I'm due at my sister's, too,' he said. 'Again, you're welcome to join us, but if you do I have a feeling there will be questions. Lots of them.'

'Let's both take a rain check,' she said, sitting up. 'And if you're off to Cambridge, you need to get going soon or you'll be late.'

'Can I get you some breakfast?' he asked.

'No, I'm fine,' she said. 'But thank you.' She pulled on her clothes, and he found a pair of pyjama bottoms and pulled them on.

'I'll see you at work tomorrow, then,' he said, drawing her into a hug and kissing the top of her head.

'Yes.' She pressed her lips against his bare chest. 'Have a lovely day.'

'You, too.'

She was smiling all the way home. Daniel had been a generous lover; and instead of finding it shy and awkward, they'd laughed and enjoyed exploring each other. And afterwards they'd lain curled up in his bed, talking for hours, too comfortable to move. Eventually they'd pulled their clothes on and gone downstairs to eat leftovers from lunch for supper. And then he'd persuaded her to stay the night—not that she'd needed much persuading, because she'd enjoyed his company so much that she hadn't wanted to leave.

Thankfully she hadn't been needed at the hospital, and she'd finally gone to sleep in his arms.

It had definitely been worth breaking her rules.

Mandy was still smiling when she'd showered, changed and taken the other Greek walnut cake she'd made over to her sister's house.

'You look very happy today,' Jen remarked when she'd made coffee and they were sitting with their mother and Gemma in the living room; Dev was outside with Jen's husband Barry, looking at the classic car he was restoring. 'Is there something we need to know?'

Mandy wasn't ready to share her delicious secret, yet. 'No,' she said. 'I just had a good week at work.' She wrinkled her nose. 'Well, mainly. Monday was rough on all of us, and you don't need to know about that.' No way was she telling that particular horror story in front of her pregnant daughter. 'But Noah, the baby who came in with infant botulism last week, is responding well to treatment.' She smiled. 'Dan's including Noah's case in the next series, and there's a tiny interview with me because I'm the one who worked out what it was. And of course you both know better than to feed honey to a baby under the age of one, right?'

'Of course,' they echoed.

'So you're on very good terms with Dr Dan?' Jen raised her eyebrows.

'Everyone on the ward calls him Dan.' Mandy willed the blush to stay down. 'He's lovely to work with. So are the rest of the team. I'm glad I made the move to the London Victoria.'

Gemma gave her a searching look, and Mandy deftly switched the conversation to babies and when Gemma's next scan was due. Thankfully it seemed to distract her mum, her sister and her daughter, and she managed to keep the conversation on babies until lunch was ready.

'There's something different about you,' Ally said, narrowing her eyes and holding Dan at arm's length. 'You look…hmm…*relaxed.*'

'It's probably because we've just started filming. That always gives me an energy boost,' Daniel said.

'Hmm,' Ally said.

Daniel enveloped her in a hug. 'Plus I don't have to cook my own Sunday lunch today.' He gave her the roses he'd bought on the way to Cambridge, and a bottle of New Zealand Sauvignon Blanc.

'My favourites,' she said. 'Thank you.'

'My pleasure.' He handed over a packet of dog treats. 'Not forgetting Dora.'

The miniature dachshund, hearing her name, trotted over and nudged him with her nose. He bent down to scratch her behind the ears. 'Hello, gorgeous. You're nearly as gorgeous as my favourite sister.'

'Your only sister,' Ally said drily, but to his relief she let the conversation centre around her beloved dachshund.

He enjoyed the day, especially as his nephew and niece and their partners also turned up for lunch, and Ally suggested that as it was a lovely day they should all walk off the rice pudding with Dora in the grounds of the local stately home. The last bits of autumn colour sparkled in the late autumn sunlight, and the reflections in the river were stunning. This, he thought, was a place that Mandy would like.

He left his sister's house at the same time as the children, pleading Sunday night London traffic; back at the house, he texted Mandy.

Had a good day?

He debated putting a kiss, and decided that might be over the top, so he sent it as it was.

She texted him back within a minute.

Lovely. You?

Went for a walk after lunch.

He sent her the photograph of the woods reflected in the river, and one of Dora.

She rang him. 'That's gorgeous—and so's the dog.'

'Dora the Daxie. She's a sweetie,' he said.

'Where did you go?'

'A stately home near Ally's. Daisy and James were there, too, with their partners.' He paused. 'I had to use a few distraction techniques. Ally's first comment was that I looked *relaxed* and she wanted to know why.'

She chuckled. 'I had a similar problem.'

Oh, that chuckle. Right at that moment he really wanted to see her. But he didn't want to put pressure on her. 'Are you busy tomorrow night?'

'No—my book club's only on the first Monday of the month,' she said.

'Fancy joining me at the cinema? They're showing a season of nineties' films just round the corner from me. *Good Will Hunting* is on tomorrow evening.'

'I love that film,' she said. 'Yes, please.'

'I'll book tickets. It starts at eight, so we've got time to eat first,' he said.

'I'll look forward to it. See you tomorrow,' she said.

'Sweet dreams.'

'You, too,' he said.

At the hospital on Monday, they managed to act as if they were merely colleagues. Mandy was teaching, while Daniel was busy on the ward and in meetings. They left the hospital separately, took the Tube separately, met up at Sloane Street and walked to the French bistro Daniel had booked not far from the cinema.

The cassoulet and tarte tatin with Chantilly cream were both fabulous; but Mandy enjoyed Daniel's company even more. He was easy to be with, and she thoroughly enjoyed talking about favourite films and plays with him, particularly when she learned that his taste chimed with hers as much as their musical tastes did.

He held her hand through the film, and it made her feel as if she were a teenager, holding hands in the dark.

'Let me drive you home,' he said when they left the cinema. 'I know you're perfectly capable of getting the Tube, but I'm not quite ready to say goodnight to you yet.'

She felt the same way. 'All right,' she said.

They walked back to his street to collect his car, and he took the pretty route along Chelsea Embankment towards the Strand; the river reflected the lights from the bridges and the buildings and looked incredibly pretty. The narrow steeple of St Mary Le Strand rose up before them, brilliant white, followed by the iconic dome of St Paul's. Daniel didn't bother putting any music on through the car's sound system, because they didn't stop talking on the way, about anything and everything.

When they neared King's Cross, Mandy directed him to her address, and Daniel found a parking spot close to her flat.

'Would you like to come in for a coffee?' she asked.

'I'm incredibly tempted,' he said, 'but we both have an early start tomorrow, so I'll say goodnight now.'

This was their second date.

What now? Mandy wondered. Was his refusal to come in his way of preparing her for the last date? Would the next date be their last? Or would he, like her, break his rules and see where this thing between them went?

'Goodnight,' she said.

He kissed her lingeringly. 'I'll see you at work tomorrow. I know you have a class tomorrow night, but are you free on Wednesday evening?'

'Yes. You could come over and I'll cook for us,' she suggested.

'Thank you—I'd like that. I'll bring pudding,' he said. He took her hand, pressed a kiss into her palm and curled her fingers round it. 'See you tomorrow,' he said.

How did this man manage to make her knees turn to jelly, when nobody had done that since Laurence? she wondered. And it wasn't just that sweet little gesture of a kiss, but the fact that he waited until she'd let herself in safely through her front door before driving off. It made her feel cherished. She was perfectly capable of looking after herself, but it was nice to date someone who wanted to look out for her, too.

On Tuesday afternoon, Daniel caught up with her. 'Do you have time for a quick chat? I have a patient I'd like you to meet. He actually asked me if he could be on the show—he enjoyed telling me that his mum has a crush on me, and the poor woman turned beetroot— but, actually, I think he'd be a natural on television. He's also said that he's happy for the students to come and ask him questions, and I think he'd be an excellent case for them.'

'Sure,' she said. 'Can I have a patient history?'

'Joe Lavery, aged thirteen. If I tell you he's missing school because he's too exhausted to get out of bed, and he gets sharp pains in his stomach, what would you say?'

'I know what that makes me suspect, so I'd ask about bowel movements,' she said.

'There's diarrhoea and blood in his faeces,' Daniel said.

Which was what she'd expected him to say. 'Would I be right in guessing that he's very thin?'

Daniel nodded. 'His older brothers are tall and slim, but Joe's painfully slender, and his mum thinks he's stopped growing upwards. Joe himself says that he still has a baby face when some of his mates are starting to get fuzz, and he's not very happy about it because he thinks it'll put the girls off.'

'Bless him. Have you done an endoscopy and colonoscopy?' she asked.

'Yes. I've just had the results back. Want to see?' Daniel asked. At her nod, he brought up the images on his computer screen.

'Poor kid. He must've been in agony,' she said, seeing the extreme ulcerations from his throat right down to his anus. 'That's textbook Crohn's.'

'Which is why I thought of your students,' Daniel said. 'I'm going to admit him and put him on meal replacement drinks to help him gain weight. A couple of weeks of that, and then we can give him monthly infusions of infliximab to stop the inflammation.'

'Have you talked to him about the diagnosis?' she asked.

'He's round from the sedation now, so I'm just about to see him and his mum, if you'd like to join us.'

'All right. I'll just have a quick word with Kelly—' one of the other senior doctors on the ward '—and ask her if she'll keep an eye on the students for me, and I'll be with you.'

'I'll be in consulting room four,' Daniel said.

Once she'd made sure that her students all had someone to ask if they were stuck on anything—and told them they'd get to meet another patient shortly—she knocked on the door of consulting room four.

'Joe, Abigail, I'd like you to meet Mandy Cooke, who job-shares with me,' Daniel said. 'Mandy, this is Joe Lavery and his mum, Abigail.'

Joe was very thin and pale, with a shock of blond curly hair and cornflower-blue eyes. Despite the fact that he was in obvious pain, he smiled at her. 'Hello.'

'Nice to meet you both,' Mandy said. 'Dan told me that you'd agreed to talk to my students. Thank you very much, Joe. I know it can be a bit embarrassing, so it's really appreciated.'

'It's important to talk about poo,' Joe said. 'Since I've been ill, my mates and I all talk about it more. You know, like if something doesn't feel quite right.'

'Talking's a good thing,' Daniel said.

'So did the camera tell you what's wrong with me?' Joe asked.

'Yes. We think you have Crohn's disease,' Daniel said. 'It's a sort of inflammatory bowel disease. Part of your gut becomes swollen, inflamed and ulcerated—that's why you get diarrhoea, blood in your poo and stomach pains, and why you feel tired.' He looked at Joe. 'Do you want to see the pictures?'

'Definitely,' Joe said.

Dan brought them up on the screen.

Joe's eyes widened. 'Wow. I wasn't expecting that.'

'You can definitely see why you're in pain,' Daniel said gently.

'What causes all the ulcerations?' Abigail asked. 'Is Joe allergic to any foods? And how do we know which ones?'

'Crohn's isn't caused by diet,' Mandy said. 'We don't

know for sure what causes it. Sometimes it runs in the family.'

'Nobody else in our family has had any symptoms like Joe's, not even mildly,' Abigail said.

'Sometimes it's an autoimmune disease—that means your body's immune system, which defends you against infection, attacks your digestive system,' Daniel explained. 'Though, as Mandy said, we don't always know why it happens.'

'Can you cure it?' Joe asked.

'No. It's a lifelong condition, and it can be unpredictable,' Daniel said. 'You're likely to go into remission—that's when you feel really well—and at other times you'll have a flare-up, where your symptoms will be worse. The good news is that we can give you medicine to keep you in remission for long periods.'

'We can give you steroids, either as injections or a tablet, to calm the inflammation down,' Mandy said.

'Aren't they what body-builders use? The dodgy ones, I mean, and they're angry all the time with Roid Rage?' Joe asked.

Mandy could see exactly why Daniel had suggested the teenager as a case study for her students as well as for his show. Joe was bright and slightly cheeky, even though he was obviously in pain, and she rather thought he'd enjoy testing the students. She smiled. 'It's a different sort of steroid. These are ones like your body produces naturally. Though they do have side effects—they can cause problems sleeping and make you more prone to picking up infection. You might find you put on weight.'

'That won't be a problem. I worry that he's all skin and bone as it is,' Abigail said.

'Sometimes steroids affect your growth,' Daniel said, 'so for the next couple of weeks we're going to put you on a liquid diet that contains all the nutrition you need. It'll help counteract that and help build your strength up.'

'Milkshakes?' Joe asked.

'Something like that,' Mandy said. 'We'll need to give you some biological medicines as well, when you've built up some strength.'

'Biological? Like laundry liquid?' Joe asked.

Mandy smiled. 'No. It just means they're medicines made from cell cultures rather than synthetically.'

'The one I want to prescribe is called infliximab,' Daniel said. 'The latest research shows that if we give it to you soon after diagnosis, you're less likely to need surgery in the future. We'll give you an infusion—that means we'll put you on a drip for a couple of hours so the medicine goes straight into your vein—and we'll need to do that once a month.'

'How does the medicine work?' Abigail asked.

'It's an antibody-based medicine and it targets a protein in your body called TNF-alpha—that stands for "tumour necrosis factor", but that isn't the same as cancer,' Mandy explained. 'TNF is naturally produced by your body and helps fight off infection, but too much of it can damage the cells lining the gut. What infliximab does is bind to the TNF-alpha and that reduces inflammation.'

'How long does it take to work?' Joe asked.

'Everyone responds differently. It might start helping straight away, or it might take two or three sessions,' Mandy said. 'We'll see how it goes, but if it suits you we'll suggest taking it for a year and then we'll review it.'

'Are there any side effects, like the ones with the steroids?' Abigail asked.

'There might be a bit of redness or swelling around the site where we give you the infusion, and you might get a headache or feel a bit sick,' Daniel said.

'You're also likely to pick up infections more easily,' Mandy added. 'We'll give you a leaflet so you know what to look out for, and you need to tell us if you've got a fever or you're worried about anything. I'd advise having a flu jab every year, and give us a call if you've been in contact with anyone who has chickenpox, shingles, measles or TB.'

'That's a big list of things,' Abigail said, looking daunted.

'I know it's a lot to take in. As Mandy said, we have patient information leaflets that can help you,' Daniel said, 'and we can also give you details of support groups. I know the diagnosis might feel like a bit of a shock right now, but there's no reason why Joe can't live a normal life. Yes, it's a lifelong condition and you'll need treatment, Joe, but that treatment will let you live a healthy life.'

'Thank you,' Joe said. 'So I can still play football, do computer stuff and see my mates.' He smiled. 'And, if I'm on telly, that means I might even get a girlfriend...'

# CHAPTER EIGHT

ON WEDNESDAY EVENING, Daniel stopped at the deli round the corner from his house to buy a box of *macarons*, some out-of-season raspberries and a bottle of wine; he picked up a nice but not over-ostentatious bouquet of roses, gerbera and antirrhinum in autumn tones at the florist's, then caught the Tube from Sloane Square to King's Cross.

Mandy's flat was a short walk away, in a row of four-storey Georgian townhouses that were similar to his own but had clearly been split into flats. He pressed the button for her flat; a few moments later, he heard her voice. 'Hello?'

'It's Dan.'

'I'll buzz you in. Come straight up,' she said. Seconds later, he heard a buzz and a click, and he opened the front door.

Her flat was on the second floor, and she was waiting for him at the top of the stairs.

'Hi.' He kissed her cheek and handed her the bag with the wine, raspberries and *macarons*. 'For you. I'm afraid I cheated and bought pudding rather than making it.'

She looked inside the bag. 'Ooh, I love these. Thank you.'

'And also for you.' He gave her the flowers.

She smiled. 'They're beautiful. Thank you. Come through to the kitchen while I put the flowers in water. The bathroom's just here—' she indicated the door between what were clearly the living room and the kitchen '—if you need it.'

Her kitchen was square and compact, with pale primrose walls, beech cabinets, dark grey worktops and dark grey tiled flooring. There were a couple of pots of herbs on the windowsill, a wok set on the hob, and three bowls on the worktop next to it; one contained diced chicken, one contained diced vegetables, and one contained what looked like a home-made sauce. Next to them was a saucer containing grated fresh ginger and crushed garlic, and a wooden spatula.

He raised an eyebrow, smiling. 'You could be a TV cook, with everything prepped like that.'

She laughed. 'It just saves a bit of time. It'll take literally five minutes to cook this lot, boil the kettle and do some noodles to go with it.' She looked at him. 'Did you drive?'

'No. I came by Tube,' he said.

'Then there's a bottle of white wine already chilling in the fridge, if you'd like to pour us both a glass. Or I can offer you sparkling water, with or without elderflower; or make you some jasmine tea, if you'd prefer?'

'Jasmine tea?' He blinked.

She opened the door to the cabinet above the kettle. 'Behold my tea collection. Breakfast, Earl Grey, jasmine, peppermint, lemon and ginger, camomile and three different fruit teas.' She grinned. 'Gemma used to tease me about them.'

'Teasing about tea,' he said.

Her grin became a rich chuckle. 'Indeed. Anyway, when she fell pregnant and discovered she couldn't stand the smell of coffee, she was very grateful for my tea collection.'

'If you're having wine, so will I,' he said.

'The glasses are on the table in the living room,' she said, 'if you'd like to grab them.'

'Sure.'

Her living room was also square; there was a small table and four chairs placed against one wall, set with two places. A comfortable-looking dark red sofa sat opposite, with scatter cushions that matched the curtains of the two sash windows overlooking the street. Daniel recognised them as his sister's favourite William Morris design, in an elegant dark navy. The elegant fireplace was flanked on each side with shelves stuffed with a mix of what looked like medical textbooks and classic novels. He glanced at the photographs on the mantelpiece. One was clearly Mandy's daughter on her graduation day; one was Gemma's wedding; another was Mandy's own graduation day with her sister and her parents; and the final one was of Mandy as a bridesmaid. He guessed that the bride was probably Linda, her best friend.

Next to the sofa was a small table with lamp and smart speaker, and in the middle of the polished wooden floor was a navy rug with the same William Morris pattern as the cushions and curtains. Like the kitchen, the room was compact, but the overall effect was cosy rather than cluttered.

Mandy had put the flowers in a vase by the time he returned with the two wine glasses, and heated oil in the wok ready to cook the stir-fry.

He took the chilled bottle of wine from the fridge and poured two glasses of wine; he placed hers on the worktop next to the hob. He could smell the delicious aromas of the garlic and ginger sizzling.

'You have a very nice flat,' he said.

'Thank you. It's small, but it suits me—plus it has a spare bedroom next to mine, upstairs,' she added, 'which means I can have my grandchild to stay if Gemma and Dev are going out somewhere.'

She clearly had her life worked out, Daniel thought. He really wasn't sure if she would have room in her life for a relationship. Then again, neither did he. Besides, they'd both said that they didn't want a proper relationship. This was a fling, he reminded himself. For fun, not for ever.

He glanced at her fridge as he put the bottle back in to chill again. There were postcards stuck to the front with magnets, plus a couple of photographs, one of which appeared to be a group of people outside the Royal Opera House.

'Is that your ballet class?' he asked.

She glanced round to see what he was looking at, and smiled. 'Yes. We went to see *Swan Lake* together at Covent Garden earlier this year. We had amazing seats, and I think it was the best performance I've ever seen—everything was just perfect. We did the backstage tour, too, and it was fascinating. Did you know there used to be nine gin palaces on Bow Street? There's only one left now, though obviously it's a modern pub.' She grinned. 'And of course we had to visit it. We begged our teacher to do us a simplified bit of *Swan Lake* choreography, that half term.'

'What are the chances,' he asked, 'of you dancing it for me?'

'None, because I can't quite remember the whole thing, now.' She smiled. 'But if you really want a demo, I can do you a simplified "Dance of the Sugar Plum Fairy". That's what we've been doing this term—obviously it's *Nutcracker* season.'

'I'm so in for that,' he said. 'Do you happen to have a tutu?'

She laughed. 'No. But I'll wear my practice skirt so you get the full effect of the swishy bits in the routine. After dinner.'

'I'll look forward to that,' he said.

As she'd suggested, it only took a few minutes to cook the stir-fry and the noodles. She served up, and took the bowls into the living room while he brought the glasses through.

'This is fabulous,' he said after the first mouthful.

'It's an easy recipe,' she said. 'From my favourite recipe website.'

As soon as she named it, he nodded. 'Mine, too. Which makes me sound horribly domesticated.'

'Nothing wrong with being capable,' she said.

He glanced up at the framed pictures of flowers on the wall. 'Is that cross stitch?' he asked.

'My guilty pleasure,' she said. 'I normally sew for an hour in the evening; it helps me decompress. I'm currently making a birth sampler for my grandchild.' She left the table to lift the cloth off a stand in the corner.

It was a charming design, with foliage in the shape of a heart and woodland animals peeping out of it—a fox, a squirrel, a rabbit and an owl—plus room in the centre of the heart for the baby's name and weight.

'Gemma and Dev chose a woodland theme for their nursery. I was so pleased when I found this pattern.'

'It's lovely,' he said. 'She'll be thrilled.'

'I hope so.'

He kept the conversation light, and insisted on helping her clear the table after they'd finished eating. Then he sneakily washed up while she went upstairs to change into her ballet clothes.

'You weren't supposed to do the washing up,' she said when she came back down to join him. 'I didn't wash up at your place.'

'You didn't need to. I have a dishwasher and a cleaner,' he reminded her.

'Even so. You're my guest. I should be waiting on you, not the other way round. Though thank you.' She rolled the rug up, to give her room to dance on the wooden floorboards. And she looked incredibly cute, he thought, in a black leotard, black footless dance tights, and a floaty chiffon skirt that reached down to just above her knees, plus pale pink ballet shoes.

'I need a two-minute warm-up so I don't pull a muscle,' she said, and proceeded to do what he assumed was the usual warm-up routine at her class. Then she switched on her smart speaker, connected it to her streaming service and called up 'Dance of the Sugar Plum Fairy'. The ethereal notes of the celesta shimmered in the air and she began to dance—not on pointes, as she'd already told him, but still on tiptoe. He was captivated by the graceful way she moved her arms and legs, the arabesques and turns, the tiny bourrée steps—and all with a smile on her face.

When the music ended, she swept into a deep curtsey, and he clapped.

'I loved that,' he said. 'You're amazing.'

She went pink. 'It's hardly in the same league as Sadler's Wells or the Royal Opera House. But I enjoy the music and the dancing. It's taken our class a while to learn this piece, even though it's only a couple of minutes long. And I'm sorry it's not the flashy one with all the fouettés and pirouettes that you've seen in a proper performance—this is a beginner's version.'

'I loved the routine,' he said again. 'And I love the way your skirt swished when you danced. It's given me all kind of ideas.'

'Oh, yes?'

He stood up and walked over to her. 'Do a twirl for me? Please?'

'I'm not very good at it, but I'll do you a soutenu turn,' she said. One leg came out, then as she drew her leg back in front of the other one she went on tiptoe, spread her arms, spun round and faced him with her arms posed above her head like a ballerina in a musical box.

'One more?' he begged.

She did so; this time, when she faced him again, he drew her into his arms and kissed her until she was breathless.

'Just as I dreamed it would be,' he said, his voice husky.

This time, she kissed him.

And he scooped her up and carried her up the stairs to her bedroom.

\* \* \*

Afterwards, they lay curled in bed together.

'So tonight was pretty much our third date,' she said. 'Is this where you tell me that you've enjoyed my company but you'd rather we go back to being just friends— and I've done nothing wrong, it's just the way you are?'

Daniel gave her a wry smile. 'That's what I'd normally do, yes.' He paused. 'But you broke your rule for me by seeing me in the first place. I ought to break my rule for you.'

'But?'

The word that had echoed in his head; clearly she'd noticed. 'You really are brave,' he said. 'Asking the difficult question.'

'It needs asking. And it does neither of us any favours if we sidestep it,' she said.

'All right. The thought of going past my three-date rule makes me antsy,' he said. Which was an understatement. It made his stomach turn to water. What if they kept seeing each other, got closer, and they fell in love? What if he let her down, the same way he'd let Roxy down? What if, deep down, he was still just like his father and he hadn't learned to be different?

The last thing he wanted to do was to hurt Mandy.

On the other hand, going back to being just colleagues and friends would be more than difficult, now. He really liked the woman he was getting to know. Liked her more than he'd liked anyone in a very long time. And she seemed to like him, too...

'Dan?' she asked gently. 'What do you want?'

*To be sure I'm not my father's mini-me.*

Not that he could explain that. Everything was too mixed up in his head. 'If I'm honest, the thought of not seeing you any more makes me antsy, too,' he admitted.

'So what do we do now?' she asked.

Panic? Oh, for pity's sake. 'I think maybe we keep going until one of us is ready to say stop,' he said.

'And keep it just between us, for now,' she said.

'Just between us,' he agreed.

For the next couple of weeks, Mandy and Daniel sneaked in dates between work and her classes. Sometimes they went for a drink, sometimes they did the crossword together over a videocall, sometimes they went for a walk—and even on a rainy evening it was fun, holding hands and laughing as they dodged the puddles. He even let it slip to Ally that he was seeing Mandy. But on Saturday afternoon, when Mandy was sitting on Daniel's lap on her sofa and being thoroughly kissed, her phone rang.

She glanced at the screen. 'It's my daughter.'

'Answer it, or you'll worry yourself silly that there's a problem with the baby—and everything might be just fine,' Daniel said.

She nodded and answered the phone. 'Gemma? Is everything all right, darling?'

Gemma laughed. 'Don't panic, Mum. I've been shopping, and I found this incredibly cute cardigan for the baby, and I wanted to show you.'

Mandy closed her eyes in relief. 'That sounds great. Shall I come over tomorrow?' she asked.

'Actually, I went shopping not far from you and I'm nearly at your front door,' Gemma said.

'You're nearly at my front door now?' Mandy almost squeaked in horror.

That meant there wasn't enough time for Daniel to make a quick exit. But if Gemma saw him in her mother's flat, she'd ask questions. Questions that Mandy didn't know how to begin to answer.

*Sorry*, she mouthed at Daniel.

He mouthed back, *It's fine*.

'I'll put the kettle on. Is Dev with you?'

'No. It's just me,' Gemma said.

'All right. See you in a minute, sweetheart,' Mandy said, and disconnected the call. 'Sorry. I'll tell her you're just my friend. That you came over because you wanted to talk to me about something to do with the ward. Or about a case for your show—we could tell her about Joe.'

'Even though it's plausible, she's not going to believe a word,' Daniel said drily. 'Even if you comb your hair, you'll still look as if you've just been kissed until you're dizzy.'

She stared at him, and felt her eyes widen. 'That's how you look, too.'

He winced. 'Let's play this by ear. She might not notice.'

But of course she did. As soon as Gemma walked up the stairs and saw Daniel, and looked at her mother's face, she said, 'How nice to meet you, Dr Monroe. I enjoy watching your show. Mum, let me help you make that cup of tea.'

'It's not what you th—' Mandy began as Gemma bundled her into the kitchen and closed the door.

'No? You can't even meet each other's eyes,' Gemma said. 'You look like a pair of guilty teenagers.'

'How would you know?' Mandy retorted. 'You teach Reception class, not high school.'

'It's not that long since I was a guilty teenager myself,' Gemma reminded her. 'And it's pretty obvious you've just been snogging each other's faces off.'

Mandy groaned and rubbed a hand across her face. 'Oh, for pity's sake.'

Gemma hugged her. 'And I'm delighted you're seeing him. You know I worry about you being lonely. This will stop me fretting quite so much.'

'It's very, very early days,' Mandy warned. 'It might not come to anything. We're just seeing how things go.'

'If he makes you happy for now, that's enough for me,' Gemma said. 'Having said that, if he hurts you, he'll have me to deal with. In Mama Bear mode.'

Mandy hugged her daughter back. 'He's not going to hurt me, Gem. We're friends. Well, a little bit more than friends,' she admitted. 'Neither of us was expecting anything to happen, and we're finding our way round it.'

'Just live in the moment and enjoy it. It's about time,' Gemma said, and proceeded to take over making the tea, finding the biscuits and then shooing her mother out of the kitchen.

'Well?' Daniel whispered.

'We didn't get away with it,' Mandy whispered back. 'She says we look like guilty teenagers.'

He chuckled, and stole a kiss—just as Gemma brought the tea and biscuits through and caught them.

'The pair of you really have both regressed three and a half decades, haven't you?' she asked, but she was smiling.

'Born-again teenagers who are trying very hard to

persuade everyone that they're just good friends but not making a very good job of it,' Daniel said cheerfully. 'Sorry, Gemma. Though I want you to know that I like your mother very much. She's a brilliant doctor and she's perfect as my job-share. I'm not going to do anything to jeopardise that. More importantly, even though neither of us really knows where this is going or what we want, I'm not going to do anything to hurt her.'

'Good,' Gemma said. 'Because you really don't want an angry pregnant woman on your case, Dr Monroe.'

'Call me Dan,' Daniel said. 'And I hear what you say.' He paused. 'You're thirty-two weeks, aren't you?'

She nodded. 'I've been really lucky—I've only had a little bit of morning sickness.'

'That's good,' he said.

Gemma raised her eyebrows. 'I hear Mum's going to be on your show.'

'She's the one who spotted the infant botulism, so she deserves the credit,' Daniel said. 'Plus I like the way she teaches. Some of her students might end up on the show as well.'

Gemma chatted happily to both of them until she'd finished her tea. And then her eyes widened. 'I nearly forgot to show you the cardigan.' She rummaged in her shopping bag. 'Look. It's fleecy, and there are teddy bear ears on the hood.'

'That's seriously cute,' Mandy agreed.

'And I'd better get back before Dev starts worrying I'm late,' she said. 'It really was nice to meet you, Dan.'

'You, too,' he said.

'Have a good evening,' she said.

'Text me when you're home,' Mandy reminded her.

'I will. Don't fuss.'

Mandy laughed. 'Six months' time, it'll be me telling you not to fuss…'

'I'm a primary school teacher. Nothing fazes us or makes us fuss,' Gemma said, laughing back. 'But, yes, I'll text you when I'm home.'

'She's lovely. Very like you,' Daniel said when Gemma had gone.

'Thank you.' Mandy drew a breath. 'You do know she's going to be straight on the phone to her gran, her aunt and her godmother now she's left us, don't you?'

'Her godmother being your best friend?' he guessed.

She nodded. 'Gem will be telling them all about you. And there will be "casual" invitations.' She emphasised the word with finger quotation marks.

'So they can meet me and see for themselves if they're happy that I'll be good to you?' Daniel asked.

'Yes.' And the idea scared her witless. Until they knew where this thing between them was going, she'd rather keep it between themselves.

'I'm afraid my family will do the same kind of thing.' He paused. 'Maybe we ought to pre-empt it.'

She wasn't brave enough to do that. And she needed to be honest with him about it. 'I'm not sure I'm really ready for that,' she admitted.

'Me, neither.' Was that relief or trepidation she could see in his eyes? She wasn't sure. 'Perhaps it's better if we take each day as it comes and make excuses until we're ready.'

'That works for me,' she said.

The following week, on Tuesday evening, Mandy picked up a text from Daniel after her aerobics class.

Hope you had a good class. Ally's taking Jake to a show tomorrow night because the friend she was going with has flu. They want to have dinner with me—and you, too, if you're free. I can tell them I'm busy, or you can meet Ally and Jake. No pressure either way: your choice. D x

'Oh, help,' she said to Linda. 'What do I do?'

'What do you want to do?' Linda asked.

'Dan met Gemma at the weekend and they got on fine. Me meeting his sister would be the next step,' Mandy said. It meant taking their fling another step closer to being a proper relationship, and she wasn't entirely sure how she felt about that. Dan had swept her off her feet; she'd swept him off his feet, too. Were they ready for this, or had they already rushed everything and meeting each other's families properly would be a step too far? 'On the one hand, I'd like to meet her.' She bit her lip. 'On the other hand, what if she doesn't like me and thinks I'm completely wrong for Dan?'

Linda scoffed. 'The idea of anyone not getting on with you is so ridiculous, I'm not even going to dignify it with a response. Of course she'll like you.' She paused. 'I'd actually like to meet him, too. Obviously, only when you're ready.'

'I'm not sure I'm ready, yet.' Mandy bit her lip. 'This is ridiculous, Lin. I'm fifty-two years old and about to become a grannie. Yet I feel like a teenager, in a spin every time I think about him. I don't think I've ever blushed so much in my life, this last month or so.'

'You've been a brilliant mum to Gemma, a good support to your mum and your sister, and you're a legend among the students,' Linda said. 'You've put everything else on the back burner. Maybe it's time you put that part of your life first, just for a little while.'

'While my fling with Dan lasts, you mean?'

'Don't put limits on it,' Linda advised. 'Be open to… well, whatever happens. See where it takes you. You like him, and he likes you. Thinking about anything else will just overcomplicate it.'

'I guess…' Mandy texted him back.

Love to meet them. Let me know where and what time. M x

Half an hour later, her phone pinged with a message giving her the restaurant's address in Leicester Square.

Table booked for 6.15. (Their show starts 7.30) D x

On Wednesday, she and Daniel were both caught up in meetings all day and didn't get the chance to catch up with each other, but Mandy managed to get home in time to change into a little black dress before catching the Tube to Leicester Square. It was a short walk to the restaurant; when she gave Daniel's name at the reception, the waiter ushered her over to the table.

Daniel stood up, kissed her cheek, and seated her at the table. 'This is Ally, my sister, and Jake, my brother-in-law. Ally, Jake, this is Mandy.'

'Lovely to meet you,' Ally said.

'And you.' Daniel's sister looked like a feminine version of him, with the same deep brown eyes and dark hair shot through with grey, and she had the same warmth about her.

'How have you settled in at the hospital?'

'Really well. The team's great,' Mandy said. 'Dan said you were going to the theatre tonight.'

'It's a new production of *Oedipus*,' Ally said. 'I was going with a friend who teaches Classics at my school—I don't know if Dan told you I teach English at sixth form?—but she's gone down with a bug and I nagged Jake into coming with me because I didn't want to miss it. I asked Dan to meet us for dinner—and then it struck me, it'd be the perfect chance to meet you.'

'Thank you for asking me to join you,' Mandy said. 'Your dog's gorgeous, by the way. Dan showed me the photos he took from your walk.'

'Dora. Which is also short—like her legs—for "adorable",' Ally said with a grin.

'Excuse me. *I'm* the one who does the terrible jokes and puns,' Daniel interrupted.

'Believe me,' Jake said drily, 'your sister can give you a run for your money.'

'So can Mandy. Her daughter teaches Reception class,' Daniel said.

'Five's such a lovely age,' Ally said.

'Isn't it just? Though my source of jokes for my patients will be drying up for a little while,' Mandy said, 'when Gemma has the baby.'

'Is it her first?' Ally asked.

Mandy nodded. 'I'm so looking forward to being a grannie—in somewhere around seven weeks' time.'

'I would be, too,' Ally said. She smiled. 'It'll be a while until either of my two settle down and think about babies.'

'Daisy's the music therapy specialist and James is

the archaeologist, right?' Mandy checked. 'Dan told me about them.'

'Thankfully they both live in London, so they're not that far from us,' Ally said. 'Dan's always been good with them. Especially Daisy—he got through to her when nobody else could.'

'I just did what you all would've done, if she'd let you,' Daniel said. 'She hated the pressure of her course. She would've made a good doctor, but she didn't enjoy it, and she simply needed someone to show her that she had options. That she didn't have to follow in anyone's footsteps and be a hospital doctor or a GP. She could still help people, but she could do it her way.'

'He took her to the beach for the day and made her walk for miles,' Jake said. 'And he told her to remember the little girl who used to dance and sing all the time. What did *she* want to do?'

'I wasn't trying to get her to drop out of uni and become a busker,' Daniel explained. 'But I said that there was a way she could use the music she loved in a medical setting. We talked about how some of my patients have play therapy, and how music therapy helps a whole range of people. I merely suggested that she could look into trying a different route that might make her happier.'

'Now she's working as a music therapist, and she's got a research project about dementia and music,' Ally said proudly. 'But, most importantly, she's happy in her job. I hated seeing her trying to force herself into the wrong-shaped hole, and she was so stubborn about wanting to follow the family tradition of being a doctor. Her grandfather, her uncle and her cousin.'

Was it her imagination, Mandy wondered, or had

Daniel flinched slightly when Ally mentioned their father? And he hadn't mentioned before that his dad had been a doctor. She wondered why. Had he not got on well with his dad?

'I wonder where Daisy gets her stubbornness,' Jake teased, nudging Ally.

She nudged him back. 'Some of it's from you,' she retorted.

They didn't have time for a pudding, and Daniel glanced at his watch and shooed his sister and brother-in-law from the table. 'My bill,' he said. 'Don't argue. You can treat me some other time. Go and enjoy the show.'

Ally hugged him warmly. 'Best baby brother ever,' she said. Mandy got a hug, too. 'The next weekend when you're free, come to Cambridge—with or without Dan—and we'll have that walk.'

'Definitely,' Mandy promised.

Then Ally murmured in her ear, 'I think you're good for him. Thank you for making him relax.'

That was incredibly cryptic, but there was no way she could ask for an explanation. At least, not when Ally and Jake had to get to the theatre in time to take their seats. Why would Daniel not be relaxed?

Clearly there was something else he hadn't told her. She didn't have a clue what it might be, or how to persuade him to open up to her. She'd just have to wait until he was ready.

She was still thoughtful after Ally and Jake had left, Daniel had paid and they'd gone back to her place for coffee because it had started to rain and her flat was nearer the Tube station than Daniel's was.

'You've gone quiet. Everything OK?' Daniel asked when they were curled up together on her sofa.

'It's fine,' she said with a smile. 'I liked your sister. She's very like you. Straightforward and easy to get on with. Jake seemed nice, too.'

'Yes, he is.' He dropped a kiss on the top of her head. 'I'm glad Ally didn't grill you. Mind you, she'd already asked me a lot of questions about you.'

'I think,' she said, 'our families think we're set in our ways and they worry about us.'

But were they too set in their ways, she wondered, for this thing between them to work? And what was Daniel holding back?

# CHAPTER NINE

ON THURSDAY, MANDY WAS working in the Paediatric Assessment section with one of her students when five-year-old Isabella Moran was brought in. The little girl was listless and had a temperature. Every so often, she coughed.

'She caught a cold at school,' her mum said, 'but she hasn't managed to shake it off. She's gone off her food, and last night her temperature spiked and I just couldn't get it down. And her breathing's funny, this morning. I rang the doctor and he told me to bring her straight here.'

'Absolutely right,' Mandy said. 'I'm Dr Mandy, and this is Tom, one of my students. Are you OK for Tom to sit in and maybe do some of the checks under my supervision?'

Isabella's mum nodded. 'I just want Bella to get better.'

'Let's have a look at you, sweetheart,' Mandy said, lifting the little girl onto the examination couch. Her temperature was just over thirty-nine centigrade, and her breathing was faster than Mandy was happy with. 'Is it all right if Tom and I have a listen to your breathing with our stethoscopes? When we're done, you can listen to Mummy, if you like.'

The little girl didn't even smile or nod, just looked weary, and the anxiety in her mum's face grew deeper.

'It might feel a little bit cold on your back,' Mandy warned.

Isabella's mum lifted the little girl's sweater at the back so Mandy could listen.

'Can you do me a big breath in and a big breath out, please, Isabella?' Mandy asked.

The little girl did so. As Mandy had suspected, she could hear crackles: a bubbly sound, like Velcro being ripped open. But, more worryingly, she could hear a pleural rub as well.

'Tom?'

Her student placed his stethoscope in the same place that Mandy had. 'Big breath in for me, please, Isabella?' he asked. 'And out?' He frowned and looked at Mandy. 'It sounds bubbly,' he said. 'That's coarse crackles, right?'

She nodded. 'And what causes that?'

'Mucus in the bronchi—that's the tubes that connect your windpipe to your lungs,' he said.

'Did you hear anything else?'

He frowned. 'Not sure.'

'Something a bit like a snore crossed with someone walking in fresh snow?' she suggested.

Tom listened again. 'Yes, but I don't know what that is.'

'It's called a pleural rub, or sometimes a friction rub,' Mandy said. 'Mrs Moran, given that Isabella's temperature's still high, her breathing's fast and she's coughing, I think she has pneumonia. We can treat that, but I want to send her for a chest X-ray and possibly an ultrasound as well, because I think she has an infection.'

'Will she have to stay in, or can I take her home again?' Mrs Moran asked.

'That depends on the X-ray,' Mandy said. 'I'll be able to give you a better idea after that's done.'

She sent Tom with Isabella for the X-ray, then reviewed the images with him and sent him off to sort out an ultrasound. When the results were back, she went to see Isabella and her mum.

'She's got a condition called empyema,' Mandy said. 'Normally, the narrow space between your chest wall and your lungs is filled with pleural fluid. When you have pneumonia, the amount of fluid increases faster than it can be absorbed, and it gets infected.' Usually with *Streptococcus pneumonaie* or Group A Strep; she thought of baby Aarya and sighed inwardly, though she was careful not to let any of her sadness show. 'The infection causes the fluid to form pockets of pus, which coat the outer layer of the lungs and stop them expanding properly so it's harder for someone to breathe. The X-ray shows those little pockets of pus on Isabella's lungs, so we need to treat that. With young children, we tend to try conservative management first. I'm going to get her to cough up some sputum and I'll get the sample tested to find out which bacteria's involved, but it does take a couple of days to grow the culture, so in the meantime I'll give her broad-spectrum antibiotics on a drip. She'll be able to walk about and do things—we encourage that— as long as you're careful not to let her knock the drip. We'll keep her in for a couple of days and see how she responds to them; if she seems a bit better, you can take her home to finish the antibiotics in tablet form.'

'What if she doesn't get better?' Mrs Moran asked.

'Then we'll need to insert a tube called a chest drain to get the fluid and pus out,' Mandy said. 'It's something the paediatric surgeon will do under a general anaesthetic or sedation, so she won't feel any pain. Then she'll stay in for another three or four days, until the infection has cleared and her lungs are fully expanded again, and her temperature's down. But we'll start the antibiotics now, and Tom will take you both to the ward to settle her in. I'll pop in after clinic to see how she's doing, but if you're worried about anything have a word with one of the nurses. They're all really lovely and good with little ones. And if they're worried about anything they'll come and get me.'

The following day, during ward rounds, Mandy noted that Isabella hadn't shown any signs of improving.

Mrs Moran was at her daughter's bedside. 'Is Bella getting better?' she asked.

'Not according to her charts.' Mandy gave her a sympathetic smile. 'We'll need to get the surgeons to put a chest drain in.'

'You told me about that yesterday.' Mrs Moran looked anxious. 'An operation.'

'They'll use a really light anaesthetic so she'll come round very quickly,' Mandy reassured her. 'Once it's in, we'll put a dressing on to keep the area clean. It's sometimes a little bit uncomfortable so we'll make sure she has pain relief. And as the pus drains out she'll find it easier to breathe.' She paused. She'd mentioned Isabella to Daniel, yesterday, and he'd said that it sounded like a potential case for the show and asked if she'd mind introducing him. 'My colleague Daniel Monroe presents the *London Victoria Children's Ward* series. Would you consider having a chat with him about maybe including Isabella's case in his show?'

'She'd be on television?' Mrs Moran's eyes widened.

'It'd be just a chat at this stage,' Mandy said. 'But he's very keen on including the kind of cases we see quite often, as well as the rare ones. Seeing Isabella would help other parents to keep an eye out for the symptoms of pneumonia and maybe get treatment earlier than they would've done—as well as reassuring them that lots of other children go through this and get better.' She smiled. 'Dan's really nice. Apart from being a good doctor, he really cares, and children respond to him. I've seen him read stories to comfort a tearful toddler, and tell terrible jokes to make a teenager laugh.'

'I watch the show,' Mrs Moran said. 'He comes across as really lovely.'

'He is,' Mandy said, and meant it. Daniel was the kind of man who made the world feel like a better place.

Mrs Moran nodded. 'All right. I'm happy to have a chat with him.'

'Thanks. I'll go and have a quick word with him when I've finished ward rounds, and I'll introduce you to him,' Mandy said.

'Pneumonia and empyema,' Daniel said when Mandy had finished giving him a quick rundown. 'And we're looking at a chest drain, so with the parents' permission we can film in Theatre,' he added thoughtfully. 'Parents get twitchy about anaesthetic and sedation. It'd be nice to be able to reassure them and show them what happens.'

'I've spoken to the surgical team and they're going to

put the chest drain in this afternoon,' Mandy said. 'And Mrs Moran says she's happy to have a chat with you. Is now a good time to introduce you?'

'Yes,' Daniel said. Shalmi, Carey and Keisha were busy examining the footage they'd already taken that morning and making notes about what they needed to film to complete the story. 'OK for me to dip out for a few minutes to talk to the mum of a potential case?' he checked with Keisha.

'Fine,' she said with a smile.

'Great. See you soon.'

Daniel walked with Mandy to Isabella's bedside, where she introduced him to Mrs Moran and Isabella.

'Hello, Isabella. I'm Dr Dan,' he said, sitting on the edge of her bed. 'I work with Dr Mandy. She tells me you're feeling poorly.'

The little girl nodded.

'We're going to make you feel much better,' he promised. 'I see your mum has been reading you one of my favourite stories ever. I used to read this book to my nieces.' He gestured to the book about a ballet-dancing mouse. 'Can I read a bit to you?'

The little girl looked to her mum, who smiled. 'If you'd like that, Bella, it's fine.'

'You like ballet?' Dan asked.

Isabella nodded.

'She goes to lessons,' Mrs Moran said. 'She's missing it at the moment.'

'My niece Daisy did ballet lessons, too, when she was your age,' Dan said. 'And she still remembers me reading this story to her.' He read a little bit of the book, doing a special squeaky voice for the mouse when she talked, and Isabella smiled.

He finished the page, and gave the book back to her. 'I'll read you a little bit more later, if you like.'

The little girl looked pleased. 'Thank you.'

'And I'll tell you a secret, Bella,' Dan said in a stage whisper. 'I know someone else who does ballet. Someone standing right near us. Can you guess who?'

'Mummy?'

'Your mummy dances, too? That makes *two* other people, then.' He added in a stage whisper, 'Dr Mandy goes to ballet lessons.' Then he gave an exaggerated frown. 'Oh, dear. That means I'm the only person here who doesn't do ballet. You know what? When you're feeling better, maybe you can teach me how to do a ballerina twirl.'

Isabella gave a tiny giggle, and he laughed back. 'Bella the Ballerina, and Dan the Dancer. We're going to be a great team. Give me a high five.'

The little girl did so.

'Now, I'm going to have a chat with Mummy.' He glanced at Mandy.

'And I'm going to take over reading, though I'm not as good at the voices as Dr Dan,' Mandy said. 'Can you show me which is your favourite picture, Isabella?'

Daniel ushered Mrs Moran a few metres away, so Isabella wouldn't overhear but was still in her mother's view.

'That's the first time I've heard her giggle in a week,' Mrs Moran said. 'Thank you. That's amazing.'

'I remember having my tonsils out when I was only a year or two older than Bella,' he said. 'I didn't feel very well, and I didn't know how to explain how I felt. And hospital was *horrible*. Everyone had to be really quiet, there were weird smells and beeps that I didn't understand, and nobody smiled. When I became a doctor, I was determined that my ward wouldn't make children feel worse, the way I'd felt when I was small.' He smiled. 'That's why I have a stock of terrible jokes and a book of stickers in my pocket. I know a couple of basic magic tricks, too. But when children have favourite books, that makes it easier for me to connect with them and reassure them.'

'Dr Mandy said you might want to include Bella on your show.'

'With your permission, obviously. And we'd have a chat with you as well, to get the parent's point of view.'

'I'm not sure I'd be any good on television,' Mrs Moran said.

'My production team are brilliant,' Dan said. 'It's not all the scary, glamorous stuff. We film ordinary people who know what it feels like to worry about their child. The show's about reassuring other parents that how they're feeling is normal, and other families have been through it and come out the other side. And you don't have to learn a script or read cue cards—it'll be like sitting on a sofa in your living room, having a cup of tea and a chat with me. Just like we're chatting now.'

'You made my Bella smile,' Mrs Moran said. 'So all right, we'll do it.'

'Thank you,' Daniel said.

Later that afternoon, Isabella had been to Theatre; the chest drain was in place, along with urokinase, a clot-busting drug that helped to break up the pus. The little girl was asleep when Mandy checked in on her but appeared to be breathing a little more easily, to Mandy's relief.

Mrs Moran couldn't stop talking about how wonderful Daniel was. 'You were right. He's lovely,' she said. 'You've been lovely, too, but there's something so calming about him. And the way he read to Bella and chatted to her about ballet and made her brighter than she's been in a week—I bet he's a wonderful dad.'

Except Daniel didn't have children, Mandy thought. Because he'd never let anyone close enough to him to make a family, after his divorce. 'All the children on the ward love him, from the toddlers to the teens,' she said instead. 'He makes time for them, and that's important.' She smiled. 'Did you enjoy the filming?'

'Surprisingly, yes. Dr Dan was right; it really was like having a cup of tea and a chat in my living room.'

'If I know Dan,' Mandy said, 'there was tea or coffee involved. And biscuits.'

'Chocolate ones,' Mrs Moran confided.

Mandy smiled. 'Excellent. I'll pop in and see how she's getting on tomorrow. The sputum test probably won't be back, but I'll check anyway.'

'It's your weekend on shift?' Mrs Moran asked.

'No. The nice thing about being a senior consultant is that I'm on call alternate weekends, but I don't have to come in unless I want to say hello to a special patient,' Mandy said with a smile. 'And Bella counts as special.'

Daniel met Mandy at her flat after ballet class.

'Sorry if I put you on the spot with Isabella, earlier, when I told her about your ballet lessons,' he said.

She smiled. '"Spot" has a very different meaning in a dance class; you look at a spot on the wall when you do a turn and make sure you keep looking at the same place. It helps you control the movement, keep your balance and prevent dizziness.'

'Am I going to get a demo?'

'From Bella, maybe,' she teased. 'Dan the Dancer.' She couldn't help a chuckle. 'Perhaps I should teach you how to do a pirouette, or at least a kind of turn.'

'If I can let Daisy and Hannah put sparkly slides in my hair and paint my nails, then I can learn to do a pirouette for a poorly little girl.'

He'd been that patient with his nieces? Then again, she wasn't surprised. She'd discovered that Dan had a very soft centre, behind the charm and the humour. 'All right,' she said. 'I'll teach you.'

'Wearing that swishy skirt?' he asked, sounding hopeful. 'It'll help me concentrate.'

'Oh, really?' she teased.

He grinned. 'Busted. I just like seeing you in your ballet clothes. And I like thinking about how I can unwrap you, afterwards.'

'You have to earn that,' she warned.

'Change back into your ballet stuff,' he said, 'and teach me.'

'Roll the rug back while I change,' she said. 'And you need to be in socks. Roll them down over your heel to the middle of your arch, so you can slide on your toes and use your heels to stop yourself sliding.'

He gave a little hum of pleasure when she was ready. 'Have I told you how hot you look in that skirt, Dr Cooke?'

She laughed. 'I think I've got the message. Right.

We're going to warm your muscles up first. I assume you've gone to some kind of exercise class in the past and know you just mirror the teacher?'

'Yes,' he said.

She got him to roll his shoulders forward and back, singly and together, and then taught him the basic arm movements of ballet. 'Make it flow,' she said. 'And now I want your arms up, in fifth position. Just how children do when you're playing "Simon Says" and tell them to put their arms like a ballerina's.'

He did so. 'Is that right?'

'Pretty much. I'm not going to fuss about your fingers.'

'What's wrong with my fingers?' he asked.

'I'll let Bella tell you,' she said. 'And now I want you on your tiptoes. Right foot in front of your left, feet close together. Keep looking straight ahead, and you're just going to take tiny steps—that's a bourrée,' she said. 'Turn as you step. Tiny, tiny, tiny steps.'

'That wasn't a pirouette,' he said, when he'd turned round and she'd said he could stand on flat feet again.

'It's nearly as good as one,' she said. 'It'll be good enough for Bella to enjoy it.' She gave him a wicked grin. 'And I might just mention it to Keisha.'

'I'll do this for Bella, but *not* for the show,' he warned.

She spread her hands. 'If you can let a child put sparkly clips in your hair... Hey, if you do a pirouette, they might even ask you to go on *Strictly*.'

'No. I only do celeb stuff if it's going to benefit the hospital. And now I claim my reward,' he said. 'Unwrapping you.' He pulled her to him, undid the bow she'd tied to keep her dance skirt in place, and slowly spun her round as he unwrapped her skirt. 'You're doing bour-rées,' he said, narrowing his eyes at her.

In answer, she put her arms up, the way she'd just taught him to do, and hummed a bit of the Sugar Plum Fairy.

His retort was to scoop her over his shoulder in a fire-man's lift and carry her up the stairs to her bed.

Afterwards, he went down to raid her cupboards and fridge for cheese and crackers, and brought a glass of wine with the plate to share.

'Are you staying tonight?' she asked.

'If you're asking.'

She kissed him lightly. 'I'm asking.'

'Then I'm staying,' he said softly.

# CHAPTER TEN

THE NEXT MORNING, Daniel woke before Mandy. Her head was pillowed on his shoulder and her arm was wrapped tightly round his waist. And this felt oh, so right.

He'd been seeing her for a month now, and it felt as if he'd known her for always.

In some ways, it worried him. This was getting way too close to a proper relationship—something he'd avoided for years. He'd never forgive himself if he hurt her. Maybe he should back off. Take things a little more slowly. Be really, *really* sure about what he was doing.

On the other hand, waking with her in his arms made the mornings feel brighter. It was the perfect start to the day. Maybe he should brush his worries aside. After all, he was older now, and much wiser than he'd been when he'd wrecked his marriage. And what if Mandy was the person he'd been waiting to share his life with?

He wanted to believe in love. Yet at the same time it scared him stupid that this relationship was going to go wrong. That he'd let her down, the way he'd let Roxy down. That deep down he was just as bad as his father had been and he'd never be able to settle.

Eventually she stirred. 'Good morning.'

And there it was, the almost shy smile that took his

breath away and made him forget his worries. 'Good morning,' he said. 'What do you want to do today?'

'I'm on call,' she said.

'If it's a major emergency,' he reminded her. 'There are other consultants who'd be called in before you.'

'True. But I want to pop in to the ward, this morning.'

'To see how Isabella's doing?' he guessed.

'And to check on the sputum culture results. They probably won't be there until Sunday, but it's worth a look, just in case,' she said.

He stroked her hair from her face. 'You know, if it is Group A strep, rather than *strep pneumoniae*, we're not going to have a repeat of what happened to Aarya. Bella's a lot older and her system's strong enough to cope.'

'I know,' she said lightly.

'But you worry anyway,' he said. And that was what made her a good doctor. Attention to detail. Making sure things were checked. 'Do you want me to come in with you?'

'No,' she said. 'Because then people might put two and two together.'

He knew she was being sensible. They weren't going public with what was happening between them; only their closest family and friends knew. But at the same time it made him feel like a dirty little secret; and again his doubts flooded back. Was this all a huge mistake? Was he kidding himself that he could make it work? Was he expecting too much of himself? 'I'll go home and shower and change,' he said. 'What do you want to do after you've seen Bella?'

'What's the weather forecast?' she asked. 'If it's wet,

then something indoors. If it's dry, it'd be nice to go for a walk.'

He checked the weather forecast app on his phone. 'Dry. How about Hampstead?'

'The Heath?'

'Sort of,' he said. 'It's an unusual garden. And then maybe we can have lunch in Hampstead and wander round the shops.' Somewhere public. Somewhere with no pressure. And maybe he could stop himself worrying that it was all going to go wrong. Stop himself worrying that he couldn't be the man she needed him to be.

'Sounds perfect,' she said.

After breakfast, Mandy went to the hospital while Daniel went back to Chelsea; they agreed to meet on the platform for the Jubilee Line at Westminster.

At the London Victoria, Mandy discovered that the sputum culture results weren't back yet, but Isabella had a little more colour in her cheeks and wasn't coughing quite so much. Plus, to Mandy's relief, Isabella's breathing seemed to be easier. 'It looks as if she's turning the corner,' she said to Mrs Moran.

'I hope so,' Mrs Moran said feelingly.

'You look exhausted,' Mandy said gently. 'I know you want to be with her, but I promise the team here will look after her tonight. Go home and get some proper rest.'

Mrs Moran sighed. 'I know that'd be the sensible thing to do—but she's my only one, and I can't bear to leave her.'

'I get that,' Mandy said. 'My daughter's my only one, too.' She squeezed Mrs Moran's hand. 'But, seriously, the best way to help look after her is to look after yourself. Go home and get some sleep. We'll ring you straight away if she wakes and calls for you, or if we're worried that her condition's worsening—though that's unlikely, now, as she's responding to the treatment.'

'Maybe I will,' Mrs Moran said.

'It's your choice,' Mandy said. 'But my advice—as a doctor and as a mum—is to get some proper rest tonight.'

Daniel was waiting for Mandy at Westminster station.

'How's Bella?' he asked.

'Her breathing's better, the cough's improving and she's got more colour in her cheeks. Though the sputum culture results aren't back yet.'

'She's got another day and a half of urokinase,' he said, 'and we'll know on Monday if we need to change to a more narrow-spectrum antibiotic. I think we can safely say she's on the way to recovering.'

'Agreed,' she said.

They got off the Tube at West Hampstead, then walked through Golders Hill Park, hand in hand, enjoying the last of the autumn colours. It had rained overnight, so the trunks of the trees were very dark and the brightness of the sun made the yellow leaves stand out.

'"That time of year thou mayst in me behold,"' Daniel quoted.

She smiled and chimed in with him. '"Where yellow leaves, or none, or few, do hang."'

OK, so the Shakespearean sonnet was one of the most famous ones: but even so they seemed to be finishing each other's sentences, she thought. Their minds seemed to work the same way. She'd never felt like that with anyone before, even Laurence; maybe, just maybe, her family and friends had a point after all and she'd been missing out by cutting relationships out of her life.

Or maybe, a little voice said in her head, maybe she'd just been waiting for the right person to walk into her life. Even though, technically, she'd walked into his.

They wandered past the small zoo and the playground. 'I'm looking forward to enjoying the toddler years again with my grandchild,' she said. 'The swings and the slides, and a little face all bright with excitement.'

'I think the beach is still my favourite place to take kids,' he said. 'Building sandcastles with a moat, splashing in the sea, and peering in rockpools. And I'll never forget the time we had a family holiday up in Yorkshire with all of us staying in this huge converted barn. James must've been about seven at the time. He'd always been into dinosaurs, and he begged us to take him fossil-hunting. We went to the beach at Staithes, and he rushed ahead, desperate to be the first one to find an ammonite.' He laughed. 'He was indeed the first to find an ammonite—but what we all remember more is that he jumped up and down in utter joy with his hands held up in triumph…and then he slipped and landed bottom-first in a puddle! He's never quite lived it down.'

Again, Mandy thought what a good father Daniel would've made. She knew he was wary of relationships after the break-up of his marriage, but he'd denied himself something so special. Why hadn't he believed in himself?

'I can just imagine it,' she said. 'We never managed to find any fossils when Gemma was small, but we used to go to the Natural History Museum on a very regular basis to see the dinosaurs.'

'That was James's favourite place, too,' he said. 'And

I can remember building a balsa wood *Tyrannosaurus rex* with him.'

'Oh, look—fallow deer,' she said, pointing over to the trees, where a small group of fallow deer were grazing, their deep russet coat dappled with pale spots. 'They're gorgeous. The park here is definitely going on my list of places to bring the baby.'

A narrow path had them crunching over the fallen leaves of orange and russet and gold; at the end there were metal railings leading to a wrought iron gateway, and there were elegant stone columns topped with wooden trellises. Ivy twined round the columns, and climbing plants that she didn't recognise, full of richly coloured berries.

'That's gorgeous. I didn't expect it to be like this,' she said.

'It was built by Lord Leverhulme at the beginning of the last century as a place to entertain his guests and hold summer parties,' Daniel told her. 'Did you know, the pergola itself is as long as Canary Wharf tower is tall?'

'Been reading a guidebook, have we?' she teased.

'Websites,' he admitted. 'I wanted to know a bit more about the place. Guess what it's built on?'

She could see his eyes glittering with amusement, and remembered what they'd been talking about earlier. 'Dinosaurs?'

'Nope,' he said. 'It's the debris from where they dug out the extension of the Northern Line to Hampstead. The designer used the rubble to raise the hill and make the terraces.'

They climbed up the steps to the pergola and wandered through the walkways; there was a stunning view of the red brick arches supporting the pergola, and the formal terraced gardens below.

'Apparently it's really pretty in spring, with loads of wisteria,' Daniel said, 'and in the summer it's full of roses.'

'I can just imagine Edwardian garden parties here, the women all in elegant dresses and sipping champagne from coupe glasses,' she said. 'A string quartet playing...' She smiled. 'I loved all the Merchant Ivory films from the eighties.'

'This place was all pretty much in ruins, back then,' he said, 'or it would've made a good film set.'

Once they'd had their fill of the gardens, they headed down through the heath to Hampstead itself.

The village was seriously pretty with narrow winding streets; there were Regency townhouses with sash windows and gorgeous metal porches with trellised stands supporting roses and climbing shrubs; the shopfronts were picture-postcard, each one different, and a mixture of everything from florists to upmarket grocers to antique shops.

'All that walking's made me hungry,' Daniel said.

They found a little café, and ate a fabulous roasted tomato and red pepper soup served with artisanal bread and excellent coffee. Once restored, they continued wandering through the little side streets. They spent a while browsing in a second-hand bookshop; Mandy found a collection of Daphne du Maurier short stories she hadn't yet read, while Daniel came out with a volume of Cornell Woolrich's short stories.

'I've not read anything by him,' she said.

'He was one of the pulp fiction authors of the nineteen-forties,' Daniel said. 'A few of his stories were made into films—you'd definitely know *Rear Window*.'

'The Hitchcock film?' At his nod, she smiled. 'I love the James Stewart films.'

'Including the best Christmas film ever,' he said.

'I watch *It's a Wonderful Life* every year,' Mandy confessed. 'It always makes me a bit sad and cross at the very end, though, because Henry Potter gets away with stealing the money.'

'But money and greed can't buy him the love that the people of Bedford Falls give George Bailey for being the man at the heart of their community. George stood up to the bully and he prevailed. Potter has to live with knowing that,' Daniel pointed out. 'And his plans for Pottersville never happen.'

'I would just have liked a bit more justice. And for Potter to apologise to George,' Mandy said.

'But it wouldn't have been a genuine apology. It would've been lip service,' Daniel said. 'How do you even start to apologise when you've done that much wrong to someone?'

There were shadows in his eyes that made Mandy wonder if he was talking about himself. But surely he'd paid his debt to Roxy, with that life of loneliness—never letting anyone close? She tightened her fingers round his. 'I think if you're genuinely sorry, it shows. And it changes you for the future. You learn from your mistakes,' she said.

'Maybe.' He didn't sound as if she'd convinced him, but he distracted her from taking the conversation further by pointing out an old-fashioned toy shop. 'Detour alert. I have something I need to buy.'

She raised an eyebrow. 'For your nieces and nephews?'

'No. For the kids on the show. I normally buy them a little something, just a token, to say thanks for their help.' He smiled. 'I'm still in touch with the kids from the first series. Even the ones who aren't still treated by our department, because their parents send me a Christmas card to the hospital every year with a photo and an update.'

'That's lovely,' she said.

Looking round the shop, Mandy found the softest, cutest little white rabbit and couldn't resist buying it for her grandchild-to-be. And Daniel was delighted to find a mouse dressed in ballet shoes and a tutu. 'This is perfect for Isabella,' he said.

'And you know what you have to do when you give it to her. Even if you do it in your normal shoes,' she said.

In response, he stood on tiptoe with his arms up, and did the turn she'd taught him, not caring that they were in the middle of the shop and people were staring.

'Perfect,' she said, clapping her hands.

Mandy was beginning to think that maybe this time she'd got it right, because Daniel was one of the good guys. A man with a huge heart who cared about his family, who supported his colleagues, and who tried to make a difference to people's lives with his television work as well as his hospital work.

Could she trust him with her heart?

Yes, he'd made a huge mistake, all those years ago. He hadn't fought hard enough to save his marriage to Roxy, and he'd let himself be dazzled by Leila. He'd broken the vows he'd made before his family and friends, to love and honour and cherish—just as Laurence had broken his vows to Mandy.

But Daniel wasn't like Laurence. He truly regretted what he'd done: to the point where he'd never put himself in a position where he could hurt someone again.

Though it had all happened half a lifetime ago. He wasn't the same man now who'd married Roxy and cheated with Leila. So maybe it was safe to take the risk that he wouldn't cheat on her. Safe to ask him to make a proper go of things.

'What do you want to do this evening?' she asked. 'Do you want to eat out, or shall I cook for us?'

'It's my turn to cook,' he said. 'Let's pick up something while we're here.'

And of course they ended up in the bakery section of the deli. 'Blueberry polenta cake,' Daniel said, looking gleeful. 'Does that work for you?'

'That'd be lovely,' she said. 'Though pudding and wine will be my contribution to dinner.'

Back at Daniel's house, Mandy enjoyed sitting at the table chatting to him about books while he cooked, sipping a glass of perfectly chilled Sauvignon Blanc, with gentle classical music playing in the background.

Dinner was perfect: chicken in a tarragon and crème fraiche sauce, served with roasted Mediterranean vegetables and fluffy basmati rice, followed by the polenta cake and vanilla ice cream.

And then they curled up on the sofa together.

'Shall we watch *It's a Wonderful Life*?' he suggested.

'Great idea.' She smiled. 'Especially as you've taught me to look a little bit differently at the ending—at the bit that bothers me.'

'I'm glad,' he said.

She stole a kiss. 'You've taught me to look at other things differently, too.'

'How do you mean?' he asked.

This was a risk. But it was one she was willing to take. 'About dating someone. This last month, I've had such a good time with you.' She took a deep breath. 'I like who you are, Dan, and I think you like me, too.'

Ice slithered down Daniel's spine. He had a nasty feeling he knew where this was going.

Her next words confirmed it.

'I want to change the terms of our fling,' she said. 'I'd like this to be a real relationship. And I was thinking, I know you've already met Gemma, but maybe tomorrow you'd like to come for lunch and meet my family properly.'

*A real relationship.*

*Meet her family properly.*

The words screeched like an alarm in the back of his head.

This would mean a relationship without strictly defined boundaries—and he brushed aside the fact that that was exactly what had been happening since their first week together. There was a huge difference between saying they were seeing where something was going, keeping things on a more or less casual basis, and officially dating where everyone knew about it.

What if things went wrong?

It was incredibly brave of Mandy to suggest taking such a risk on a proven cheat, when her marriage had broken up because of her ex's infidelity. Daniel knew he wouldn't be carelessly unfaithful to her. But he still couldn't shift the fear that, deep down, he was a carbon copy of his father, shallow and selfish. And that meant if he had a proper relationship with her, there was a risk he'd end up hurting her.

Plus he knew he didn't have to cheat for things to go wrong between himself and Mandy.

His job was partly in the public eye. He'd seen the kind of things people said about him on social media. That ridiculous nickname of being the thinking woman's crumpet—his team teased him about it, but it was still a real issue. When people saw you on the TV, they formed an opinion about you and they felt that they knew you. And they talked about you. Misinterpreted things. A social kiss on the cheek, an arm round someone's shoulders in a gesture of sympathy, the squeeze of a hand to bolster someone's confidence—it could all be so easily misconstrued.

Sure, these things could be resolved by talking about them.

But it would be like water dripping on a stone. Each tiny droplet of doubt would add to the one before, until eventually it wore away the trust.

And he didn't want that for either of them.

There was only one way he could think of to protect her from that. To protect himself, too. He needed to end things between them. *Now.*

Knowing that this was going to hurt her, but convinced that it would hurt less now than if he let things continue so they got even closer and then it went wrong, he said, 'I like you too, Mandy. Very much.' He steeled himself and added, 'But I'm sorry—I don't want a relationship.'

Shock and hurt flared in her eyes. 'But...we've been getting on so well. I thought that was what you wanted, too.'

'I'm sorry,' he said again. 'I think it's better if we stick to being just colleagues, from now on. I know we're both professional enough not to make things awkward at work.'

For a moment, he thought she was going to argue.

If she did, there was a very good chance he'd fold. Right now, every sinew, every muscle, was screaming out to him to wrap his arms round her and tell her to ignore whatever he'd said because he was panicking and he was being an idiot. Keeping his distance from her felt like physical pain—as if he couldn't breathe. As if he was drowning in fear.

She stared at him for a long, long moment. He saw a muscle flicker in her jaw. Then she said, quietly and tonelessly, 'Then I think I'd better go. I'll see myself out.'

He made no move to stop her when she stood up, slipped her shoes back on and collected her bag and coat from the coat pegs in his hallway. He didn't follow her to the front door, or open it for her.

Only when he heard the door close did he close his eyes and rest his head in his hands.

It was over.

At his own instigation.

And how he wished that things could've been different. That *he* could've been different. That he could've been the right one for her.

But the fear that he wasn't had been too much for him.

# CHAPTER ELEVEN

ALL THE WAY HOME, Mandy went over the day in her head. They'd had such a nice time, taking a leisurely stroll round a beautiful hidden garden, enjoying lunch and then browsing in the little shops in Hampstead. They'd laughed, they'd held hands, they'd been close...

And then everything had changed.

Well, she knew what had changed. She'd suggested making their relationship more formal. Going public.

But Daniel had already met her daughter. He'd got on well with Gemma.

He'd introduced her to his sister and brother-in-law, too, and she'd got on well with Ally and Jake.

It worked between them. The last month had been one of the happiest of her life, and he'd seemed happy, too. So why had he backed off? Was it her fault? Had she done something wrong?

She thought about it for the rest of the evening, and still couldn't come up with a convincing reason.

She still hadn't found an answer, the next morning; but at least she could keep herself too busy to think about it by preparing lunch for her mum, her sister and brother-in-law, and Gemma and Dev. And she was super-smiley all afternoon, sidestepping the subject of Daniel when

Gemma tried to raise it and instead telling them all about the garden she'd visited with a friend.

They didn't need to know that her 'friend' was now strictly her colleague.

On Monday, she didn't have the usual spring in her step when she walked from the Tube station to the hospital. As she walked down the corridor to the children's department, adrenaline made the ends of her fingers tingle. Facing Daniel was going to be awkward—but it would be even more awkward if other people noticed and started asking questions. She was just going to have to be super-professional about it.

He was already at his desk when she walked into their shared office. 'Good morning, Mandy,' he said, glancing up.

'Good morning, Daniel.' She couldn't think of any small talk to save the situation. She could hardly ask him if he'd had a good weekend, given that he'd called it off between them and the shadows under his eyes looked as deep and dark as hers. What now? Did they talk about the weather? 'I, um—just going to check on a couple of patients,' she said, and fled for the safety of the ward.

Isabella was definitely looking brighter. She still had a slight temperature, but she was smiling and chatty, and her skin wasn't so pallid.

'Look what Dr Dan bought me to say thank you for being in his film!' she said, showing the tutu-wearing mouse to Mandy. 'And, guess what? When he gave it to me, he did a turn just like a ballerina, with his hands up and everything!' She giggled. 'Except he had crabby hands!'

The turn Mandy had taught him, and would've liked

to see—except today that might've made her heart crack into pieces. 'That's lovely,' she said, forcing herself to smile broadly. 'Did you tell him they should be flowers?'

'I showed him how and then he did it right,' Isabella confirmed.

'How are you feeling?'

'Ever so much better. Thank you,' she added swiftly at her mum's raised eyebrows. 'Can I go home now, please?'

'In a couple of days,' Mandy said. 'We still need to give you a little bit more medicine.'

Mrs Moran was smiling and looking a lot less anxious. 'It's going to be hard to keep her in bed, now she's back to her usual self.'

'She can get up and walk about—that's walk, not dance, Bella,' Mandy said. 'Just be careful that she doesn't knock the chest drain or the line where the antibiotics go in. The sputum culture results should be back today, so we'll know if we need to give Bella a different antibiotic, and once the chest drain is out and her temperature's back to normal she can go home.'

'It'll be good to have her home,' Mrs Moran said. 'And thank you for everything you've done, you and Dr Dan.'

*You and Dr Dan.*

Except they weren't a couple any more. Maybe she'd been kidding herself and they'd never really been one in the first place. She pushed the thought away and made herself smile. 'It's what we're here for.'

Dan loathed himself. He'd seen the shadows under Mandy's eyes, and he knew he'd put them there by breaking up with her. He'd made her miserable.

But what else could he have done?

He focused on running the ward while she was teaching. On Monday evening, he forced himself to ignore how much he missed her and how he wished he was at the cinema with her, or talking to her about all the deep questions over a glass of wine, or lying with her in the bed that suddenly felt much too wide.

Though he missed her.

Really, really missed her.

In the few short weeks they'd been together, he realised that he'd fallen for her. Head over heels. He liked her warmth and her brightness. He liked the way she saw solutions instead of problems. He liked how easy it was to just *be*, in her company.

Right now he was miserable. Nothing in his life seemed to fit, any more, except his job. And that no longer felt like enough.

Mandy was glad that Tuesday was Linda's husband's birthday, so her best friend was taking him out to dinner instead of doing their usual aerobics class. It gave her a couple more days to work out how to avoid Dan's name coming up in conversation.

Wednesday was trickier. She and Dan were scrupulously professional on the handover day. Isabella was going home, the next day, so Dan would be doing a last bit of filming with her; baby Noah was finally able to breathe on his own and was starting to get better; and Joe, despite saying that the liquid nutrition was the most disgusting stuff he'd ever tasted, had responded well and was putting on weight. He was due to start the infliximab, the following week.

But Daniel looked tired, Mandy thought. He wasn't quite as smiley as usual.

Maybe he felt as sad as she did about the way things had gone wrong between them. But his whole 'I don't want a relationship' stance made her wonder if that was the root of the problem. He'd said that he'd forgiven himself for his mistake all those years ago—but had he really? Because he'd struck her as very much a family man, close to his siblings, his nephews and his nieces. The 'book' they'd made him for his fiftieth birthday had been full of love. He would've made a fantastic dad; had he missed out on having children because he didn't trust himself to get it right in his next relationship?

They needed an honest talk.

When he came in to write up his notes, she said, 'Do you want a mug of tea?'

'Thanks, but I'm fine.'

'Are you all right, Dan?' she asked.

'Yes, thank you,' he said coolly.

'You don't look it,' she said. And then, because he was obviously not going to admit to anything unless she said it first, she added, 'You look as miserable as I feel.'

'We're not having this conversation,' Dan said.

'Not here,' she agreed. 'But we do need to talk.'

'We're fine as we are. Colleagues.'

'If you're trying to fake it until you make it, don't. You *know* we're not fine,' she said softly. 'So either we have this conversation here and now, or we go for a drink somewhere quiet after work.'

He didn't say anything, just looked at her. And she was certain she could see a hint of longing in his eyes—

that he missed her as much as she missed him. Or was she simply seeing what she so desperately wanted to see?

But then he sighed. 'There's no point, Mandy.'

'No? Then perhaps you can explain this to me. I've seen you working with patients and their parents. I've seen you working with colleagues—from the most junior to the most senior. I've seen you with the film crew. I've seen you with your sister. And the man I see has the most huge heart. He's generous with his time. He's kind. He's thoughtful. But I think he hasn't forgiven himself for a mistake he made nearly thirty years ago. He's shut part of his life off because of that—and I don't understand why.'

'You don't need to understand why,' he said, which told her that she'd been on the right track.

'Oh, but I do,' she said. 'I need to understand why a man who's clearly deeply loved by his nieces and nephews—a man who would've made a wonderful father—denied himself the privilege of having a family of his own.'

He walked over to the open office door and closed it. Then he leaned back against the door. 'All right. If you really want to know, it's because of who I am, deep down. I look like my father—and I behaved like him, too. I cheated and I hurt my wife.'

She blinked, shocked. 'Are you telling me your dad cheated on your mum?'

'Multiple times. I was fifteen when I found out. I asked him why, and he said he'd fallen head over heels for someone else and he couldn't help himself.' Daniel's face tightened. 'But Mum took him back. I thought maybe he'd just made a mistake. Except he did it again. And again. And then I discovered that what I'd thought was the first time was very far from it. He'd cheated all the way through their marriage, and Mum put up with it because she didn't want to drag us all through a divorce.' He dragged in a breath. 'Then, when I fell for Leila...he said I was just like him. It terrified me, because I knew he was right. I'd fallen for someone else when I shouldn't have. And I didn't want to spend the rest of my life being selfish and shallow and unreliable, not caring if I hurt people—always saying sorry and never meaning it, the way he did.'

'But you're not selfish, Dan,' she said. 'Surely you can see that? You're not shallow and unreliable. You made a mistake and you learned from it.'

'Did I? I can't take the risk,' he said. 'I can't risk hurting you.'

'Does it occur to you that you might be hurting me more by not being in my life?' she asked.

'Yes, and I'm sorry I've hurt you at all, but I can't risk making it worse,' he said. 'I don't trust myself. The apple doesn't fall far from the tree, does it?'

'Your dad might have been a cheat, but your mother wasn't. How do you know you're not more like your mother?' she asked.

'Because if I was, I wouldn't have cheated on Roxy in the first place.'

He was the most stubborn, aggravating man, she thought, circling back to the same argument and not giving himself a chance to break free from all the pain. She tried another tack. 'Don't you think people can change, over time?'

'Some people do. I haven't,' he said. 'Which is why this conversation is going to end now, and we're going back to being strictly colleagues.'

And he flatly refused to discuss the subject with her any more.

It was stalemate. Much as she wanted to yell at him for being stubborn and blinkered, she realised it wouldn't change the situation. Until he was ready to recognise the truth for himself, there was nothing she could do or say to change his mind. And maybe he was so stuck in his ways, after all these years, that he'd never let himself recognise the truth.

So she avoided him as much as she could without making it obvious, told Gemma and Linda quietly that things between her and Dan had simply fizzled out and there wasn't any point in discussing it, and concentrated on her job.

Over the next week, Mandy's cool, professional distance was hard to bear. Daniel *missed* her. He missed the lightness of spirit he'd felt when they were together. He missed her sense of humour.

But he'd been the one to call a halt. He'd been the one to push her away. He knew he only had himself to blame.

On Tuesday morning, he was dealing with a pile of admin when the phone he shared with Mandy shrilled; he picked it up and answered absently. 'Daniel Monroe.'

'Could I speak to Dr Cooke, please?' a voice asked.

'I'm sorry, she's with a patient,' Daniel said. 'Can I help at all? I work with her.'

'Could you get a very urgent message to her, please? It's Dev, her son-in-law,' the voice on the other end of the phone said. 'I'm on my way to the hospital now. Gemma's being brought in by an ambulance. I know she'll want her mum.'

'Of course I will.' Daniel did some rapid calculations in his head. Gemma must be thirty-six weeks pregnant. A month before her due date. That wasn't good. 'Sorry to ask, but can I give Mandy any idea what's happened, so I can prepare her a bit?' he asked.

'Gemma had a bit of a headache this morning, but she still went into work. At the end of the first lesson, she was sick, having stomach pains and her hands were swollen. The school secretary called an ambulance. The paramedics weren't happy with her blood pressure so they're bringing her to hospital.'

'OK,' Daniel said. It had been years since his rotation in the maternity department, but he recognised the symptoms of pre-eclampsia. If it was severe, the only cure was to deliver the baby. Four weeks early wasn't as tough as it could be, but it was still worrying. And there was still the chance that before delivery the pre-eclampsia could progress to full-blown eclampsia. 'I'll go and find her now,' he said. 'Dev, try not to worry. They might need to deliver the baby early, but they're really used to dealing with babies born a bit early, and thirty-six weeks isn't super-early.'

'Uh-huh.' Dev was clearly worried sick but trying to stay calm.

'I'll go and find Mandy now,' he said. 'Can I take your number in case she needs me to pass on a message?'

Dev dictated his number and Daniel read it back to check he'd taken it down correctly. 'Try not to worry,' he said again. 'And call again if you need to.'

He called down to the Emergency Department to see if Gemma was there yet; she wasn't, so he checked the board and discovered that Mandy was in consulting room two. He knocked on the door and stepped inside the doorway. 'Dr Cooke, I'm so sorry to interrupt, but I need an urgent word, please.'

She frowned, but apologised to her patient, their parents and her student for the interruption. 'What is it?' she asked when she'd followed him out of the room.

'I don't want you to worry,' he said, 'but Dev just called.'

'Dev?' Her face blanched. 'What's happened to Gemma?' Her eyes widened with fear. 'If she was too ill to call me herself...'

'She started vomiting at work,' he said, 'and she's got a headache and stomach pains. The paramedics weren't happy with her blood pressure. She's on the way in, and so is Dev, but I think she's going to need her mum.'

Mandy was shaking. 'Oh, God. That sounds like pre-eclampsia.' She didn't say it, but he could see in her expression what was worrying her: *what if it progresses?* 'What was her blood pressure reading?'

'Dev didn't say. But if it's not super-high they might manage her conservatively on the ward.'

'Or they might deliver the baby early.' Mandy bit her lip. 'She's thirty-six weeks. But she never gets headaches. Are her hands and feet swollen? And—'

'We're not going to know any more until the ambulance gets here,' he cut in gently. 'I rang down to the Emergency Department, and she's not here yet. Go now, and Dev's on his way in as well. I'll sort out your patient and your students.'

'But—'

'We're still a team on the ward,' he said softly. 'Gemma needs you. I'll cover for you, and I'll explain to everyone that you're dealing with a family emergency. Call me if you need anything. Otherwise I'll presume you're all be on the maternity ward and I'll check in with you at the end of my shift.'

'Thank you.'

He took her hand and squeezed it. 'Gemma's going to be in the right place if anything happens. Try not to worry.'

Mandy got to the Emergency Department about five minutes after Gemma did.

'Mum.' Her daughter was pale and shaking. 'I…'

'I know, darling, and it's going to be all right,' Mandy soothed, holding her free hand tightly. 'You're in the right place. We'll get this sorted out.' And at least she knew the doctor who was assessing Gemma, having worked with him on a couple of her patients. 'I'm not going to get in the way, Alan,' she reassured him.

'I know,' the younger doctor said, smiling. 'Your mum's one of the good ones, Gemma.'

It was scary to see her daughter with a cannula in her hand to give intravenous access and a monitor on her finger to measure her pulse and blood oxygen saturation, even though she knew they were the first procedures the Emergency Department staff would do.

The next few minutes were a blur while Alan examined Gemma, took bloods and a temperature reading, then a manual blood pressure reading, had a quick conversation with one of the obstetricians and then gave Gemma medication for her blood pressure.

'We're going to transfer you upstairs to Maternity, Gemma, and they'll catheterise you there—we need a wee sample now, and then in Maternity they'll monitor your fluid input and output,' Alan said. 'If your husband checks in at Reception, they'll tell him where to find you. And you've got your mum here to keep an eye on you, too.'

'But you're meant to be at work, Mum,' Gemma said.

'It's fine,' Mandy reassured her. 'Daniel's looking after my students and clinics for me, and I'll sort some of his paperwork in return. I'll message him so he knows what's happening.'

By the time they were in the maternity unit—and Mandy had reassured her daughter that being in the high-dependency section of the ward simply meant the team could keep a really close eye on her, plus it would be quieter than the main ward—Dev had arrived.

'We'll try to get your blood pressure down, Gemma,' Connie, the midwife, said. 'The consultant and the anaesthetist both know you're here, and we'll be keeping regular checks on your blood pressure and your pulse, as well as regular checks on the baby.'

'What's made me ill?' Gemma asked.

'We think you have pre-eclampsia,' Connie said. 'Your mum will be able to tell you about that.'

Mandy smiled. 'It's been a while since I did my maternity rotation. You're more up to date than I am—plus *you're* her midwife. I'm simply here as Gemma's mum.'

Connie gave her a smile of understanding and turned to Gemma. 'It's a complication of pregnancy where your blood pressure's too high and protein leaks from your kidneys into your urine. And sometimes it can affect how your blood clots.'

'What causes it?' Dev asked.

'It's not fully understood, but we know it's a problem with the blood vessels that supply the placenta. It's nothing you've done wrong,' Connie said. 'It's most common in the third trimester, and it's usually picked up at a routine antenatal. Up to six per cent of first pregnancies are affected by it. Some people don't have any symptoms at all; but a headache that just won't go away is a common one, along with being sick, having a pain under your ribs and having swollen hands and feet.'

'How does it affect the baby?' Gemma asked.

'It affects how well the placenta works and the baby's growth,' Connie explained. 'We're keeping an eye on the baby to make sure they're not in distress; you'll have an ultrasound shortly to check the blood flow through the placenta, measure the baby's growth and see how much amniotic fluid there is. We're also going to monitor the baby's heart rate. If we can keep you going with medication and monitoring until thirty-seven weeks and the baby's not in distress, that's when we'll advise you to have the baby—either by induction or by a caesarean section.'

'What if the baby's in distress?' Dev asked.

'Then we'll suggest delivering the baby now,' Connie said. 'You're at thirty-six weeks, so the baby will be only a tiny bit premature. If it makes you feel any better, we often deliver twins at thirty-five weeks. Try not to worry.'

Gemma looked relieved.

'We'll need to keep you in a little bit longer than usual after delivery, to make sure there aren't any complications, and your little one might need a short stay in the neonatal unit so we can keep a close eye on them, but try not to worry. The main thing is we'll keep an eye on you both and keep you safe. And your midwife and health visitor will check your blood pressure more regularly until it's back to normal and you stop needing the medication.'

'Will I get it again if we have another baby?' Gemma asked.

'It's possible, but because we know it happened in your first pregnancy we can monitor you more closely in any future pregnancies,' Connie said.

The rest of the morning felt like an endless round of tests and discussions, though Mandy was pleased to see that the maternity team took the same approach as the children's ward, making sure their patients understood the choices.

Finally the consultant said, 'I'm not happy with your blood pressure, Gemma. Obviously it's your choice, but I'd like to deliver the baby.'

'Will I at least be awake for it?' Gemma asked.

'Yes. We can give you spinal anaesthesia,' he said. 'And Dev can be in there with you to hold your hand.'

'Then I'll pop back to my ward for a few minutes,' Mandy said. 'Everything's going to be fine, Gemma. I'll see you very soon.' She kissed her daughter and her son-in-law, then headed back to the ward.

Daniel was in their joint office. 'How's Gemma?' he asked.

'She has pre-eclampsia,' Mandy said. 'Her blood pressure's been a bit stubborn, so she's having a section now.' She bit her lip. 'This is when being a doctor isn't so great. You know all the complications.'

'And you also know the solutions,' he reminded her. 'She's in the right place.'

'I know. But it's my job to worry about her,' Mandy

said. 'Thank you for covering my clinics this morning—and the first half of this afternoon.'

'Not a problem,' he said. 'I had a couple of meetings that were easily moved. It's all fine. I assume you're going back to Maternity now?'

'I ought to finish my clinic, first,' she said.

'Go back to Gemma,' he said. 'I'll handle your clinic. You'd do the same for me, if I were in your shoes.'

'True,' she admitted.

'Go. And I'll come and see you at the end of the shift and fill you in.' He smiled. 'And sneak a cuddle. There's nothing like newborn cuddles.'

'Thank you. I really appreciate your support,' Mandy said.

It was the least he could do, Daniel thought, but he didn't say it.

At the end of his shift, he went up to see Gemma and Dev. He found them by their newborn's crib in the neonatal unit; Gemma was in a wheelchair.

'Thank you for everything you did for us today, Daniel,' Gemma said. 'Sorry I can't stand up to greet you properly. It'll be another couple of hours before the spinal block's worn off.'

Dev shook his hand warmly. 'Thank you for getting Mandy to be with Gemma so quickly.'

'You're very welcome,' Daniel said with a smile. 'And your baby's beautiful.'

'He needs a little bit of special care right now,' Gemma said, 'but we're hoping in a day or two he can join me in my room.'

'They'll want to keep an eye on his breathing, temperature and blood sugar, and catch any jaundice early,' Daniel said. 'Though you should be able to feed him yourself, if that's what you'd planned. The neonatal team will teach you and Dev things like kangaroo care—where you hold him against your chest, skin to skin—and "comfort holding". And they're very used to questions, so feel free to ask them anything.'

'I feel a bit daft, asking if a thirty-six-week-old baby counts as premature,' she said, wrinkling her nose.

She had Mandy's lovely brown eyes, and it made him feel warm inside. 'Thirty-six weeks officially counts as late preterm,' Daniel said, 'but remember that full term is anything from thirty-seven weeks. So he might be in the unit for a few days, but during that time his care will transition to you.' He paused. 'Where's your mum?'

'She's gone to pick up my hospital bag,' Gemma said. 'Actually, I could do with a drink of water. Would you mind pushing me back to my room while Dev stays with the baby, please?'

Daniel was pretty sure there was a water cooler in the unit, but clearly Gemma wanted to talk to him about something in private. 'Sure,' he said.

She waited until they were back in her room. 'I don't know what went wrong between you and Mum,' she said gently, 'but I wish it hadn't. She was happier with you than she'd been in a long time.'

He winced. 'It's complicated.'

'Does it have to be?' she asked. 'When I saw you together, it was pretty clear that you were in love with each other. I know Mum can be a bit guarded sometimes, but she's special.'

'She deserves someone who'll treat her properly,' he said.

'She does,' Gemma agreed. 'And I thought that someone was you.'

'I'm the worst person she could get involved with,' Daniel said. 'My marriage broke up because I was unfaithful.'

'Obviously you must know my dad cheated on her, if infidelity's the reason why you think you're wrong for her,' Gemma said. 'Can I be rude and ask, did it happen very long ago?'

'I was about your age,' he admitted.

She raised her eyebrows. 'That's a whole generation ago. And you've really not forgiven yourself in all that time? I think you've been too hard on yourself, Dan. Everyone makes mistakes. Sometimes really terrible ones. But that doesn't mean you should just give up. So learn from whatever you did and move on.'

He couldn't. He was stuck. So he just stared at her.

'I can't remember the last time my mum dated someone. But she trusted you enough to let you close,' Gemma said thoughtfully. 'And—my dad aside, obviously—she's a good judge of character. If Mum can trust you, maybe you should follow her lead and trust yourself.'

'Maybe,' he said, not wanting to argue with her. 'Let me get you that glass of water and push you back to join your husband and son.'

Just as he'd handed Gemma the water, Mandy walked in.

'I've got the hospital bag for you,' she said.

'Thanks, Mum.' Gemma gave her a grateful smile.

'Your grandson is gorgeous,' Daniel said. 'I'm not

going to ask for a cuddle now, because I know he's more vulnerable to infections and he needs to rest—which doesn't happen when he's being passed round to people. But I'm definitely claiming a cuddle when he's ready to socialise.'

'You've got it,' Gemma said. 'Can we go back, now?'

'Sure.' He wheeled her back to the neonatal unit.

'Mum, you need a break. You've been watching over me or running errands all day,' Gemma said.

'So unsubtle, Gem,' Dev said with a sigh. 'You're supposed to point out that our baby can only have two visitors at a time, and right now that's you and me, and my parents are on their way down from Manchester and will be here any minute now, so maybe we can catch up with your mum tomorrow?'

'Very tactful, Dev,' Gemma said.

'We get the message. We'll leave you in peace,' Mandy said.

At the door to the neonatal unit, she said to Daniel, 'You've clearly been looking after Gemma in my absence. Thank you.'

'You're very welcome. She's lovely.'

And her words echoed in his head. *If Mum can trust you, maybe you should follow her lead and trust yourself...'*

Could he try?

'Mandy.'

'Yes?'

'You've had a day of worrying yourself sick,' he said. 'Come home with me. I'll feed you and drive you home.'

'I don't think that's a good idea,' she said.

'And I'd like to talk,' he added softly. 'I know I haven't

been fair to you. I understand if you don't want to go to my place. Maybe we can just find somewhere quiet in King's Cross where we can grab something to eat and have the space to talk? Neutral territory.'

For a very long and very nasty moment, he thought she might refuse.

But then she huffed out a breath. 'I'm too tired and too stressed to cook tonight,' she admitted.

'No strings,' he said. 'Something to eat, and a quiet chat.'

'All right.'

They didn't speak much on the way to King's Cross, but it wasn't an awkward silence so he didn't mind.

'Fancy some comfort food?' he asked.

'I'm thinking macaroni cheese,' she said.

'Good call.'

They found a café offering what they wanted, and ordered two big bowls of macaroni cheese with a dish of steamed tenderstem broccoli cooked with garlic and lemon. Daniel added a jug of water and two glasses of prosecco to their order.

'Prosecco? Seriously?'

'We're both too tired to drink a whole bottle between us, and we need to toast the baby,' he said.

She gave him a weary smile. 'We do. That was scary, today. I didn't tell Gemma, obviously, but in my head I was running through the stats of how frequently pre-eclampsia turns to eclampsia.'

Just what he'd guessed. 'One less worry is that he's thirty-six weeks,' Daniel said, 'so he didn't need steroids to help mature his lungs.'

'But there's the risk of jaundice.'

'Which is easily fixed with phototherapy,' he countered.

'True.' She closed her eyes. 'That's the thing about your children. When you see them upset and worried and ill, you want to take it all from them so everything's OK again. You'd do anything to have a real magic wand.'

'That goes for nieces and nephews, too,' Daniel said. 'At least for me, as they're the closest I have to children.'

She opened her eyes again. 'You would've made a good dad.'

'I made a different choice,' he said. But maybe, just maybe, he could be a grandad…

Though that was running before he could walk. He needed to be totally honest with Mandy before he could even think about suggesting something like that. Take the risk and really open his heart to her.

He was about to open his mouth and tell her when the waiter came up with their prosecco.

So instead he smiled. 'To Gemma, Dev and the baby,' he said, lifting his glass.

'Gemma, Dev and the baby,' she echoed.

They lapsed into silence again when their food arrived. She picked at her meal, he noticed. 'Sorry,' she said. 'The food's good. I think I'm just too tired to eat.'

'It sounds as if you've hit that point when you know you can stop worrying quite so much, and at the same time you realise just how much you *have* been worrying and it wipes you out,' he said. 'I've been there.' He pushed his own plate away and looked at her. 'Gemma said something that made me think. If you can trust me not to cheat on you, maybe I should follow your lead and trust myself.'

'Gemma said that?' Her eyes widened. 'I didn't tell her anything about what you told me in confidence.'

'I know. I told her about it myself,' he said. 'But she didn't judge me. She asked me how old I was at the time, and pointed out that it happened a whole generation ago.'

Mandy laced her fingers together, resting her elbows on the table and her chin on her linked fingers. 'Did you listen to her?'

'I should,' he said, 'have listened to *you* when you said something very like it in the first place.' He sighed. 'The idea of a proper relationship terrifies me. I was desperate to make a go of my marriage with Roxy, prove to myself that I wasn't my dad. And what happened? I did exactly what my dad would've done.'

'Maybe,' she said, 'you rushed into marriage. You met Roxy when you were both eighteen, and people change hugely between that age and twenty-five.'

'I know,' he said softly. 'I thought we'd change together. But we grew apart, instead. I don't think either of us knew how tough those years would be, with me working stupid hours and studying and not spending enough time with her. I wouldn't have blamed her for leaving me for someone else—someone who was prepared to put the work into their relationship. For me, that made it even worse that I was the one who looked elsewhere, not her.'

'So you've punished yourself ever since, convinced that you're shallow and unreliable,' she said. 'When you're not. The truth is, you were both young and you found yourselves in a situation neither of you really had the tools to cope with at the time.' She paused. 'You said Roxy forgave you.'

'She did.'

'So follow her lead,' she said. 'Forgive yourself.'

'The thing is, I've thought of myself in those terms for so long, I don't even know where to start,' he said.

'People are capable of changing, if they really want to,' she said gently. 'It sounds to me as if your dad didn't want to change; he was quite happy putting himself first. Whereas you—you don't do that.'

'Don't I?'

'No. Would your father have taken Daisy for a walk by the sea and told her she didn't have to be a doctor, then made her think about doing something that combined the caring side of medicine with the music and dance she loved so much?' she asked.

'Well, no. He would have seen her as the third generation of medics in our family. And he probably would've tried to pressure her into following in his exact footsteps and becoming a surgeon,' Daniel said.

'Exactly. Putting himself first. Not like you. And you're the same at work. You put yourself in other people's shoes. You thought how I'd react to the news about Gemma coming into hospital, and knew that I'd want to be with her—so you told me to be with her while you sorted everything else out.' She looked at him. 'And I knew I'd be safe to leave my patients and my students in your hands, because you're reliable.'

'Even though I let you down?'

'You've spent so long thinking about yourself as the bad guy, you've forgotten to remember the good stuff you do,' she said. 'You learned how to do a ballet turn, just to make a little girl smile.'

'She was so pleased,' he said. 'And you were right. She told me I was holding my fingers wrong. She said they were crabby and they should be flowers.' He smiled. 'It was good to see her giggle, given how pale and poorly she was when she came in.'

'That's why I didn't tell you how to hold your hands,' Mandy said. 'I thought she'd enjoy teaching you.'

'She did.'

'And there's Matty. I bet you end up going to watch him play cricket.'

'Busted,' Daniel muttered. 'I was planning to do that in the summer.'

'So are you going to start trying to see your good side?' she asked.

'I want to. I really want to,' he said. 'But I think I'm going to need help.'

'You told our team that asking for help when you need it is a sign of strength,' Mandy said. 'Maybe you should take your own advice.'

Hope flooded through him. If she meant that... 'Will you give me a second chance, Mandy?' he asked. 'And help me learn to give myself a second chance?' He shook his head. 'No, that's coming out all wrong. It's all me, me, me, and that's not what I want.'

'What do you want?' she asked.

'Love,' he said simply. 'I love you, Mandy. I think I fell for you the first day I met you, when you told me terrible—and literally—cheesy jokes. You make my world a brighter place, and I want to do that for you, too. I want to share my life with you. Explore things with you, to learn and laugh and...love,' he finished.

'That's what I want, too,' she said. 'But that means opening up to me. Trusting me, and trusting yourself. Can you do that?'

'With you by my side, yes. I'm always going to worry,' he admitted, 'but knowing that you believe in me will help to stem the doubts.'

'You're a good man, Daniel Monroe,' she said. 'I love you. Let's see if we can change the way you think about you.' She reached over to take his hand. 'Starting now.'

# EPILOGUE

*Three months later*

ON AN UNUSUALLY sunny Saturday morning in late February, Mandy walked hand in hand with Daniel through the grounds of the gorgeous seventeenth-century Ham House.

'That's an amazing house,' she said. 'I bet the gardens are full of roses in the summer.'

'We'll come back and find out, but I wanted to come this weekend because I had something specific in mind,' Daniel said. And suddenly he felt ridiculously nervous. What if…?

But Mandy had taught him to believe in himself over the last three months. And his world had really opened up. Everything from hosting family lunches where everyone brought a dish to add to the kitchen table already groaning with what he'd cooked, through to baby James Devendra Shastri's christening, the previous week—where he'd been incredibly touched and proud that Gemma and Dev had asked him to be one of the baby's godfathers.

He encouraged Mandy to keep up with her book group, dance aerobics and ballet class, just as she encouraged him to keep up going to the gym with his best friend;

and he and Mandy had a regular Wednesday night slot babysitting James to give Gemma and Dev a chance of spending time together. He'd loved bathtime, lullabies and storytime; being an unofficial step-grandparent had really enriched his life.

And in between, he got to wake up with Mandy in his arms every morning—either at his place or hers—and to spend time with the loveliest woman he'd ever met.

She nudged him.

'What?' he asked.

'You were away with the fairies. What's this specific thing? Have you been reading guidebooks again?'

'Websites,' he said. And the picture he'd found had made him realise this was going to be the perfect back-drop for what he had in mind. He'd checked with Gemma first, on the quiet, and she'd given him the most enormous hug, followed by asking a question that had actually brought tears to his eyes and a lump to his throat.

'And...?' Mandy prompted.

'There was something I wanted you to see in the gardens,' he said.

'Snowdrops?' she asked. 'I love snowdrops.'

'There are snowdrops,' he said, 'but that's not it.' As they walked through the grounds towards the back of the house, he said, 'Would you humour me and close your eyes until I say you can open them?'

She laughed. 'I don't have a clue why you're asking that, but all right. I trust you not to let me walk straight through a puddle or fall flat on my face.'

He led her along the gravelled path until they reached the back of the house—and the photo he'd seen from the previous spring that had caught his eye barely did it justice.

'All right,' he said, drawing them both to a halt in front of one of the large rectangular areas. 'You can open your eyes now.'

She did so. 'That's gorgeous! A purple carpet—of crocuses? I've never seen anything like this. My favourite colour, too.'

He knew. It was why he'd chosen this spot.

She grinned. 'No wonder you sounded so pleased with yourself when you asked me to close my eyes.'

'I wanted the perfect backdrop.' He went down on one knee. 'Amanda Cooke, I think I fell in love with you the first day I met you—and it's not just cupboard love because you make the best brownies. You've changed my life for the better, and you've taught me to do something I haven't done for half a lifetime: to trust myself. I asked Gemma's permission, and she said I could ask you.' The words spilled out in a rush. 'Will you marry me?'

Her smile broadened and she opened her arms to welcome him. 'I love you, too, Dan. Yes.'

He stood up, wrapped his arms round her, and kissed her until he was dizzy. 'Thank you,' he said. 'I haven't bought a ring, because I thought it'd be nice to choose it together. Maybe we can go shopping this afternoon.'

'I'd like that,' she said. 'But backtrack a moment. You asked my daughter's permission?'

'She was really pleased that I'd asked.' He swallowed the lump in his throat. 'And she asked if she could call me "Dad".'

'Oh!' Mandy's eyes filmed with tears, telling him that she was affected in the same way that he'd been.

'Shall we give her the answer?' he asked, taking his phone from his pocket and flicking into the camera app. They stood with their arms wrapped round each other, smiling, and he angled the screen so the carpet of purple crocuses was the full background.

And then he sent the picture to Gemma.

The answer's yes. To both questions. xx

\* \* \* \* \*

# Nurse's Twin Baby Surprise

Colette Cooper

MILLS & BOON

*Nurse's Twin Baby Surprise*
is **Colette Cooper**'s debut title.

Look out for more books from Colette Cooper.
Coming soon!

Discover more at millsandboon.com.au.

As a child, reading the Ladybird book *The Nurse* sowed the seeds for **Colette Cooper**'s future career. Using her experiences as a nurse to write medical romances with vibrant, interesting heroes and heroines to fall in love with is a dream come true. Colette lives in a beach house in Australia in her daydreams, but in reality she lives in the Heart of England—just about as far from the sea as it is possible to be in the UK, but very close to the home of Mr Fitzwilliam Darcy! As well as writing, she practises yoga, which she isn't bad at, and French, which needs much more practice!

To my biggest cheerleaders, my lovely family.

# CHAPTER ONE

THE ANTICIPATION OF meeting the new consultant was undoubtedly the cause of Lois Newington's butterflies and the excited, almost tangible buzz in the air. He'd arrived two days ago, when she'd been away on a course, so she hadn't yet met him, but he seemed to be the subject of every conversation between the staff. She was ready for him, though. Ready and determined not to fall at his feet as it seemed most of the rest of the hospital staff had done. TV's Dr Sex-on-a-Stethoscope might well look like a movie star, but Lois was off men...totally.

The cool and not unwelcome swish of air around her bare legs as the cubicle curtain was pulled back told her that they had company. Otherwise ignoring the newcomer, she instinctively took a step forward to allow them into the cubicle behind her. She wasn't going to allow whoever it was to distract her even for one second from the emergency she was dealing with.

It was probably a junior doctor. Junior staff often wanted to watch a cardiac arrest to gain experience—well, they could watch, as long as they didn't get in the way.

The clear, confident instructions she called out were completely by the book—a CPR masterclass. She'd done this a thousand times, and even though the understandable adrenaline surge made her heart bang against her ribs, she controlled its rate with accustomed resolve, kept herself two steps ahead of the rest of the team and appeared as cool as the proverbial cu-

cumber. If there was one thing scumbag Emilio couldn't have criticised her over, it was the fact that she was good at her job.

'Airway secure?'

'Secure and air entry all areas, Sister.'

Lois glanced at the cardiac monitor. 'VF. Shockable rhythm. Charge, please.'

The shrill tones of defibrillator rang out as it fuelled itself with electrical charge, but the doctor's gaze wasn't focussed on the patient—it was fixed on the newcomer who was standing silently, right behind her. The back of her neck prickled.

She looked around the cubicle. Senior nurse, Tom, on chest compressions, was counting aloud, but everyone else was looking past her right shoulder, and they all seemed to be standing a little bit taller and a little bit straighter than they had been before the stranger's arrival.

Her stomach lurched. She didn't need a sixth sense to know instantly who they were looking at. The newcomer was Max Templeton, surgeon to the stars and Emilio the scumbag's much anticipated replacement. She didn't turn around. The defibrillator's beep signalled that it was ready.

'Stand clear.'

Everyone moved away from the bedside.

'Shock, please.'

A dull thud of electricity shot, bullet-like, into the arrested patient, causing his body to arch in response.

'Checking rhythm…'

She held her breath, silently praying that the erratic ECG trace on the monitor would settle to a normal sinus rhythm. If it didn't, this patient's chance of survival would plummet.

'VF.'

The commanding male voice from just behind her, almost made her jump.

'Shock again…now.'

'Charge,' called Lois.

*What was he doing? He couldn't just turn up and take over.*

A junior doctor took the command and depressed the charging button. The defibrillator whined as the electrical charge built within it.

'Stand clear,' she called.

'Shock.'

Max Templeton's command rang out loud and clear, the command on her own lips silenced by his. She didn't have time to turn around and explain that *she* was leading the arrest and had been for the last five minutes. Didn't he know the protocol? He must do. He was just making his presence felt—just like Emilio, and just as she'd expected he would.

Emilio had gone, leaving her to try to put her life back together, but his replacement was going to be exactly like him—she just knew it. The only difference was that she wasn't going to fall ridiculously head over heels for Max Templeton—not in a million years.

The dull thud of the electric shock entered the patient and Lois turned her attention to the monitor as the spikes on the ECG settled.

Damn, he was still in...

'VF. Shock again.' The male voice behind her cut in with an air of authority no one could ignore. 'Get me some wire cutters and a thoracotomy set. I may need to reopen his chest. He's had adrenaline, I assume?'

He moved from behind her and stood at her side, almost but not quite touching her arm with his. Still she didn't look at him, but there was no doubt who it was standing beside her, ignoring protocol, taking command, flooding the air between them with crackling anticipation.

So here he was at last, the much anticipated, famous and infamous Max Templeton. His reputation as a brilliant surgeon wasn't in doubt, and she was keen to see him in action. But what she knew she *wasn't* going to appreciate was his reputation as a man who thought he was God's gift to medicine...and women. By the time Emilio's six-month contract had been drawing to a close, and he'd been preparing to go back to Italy—back to his wife and the toddler daughter that he'd somehow neglected to tell her about—she'd have welcomed whoever replaced him. Anyone was better than the deceitful, lying cheat she had the misfortune to call her ex. But he was being replaced with another smooth operator… TV heartthrob Max Templeton.

She wasn't going to give him the satisfaction of turning around to look at him; much as she wanted to.

'Dr Harper—charge, please.' The junior doctor depressed the button. She had his attention back.

She swept a glance around the bed. 'Stand clear…'

'Shock.'

Max Templeton's clear command came only a split moment before hers. She swung round to face him as she heard the shock being delivered. He was overriding her. Did he think she was incompetent? Or was he just being the arrogant egomaniac she'd expected he would be?

'Was that a yes or a no to the adrenaline?'

His tone was composed but firm. Two deep blue hypnotic eyes burned into her, requiring an answer—eyes she'd seen hundreds of times on screen, in newspapers and in magazines. Eyes whose true power could only be felt when face to face with them.

'Begin chest compressions.'

She tore her gaze away from him to instruct the team. She had exactly two minutes to reply to him whilst the next cycle of CPR continued. Turning fully towards him, she let her gaze travel upwards over his tall frame, and the further up his body her eyes rose, the harder her heart banged in her chest.

He was a finely tuned athlete, with an impressive, strong-looking physique, sun-kissed skin, broad shoulders and well-defined pecs not hidden by the navy scrubs he wore. He looked like a glossy ad for designer aftershave. Only the scrubs and the stethoscope draped casually around his neck made him look like a doctor and not an Olympian.

She swallowed. It *was* him.

*Don't look at him with 'starstruck' written across your face like everyone else is.*

Somehow, she found her voice. Professional Lois kicked in and she briefed him on the situation with the patient.

'Yes, as protocol. The patient suddenly dropped his BP to sixty over thirty, central pressure was down at two, heart rate one ten, and then he went into VF. He's had two cycles of CPR and that was the third shock of the second cycle. And you are...?'

Impossibly, her heart rate notched up further still.

*Had she really said that?*

There was little doubt as to who he was, but he shouldn't just rock up and expect everyone to know him. He wasn't wearing any ID and, a stickler for correct protocol, Lois felt a need to point it out to him right there and then that was almost overwhelming.

She turned back to the team. 'That's two minutes. Check rhythm again, please.' She'd timed her reply perfectly.

The team paused to let the chaotic green lines on the monitor settle, but the high-pitched, continuous beep told anyone who wasn't staring at it that it had settled into an ominous flat line.

'Asystole.' *Damn.* 'Continue CPR.'

'We need to do a thoracotomy.'

Again, his tone was calm, but his words made Lois draw in a breath. He wanted to perform open heart surgery on the intensive care unit? It was unheard of.

But Max Templeton had taken a sterile pack from the shelf and stepped forward, claiming his space, and all eyes were fixed on him. Ripping the pack open, he dropped it onto the bed and spread the sterile field flat to reveal the array of silver surgical instruments within it.

'Continue CPR until I'm gloved up and ready,' he ordered.

The team did as they were instructed, swiftly swinging into action, restarting the methodical, well-practised processes which they hoped would prolong this man's life long enough for Max Templeton to remedy the underlying cause.

Despite the fact that he hadn't introduced himself, and wasn't wearing his ID, everyone knew it *was* him, of course. He was one of the best-known faces on the planet. But he'd just assumed everyone would know who he was and that just reeked of arrogance. No one else had questioned him, but charlatans had been known to masquerade as medical staff in hospitals, often by being brazen. And this man certainly had more than a touch of the brazen about him. He shouldn't just stride in here and expect that everyone knew him…but that had been exactly what he'd done.

Well, she wasn't having it. She spoke quietly but directly.

'I can see you're dressed in scrubs, but I can't just let you crack open this man's chest without confirming your identity.'

Glittering sapphire eyes met hers and her breath locked in her throat. He was even more stunning in the flesh than he was on screen…almost impossibly so. She was aware the team around them were continuing with CPR—compressions were being quickly but steadily counted aloud, and monitor alarms still rang out, reminding them the patient's vital signs were critically outside of normal parameters.

She knew what was going on around her, but for a moment the centre of her focus was the two deep blue eyes looking back at her, laser-like, penetrating, silently assessing. Her determined resolve not to find him attractive wavered. Straightening the front of her uniform, her instinct telling her to look away, she held his gaze.

'Max Templeton, cardiothoracic consultant,' he replied, one dark eyebrow raised, clearly having completed his appraisal of her.

*Was he trying to suppress a grin?*

But it was gone before she could decide, and then, much to her astonishment, he took her by the shoulders and gently but firmly moved her to one side before snapping on the sterile gloves.

'I operated on Mr Ferns yesterday and replaced his aortic valve in order to keep him alive. I'm not about to let him die today.' He picked up the wire cutters. 'Dressing.'

Everyone had been right—he was something else. Most surgeons wouldn't attempt this procedure outside of a theatre.

She watched him like a hawk as she too quickly drew on a pair of sterile gloves. If he was going to attempt this they had to move fast.

Reaching out in front of him, she tore the dressing off the patient's chest. 'This is pretty irregular, Mr Templeton.'

'He has a cardiac tamponade,' he replied, slicing through the chest sutures with ease. He glanced at the three junior doctors opposite him across the bed. 'One of you needs to glove up to hold a retractor.' He addressed Lois again as he began to cut through the wires holding the patient's sternum together. 'He'll die if I don't drain the blood from the pericardium.' He snapped through a wire. 'And I'm not about to let that happen.'

*Clearly.*

But she wasn't going to be silenced that easily. 'You can't do a thoracotomy on the unit.'

'Watch me.'

'You could attempt pericardiocentesis.'

'I know.' He cut through another wire with a snap.

'It's less traumatic.'

'I know.' He snapped through the last wire and eased the sternum apart, placing a retractor inside the cavity and handing the end of it to one of the juniors, instructing him to pull gently but firmly.

'But you're not going to.'

His swift glance and raised eyebrow gave her his answer.

Lois threaded her arm through his. The jolt as her skin met his was as unwelcome as it was shocking. She pressed thick piles of swabs against the edges of the wound, stemming the bleeding, applying pressure. The oozing red liquid soaked through the gauze, warming her gloved fingers. She had no qualms about calling for help if Max Templeton didn't pass muster, but up to now she was satisfied with all his actions.

All his actions, that was, except the way he looked at her and made her insides quiver. *That* was completely unsatisfactory.

'Tamponade. Pass me a—'

Lois placed a large syringe and long needle firmly into his outstretched palm. The faint look of surprise in his eyes was just a tad satisfying. She hadn't been an intensive care and theatre sister for four years without knowing how to assist with a thoracotomy.

'Thank you, Sister…?'

'Newington.' She pointed to her name badge whilst holding out a tray ready for the syringe, her forearm brushing his and sending a spark into her which could rival the jolt from the defibrillator.

*Why did these cubicles have to be so damn small?*

The staff had all been correct in their assessment of this new consultant. He was undeniably gorgeous and, much to her surprise and annoyance, she'd been ridiculously conscious of her heart hammering in her chest since the moment their eyes had locked minutes before.

*She didn't want this.*

Emilio had slunk back to his family in Italy, leaving her self-esteem battered and bruised, six months ago. The last thing she needed was to fall for the charms of another schmoozer. Well, she wasn't going to.

*Get a grip, Lois. This man lives in a different world—he's surrounded by glamour. He isn't even going to notice your existence beyond what you can do for his patients. And if you didn't know that before Emilio slimed into your life, you certainly do now.*

Max Templeton's reputation went before him. Since leaving medical school he'd quickly made a name for himself as one of the world's leading heart surgeons, and soon celebrity patients had been queuing up to be treated by him. His film star good looks and charismatic charm had made him the perfect TV doctor, and he seemed to spend as much time on the red carpet as he did operating. He'd recently returned to his roots in the NHS to pioneer an antenatal cardiac screening programme, but he'd only signed a four-month contract for some reason.

The only other thing she knew about him was that his reputation for mending hearts rivalled his well-known reputation for breaking them. And after the recent dark chapter in her life that had been Emilio, she wasn't going anywhere near his replacement, clearly cut from the same cloth. No one was ever going to crush her like that again.

'Fifty mils aspirated.' He was utterly focussed and completely in control. 'He's very bradycardic—there's not enough pressure.'

Reaching back into the chest, he began internal cardiac massage, rhythmically squeezing and releasing the heart, attempting to bring it back to life.

Lois watched the green lines on the monitor. They were either flat or barely moving. The numbers were flashing, telling them what they already knew—that they were into desperate measures territory, and the patient's life was balanced on the thin knife-edge between life and death.

Shifting her gaze, she watched as Max, calm but still intensely focussed, his jaw set, tiny beads of sweat appearing on his forehead, continued to demand that life return to his patient. He appeared to be true to his word—he really didn't want this patient to die.

No one dared to breathe. Only the rhythmic hissing and clicking from the ventilator and the long, continuous flat beep from the monitor filled the silence. All eyes were on Max Templeton, his gloved hand inside his patient's open chest. Time stood still.

*Was this much-esteemed surgeon as good as he was cracked up to be?*

'Suction.'

It wasn't a question or a request. Already poised with the suction tube in her hand, Lois inserted it into the pool of ruby blood which had collected in the chest cavity, clearing it so that Max could see.

'Better pressure on the arterial line,' she advised, glancing at the monitor at the side of the bed, breaking the silence, taking charge, in control as always.

She might not be svelte, slender and beautiful—*thanks, Emilio, for confirming that*—but this was something she was good at. At least no one could argue with that.

'Over sixty,' agreed Max. 'Enough to perfuse his brain. But the acid test is what happens when I take my hand off the heart. Ready?'

It was intoned as a question, and no one in the cubicle was going to say they weren't. He stilled his hand and focus moved to the cardiac monitor where, if the intervention had worked, the wavering, erratic green lines would show signs that life was returning.

'Sixty-five.' Lois willed the screen to give her the figures she wanted. 'Pressure's seventy.'

Suddenly there was hope.

'Good.' He withdrew his hand from the open thorax, wiping his brow with his forearm. The tightness in his face, jaw and neck slipped away as he let out a slow breath. 'How do we know the patient isn't still bleeding and won't tamponade again?'

The three junior doctors looked back at him—deer in headlights.

And that was when his whole demeanour changed.

'Any ideas, guys? No problem if you don't—this is a great learning opportunity.' He gave a wry grin. 'Not that the patient would see it that way.'

Taking the retractor from the junior doctor, he placed it back into the sterile tray before resting his fingers on his patient's wrist. He studied his audience as if awaiting a response, his famous smile completely changing his face.

The act was so sudden and the effect so startling that Lois was forced to make sure her mouth wasn't gaping open.

*How could someone go from Mr Cool and Arrogant to Mr Relaxed and Happy in a second?*

'The answer, is that we don't,' said Max. 'We have no way of knowing if the pericardium will fill up again. If it does, and any of you are on duty, you can call me—day or night, whether I'm on call or not. Okay, thanks everyone. Show's over, let's get back to work.'

*Had the Max Templeton who'd first walked in and so rudely taken over suddenly been replaced with another Max Templeton, who knew what politeness was and even had a sense of humour?*

Suddenly, her perception of him as irretrievably arrogant as hell had a severe dose of doubt thrown over it. She let out a breath. It sure as hell was going to be interesting working with this man—she'd never seen anyone like him.

*So what was it that made her feel so uneasy?*

His star status? His super-confidence? His apparent lack of respect for protocol? His willingness to push the boundaries to save a patient?

Or was it the fact that when he'd locked his eyes on hers he'd made her heart skip a beat or ten?

The junior doctors filed out, the very attractive female of the three smiling at Max as she drew the curtain behind her in an unnecessarily coy way, making Lois roll her eyes in disbelief. She was so glad she wasn't one of those fawning females who were so obvious it was embarrassing.

'Do you want an echocardiogram?' she asked.

*Why was she suddenly so annoyed? What did she care if staff flirted with him?*

As long as it wasn't done in an unprofessional way or in an inappropriate situation.

But the reason her question to Max had come out so abruptly was as obvious as it was annoying—the junior doctor was slim and pretty, and had enough self-confidence to allow her to flirt openly with someone and even maybe to think that the other person might welcome it.

Lois had never been able to flirt. Whenever she'd tried it, she'd felt silly. It was probably a skill you learnt as a teen— going out with friends...at the school dance. And she'd never done any of those things, had she? As her mother's carer, she'd never been able to indulge in those rites of passage. She'd never been round to friends' houses, excitedly getting ready for a night out, talking about boys, experimenting with make-up, trying each other's clothes on. Flirting was untrodden territory for her.

She hadn't even flirted with Emilio. Lord knew how they'd ended up getting together. He'd done all the running, though, hadn't he? And she'd been stupid enough to fall for what had turned out to be empty compliments.

'No,' Max replied now. 'The tamponade has been drained, and the figures are good. Shall we suture him up?'

Tom slipped out of the cubicle, returning a moment later with a suture pack, which he placed on the bed before turning to Lois.

'Okay if I carry on now?' he asked.

Lois opened her mouth to respond, but once again Max was quicker.

'Sure.' Then, placing his stethoscope in his ears, he bent to listen to his patient's chest.

Tom raised an eyebrow at Lois and grinned at her, mouthing *Told you!* before slipping out of the cubicle, leaving them alone. Lois bit her lip.

'I just thought you'd want a scan to check the valve.'

That was normal procedure, and she was duty-bound to remind him—even if he was one of the most eminent cardiac surgeons in the world.

'There's nothing wrong with my valve, Sister Newington.'

He spoke with uncompromising certainty, reaching for the sterile gloves from the suture set Tom had opened, snapping them on before looking at her directly with his laser blue eyes and flooring her with his completely disarming smile.

'A scan won't be necessary.'

Lois watched him as he began to close the patient's chest, absorbed once more in his work. There was no doubt that his clinical reputation as the best was completely justified. He'd just cracked open this man's chest, and that was pretty rare outside of an operating theatre setting. He'd saved a patient's life and he looked as if he wasn't even trying.

He'd made an impressive first impression…on the whole. But he blithely ignored protocol, wasn't wearing any ID, and spoke to the staff as though *he* ran the unit instead of her.

What everyone had told her seemed to be correct—Max Templeton was something else, and she knew she was gaping at him in exactly the same starstruck way everyone else had been. Well, she wasn't about to allow another consultant to stroll into her unit, rinse and repeat…

'You seem a little irked about the lack of ID badge, Sister.'

His voice broke into her thoughts sharply. She straightened up but he wasn't looking at her. He was working intently on his patient, dark head bent, long fingers moving to and fro with swift expertise as he sutured. He was mesmerising…in more ways than one. But his professional expertise was all she wanted to be mesmerised by—she wasn't interested in anything else.

'ID should be worn at all times,' she managed, a little surprised that she could speak. Suddenly, after what he'd just pulled off, her issue with him not wearing his ID seemed trivial.

*But was he trying to make a point?*

'I was about to start a theatre list when I got the arrest call and I hadn't quite finished getting dressed.'

He turned to face her, the intensity of his blue eyes making her breath catch in her throat and her thoughts spin so she couldn't find the words she needed to speak.

*What was he doing to her?*

Whatever it was it was completely unwelcome. She was off men…period.

He turned back to the patient and she took a moment to breathe again.

'And if I can't trust my ability to place an aortic valve correctly…well, it's time to give up, frankly.'

Lois knew full well that she was staring at him with very poorly disguised incredulity. Humility wasn't one of his strong points, then.

But then he smiled, and his blue eyes twinkled, lighting up with shining stars of mirth.

'I know what you're thinking, Sister Newington.'

*That you're astoundingly gorgeous?*

'I doubt it, Mr Templeton.'

He lowered his gaze, focussing once more on his patient. 'You think I'm an arrogant ass.'

Lois couldn't help it that her mouth fell open. He was right, though—that was what she'd been thinking. As well as thinking that she wanted to spend for ever gazing into his eyes. Which was such a contradiction she couldn't quite believe she was thinking it.

*Don't do this, Lois—get your sensible head on again.*

'Wearing ID is mandatory for all staff, whether you're a cleaner or a surgeon, and I'd be grateful if you could remember that the next time you step into my department—there's good reason for it.'

There…sensible Lois was back in the room.

Snipping the end of the last suture, he tossed the needle and forceps into the opened thoracotomy pack and checked his watch, apparently ignoring her comment.

'Finished?'

She wasn't usually one for stating the obvious, but the quizzical look in his piercing eyes told her she'd probably done just that. She swallowed, managing to hold his gaze even though she desperately needed to look away. Max Templeton had people falling at his feet all the time. Well, she wasn't going to be one of them.

'All yours, Sister Newington.' He swept an upturned palm towards the patient.

*Focus, Lois.*

Stepping forward, she leant in to clean the wound. But Max didn't stand aside, and her arm brushed his once more, sending a bolt of electricity through her.

*Why didn't he move?*

His nearness was warming her—way too much.

'I can take care of everything now.'

*Please leave.*

She needed to breathe normally again.

'I'm sure you can, Sister. Please, carry on—I'm just monitoring his heart rate a moment longer.'

Trying to pretend he wasn't there, she tore the backing from a dressing and placed it over the suture line, smoothing it down carefully, her mind whirling, weighing him up, trying to process what had happened over the last hour, wishing he hadn't made her knees suddenly struggle to take her weight.

*Was he good at what he did?*

Undoubtedly.

*Did she think she could work with him?*

Of course she could—she'd managed it before, hadn't she? Working with surgeons who thought they were the best thing since sliced bread was an all too familiar challenge. She'd ridden the storm that was Emilio Bartello and survived—just.

*Did she like him?*

Not so easy to answer. How could she like someone who had his reputation with women? Men like him thought they could do whatever they liked, with whoever they liked. And if she'd learned anything in the last year…if her relationship with Emilio had taught her anything…it was not to trust men. Especially good-looking, successful men.

But for the last hour her heart had been hammering in her chest as if it was trying to break out—and that hadn't been solely due to the clinical situation they'd found themselves in.

# CHAPTER TWO

HE'D LIED—he didn't need to look at the monitor. The rhythmic beeping told him everything he wanted to know about the condition of his patient's heart. But it had been a close call, and dealing with close calls brought out both the best and the worst in him.

On the one hand, it focussed him so acutely that he was able to give the patient everything he had, calling to mind everything he'd ever learned and giving that patient the very best chance they had of survival—the very thing he wished he'd been able to do all those years ago, when his own brother's life had been in his hands and he'd failed him.

On the other hand, it turned him into what others might interpret as an arrogant ass. He knew he had work to do on that score, and although he tried to control his reactions to being in life-threatening emergencies, and not to come across as over-confident and condescending, he knew he didn't always achieve it.

He'd have loved to be able to rock up to an emergency and feel nothing—churn out the correct interventions with a cheery smile and an easy manner, make everyone think he was cool, calm and a ray of sunshine as he made life-and-death decisions. But life-threatening emergencies churned up memories from long ago that he'd spent his life desperately trying to keep buried, and when he was suddenly confronted with them he feared becoming the twelve-year-old boy who'd failed his twin.

The day William had died—the day that had destroyed everything—he'd made a promise. He wouldn't ever let the same thing happen again. Becoming a heart surgeon had made good on part of that promise—doing everything in his power never to lose a patient—and what he'd come here to St Martin's to do now would complete it.

Sister Newington currently thought him an arrogant ass—he'd seen it in her eyes. He wasn't. He just couldn't lose a patient. This patient had been lucky; his condition was stable. Which meant he could turn his attention fully to the ICU sister who'd clearly got the wrong impression of him and did not feel the need to hide it.

Looking at her was now both possible to do and impossible not to. He'd been briefed about her by the hospital's CEO when she'd been trying to persuade him to come here to St Martin's. Not that he'd needed persuading—he had his own reasons for coming. It was to fulfil a long-held promise from many years ago—a way to make up for what had happened to William… possibly. Learning that the sister at the helm of the intensive care unit was a consummate professional who ran the place like a well-oiled machine was simply a bonus.

No one had warned him, however, that Sister Newington had seductive come-to-bed eyes, curves to die for and a seriously kick-ass attitude which had shot a dose of undeniable lust through him. He knew his ranking in the world of cardiothoracic surgery was as a world-leading heart surgeon, but somehow she'd just turned him into a first year again, questioning his decision to open the patient's chest and berating him for not wearing his ID.

She was right, of course, to question him. But no one had questioned him over anything in a long while. It was oddly alluring…

'Well done, by the way.' He lifted his eyebrows, mildly surprised at the words which had left his lips.

'For not kicking you out and sending you to get your ID?'

She began to gather up all the strewn empty packages from the bed and bundle them into a disposal bag.

'Not in the best interests of the patient at that particular point.'

She lifted her eyes and met his gaze, holding it as time stood still.

And then she smiled.

And his stomach tightened.

Her green eyes were exquisite. No one had warned him about those either.

'I meant for dealing with me performing open heart surgery in the middle of your unit. I got the feeling you weren't keen.'

She clearly hadn't been, but it had been the only option and she'd dealt with it like the consummate professional she'd been described as—much to his admiration and relief.

'Just don't make a habit out of it.' She glanced at the post-arrest untidiness of the cubicle with an exaggerated theatrical sigh. 'It makes a hell of a mess.'

Her eyes sparkled and suppressing his own smile became impossible.

'Apologies, Sister; let me help.'

He picked up the used wire cutters, fully expecting her to tell him to get back to Theatre and do his list. Most nurses didn't allow consultants to clear up.

'Very good of you.' She threw a pair of artery forceps into the receiver he was holding. 'Many hands make light work and all that.'

Lois Newington was evidently not most nurses. And he didn't want to look away.

*Stop it—that's not why you're here.*

He picked up one of the discarded retractors. She certainly lived up to her reputation—confident, competent, in control… The perfect combination for her role as Sister on the ICU.

'Well, your intention was good, but so far you've picked up the sum total of three items.'

She nodded towards his hands and he looked down at them. He had indeed contributed very little to the clearing up operation.

'Not used to it, I assume?' she said.

He looked at her, confused. 'To what?'

'To clearing up.' She rolled her eyes and took the receiver dish from his hand. 'Typical. You might as well get back to Theatre, then.'

And he was a first year again.

'Yes, I've got a bypass to do.'

*What was she doing to him? He was a consultant surgeon—the best in the land—and he was being told off.*

The odd thing was…he didn't mind—in fact, he was rather enjoying it.

*What?*

'I know.'

She turned, reaching up for the curtain to pull it open. His errant gaze wandered down her body and his breathing deepened as her uniform rose to reveal the backs of her bare knees.

'Mr Swain. He's coming here post-op. He'll be in bed three. I promised him I'd be here.'

'Right…'

His difficulty in processing the thoughts suddenly flooding his mind took him by surprise, and somehow, unnervingly, he couldn't suppress them. But Sister Lois Newington wore that blue uniform like he'd never seen anyone else wear it…

*Stop.*

He'd come back for one reason only—and it didn't include getting involved with anyone. His reason for becoming a heart surgeon had been no random choice. Neither had the fact that he'd given so much of his time, energy and own money to St Martin's either. Getting this project over the line wouldn't bring William back, but it would help to prevent any more families from being torn apart. And that required giving it everything he had. Because he'd promised his twin that what had happened to him wasn't going to happen to anyone else—not if he had anything to do with it.

'I'll see you after, then,' he said now. 'If you're still on duty.'

*Was he asking her? Did he want to know?*

The shocking answer to both questions was yes.

'Well, that depends on how long you take with Mr Swain.'

She pulled the curtain back to reveal the rest of the unit going about its daily business as usual—ventilators clicking, monitor alarms pinging—and suddenly he remembered where he was. He needed to be in Theatre. Yet here he was, being drawn to this sassy, captivating woman, hoping she'd still be on shift later when he came to check on his patients.

'I'll be here.' She turned back to face him. 'I never leave the department until all the patients are settled in post-op—I'd never sleep.'

Inexplicably and confusingly, his shoulders relaxed at the thought. He wasn't surprised at her answer. He could well imagine that she wouldn't sleep unless she knew the patients under her care were as stable as they could be and were being well looked after. She looked completely earnest, and again the surprise that he found it was utterly natural to smile at her shocked him.

It was because he valued dedication.

It wasn't for any other reason.

He wasn't interested in engaging in anything personal. He enjoyed the company of women—of course he did—and there were always plenty of women who were happy to spend the odd night or so with him…mostly because of who he was and his connections in the TV business. But longer term? No, thanks. Long term meant allowing someone else into your head, and his head was a mess no one needed or would want to get to know.

Their eyes met once more, kicking his pulse into overdrive as the ever-present lively hum of the busyness of the unit faded into the background, leaving just the two of them, locked in a long moment, rooted to the spot, standing alone amongst the hustle and bustle.

Suddenly she lowered her gaze and turned away, hiding that gorgeous smile, digging her hands into her pockets, glancing around the unit, her sassy confidence gone.

*What had changed?*

He had to go, but wanted to stay.

*Keep it professional, Templeton.*

Professional and superficial. He didn't want to get involved with anyone, even briefly. There was too much else to do. The promise he'd made to William over twenty years ago was about to come to fruition.

Remaining in London for all those years when all he'd wanted to do was run away had been hell at times, but necessary, and he'd promised himself that if he achieved his goal he'd leave London for a new job in California—finally get away from the city he'd grown up in…the city where his life had changed for ever and his young world had come crashing down around him.

Now being able to leave London was so close, and he wanted to do it as quickly as possible and get the hell out of there.

'I should get back to Theatre,' he said.

'Yes.' Glancing at her fob watch, she took a pen from her breast pocket and began busying herself jotting obs down on the huge chart at the end of the bed. 'The sooner you get started on Mr Swain, the sooner we can get him settled in and comfortable here.'

And just like that, sassy Lois was back in the room.

'Thank you again for your help.'

With a reluctance he didn't want to admit to, he walked away, feeling compelled to look back and struggling not to. Pushing open the swing doors leading into theatre suite number four, he called out to a passing nurse.

'Call for Mr Swain from Ward Six; I'll be ready in five.'

He strode into the scrub room and stood before the long

trough sink, turning the taps on with his wrists. He smoothed the dark orange iodine solution up his arms, lathering, scrubbing, rinsing, lathering a second time, his mind swimming with unwanted images of Lois that wouldn't go away. Drying his arms roughly he eased them into the sterile gown and shrugged it onto his shoulders.

*Lois Newington.*

He had to clear her from his head.

*Those eyes.*

Reaching for sterile gloves, he snapped them on.

*Those curves. That sassy, sparkling confidence.*

And yet there was vulnerability too—she'd exposed just a flash of it before she'd hidden it by busying herself. What was the cause of it? She intrigued him.

'Ready, Max?'

He looked up sharply. It was Toby, his anaesthetist.

'Patient's asleep—whenever you're ready.'

'Ready.'

Thinking any further about Lois would have to wait. Actually, he really didn't want to think any further about Lois at all, did he? He'd be leaving soon. London had stopped being his home a long time ago and had become just a place he needed to be so that he could fulfil his duty. And as soon as that duty was done he'd leave. He had to...had to get away from the place and the memories it held. Leaving the city was the prize he'd promised he'd award himself for all the years of training, exams and long shifts, all the years of research. The prize for staying even when it was the last place on earth he wanted to be.

That was the plan and nothing would change it.

'That was all very dramatic, wasn't it?' said Tom as he and Lois prepared infusions in the clinical room.

'The thoracotomy?'

She held up a bottle of anaesthetic, piercing the rubber

stopper with a needle, watching as tiny bubbles of air rushed through the fluid, allowing it to flow.

'He swept in like a superhero—were his underpants on over his scrubs?' Tom grinned. 'It's the first time you've met him, isn't it?'

'Um-hum...'

Lois held up the giving set, rolling the regulator with her thumb, sending the milky liquid into the tubing. She was trying to forget how Max's intense blue eyes had locked onto hers and made her heart thud heavily in her chest, but it had proved impossible all afternoon. And now even the mention of his name had a similar effect.

'Welcome to the fan club.' Tom wore a dreamy but then suddenly pained look on his face. 'Why are all the handsome men straight?'

He sighed dramatically, making her laugh.

'Don't give up, Tom, your knight in shining armour will come along one day. Come on—let's get these up.'

Nodding towards the infusions, she was glad to end any talk of Max Templeton. His dark, handsome profile as he'd held his patient's heart in his hands and saved his life was etched on her mind, even though she'd spent half the afternoon trying to shake herself free of it. But she wasn't interested in Max Templeton in any other way than for his surgical ability. And she most definitely wasn't interested in romance.

*But he'd be back on the unit later...after Theatre.*

Her heart rate picked up again. The devastating smile he'd flashed at her when they'd been clearing up had flooded her face with heat and made her turn away from him to hide it. Hopefully he hadn't noticed. Hopefully she would be able to control it the next time she saw him. But Max Templeton was like no other man she'd ever met—and, damn it, her unruly, misbehaving heart flipped once more in her chest.

# CHAPTER THREE

BUSYING HERSELF AT the bedspace, Lois ran through the checklist. Oxygen and suction, infusion pumps and paperwork—all ready to receive the patient. The double doors behind her clunked open.

Her heart missed a beat. *Max*. He was early.

The porter grinned as he steered the bed carrying the patient into the space, slotting it between the banks of equipment before locking the brakes.

'Evening, Sister.'

'Evening, Dom.'

No Max Templeton.

Lois returned Dom's smile, but the fluttering butterflies had become stones and they sank to the pit of her stomach as the anticipation of seeing him again dissolved into unmistakable disappointment.

Straightening her uniform, she looked to Toby for handover.

'All went well,' advised the anaesthetist as he disconnected the oxygen from the portable cylinder, handing the tubing over to her. 'On pump triple bypass, as planned. Vein graft from left leg: two units of blood. Norad is on four mils an hour. PCA. Last blood gases were okay. Chest drain in situ and patent. Obs stable. Post-op instructions in the notes.'

'Family?'

Lois transferred the leads from the small portable monitor to the large monitor above the bed, which sprang into life as different coloured lines of varying waveforms appeared on it, showing the patient's vital signs.

'They're all up to date and will visit tomorrow. Templeton's happy with everything. Anything else?'

'No, I think that's everything. Thanks, Toby.' The butterflies in her stomach fluttered into action again, dancing at the mention of his name.

'Well done, Mr Swain.' Toby touched the patient's arm. 'Get a good night's sleep; you'll be well looked after here.'

Trying to control the fluttering, Lois smiled at the anaesthetist. She liked Toby—he was warm, gentle, and he cared about his patients. His was a friendly, comforting face, and he was down to earth and immensely likeable. He'd married her best friend, Natalie, one of the staff nurses who worked on the unit. They were expecting their first baby and were incredibly happy.

It was lovely to see two people so in love.

What must it feel like to be loved by someone so much?

Maybe she'd never know. All her life her mother had told her she wasn't lovable—wasn't attractive enough for anyone ever to love her. After her death, she'd eventually come to realise her mother's cruel words about her weight and plainness had probably been her way of keeping her there in the family home, to look after her. She hadn't wanted her to get ideas above her station and believe she could leave home to be with a lover, or even a husband one day.

And it had worked. In fact, it was still working. Unpicking the reasons behind those cruel taunts had been a long, difficult process, but Lois had been making some slow, steady progress. Right up until the time Emilio had come along, taken her for a mug, and smashed that progress into the rocks so hard that now there was nothing left of it.

'I'll see you in the morning, Mr Swain.' She touched his hand lightly, having satisfied herself that he was stable. 'Get some sleep now.'

'Thank you, Sister…for keeping your promise.'

She hadn't eaten and it was late. Making her way out of the hospital, she told herself she was looking forward to a quick cheese on toast when she got home. She walked past the chapel and stopped. It would be quiet in there, and empty—a good opportunity for her to practise for the service on Sunday. Supper could wait another half an hour—and anyway, she had enough reserve on her hips to keep her going for a while.

The door to the chapel creaked slightly as she pushed it open. It was dark save for the small collection of flickering prayer candles on a table. The sweet scent of melting beeswax filled the air. Flicking the end light switch, to illuminate the soft lights on the altar, she made her way to the front, slipping off her fleece and placing her bag on top of it on one of the wooden chairs. The light partially lit up the coloured stained-glass window behind the altar and the jewel-coloured panes glowed richly. The chapel was silent save her footsteps on the terracotta tiled aisle, and at this time in the evening it was highly unlikely she'd be disturbed.

Perfect—just how she liked it.

Church choir had been one of her very few escapes when she'd been growing up—one of the few places, apart from school, she'd been allowed to go. It had provided her with some much-needed warmth and friendship over those difficult years as she'd tried to navigate her way through school and college whilst also being her mother's carer.

'Ave Maria' was perfect for her mezzosoprano range. The melody was exquisitely beautiful, delicate and emotional. But the only way Lois had ever been able to sing it aloud in front of other people had been to imagine no one was there—always ensuring she was on the back row of the choir, hiding away behind the others and pretending no one else was there to hear her, see her, judge her.

She'd vowed that if she ever had children, she'd encourage them to sing at the tops of their voices, whenever they liked.

But it wasn't something she herself had ever been able to do...
unless she was alone.

Imagining the opening notes, she closed her eyes and began
to sing—softly at first, but quickly building the volume and intensity as the song progressed, projecting her voice to fill every
corner of the chapel, allowing it to escape from her fully, ebb-
ing and swelling with the melody, reaching its crescendo and
falling away serenely to its end.

She drew in a deep breath, refilling her lungs with the air
she'd given to the last series of notes.

The unmistakable scraping sound of a wooden chair on a
wooden floor made Lois freeze. Suddenly alert, a shot of adrenaline making her heart bang uncomfortably in her chest, she
squinted to the back of the room. A dark figure stood up and
began to walk towards her, down the central aisle. Instinctively,
she took a step backwards as the light from the altar fell on his
tall frame, illuminating him.

Max Templeton.

What was *he* doing here?

He stopped halfway down the aisle, looking at her sheep-
ishly, his hands in his pockets. She couldn't move.

'It's only me.'

*Only me?* Probably the one person in the whole world she
would have chosen not to be there right then, and he said,
*'Only me.'* As if him suddenly coming out of the shadows like
a prowling panther was nothing.

Could he hear her heart banging like a bat out of hell against
her ribs?

'I can see that...now.'

'Sorry... I didn't want to startle you.'

He began to walk towards her again, and it was all Lois
could do to hold her ground and not step further backwards. He
stopped just before the first step of the altar, three steps below
her, his eyes level with hers, and the light from the flickering
candles flamed the dark indigo pools, drawing her into them.

'You have a beautiful voice, Sister Newington.'

Heat flooded through her, flushing her cheeks with unwanted warmth.

*You have beautiful eyes, Mr Templeton.*

'Oh… I was just practising…it's better with the music.' She plunged her hands into her pockets.

'It's beautiful without—perfect, in fact.'

His eyes were hypnotic, mesmerising… They seemed sincere.

*Did he mean that?*

She wrinkled her nose. She *wasn't* perfect.

'I don't know about that—it was okay. I didn't think there was anyone in here. Have you only just come in?'

*Please have only just come in.*

'I was already here when you came in.'

'Oh…' Her heart sank.

'It's been a hard day; I was just having five minutes.'

'In the dark?'

He was dressed now in jeans and a tieless inky blue shirt, which matched his eyes perfectly. He was no longer clean shaven, due to the late hour, and dark stubble shadowed his lower face, giving him a raw, masculine look. She wanted to touch it.

'You should've said you were here.'

'I wanted to listen.'

'To me? Why?'

He should have made it known he was there. Anyone else would have. It was only polite.

'I was curious.'

'I thought I was alone.'

She'd never have abandoned herself to the song as she had if she'd known he was there. Suddenly feeling naked before him, she instinctively crossed her arms over her chest.

'I didn't want to interrupt you.'

He was smiling at her. Not in that designer aftershave advert way he often used, but in a somehow softer way. In a way that made her feel as though she needed to sit down and take the weight off her suddenly buckling knees.

She crossed her arms more tightly. She wasn't being taken in by another handsome face and dazzling smile. He'd crossed a boundary. He should have spoken up.

'I wish you'd said you were there.'

'Well, I'm glad I didn't.' He sounded unremorseful. 'I'm glad I stayed where I was.'

'Hiding in the dark like some kind of spy?'

He'd known she'd thought she was alone—he must have. He hadn't made his presence known.

*How dare he?*

He'd spied on her, exposed her, judged her…

'More like a scout.'

She stared at him. 'A *scout*? A Boy Scout?'

He laughed. 'A talent scout.'

*This wasn't happening.*

She needed to leave. He was making fun of her. 'I should get home…get something to eat. I'm back at seven in the morning.'

'You haven't eaten? Me neither. Let's get something together. My treat…to apologise for being a spy.'

She didn't want to. In fact, she wanted to run. She wanted to be back in the safety of her home. Away from him. So she could work out how she was going to face him again.

'Please… Come on—we're both tired and hungry. There's a great pizza place just down the road. You look as though you could eat a pizza.'

He turned and began to walk back down the aisle towards the chapel door, picking up her fleece and bag, offering them to her and waiting.

He was right. She was tired, and hungry, and she knew for sure that she looked like a girl who enjoyed pizza. A little too much pizza—most of which sat on her well-rounded, apparently child-bearing hips, according to her mother. And she'd have to face him tomorrow anyway, so why not just tough it out tonight?

'They do an amazing margherita,' he said.

She sighed. She couldn't undo what he'd seen and heard, could she? And the floor wasn't going to open up and swallow her.

The rich, jewel-coloured stained glass window behind him cast shafts of ruby, emerald and sapphire onto him, making him look as if he'd been sent from heaven. She walked towards him, head held high, taking the fleece and her bag from his hands as she passed him.

'You're paying.'

Max had known even as he'd been doing it that he shouldn't have sat silently at the back of the hospital chapel in the dark, watching her. When Lois had walked in he'd expected her to light a candle, or sit for a few moments and then leave. But then she'd put on the altar lights, stood centre-stage and appeared to be about to perform. That had probably been the moment to admit he was there, but the need he'd felt to hear her had overridden the knowledge that he should speak up.

He was glad he'd stayed quiet. Her voice was amazing—exquisite—and he definitely wanted her to perform in his show. But he had the distinct impression that she wasn't too pleased he'd watched her—and really, she was right. But he'd been sitting there on his own, in the dark, and he didn't want to explain the reason for that to anyone.

The pain of William's death was with him every day, but today he felt it even more so. Perhaps other people in similar circumstances would have spent time with family, but that port of call had been denied him for a long time. And so he'd found his way to the little chapel to be alone in the darkness. And he didn't want to have to answer any questions about why that was.

'So, why *were* you sitting in the dark, spying on me?'

They'd walked the short distance to the restaurant, making

small talk about the warmth of the summer evening and how
it was easy to forget the passing of time when on shift and end
up working over.

Now Max chose a table in the corner, beside a wall with a
painted fresco of an Italian courtyard scene, complete with
pencil-thin cypress trees in terracotta pots. The waiter came
over to take their order, replacing the almost burnt down votive candle in its crimson glass jar, lighting it with a long taper.

'I wasn't spying.'

*He sort of had been.*

Lois dipped her bread into the dish of olive oil and brought
it to her lips, but stopped short of biting into it. She looked at
him, long-lashed emerald eyes gazing into his own, brim-full
of irony but still exquisite.

'Okay, I'll rephrase that. Why were you watching me co-
vertly in the chapel instead of politely making your presence
known, as most people would have done?'

She bit into the bread, the oil glossing her lips. She was definitely not happy with him but he wasn't going to explain. He
didn't want her pity. But he did want her to sing.

'It's a good place to just sit and catch your breath after a trying
day.' He wasn't lying. He wasn't telling the full truth either—
but how could he? 'How's the bread?' he asked.

She dabbed her lips with a napkin, ignoring his question.
'Why the chapel? Are you religious?'

Not after what he'd been through. No benevolent deity would
put anyone through that.

'No. It's just the chapel is about the only place in the hospital where there isn't chaos, noise and someone who wants
something from you.'

And that had been exactly why he'd gone there today—even
if it was an odd place to be on the evening of your birthday.
But he'd needed somewhere quiet to think about William, his
twin, who ought to be sharing his birthday with him but hadn't
in more than two decades.

For over twenty years their birthday hadn't been celebrated…
at all. In fact, celebrations of any kind had stopped the moment
William had died. No more birthdays…no Christmases…no
graduation celebrations. The contrast between how life had
been and how it had become was so extreme it wouldn't have
been believable if he hadn't seen it with his own eyes.

'Margherita for two?'

The smiling, dark-haired Italian waiter placed a huge pizza
between them both.

Lois looked from the pizza and back to Max with wide
eyes. 'You were right…that one is enough for two. Although I
haven't eaten since having an early lunch, so if pushed I could
manage it all.'

She smiled at him apologetically and he didn't want to look
away.

"Tuck in then," said Max. But Lois had already taken a slice
and groaned with pleasure as she bit into it. "Good?"

"Mmm," she replied, covering her mouth with her hand,
"really good but don't let me have it all. You've been here before then?"

"Too often," he said with a grimace, lifting a large slice from
the stone and stretching the cheese until it broke. "It's way too
handy to nip into on the way home and I'm not a cook so I do
rely on it a little more than I should."

"Only the Italians can do pizza as well as this." She took another slice, wrapping the stretched out cheese around her finger
and popping it into her mouth. "Just what I needed."

'I can order another if you're hungry?'

'Noo.' She patted her hips and sighed. 'I can't afford the
calories.'

*She was perfect.*

What was it with women and calorie-counting? He'd never
understood the need some women had to be stick-thin. It was
both unhealthy and unattractive.

'You don't need to worry about calories. Anyway, you're an opera singer—you *should* be voluptuous.'

His breath caught in his throat.

*How had that come out the way it had?*

Picking up his wine glass, he took a mouthful of the chianti, barely registering the taste.

*Had that sounded like flirting?*

Damn it.

'I'm going to get a coffee—do you want one?' he asked.

If she responded to his unwitting compliment and flirted back he'd have struggled not to continue it, and that would have been a dangerous game to play. But Lois wasn't a typical wannabe moocher, looking for a free ride into TV. She was a complete professional who was probably already happily part-nered up with some lucky guy.

And that thought unsettled him more than was comfortable. There was no wedding ring, though—he'd checked that earlier and berated himself for doing so.

'I'm okay, thanks.'

Pushing the plate away from her, she placed her folded nap-kin onto it and zipped her hospital fleece up to her neck.

'I should get home.'

She wasn't looking at him. Something had changed. Had she thought he was flirting? If she had, she clearly didn't welcome it. She'd suddenly closed herself off.

*Damn it, why had he said that? Voluptuous? Really?*

"Have another slice." He nodded towards the pizza.

"I'm done…thanks."

'You've got time for a quick coffee.'

The waiter came over, having noticed Max raise his hand to beckon him. 'Two coffees, please. An espresso and… Lois?'

He was stalling—trying to keep her there for a bit longer. *Why?*

To figure out the right moment to ask her about the show? Because he liked looking at her?

Because this was the best birthday he'd had for a long time…
even if he wasn't going to explain that to her?

She opened her mouth to speak, then hesitated and sighed.
'I'll have a decaf, please.'

*Good.*

But looking at her made him want to pull his chair in closer…
find out why she'd suddenly closed up…look into her eyes.

That was a very bad idea. He had a mission he needed to ac-
complish. Years in the making, now it was near to completion,
and he needed to finish it in as short a time as possible. Staying
in London—where he'd grown up, where he'd ruined lives—
had been a test of endurance. Aged twelve, he'd had no choice
but to stay, even if his parents had been so buried under the
weight of their own grief, and consumed by the blame they'd
put on him, that he was all but shunned.

He'd run away once. It had been the first anniversary of
William's death and facing them, seeing their pain and feeling
so responsible for it, had been more than he could bear. He'd
been found the next morning by the owner of the boathouse
he'd slept in by the river and taken home. When his father had
died, later that year, his mother had told him he'd died from a
broken heart, making it clear in no uncertain terms that Max
was responsible for his father's death too.

Growing up, becoming a heart surgeon had seemed like
the natural thing to do, and it had at least given him a sense
of purpose. Perhaps by saving other people he could in some
way make up for the deaths of William and his father. Maybe
even make his mother proud of him. But that had always been
nothing but a vain hope. And not everybody could be saved—
however hard he tried. Knowing that was a reality he hadn't
yet learnt to live with. And being unable to deal with losing
a patient gave him tunnel vision—nothing else mattered. Not
how he spoke to people, not how hard he pushed the boundaries, not the risks he took.

And that was why Lois thought he was a puffed-up prat.

'You really do have a beautiful voice,' he ventured.

He had to change her mind about him. He needed her to sing.

'Are you classically trained?'

She wrinkled her nose in that completely endearing way and he couldn't help but smile. It was becoming a habit.

'No, just the church choir—since I was about eight years old.'

Her lips curved into a cautious smile, and suddenly tearing his gaze away from them was impossible. He wanted to brush his own lips against them…feel the fullness of them.

*What was she doing to him?*

Lowering his gaze, aware that the beating of his heart had suddenly intensified, he tried to find words which didn't include *I want you.*

'You could be a professional,' he told her.

The caution in her smile gave way, and suddenly that sexy assuredness was back, shining out of her. 'I *am* a professional.'

'A professional *singer.*'

'A professional nurse is all I want to be.'

She reached for the sugar at the same moment he did and his fingers almost touched hers. She snatched her hand away as though she'd touched hot coals and placed her hands in her lap under the table.

So near and yet so far…

*Stop it. And ask her.*

'I'm doing a show…for charity.'

She looked at him warily, her emerald eyes narrowed.

'No.' She crossed her arms.

'You don't know what I'm going to say yet.'

'I think I do.'

She was right; but he wasn't going to accept her answer. He wanted her at the show. She'd be sensational—and he needed to sell way more tickets to make the kind of profit the fund needed.

'It's for charity,' he said again.

'I know. I've seen the posters. But I only sing in church.'

'You'd be the absolute star of the show.'

She sighed heavily, picked up her discarded napkin and re-folded it, not looking at him. 'Don't be ridiculous; Pathology are doing their magic act, Roman from Accounts is fire-eating, and the guys from Ophthalmology are doing their Take That tribute. I can't compare to that.'

'People would pay good money to see Sister Newington dressed like an opera diva and singing like a nightingale—I certainly would. Please.'

'No.'

'It's for charity.'

'That's below the belt.'

'To help save babies…'

'Stop it!'

'At least you're smiling now.'

She was, and even though she was clearly trying to suppress it, it was beautiful and it made her green eyes sparkle.

'You know you want to.'

'You're incorrigible.'

'It has been said…'

She drained her coffee and disappointment flooded through him—the evening was almost over. But spending longer with her would be a dumb idea. The more he spent time with her, the more he found she intrigued him. Why would someone with a voice like that be so reluctant to share it? He couldn't leave it there—he had to have her in the show.

'Is it a religious thing?'

'What do you mean?'

'Is it that you only perform in church and nowhere else for religious reasons?'

'No.'

'Then why won't you sing at the show?'

She sat up straight, tilting her chin. 'I don't need a reason.'

The defiance in her tone told him she wanted to end this conversation.

'I should get back. Thank you for the pizza.'

But he didn't want to end it—not until she'd agreed to be in the show.

'Lois, please… At least think about it—I really think people would enjoy it.'

He had to get over the line with this fundraising. The sooner he did that, the sooner he could leave London. His home city had gone from being a colourful, vibrant, happy childhood home into a place of dark, painful memories. He needed to get away from it. And if he could make good on his promise, that was exactly what he was going to do.

California was five thousand miles away—far enough for him to get away and maybe start a new life. And that meant not getting involved with anyone.

She stood and shrugged her bag on to her shoulder. Suddenly it was imperative that she saw how important this was.

'Lois, please. Sit down again and just listen for a moment. Let me explain the problem I have.'

Stunning emerald eyes held his, and it was all he could do not to forget what he wanted to say. But this was important—his life's work. And if he didn't succeed… Well, that wasn't even worth thinking about. It would be years of building his career, honing his skills, making the right connections, making promises, for nothing. It not working out wasn't an option.

She sat down again and placed her bag on the back of her chair.

He took a breath. This was for William, and for his twelve-year-old self who'd failed to save his twin when he'd suddenly collapsed as they'd played in the garden of their home over twenty years ago.

'You know that I want to launch the first trial of an aortic valve disease screening programme?'

'Yes. The posters are splashed all over the hospital.'

'It's taken me years to get agreement to run the trial and it means everything to me…everything, Lois. I have agreement in principle to run it, but I have to raise the funding…by the end of the month. If I don't, the deal is off and the Department of Health will cancel the trial. This screening programme will save lives, and I really believe that adding your name to the posters will sell more tickets to the show.'

He hadn't meant to reach out and touch her arm, but when he realised he had, and that she hadn't moved her arm away, he knew something had changed between them. He didn't want to, but he removed his hand.

'Sorry.'

Beautiful, intelligent green eyes searched his. 'It's okay. This clearly means a lot to you.'

'It means everything.'

The need to reach out and touch her again was almost overwhelming. She had to see he was genuine and serious. He didn't just want to *trial* the screening programme—he wanted to roll it out across the whole country. He had to. No one else should have to go through what William's death had put their family through, and it was his responsibility to ensure that. But he wasn't going to give her that last piece of information. He didn't want her pity.

'And they really might cancel it?' She said the words as though unable to believe them.

'They check where the donations come from. I can't just put the money in myself. It has to come from genuine donations.'

'I didn't realise there was any risk it wouldn't get off the ground.'

'It has to get off the ground.'

*It had to for William.*

She held his gaze, concern etched on her brow and shining from her eyes.

And suddenly she changed. Taking a slow breath, she sat up straight, her lips set in a hard line. 'Well, we can't have that can we? Okay, I'll do it.'

His heart leapt. 'You will?'

'Only one song, though.' She spoke sternly but her smile was playful.

'Whatever terms you like, Lois. I just want your name on the posters and you on that stage.' It felt entirely natural to grasp her hand now. 'Thank you.'

'I just hope you don't regret it.' She lowered her eyes, slipping her hand from his and reaching for her bag.

'I won't.'

She pushed her chair back and he stood too.

'Can I give you a lift home—it's late.'

'My car's only round the corner, but thanks.'

He didn't want her to go. 'See you tomorrow?'

'I'll be on the unit first thing.'

Fighting the urge to go after her, he watched her leave. Never had a woman filled his senses like she did. Never had he wanted to touch someone so badly. And never had he let his guard down, even if it had only been a little.

He needed to get a grip.

He might well want Lois Newington, but there was no way he was going to allow himself to go there.

*Cool it, Templeton.*

He lifted his hand for the waiter. 'The bill, please.'

His reason for being at St Martin's didn't include falling for a woman. Falling in love wasn't in his repertoire. Hell, he'd spent his life making sure he *didn't* fall in love. His propensity to ruin lives meant that people were better off not having him around. Short term, no strings was more his style. And now he didn't even have time for that. His mission here was more important than anything else. Persuading Lois to sing at the show was simply a means to help him achieve his goal...

*Wasn't it?*

Wanting her in any other way was just a distraction he didn't need, and he had to figure out a way to clear all thoughts of her from his mind. Lois had said yes, and although that in itself created new problems, suddenly reaching the fundraising target was a real possibility, and his long-held need to leave the ghosts of the past behind him was within his grasp.

# CHAPTER FOUR

'SHALL WE DO a round?'

Her breathing quickening even at the sound of his voice, Lois looked up from her desk. Max was dressed for clinic rather than for Theatre, wearing an immaculate dark blue suit, the jacket of which he was now removing. He hung it on a hook behind the door, reaching up, causing the white shirt he wore to strain against the well-defined angular muscles of his broad back. As he moved, he disturbed the air in the small office and his scent swirled around the room…fresh, aquatic, making her want to inhale deeply and take him in.

'Sure. All your patients have been fine overnight.'

She'd eventually fallen asleep last night still thinking about him, and woken up at three a.m. in a complete panic, having dreamt she'd appeared on stage at his charity concert naked.

She couldn't do it—just the thought of being on stage in front of people made her queasy.

*Why on earth had she agreed to it?*

Because she'd heard his brother had died from a failed aortic valve years ago, and she'd seen how much the screening programme meant to him.

When he'd reached out to touch her hand, his words tumbling over themselves as he'd explained about the funding and how the programme might fail at the last hurdle, he'd exposed a different side to himself. The super-confidence had vanished, just for a moment, and she'd had a glimpse of something that somehow seemed more real. Was there a deeper side to Max Templeton? One he usually kept to himself?

'Shall we go and see them?'

Lois stood and straightened her uniform dress, adjusting the silver buckle and the skirt, which had ridden up when she'd been sitting. Ridden up over her apparently *voluptuous* operatic frame.

His description of her figure last night had cut her. She wasn't quite as resilient to those kinds of comments as she'd thought she'd become, clearly. It really didn't matter that he didn't find her attractive. He didn't have to shove her size in her face, though, did he?

'Ready?'

His eyes flicked up from her waist and met her own as she looked at him, one dark eyebrow moved very slightly upwards, and he visibly checked himself when she met his gaze, straightening his features, as if she'd caught him doing something he shouldn't. He was probably comparing her to the glamorous women from TV Land whom he usually worked and played with.

'Let's go.'

She slipped past him and out into the hubbub and the busyness of the unit. She was happy with how she looked, and if Max Templeton wasn't, that was his look-out. She was done with feeling the need to conform to the societal belief that to be attractive you had to resemble a super-thin catwalk model. Emilio had spent most of their six months together telling her, in one way or another, that her mother had been right—she was plump and she was plain.

*Why had she believed his lies when they'd first met?*

He'd been sweetness and light at first, and she'd felt flattered—for the first time in her life—and had allowed herself to be seduced by his obviously empty compliments.

*How could she have been so naïve?*

Had she been so desperate to hear someone tell her she was attractive that she hadn't been able to see through him?

She took a deep breath, wincing at the memory of how easily she'd been sweet-talked into bed. And then the insinuations about her size had started—at such a low level that she hadn't really noticed them at first.

*'No dessert for her!'* he'd say to waiters with a smirk.

*'Breathe in!'* as he took photos.

And, *'I expect your prefer holidays in cold places, where you can cover up, rather than beach holidays?'*

His jibes had become increasingly barbed and cruel as time had gone on, but they had been so insidious she hadn't seen the level it had got to. But then, her mother had normalised body-shaming jibes, hadn't she?

Oddly enough, the last straw with Emilio had come even before she'd discovered his secret—that he had a wife and little daughter back in Italy. The last straw had come when he'd taken her shopping and insisted on buying a teeny-tiny dress she could never have hoped to fit into, laughing with the shop assistant and saying that he'd lock away the biscuit tin until it fitted.

Even months later, recalling that stung. And recalling it only reinforced the knowledge that she wasn't going to get up onto that stage next week and be judged by anyone else.

She wished she hadn't bumped into Max Templeton in the chapel—then she wouldn't be in this mess.

*Let's see the patients, and then somehow I'll tell him I can't do the show.*

'I spoke to the printers first thing, by the way,' said Max, following her, 'and they're going to reprint the posters for the show this morning.' He checked his watch. 'In fact, they should have done them by now. They said they'd deliver them by lunch, and I've asked my secretary to organise having them put up around the hospital asap.'

She turned around and watched him as he folded up the

sleeves of his white shirt and tucked his tie through a gap in the buttons.

*Stay professional, Lois—do not swear.*

'That was quick.' Her voice had gone up an octave.

'I didn't want to give you time to change your mind.' He grinned and walked past her, heading for his first patient.

*Oh, God. Now what?*

Following him, she felt her mind whirling.

*You'll just have to do it.*

*I can't.*

*He's left you no choice.*

Damn him.

'Good morning, Mr Swain,' said Max. 'Mind if I check your pulse?'

His patient smiled. 'You can do anything you like to me, Doctor, after the miracle you've performed.'

Max smiled, placing practised fingers on his patient's wrist. 'It wasn't just me—it's a team effort.'

*Big of him! And a little unexpected...*

'They're all wonderful here,' Jack Swain agreed. 'Especially this one.' He smiled and nodded towards Lois. 'A proper angel, she is...can't do enough for you.'

'So I hear,' replied Max, looking at her with that eyebrow raised once more, awakening the butterflies. 'How are his numbers, Sister?'

'Numbers are good.' She didn't need to check the chart. 'Norad is off.'

The butterflies had commenced their dancing.

'Perfect. That means you're holding your own, Mr Swain. If you behave yourself, we should be able to discharge you to the ward tomorrow.'

Mr Swain gave a thumbs-up and Max turned his attention to Lois as they moved towards the next patient.

'Rehearsals start tomorrow night—seven p.m. in the lecture

theatre. We can't rehearse in the Savoy itself as the ballroom is in use for a wedding.'

'Actually, I wanted to talk to you about that...'

'How's Mr Ferns been overnight? Recovering from the impromptu thoracotomy from yesterday?'

He was ignoring her. Almost as though he knew what she was going to say. Well, okay, it could wait. It wouldn't change her mind. The other acts were brilliant—he'd get the money he needed without her.

'He's been stable. Bloods show his clotting is normal; we've been titrating the heparin accordingly.'

Max glanced at the obs chart. 'I'm going to keep him on the ventilator for another day. Blood gases are pretty good, but I want to rest him after reopening his chest.'

Moving to the patient's bedside, he placed his stethoscope in his ears, bending to listen, then tugging the earpieces out and draping the instrument back around his neck.

'All sounds fine. Any concerns from you?'

*Plenty. Mainly that I can't stop thinking about you. Also that I wish I hadn't agreed to be in your show.*

'No, he's been behaving himself.'

'Just Luke Evans left for me, then, I think.'

*How to tell him?*

'We extubated him this morning and he's doing well.'

Luke Evans was sitting up in bed sipping water as they approached. He winced as he swallowed. He was indeed doing well, considering it had only been three days since the horrific road traffic collision which had given him, amongst other injuries, a punctured lung and an aortic tear—often fatal, and almost costing him his life.

Lois smiled and he looked up. 'How are you, Luke? Throat a bit sore?'

He nodded, placing the small glass of water back on his bed table.

'The breathing tube that was in your throat can cause a bit of soreness, but keep sipping at the water and it'll be fine. You're doing really well. How's your pain?'

She really felt for Luke. He was the same age as her and very nearly hadn't survived the horrific car crash. Driving home from work, he'd been hit by another driver who'd been high on drugs. His car had gone under the cab of a truck and been dragged along until it had come to a stop. He'd broken five ribs—one of which had pierced his left lung—his aortic arch had been torn, and his left leg had sustained open fractures which had required pinning and plating. The torn aorta had been enough to kill him and almost had. Only the speed with which the air ambulance had delivered him to hospital, eight units of blood and the skill of the surgeon standing beside her now had saved him.

It brought home just how a life could be changed or lost in the flash of a moment. And just how good Max Templeton was at his job.

'I'm a bit sore, but alive.' He managed a small smile, but talking made him cough and he winced. 'I'm hoping to be out of here in time to see the doc's show next week.'

He nodded towards Max, grinning, and her heart sank.

*Why had she agreed to it?*

She hated letting people down.

Max slid his stethoscope from around his neck. 'There's every chance of that—and even more incentive now, as Sister Lois has agreed to perform too.'

His stethoscope was in his ears before she could reply. Luke opened his mouth to speak but Lois hushed him with a finger to her lips. Speaking would cause him to cough, and prevent Max from being able to hear his chest properly. Besides, she was still working out how to tell him she wasn't doing it any more.

'Chest's clear.' He pulled the stethoscope from his ears. 'The chest drain can be removed later, as long as there's no more drainage, and we may be able to step him down to HDU. Keep up the good work, Luke. I'll see you later.'

'I'll bring some ice chips for your throat,' said Lois, as they began to walk away.

'Thanks, Sister.'

She glanced to Max. It was now or never. 'About the show...'

But Max was looking straight ahead to where the doors of the unit had swung open. He smiled widely as Jay Vallini, a fellow cardiac surgeon, strode in.

*Was she ever going to find the right moment to tell him?*

'Jay, how are you?'

'Good, chief. Yourself?'

Lois liked Jay Vallini. He was a good surgeon, had been around for ever and the patients loved him.

'Good. Listen, I hear you need a bed for your stent chap this afternoon. I've got a young guy—three days post traumatic aortic arch tear, pneumothorax, smashed-up leg. Extubated this morning and doing well, but I just need to keep an eye on him for a bit longer before we send him next door. You okay hanging on for a bit?'

The older surgeon beamed at Max, smacking him on the shoulder jovially. 'Don't worry, chief, I've got a couple of minors I can bump up the list and do first.'

'Excellent,' said Max, 'Oh, and spread the word...' He nodded towards Lois, who was watching the scene with increasing incredulity—Max Templeton had just done something no other surgeon had ever done: got Jay Vallini to alter his theatre list. 'Sister Newington has agreed to be in the show next week.'

Jay Vallini unfolded the large poster he was carrying, beaming and holding it up like a prize for all to see.

'I know. That's why I popped in—to see if it was true. It is, then?'

Lois knew her mouth had dropped open.

Max looked delighted. 'Oh, great, the posters have arrived. As I said...spread the word. We need to sell tickets.'

Lois watched as Daisy, one of the unit's nurses, arrived on the scene, followed by Tom.

'Oh, wow,' said Daisy. 'Put me down for a couple of tickets.'

'Never mind a couple,' said Tom. 'We need a job lot—I can feel a unit night out coming on.'

Max's famous smile lit up his face. 'You see, Sister?' There was more than a note of triumph in his voice. 'I told you having you in the show would sell it out.'

And with that he turned and left, and suddenly she didn't know if she admired him or loathed him. What she did know was that there was no way she could possibly get out of the damn show now, and the heart-racing, breathless panic of her dream last night sprang from its slumber and rushed like water from a burst dam through her veins.

Nausea swept through her and her legs felt as if they wouldn't support her. Singing in the back row of the choir, hidden from view by the collective comfort of the other choristers around her, was one thing—exposing herself to the scrutiny of colleagues…on her own, on stage…was way out of her comfort zone. That was something other people did—people with confidence in themselves…people who looked as if they should be on stage.

Not people like her. Not plain, plump Lois Newington, who couldn't even get a date for the school prom and whose only grown-up relationship had been with a lying, cheating narcissist. Again, she winced at the thought of him, and at the exquisite, embarrassing shame his lies had caused.

*Emilio.*

Even thinking his name gave her a bad taste in her mouth. The memory of when she'd caught him video calling his wife back in Rome and how he'd looked puzzled at her shock resurfaced, making her squirm inside. He'd had the audacity to say he'd thought she already knew he was married. It had been unbelievable.

'I have to get some ice chips for Luke.'

She needed to get away and headed for the kitchen with a

plastic cup to collect the ice. Pushing open the door, her palm made contact with a large, brightly coloured poster advertising Max's show.

St Martin's Hospital Vaudeville Variety Show
*Now featuring operatic sensation*
*ITU's very own*
Sister Lois Newington!

Her legs wouldn't work, and she desperately wanted to run. Max Templeton had played a blinder. There was no way out of it now. She wanted to help the charity, but how on earth was she going to get up on stage on her own? For a start, she had nothing suitable to wear. Singing in church required simple choir robes, which covered a multitude of sins. Singing for this—what had he called it? *A Vaudeville Variety Show?*—was something entirely different.

Her phone vibrated in her pocket as she filled the plastic cup with ice chips from the machine. She pulled it out, glad of the distraction.

'Nat, I was just thinking about you,' she said.

Natalie had been the one to pick up the pieces when she'd discovered Emilio's other life in Italy. She'd been such a huge support when she'd felt so humiliated after he'd left and everyone had discovered the truth. That she'd been so desperate to hear the sweet nothings he'd so readily whispered into her ear to get her into bed that she'd allowed herself to be used by someone everyone else had seen straight through.

'We need to go shopping.'

Natalie's tone told her she was not to be argued with.

'Do we?'

'Unless you have a ballgown fit to wear for your stage debut hiding in your wardrobe, yes.'

'Oh, you heard.' Lois's heart, already in her stomach, sank further. Word really had got around.

'Toby texted me. I think it's amazing you're doing it, Lois. I'm a tad surprised, I have to say, but I'm so pleased. You'll be brilliant. But we do need to find you a fabulous dress. Are you still on a day off tomorrow?'

'Up to now, yes.'

'Right. Well, don't go putting yourself down for an extra shift; we have to hit the town.'

Suddenly, the whole nightmare seemed very real. She had to take the ice to Luke, but didn't want to go back onto the unit—she wanted to run a long way away and hide from every reality that had hit her in the last twenty-four hours. From the prospect of standing up on stage and singing to her colleagues in a vaudeville show to the realisation that she wanted Max Templeton.

She wasn't sure which scared her the most.

# CHAPTER FIVE

THE BALLROOM AT the Savoy exuded elegance and opulence. Huge crystal chandeliers hung from the ceiling of the ornately decorated Edwardian-style room. Dining tables had been exquisitely decorated with fresh white linen, vases of summer flowers, pillar candles and gleaming cutlery. The famous London ballroom had cost a pretty penny, but the celebrity friends Max had invited would expect nothing less, and getting them to attend his fundraising event would reap rewards in much-needed ticket sales and donations.

This had to work. Everything depended on it.

He headed backstage to check everything there had been prepared as he'd instructed. The acts would be arriving in the next hour or so and everything had to be perfect for them. It was they who were making the show possible, after all, and he was grateful to each and every one of them. The work he'd put into fundraising over the last couple of years was hopefully about to pay off, and this generous group of performers were going to be treated like royalty for making this happen.

The corridor backstage was quiet, for now, and his footsteps on the wooden floor unnaturally loud. It was the calm before the storm of the arrival of the cast. Before the banter, warming up of voices, tuning of instruments and general getting ready noise that would ensue.

He'd instructed that each act should have their own dressing room, furnished with everything they might need. He'd even had gold stars attached to the doors with the performers' names printed on them. Names he found himself searching now as he walked along.

LOIS NEWINGTON

He stopped searching, his heart suddenly banging in his chest a little harder than it had been.

*Would she turn up tonight?*

Guilt pricked his conscience. She clearly thought he'd acted a little fast getting the posters reprinted last week, and apart from making one barbed comment about him being a fast worker had all but avoided him since. Part of him had wanted to tell her that if she wasn't sure about doing the show she could duck out, but a larger part of him just couldn't. That larger part of him wanted her to sing tonight—and it wasn't entirely because she'd make money for the fund. *He* wanted to hear her sing again. The reason why had nagged at him all week, but he'd stopped trying to kid himself that it was simply because she'd be sensational and would get the audience reaching into their pockets for donations.

She'd turn up, he was sure of it.

*Wasn't he?*

If she really wanted to get out of it she could suddenly find she had to stay on the unit to cover for staff who were coming tonight. But she wouldn't do that. The concern he'd seen in her eyes in the restaurant when he'd inadvertently reached out and touched her hand told him she cared, and he was certain she'd hate to let the side down. But there had definitely been a reluctance too. So which was going to win tonight? Her need to do the right thing or that part of her he'd seen only glimpses of—those sudden, fleeting, quiet moments of reserve that caused her to close down and lose that exhilarating sassiness that made him forget everything else?

He needed her tonight. He just had to believe she knew it.

weekend. It was indeed beautiful. Simple in its design, but elegant. 'I'll be okay. Thanks for offering, though.'

She wanted a few moments before the final, decisive act of actually putting on the dress.

'Well, break a leg, then, I guess.' She nodded towards the dress. 'It's stunning. I'm going to see if I can sneak in at the back to watch the show. See you on the other side.'

She picked up her case and was gone, leaving Lois staring at a face she didn't fully recognise now that it had been painted and powdered, and knowing that, very soon, she'd have to put on a dress which would feel more than a little alien too.

There was another knock at the door. She froze.

'Lois?'

*Max.*

He tapped again.

*Could she pretend she wasn't there?*

The handle dipped.

'Don't come in… I'm getting changed!'

The handle moved back to its original position and she could breathe again.

'It's me—Max.' He spoke though the closed door.

*I'm aware of that.*

'I just wanted to check you're okay.'

'I'm fine, thanks.'

'And that you haven't run away.'

'I haven't…yet.'

'Don't say that. Everyone's really excited to see you on stage. Do you need anything?'

*Just to be anywhere else.*

'No, thanks.'

'Can I come in?'

'No, I've told you. I'm getting changed.'

There was a pause.

*Had he gone?*

'Okay.'

Another pause, but somehow she knew he was still outside the door.

'Lois?'

'Yes?'

'Thank you for doing this.'

She swallowed. This really did mean a lot to him, didn't it?

'You're welcome… But the same goes for this as goes for performing open heart surgery on my unit.'

'How's that?'

'Don't make a habit out of it.'

Out in the corridor, Max Templeton smiled. He didn't understand why someone with such an amazing voice would shy away from public performance, but he knew that Lois did. He was grateful to her, as he was to all the performers who'd agreed to do the show, but he knew that Lois was doing it against her natural instinct not to. She was here, though, and the pangs of guilt he'd felt all week were now mixing in a heady cocktail with the anticipation of seeing her on stage.

He strode back along the corridor and into the ballroom, where the tables had now been cleared and the guests were mingling, drinking and chatting. Time to go back into host mode. Everyone here this evening was here because of him.

Because he'd asked them.

Because he needed them.

Years of work, planning, organising, talking to the right people, persuading, researching—all were culminating in this night. Tomorrow he had to go back to the committee in Parliament to tell them if enough money had been raised for the trial to go ahead. And if they finally signed off on the programme he would allow himself his reward—his new life in California as a non-practising professor, helping to train heart surgeons there. His new start.

Before that he would pay a rare visit to his mother. Rare because seeing his childhood home brought him face to face with the agony of what had happened there, and because he knew he wasn't welcome. But if the programme got the go-ahead he would walk back in and perhaps show that he'd done something good with his life—not made amends for what had happened, but at least done something positive—turned something that had been devastating into something to help others.

The hope that his mother might be able to forgive him had long since been obliterated, but there was still a chance that she might believe he'd achieved something to be proud of.

He straightened his bow tie. The nerves were real. This was for William.

And instantly he was twelve years old again. In the back garden, having a kick-about with his twin. Suddenly William had hit the ground before he'd seen it coming.

And Max had laughed. Breathless from running around. Bending forward, his hands on his knees, catching his breath.

'Stop messing, Will!' he'd called. 'Just because you're losing.'

But William hadn't moved…

Max took a breath and strode to the nearest table. Picking up a jug of water, he poured a glass, taking a drink, and a moment to clear his mind. He had to paint on the smile that everyone expected…ensure they enjoyed the evening and reached deep into their pockets. Time for TV's 'Surgeon to the Stars' to make an appearance. Now wasn't the time for self-pity.

'Max!'

An ex-patient strode towards him, hand outstretched, beaming a bright white Californian smile. One of Hollywood's elite—an actor of high renown—last year he had flown to the UK to be treated by him.

'It's been too long, my friend.'

And so it began. Everyone was here for him, and he was there for William. And this time he wasn't going to let him down.

\* \* \*

The atmosphere in the ballroom was one of joy, fun and energy. The acts so far had been excellent. But by nine p.m. Max had begun to wonder why he'd not put Lois first on the bill. No one had come to tell him she'd hightailed it out of there, but the longer time went on, the more he wondered if she might get cold feet.

Standing in the wings, straining to see through the bright lights to the opposite side of the stage, where she'd make her entrance, he felt his heart beating way too fast for comfort.

She wasn't there.

Maybe she was just standing too far back behind the curtains.

Maybe the blinding brightness of the lights was the reason he couldn't see her.

As the last act exited stage left, to much applause, he took the microphone and strode out from the wings. A beam of spotlight hit him, following him as he strode to the centre of the stage—TV's most well-known doctor, smiling his famous wide smile, raising his hands and joining in the applause.

He lifted the microphone. 'Wasn't he amazing? How does he *do* that?'

Whistles and cheers demonstrated that the audience agreed with him.

The applause died down.

His heart rate notched up.

*She had to be there.*

There was no way of checking now. The show had to go on.

He stood in front of the microphone stand, every cell in his body hoping she was standing in the wings.

'Ladies and gentlemen, next up, for your delight and delectation, I am thrilled to introduce to you someone we all know as a consummate professional…someone who runs our hospital's intensive care unit with supreme skill…someone who cares for her patients and her staff with compassion, professionalism and superb talent—and someone who has a hidden gift which she's going to share with us tonight. So, without further ado—and for one night only—it gives me great pleasure to introduce to you... Lois Newington!'

The applause began again and Max held his breath, unable to see anything except the blinding bright light that was on him.

*Was she there?*

The applause suddenly grew louder and a stunning woman in a floor-length, dark forest-green velvet dress appeared from stage right.

*Lois.*

She was all he could see. Everything else—all sights, all sounds—faded into the background. It was her...but it wasn't. Her golden blonde hair was down, cascading around her bare shoulders. She walked towards him, eyes down, dark lashes fanned on her cheek, and he was sure he gasped as she raised those emerald eyes to look at him as she arrived centre-stage. They matched the dress perfectly, and when the diamond and emerald necklace she wore drew his eyes down to a deep, rounded cleavage, his body reacted in the most instinctive way.

Lifting his eyes to meet hers, he smiled, and his breath caught in his throat when she returned it. Not a beaming, showy, TV smile that a professional diva might grace him with, but a tentative one, a shy one, a brave one.

He turned, managing somehow to tear his gaze from her, and left the stage, handing the microphone to one of the stage hands. He wanted to see this properly—not from the back of a dimly lit chapel, not from the wings of the stage, but from the audience.

The strings of a guitar had already begun to play the first bars of the introduction to the song. The ballroom of this prestigious London venue was silent, save the haunting melody coming from the single guitar. The spotlight was on Lois, the most beautiful woman he'd ever seen, standing bravely, eyes closed, about to sing.

No one else was in the room.

*Open those amazing eyes, Lois. Look at me.*

And she did.

And it took his breath.

Could she see him? Or were those emerald eyes gazing out into the lights, dazzled by them, unable to see into the silent audience? Unable to see his captivation?

As she began to sing, and the first clear, pure notes left her lips, she lifted her eyes and they sparkled in the brilliance of the spotlights which had converged on her, illuminating her, making her the centre of everyone's attention.

He was lost. Her voice was ethereal…enchanting and exquisite. And she looked magnificent. Glossy golden waves framed her face and fell onto the creamy softness of her bare shoulders, drawing his eyes down to the velvet bodice of her gown, which tapered in at the waist and then flared over her hips, cascading to the floor. The melody was seductive, hypnotic—like being cocooned in a gently swaying cradle. He didn't want it to end. But he knew the end was coming.

Her breathing deepened as the song built to its crescendo, deepening the rise and fall of those tantalising glimpses of the porcelain curves of her breasts. Her eyes closed for the final notes and every inch of his skin prickled with goosebumps. He'd never hear that song again without remembering this moment. Nothing had ever connected to his soul like that.

The applause was thunderous. People were on their feet, clapping, whistling, cheering, taking stems from the flower arrangements on the tables and flinging them onto the stage. His heart soared. She couldn't regret doing this now. Surely even she could see this as confirmation of her talent.

His bleep vibrated in his pocket.

*No!*

He turned to Jay Vallini, who was next to him, cheering.

'I've been bleeped. Can you compere for me? The running sheet is with the guys up there in the wings.'

'Sure, chief, sure,' replied Jay. 'Hope it's nothing you need to go in for.'

They both left the room—Jay Vallini making his way onto the stage to help Lois pick up the flowers, and Max heading out to find a quiet corridor to call the hospital, desperately hoping it was something he could deal with over the phone.

# CHAPTER SIX

HEART BANGING IN her chest, Lois almost ran back to the sanctuary of her dressing room. Placing the armful of flowers into the sink, she ran the tap and sank gratefully into the comfy armchair, resting her head back, trying to slow her breathing.

*It was over.*

The sharp rapping on the door made her jump.

'Lois?'

*What was Max doing backstage? He was compering the rest of the show, wasn't he?*

'Hello?'

'Can I come in?'

*No! She needed to get her breath back.*

'Lois? You're dressed now.'

She sighed, unable to think up a reason to decline, went to the door and opened it. A runner dashed past, the performer in the opposite dressing room came hurrying out and the loudspeaker made some sort of announcement.

Max stood looking at her, silently, and her insides, already frazzled by the night so far, began their butterfly dance.

'You were amazing.'

She lowered her eyes. Compliments were bittersweet—nice to get, but also a reminder of the huge error of judgement she'd made with Emilio.

'Thank you.'

'I just wanted to tell you that before I leave.'

'Leave? What about the rest of the show?'

'I've been called in. Luke Evans's chest drain has dumped five hundred mils in the last hour. I need to go and see him.'

'Is he holding his BP?'

'For now... He's young, though, so he's got reserve. But if it continues draining, he could crash.'

'I'm coming with you.'

There was no way she wasn't going to make sure Luke was okay.

Grabbing her black leather jacket, she practically pushed Max out of the door. 'Let's go. Where's your car?'

'Bike.'

For a moment she just looked at him, but then remembered they needed to move fast and closed the door behind her.

They set off down the corridor. 'You cycled here?'

'Motorbike,' he called back over his shoulder.

'Do you have a spare helmet?'

'Yes.'

He pushed on one of the revolving doors in the foyer, declining the taxi offered by one of the doormen.

Half running to the motorbike, Lois struggled to keep up with him.

*Why hadn't she ditched the heels?*

His helmet hung from one of the handlebars and he put it on, handing her the spare. Thankful she'd declined an updo from the hairstylist, Lois pulled the helmet on, fastening the chin strap. Then, gathering the full skirt of her dress into her arms, she put one leg over the seat and bunched the fabric in front on her.

Max turned. 'Hold on tight; we're not going for a Sunday drive.'

Lois reached around his waist, her heart hammering in her chest. It was only a couple of miles to St Martin's—in a straight line. But there weren't many straight lines in the middle of London. She had no choice but to hold on tight.

Max kicked the engine into life and it roared as he revved it. Leaning in close, resting her head on his back, her knees squeezing firmly against the seat, skimming his backside, Lois hung on for dear life.

But there was nothing scary about being nestled into Max Templeton's wall of a back...nothing to fear about resting her head against his broad shoulders, feeling his muscles move as he controlled the bike around corners. Nothing alarming about being so close to him that the warmth of his body spread into hers and his scent filled her.

As they chased through the streets of London, her body was forced to move with his as he tilted the bike around the curves in the road. She watched the light on the Thames shimmer as they sped across Waterloo Bridge to the south bank.

There was no fear for her safety. It wasn't fear that made her heart bang against her ribs so hard she felt sure he'd be able to feel it through both their leather jackets. It was desire. And holding on to him, moving in sync with him, fear wasn't what she felt. She knew only the exhilaration of the cool wind in her face and the thrill of being almost as one with him.

Max didn't notice the open-mouthed stares from the staff as he pushed open the doors to the ITU. He could still feel Lois pressed against his back, her arms around his waist, her knees gripping either side of his thighs. If he hadn't needed to reach the hospital asap, he'd have taken a longer route just to keep her close for longer.

But the familiar sights, sounds and smells of the ITU brought him back to reality, and his focus now was Luke Evans. He strode to his patient's bedside, leaving several staff members staring after him, their gaze only leaving him when Lois followed him in, green velvet gown skimming the floor, black leather jacket undone and her usually tied back hair loose around her shoulders.

'Hi, Luke, how are you?' he asked, also acknowledging the presence of Robert, one of the doctors on his team.

Luke's chest drain had been removed a couple of days ago, but he'd been readmitted to the ITU earlier with a swinging pyrexia and a new hemopneumothorax, which had required Max to replace the chest drain.

Luke managed a weak smile, but was obviously unwell.

'Well, we'd much rather be at the show,' said Robert. 'But you really didn't need to bring the show to us.'

Max looked down at his dinner suit and then to Lois, who stood at the end of the bed, scrutinising the obs chart. His stomach clenched.

*Just look at her.*

Even the incongruity of her looking like that in this setting couldn't detract from her beauty. In fact, it enhanced it—if that were possible. She hadn't thought for a second about leaving the show and coming with him to see Luke. She should be there now—enjoying the adulation she so deserved, hearing everyone tell her how amazing she was. But she'd chosen to put her patient first and he couldn't help but admire that, even though he felt guilty that she wasn't enjoying the rest of the evening as she should have been.

He shouldn't have told her where he was going.

She glanced up at him. 'I'll check to see if the microbiology report is available…back in a tick.'

He watched her leave, hitching up her skirt a little to save it from dragging on the floor, revealing the golden glitter of her shoes.

'Just going to check this drain, Luke,' he said.

He crouched beside the bed, inspecting the tubing and the contents of the bottle. He knew what his plan was for Luke. He was concerned, but they hadn't run out of options. Lois returned with an iPad and he stood to read the report.

'What's the damage?' asked Luke, a little breathless and with a slight frown creasing his forehead.

Max gave him a reassuring smile. 'Nothing a good dose of IV antibiotics can't sort out. The fluid which collected in the pleural space where the broken ribs were has developed an infection, but it's common in this situation so don't worry.'

Luke seemed to relax, pulling his oxygen mask from his face to speak again. 'Looks like it was a very glamorous evening.'

He nodded towards Lois, who was busying herself at the end of the bedspace, making notes on his chart.

Max returned Luke's smile. 'Very.'

She'd blown his mind tonight. Her voice had filled the ballroom with its purity and power and she'd filled his senses with her beauty and her courage, bringing surprising and uncharacteristic tears to his eyes that he'd had to swallow hard to contain. She had no clue what she'd done to him. She didn't realise the gift she had. She had no idea that all he wanted to do was take her in his arms.

'Will you want a fluid challenge?'

Lois was looking at him with the same emerald eyes that had met his on the stage, but now they held certainty and confidence rather than the brave fear he'd seen before her performance. She was back in her comfort zone.

'Let's give a litre of normal saline over two hours and we'll get a chest X-ray too, please.'

She lowered her gaze, tapping on the iPad.

She hadn't let him down, despite her reluctance. She'd come to the ball like Cinderella. Beautiful, brave and humble. She should be enjoying her moment back at the Savoy, hearing how people loved her performance, getting the affirmation she deserved.

'Do you want me to review the X-ray when it's done so that you can get back to the show?' asked Robert. 'It's only ten o'clock, so there's time to get back before it finishes.'

He was right—there was time to get back. Time to get Lois there and allow her to see the impression she'd made. But he didn't want to leave Luke.

'Get Cinders back to the ball before midnight strikes,' said Robert with a grin.

It wasn't very often that he didn't know instinctively what to do, but he was torn. He wanted to make sure Luke had his first dose of antibiotics and review the X-ray. But he also badly wanted to take Lois back so she could hear the praise everyone undoubtedly wanted to lavish her with.

'I can call you with the X-ray result,' said Robert.

'Go,' said Luke.

'I can send the X-rays to your phone, if you like,' added Robert.

They were talking sense. So why did this present such a difficult dilemma?

'We don't have to go,' said Lois. 'I've already done my bit on stage. Let's get the antibiotics up and see what the X-ray shows.'

And suddenly he could make the decision. She'd read him. She'd seen his reluctance to leave, understood, and was giving him permission to stay. Admiration for this woman filled him—warmed him and swelled in his chest. She got his need to put the patient first every time, above all else, because that was what she did too. But she'd also made him realise that he wanted to put her first.

'Thanks, Robert, I appreciate it.' He turned to Luke. 'You're in good hands. I'll see you tomorrow.'

Luke gave him a thumbs-up.

Taking the iPad from Lois, Max handed it to Robert. 'Come on, let's get back—make sure all those celebs have dug deep into their pockets.'

'But...' began Lois, her hands empty but still in position as if she were holding the iPad.

'Go,' said Robert. 'I'll text Max the results.'

Max held the door open for Lois and she looked from one to the other of them.

Max swept his palm towards the door. 'Let's get you back to the ball, Cinderella.'

'I really don't need to go back,' said Lois as they headed off down the corridor, past where the Saturday night walking wounded were spilling out from A&E.

'You really do,' replied Max, ignoring with accustomed ease the stares and whispered comments from people who'd recognised him.

Lois shot him a sidelong glance which told him she required an explanation.

'I sense you don't cope with compliments very well,' he began, pushing the button on the wall to open the exit to the hospital. 'But I think you need to hear that people loved your performance tonight. I wish I hadn't told you I was leaving. I pulled you away from what should have been your evening. So I'm taking you back…to your admiring audience. So that you can hear for yourself that you were amazing.'

He pulled his helmet on and grinned at her through the visor.

'Come on, then; before this bike turns into a pumpkin.'

Lois gazed dismally at herself in the dressing room mirror. Whoever had designed the motorbike helmet had clearly not given much thought to what it did to your hair. But holding on to Max as they'd taken only a slightly more sedate ride back to the hotel had been worth getting mussed-up hair for. Ten minutes when she'd been allowed, almost been given permission to melt into him, to hold on to him tightly, grip the tops of his thighs with her knees, feel his warmth, inhale him.

He'd been reluctant to leave Luke and she understood why. He cared for his patients, and she got that and admired it completely. But Robert and the rest of the team were more than capable of looking after him and it had been safe to leave when they had. Besides, it was preferable, really, that he got back to his show. He was the main attraction—the reason everyone had turned out and paid good money to be there. She'd wanted it to be his decision, though—which was why she'd given him a get-out if he'd wanted to take it.

But he'd wanted to bring her back so she could bask in the glory he felt she deserved.

*Had he meant what he said? That people had enjoyed her singing?*

He'd smiled…kindly…genuinely when he'd said it.

He'd being paying her a compliment.

And he'd been right about that, at least—she *wasn't* good with compliments. What had led him to that conclusion?

Holding her head in her hands, elbows on the dressing table, she looked at herself in the mirror and frowned. The only compliments she'd ever had outside of the work setting had been from Emilio. And look what had happened when she'd believed *him*.

She sat up straight.

*Don't be drawn into falling for another man's lies.*

Going through that kind of humiliation again was not going to happen—not a chance. But Max clearly hadn't been about to take no for an answer and, floored by his apparently astute appraisal of her, almost without realising she'd found herself back on the motorbike, holding on to him as if he belonged to her, closing her eyes as she melted into him, feeling their bodies move as one and hot, breathtaking desire fill her once more.

She took a deep breath and looked at her reflection sternly.

'Stop it.' Picking up her brush, she dragged it through her dishevelled hair. 'He's only being nice because of the show.'

But her stern expression suddenly softened. He'd read her, though, hadn't he? Understood her. Seen the difficulty she had with compliments. The smile he'd given her through his smoky tinted visor had been warm, genuine. He knew something about her that few people did, and what he thought he knew seemed to matter to him.

Against the need he'd felt to stay with Luke, he'd made the decision to bring her back.

*Why?*

Because he felt she needed to hear that people had enjoyed her singing.

And that was thoughtful.

There was no other explanation.

The frown reappeared and she pursed her lips. There was definitely another side to Max Templeton. The problem was, that the more she saw of this kind, thoughtful, caring side, the harder it became to tell herself that he was just another over-confident, full-of-himself ass. And telling herself that was by far the safer option—it kept him away from her heart.

Picking up the lipstick Natalie had chosen for her, she slicked it onto her lips. Even if he did have some good qualities, she wasn't going to risk her sanity again by even thinking about allowing herself to fall for him.

She had to get back into the ballroom before it was all over and so, standing, she shook down her dress—which, remarkably, hadn't suffered from being gathered up around her knees for the bike ride. The velvet fabric was gorgeous, and Natalie had been right that the deep green was her colour. She didn't look bad, even if she did say so herself. The way the dress had been so cleverly cut gave her a waist she hadn't really known she had, and although the jewellery was only costume jewellery, it did complement her eyes as the shop assistant had suggested.

When she'd walked onto that stage earlier, her mother's words about being mutton dressed as lamb ringing in her ears, she'd hardly dared to look at Max as he'd stood centre-stage, looking like a film star in his exquisite satin-lapelled, tuxedo. But when she had, he'd met her gaze with a dazzling smile, and although she knew there were over three hundred other people in the room, his smile had seemed only for her.

But that was ridiculous. He was a showman. He'd spent more than enough time in front of cameras to learn how to seduce an audience and that was all he'd been doing. It was a show—that was all.

Walking down the corridor, past all the other dressing rooms with their golden, glittering stars, her golden, glittery stiletto heels click-clacking on the wooden floor, she put her shoulders back and lifted her chin.

And she could put on a show too.

For one night only, as he'd said, she was an opera singer.

Or Cinderella.

The fairy godmothers that were her best friend Natalie and Rebecca the make-up artist had waved their magic wands and helped her to do what she had to do. She'd already done the difficult bit, up on that stage, the rest would be a breeze in comparison. And then tomorrow she could go back to being Cinders—back to her comfort zone, back where she belonged. The glitz and glamour belonged to those who wanted it—to those who looked the part and felt comfortable in it. All she wanted was to be back in her department, looking after her patients and her amazing team of staff.

# CHAPTER SEVEN

THE BALLROOM WAS buzzing with noise and activity. Everyone was mingling, chatting, drinking, schmoozing. Glasses were clinking, the DJ was in full swing, the odd cork popped off a bottle of fizz and there was a crowd on the dance floor, bobbing away to the music.

Lois recognised more celebrities than she'd expected: singers, actors, comedians, a few politicians. She took a deep breath. It was only an hour until midnight—that wasn't long, and the party wouldn't go on past then, surely. She could manage an hour.

A handsome male actor she recognised but couldn't remember the name of was smiling and walking towards her, holding out a glass.

'The opera star,' he said, approaching with a wide and very white smile. 'You don't have a glass in your hand. Here—we can't have that.'

He held out a glass of something with bubbles fizzing through it and Lois took it gladly, returning his smile.

'Thank you.'

'I have to say,' the man continued in conspiratorial fashion, 'I think you were the best performer this evening.'

'Oh,' replied Lois, 'well, I don't know about that, but thank you.'

'And you're a nurse?'

'Yes, that's my day job.' She took a sip of the very welcome ice-cold drink, the bubbles tickling her nose.

'You're a woman of many talents. You were sensational on stage tonight—congratulations.' He lifted his glass, smiling before taking a long drink. 'Like to dance?'

He lifted the glass from her hand and placed it with his own on a nearby table, taking her by the elbow and leading her towards the dance floor, where the DJ had switched from dance music to a slower number.

'I'm not very good at dancing.'

Lois didn't want to dance. She felt out of place. The ballroom was full of elegantly dressed, beautiful people. She didn't belong here.

He took her hand in his and gently placed his other hand on her waist. 'Don't worry, I'll lead. You'll be fine.'

She swallowed. He seemed nice, but people had started to look at them, making her heart rate climb as though she was back on stage. She managed a smile. He was one of Max's guests and would likely make a big donation. She couldn't *not* have a dance with him.

'I'll try not to step on your toes.'

Keeping her gaze firmly fixed on the man's black satin lapels, she answered his questions about her singing. It was only the sudden sound of Max's voice that told her he was standing beside them.

'Richard, old man—how the devil are you? I just need to borrow Lois, if you don't mind…an urgent work matter.'

An excuse to leave the dance floor! Relief flooded through her, quickly followed by alarm. What had happened? Was Luke okay?

'Of course.' The actor released Lois. 'Thank you for the dance, Lois, and for not treading on my toes. Hope to see you again later.'

Max guided her away from the crowded dance floor and

didn't let go of her elbow until he'd steered her out of the ball-room and into the large, equally opulent lobby.

'Sorry,' said Max.

'Is Luke okay? Did you get his X-ray result?'

He looked puzzled for a moment. 'Oh, yes…no.'

'Good.' She frowned. 'I think. So, what did you want me for? And what are you sorry about?'

His eyes had darkened to a shade she'd never seen before, and suddenly everything going on around them faded to nothing. He looked as if he was deliberating over something significant. Her breathing deepened. There was a tension between them. The air seemed to crackle…alive with tiny particles of fizzling anticipation.

'I'm sorry for breaking up your dance with Richard.'

*It was more than that. What was going on?*

The back of her neck prickled. 'That's okay,' she replied slowly.

'It was selfish of me.'

'It was?' She held on to the glass emerald at her neck so tightly the edges of the facets dug into her fingers. She swallowed. 'Why?'

The power of his eyes was immense. She couldn't look away…didn't want to.

It was little more than a whisper, but his words were electrifying. '*I* wanted to be the one to dance with you.'

Max held out his hand towards her. She looked hesitant. She had every right to be, though, didn't she? He was well aware that he had a certain reputation with women. His celebrity status meant that the tabloids were always happy to print photos and make up stories about what they called his 'love life'. To be fair, the press stories about him had a grain of truth about them—he *was* a confirmed bachelor. But *love life*?

That was a little phrase they liked to trot out which meant nothing to him. He didn't have a love life. Love was an emotion he avoided like the plague. Love equalled pain, loss and grief. Lois, along with everyone else, was better off keeping well away from him and his reputation with love. Anyone he'd ever loved had, in one way or another, left him, been let down by him or rejected him.

He was steering well clear of love.

But she returned his smile and took his hand, her touch tightening every one of his nerves in an instant and weakening, with swift ease, his well-practised mantra not to feel anything.

'I think I can hear the opening strains of "Careless Whisper".' Her smile widened. 'I can never resist this one.'

Holding her hand, leading her back to the ballroom, through the mingling groups of guests to the softly twinkling dance floor, now packed with couples pressed together, he knew he was pushing his boundaries, trespassing into an unknown world…a world he'd never had any desire to venture into.

He felt things for Lois he'd never felt before. He knew what lust felt like, and although of course he desired Lois physically, there was much more to it than that.

*What if this was how falling in love began?*

Feelings? Caring about someone?

He smiled at people as they passed. Everyone seemed exactly as they had been before. No one else seemed to realise that the earth's tectonic plates had shifted slightly. Max Templeton was contemplating that what he was feeling might be mistaken as the first sign of something he most definitely didn't want to feel. And yet he was powerless to halt it in its tracks.

'May I?'

He moved his hand to her waist, but stopped short of touching her.

'You may.'

Her smile was shy, uncertain, but again there was bravery in her eyes. He held her waist and she placed one of her hands on his shoulder and the other in his. Pulling her closer, pressing her to him lightly, he gazed into soft emerald eyes which looked back at him, pulling him in, weakening his resolve to keep his distance.

Their race across London on the bike earlier, when she'd held on to him so tightly their bodies had almost moulded together had been exhilarating. Holding her now only confirmed that he wanted her.

*So have sex and get it out of your system.*

But it was more than that. He *felt* something. What that something was, he couldn't work out, but he knew it would take more than sex to find the answer.

*Don't do this, Templeton. Stay back. Keep feelings out of this.*

She looked up at him, a slight frown creasing her brow. 'I never really understood why this song has the power to bring couples to the dance floor—it's about heartbreak and being alone.'

'It makes *me* feel alone.'

His heart rate notched up. He knew which direction he was taking this. He was on dangerous ground, but this was travelling on one trajectory only. The need to kiss those lips was almost overwhelming.

'Does it?' she asked.

'Alone in this crowded room with you…everyone else has disappeared. Is that cheesy?'

Her eyes softened and her lips curved into a smile. His fingers ached to touch her face, to feel the softness of her cheek, the warmth of her full lips, now slightly apart, waiting to be kissed.

'Is it true?'

Emerald eyes glittered, daring him to answer truthfully.

*Sassy Lois.*

Undeniable lust shot through him.

'Yes.'

She took a breath, a moment to look into his eyes, as if to test his honesty.

*So test it.*

He *was* telling the truth.

'Then it's not cheesy.'

His breathing deepened. If this continued it could easily lead to them sleeping together. Did he want that?

*Hell, yes. Look at her.*

She was the most stunning woman in the room. And she felt amazing pressed against him. His palms ached for her.

And she'd sung for him.

Against her better judgement.

She'd strode straight out of her comfort zone and done this, tonight, for him. And even though she hadn't wanted to do it, she'd done it with style.

Every fibre of his being was grateful to her...admired her, wanted her.

Suddenly, there was no dilemma. To hell with not getting involved. He wanted Lois, and if she wanted him back, he'd deal with any fallout afterwards.

A weight lifted from his shoulders.

'You were amazing tonight. You looked stunning on that stage.'

And the glittering light in her eyes disappeared. Just like that.

His heart dropped like a stone to the pit of his stomach.

She dropped her gaze. 'I hope I did okay. I hope you get to the fundraising target you need.'

There was that vulnerability again.

He lifted his hand and touched her chin lightly, raising it, making her look up at him. 'You were much more than okay, Lois.' He wasn't flirting. He needed her to know how good she was because she really didn't know it. 'I'd say you stole the show.'

She smiled, but turned her head away. 'Thank you...that's kind. And thanks for indulging me with George Michael.'

The song had ended. The DJ was calling everyone to the

dance floor for the final rousing tunes of the evening. It was nearly midnight. Cinderella was going to go home.

'I believe Max Templeton would like to say a few words before we end this amazing evening,' called the DJ. 'Where are you, Max?'

Max lifted his hand to acknowledge the DJ, then bent to whisper in her ear. 'In the words of George Michael...please stay.'

The crowd cheered and a spotlight lit up, following Max as he made his way to the stage to take the microphone. He had host duties to perform, people to thank, hands to shake, the last donations to be elicited.

He just hoped he could do all that before Cinderella disappeared.

Lois had shaken almost as many hands as Max had. People had been very kind, lavishing her with compliments on her singing.

'You were abso-flippin'-lutely brilliant,' said Natalie, hugging her as tightly as a heavily pregnant woman could manage.

'Amazing,' said Toby, planting a kiss on her cheek.

'I was so proud of you,' said Tom, clasping her. 'We all were. How come you kept that talent such a secret?'

'And Max was most definitely impressed,' whispered Natalie with a wink as she left.

*Max.*

He'd been flirting with her when they'd danced. And she'd let him. She watched him now, as he shook hands with the last few remaining guests as they filed out. Laughing, slapping some people on the back, planting kisses on the cheeks of others, flashing that famous smile from his handsome face. Charm personified.

Was it second nature to him as it had been to Emilio? Right up until she'd given in to his charms and he'd begun to change?

The actor Richard strode towards her, smiling and shrugging on his overcoat. It was as though she'd been parachuted into an after-show party at some Hollywood awards ceremony—she'd never seen so many celebrities all in one place.

'Well, I never got that second dance with you, Lois, but I can't say I blame Max for keeping you to himself.' He grinned as Max came towards them, slapping him on the back and shaking his hand. 'Great evening, Max. Well done.'

'Thanks so much for coming,' said Max. 'Good to see you again.'

Richard tapped his forehead, turned on his heel and headed for the door, calling to a concierge to get him a taxi.

'You made an impression there,' said Max, lifting his hand in acknowledgement as his famous friend disappeared through the revolving door.

'He was very kind,' she replied, registering Max's pursed lips and raised eyebrow.

*What had Richard meant when he'd said Max had kept her to himself?*

'Great evening, Max.'

Another glamorous couple approached and shook their hands.

'Good luck with the fundraising, darling,' said the woman, air-kissing his cheek, before she swept away. *'Ciao!'*

'Well, it looks as though we're the last ones standing.'

He glanced around the foyer. A few revellers sat around, still holding on to drinks, but most had left or gone to their rooms.

'I'll get my things from the dressing room and grab a taxi,' said Lois.

*Was she glad the evening she'd so dreaded was actually over?*

At least her nightmare of appearing on stage naked hadn't come true. In fact, people had been really lovely, and Max had been grateful—she'd seen it in his eyes when she'd walked towards him on stage. Yes, part of her was relieved the evening was over—the part of her that had spent most of her life believing she wasn't worthy of a night like this. But another, unfamiliar part of her would have quite enjoyed having more time to chat with people, dance with film stars and see Max look at her like that again.

Had he just been grateful…or had there been something else in his deep blue eyes? Those butterflies reawakened.

'I'll help you with your things and get a taxi organised,' said Max.

'Oh, don't worry. I can get a taxi myself—you must have loads to do.'

'I want to make sure you get home safely. Let me at least help you with your bags.'

The butterflies danced, pirouetting, twirling. Her instinct was to lower her gaze, but somehow she couldn't. Somehow his eyes held hers.

'Thank you, that's very kind.'

She didn't *need* his help…but she did *want* it. But it was simple kindness, wasn't it? He'd be making sure *all* the performers got home safely—helping *all* of them with their bags, not just her.

*Don't kid yourself, Lois. You've fallen for all this before.*

Maybe he had been flirting with her when they'd danced. But he'd been flirting with everyone this evening—he'd been playing the charming host. His job had been to make sure everyone had a great time and that they dug deep into their pockets for his programme. He'd told her she was amazing on stage, but he'd just been showing his gratitude—he'd have said that to everyone. It was his job.

He'd said she looked stunning too, and she'd almost believed him.

*Almost.*

Just in time, she'd remembered who she was.

Anyway, she didn't want to be lured into those enchanting eyes…lulled into the false sense of security his kindness could so easily invoke…enticed by his oh, so handsome face and toned, hard body. Life had taught her not to trust in those things. It only led to heartbreak and humiliation.

Most of the performers seemed to have left and the corridor was quiet. Lois pushed open the door to her dressing room.

'Did you hear yet from Robert?' She placed her hairbrush into her case.

Max stood on the threshold, filling the doorway. 'The X-ray showed a small collection in the left base, as expected—the antibiotics should sort it out.'

She zipped the case closed and attempted to lift it down from the table.

'Here, let me get that.'

Lois stood to one side so he could reach in and take the case, but the dressing room was narrow and his arm brushed against her breasts as he leaned over. The glancing connection shot electricity through her, making her breath catch in her throat.

He turned to face her, hypnotic blue eyes locked on her own. 'Sorry.'

She swallowed.

*Why was he looking at her like that? How could he do what he was doing to her insides?*

It had been the merest brush of his arm…the most casual touch…but her breasts fizzed as though he'd poured champagne over them. She fought not to lower her gaze—it was too good looking into those eyes, feeling the warmth of his nearness, inhaling the spicy aroma of him, enjoying just for a moment the pretence that he was about to take her into those strong arms…

And then he kissed her.

It was so sudden and unexpected that for a moment she froze. A squeak of shock caught in her throat, unable to escape because his lips were crushed hard against hers.

It was over in a moment.

She let out a breath. Her lips tingled, feeling suddenly swollen, warm, desperate for more.

'I'm sorry, I—'

But Lois cut him off.

'Don't be.'

He'd lit a spark somewhere deep inside her the first moment they'd met, and that kiss had thrown fuel on it, turning it into a blazing fire that wasn't going to be quenched without more of what he'd just given her a taste of. She didn't want to fall for Max Templeton—but she didn't have to fall for him to have him kiss her like that again.

She could allow herself to be lost in the deep pools of his eyes…allow them to enchant her, hypnotise her, seduce her. She didn't have to fall for him.

'You're so beautiful, Lois…' His voice was a whisper. 'I couldn't resist. I don't know how I've resisted you all evening.'

Time stood still and she knew as she looked up into his handsome face that her lips had parted. He'd called her beautiful. She'd heard it before. From another man's lips. Another man who'd got her into bed and then changed into a narcissistic, cruel monster. No. Correction—Emilio hadn't changed. He'd always been a narcissistic, cruel monster. She just hadn't seen it.

So how could she be sure she wasn't making exactly the same error of judgement now? Emilio had taught her some harsh lessons. Lessons she'd promised herself to remember, learn from, never to repeat.

*Don't trust.*

*Don't give your heart away.*

*Don't let anyone else crush you as he did.*

She searched his face, looking for the truth.

There was honesty in his eyes.

Honesty.

And desire.

Heat flooded through her. Sometimes you had to cross your own boundaries. She'd done that already this evening, by getting up onto that stage, and that had worked out fine.

'I wasn't sure you were going to turn up tonight…'

His voice was low, edged with a seductive huskiness she hadn't heard him use before.

'When you walked out onto that stage you blew me away.'

He stoked her jawline with his finger and tilted her chin upwards.

*He was going to kiss her again.*

'You looked stunning.'

He ran his finger down her neck and across her collarbone, over the chain of glass diamonds and emeralds. She didn't move. Held in the power of his eyes, she didn't breathe. She didn't need to.

'And when you sang, I couldn't look away.'

*Kiss me.*

Her resolve had shattered. Her lips were begging him, tingling for the taste of him, and she had no intention of denying herself.

*He wasn't Emilio.*

And even if she wasn't the most beautiful woman he'd ever seen—as she clearly wasn't—it didn't matter tonight. Tomorrow was another day.

Rising up onto her tiptoes, she closed the gap between them. And although this time she was ready for it, when his lips met hers and she tasted him nothing else existed. Just the sweetness and the pressure of his mouth on hers…the warmth of his hands on her bare shoulders…the masculine scent of him filling her.

That was all there was.

All she needed.

Right up until the moment when he deepened the kiss, parting her lips with his tongue and groaning, pulling her closer. Close enough for her to feel his hard arousal through the velvet of her dress.

It was then that she wanted more.

# CHAPTER EIGHT

HIS DECISION TO kiss her had been sudden, but not out of no-where. He'd wanted her all evening. She hadn't been expecting it, though. She'd stiffened against him, and that was why he'd apologised and stood back.

What had happened between them then, when she'd looked into his eyes for what seemed like for ever, had happened without words…and without logic. He'd thought he'd overstepped the mark, misread the situation. But her eyes had softened, something had changed, and she'd been the one to reach for him. When their lips had met, much more softly this time, and she'd allowed his fingers to skim the porcelain softness of her neck, her kiss had assured him that she wanted this as much as he did.

But apart from sex, he had nothing to offer her.

He was on dangerous ground.

*Why?*

Because he'd stepped over the line—trespassed into a world he didn't belong in, one where feelings were allowed to run free with impunity.

*And he didn't do feelings.*

Besides, he was leaving, wasn't he?

'You know I'm only here for three more months?'

Emerald eyes stared back at him. There was a boldness in them he hadn't seen before and his stomach tightened.

'Yes, I was told,' she said.

Knowing that he wanted her wasn't news.

Knowing he might have her was something else.

But she deserved more than he could offer. Lois should be with someone who would love her deeply…be everything she ever wanted…give her children. Things that were pretty normal. But he couldn't do any of them. Anyway, in three more months he'd be five thousand miles away.

He didn't want to be in London. He'd stayed because it was where he'd needed to be to achieve what he wanted. As soon as the screening programme was over the line, he was leaving. His new position was all lined up, and the faraway sunshine and freedom that working in California would give him was beckoning.

He didn't want to lead Lois down the garden path and have her think a relationship was on the cards—but, hell, her eyes told him she wanted him and her kisses confirmed it.

They were both consenting adults, weren't they?

'I'm going to be living in California,' he told her.

'I know.'

She seemed okay with it. She knew he wasn't promising anything. But if this was going to go any further, it wasn't going to be in this tiny dressing room.

'I have a suite here.'

Her cheeks were flushed, her lips swollen, her breathing deep, making the jewels which nestled on her breasts sparkle in the light as they rose and fell.

Moment of truth.

'Stay with me tonight,' he said.

The tiniest nod of her head. 'Okay.'

It was no more than a whisper, but it was enough.

Max lifted the suitcase. This wasn't the way he'd expected the evening to end, but even if she changed her mind right now it had already been an evening which had far outshone his expectations. She'd turned up, for one thing, and outperformed every other act on the stage. And he'd held her in his arms, kissed her lips, seen desire in her stunning eyes.

But she lived in London, belonged at St Martin's and he would be leaving the first moment he could. That was non-negotiable.

'Shall I take your bags sir?' asked a uniformed porter in the foyer. 'The Royal Suite, isn't it?'

'It is,' replied Max. 'But we're fine, thank you.'

'Very well,' said the porter. 'Goodnight, sir…madam.'

Lois smiled at him.

Did he know where they were going? What they were about to do? Dear Lord, what had happened to her? The Lois she knew didn't do things like this. The Lois she knew and saw in the mirror every morning didn't have a one-night stand in one of the world's most exclusive hotels with one of the world's most eligible bachelors.

*Had the world shifted on its axis?*

The lift pinged its arrival and the door slid open.

'After you.'

Max nodded towards the shiny mirrored interior of the lift. Those eyes… He couldn't begin to know what they were capable of. Or maybe he did. Maybe he did this sort of thing all the time. She was probably just one in a long line.

He pushed the button for the Royal Suite. 'Are you sure about this, Lois?'

She swallowed. *Was she?*

Somehow her legs had carried her this far, and although logical Lois had put forward a reasonable counter-argument, this Lois, whoever she was, still found herself in a lift, about to go into this man's bedroom.

The lift pinged, and the sudden awareness that her heart was beating rapidly against her ribs was a warning to stop and think.

The Lois she knew was back.

The lift doors slid open. The Royal Suite was the only suite on this floor, and its large mahogany door was mere feet away, looming before her.

It was only a few steps to its threshold.

A boundary.

Her heart rate shot up further.

Logical Lois didn't want to be seduced by Max Templeton's handsome face, athlete's body and persuasive kisses. Logical Lois most definitely didn't want a relationship.

But he wasn't offering a relationship, was he? He was in London for three more months and he'd just made sure she was aware of that fact.

He held the door open for her to go first, dark indigo eyes sultry, watchful.

*Could he read her mind? Could he tell she was struggling with this? Torn between desire, fear and logic?*

'I can't offer anything long term, Lois. I don't do relationships and I'm going to be living over five thousand miles away.'

'I know.' She tried to keep her voice light—not show that she didn't do this sort of thing all the time—but knew she probably didn't sound convincing. 'I understand.'

Logical Lois knew exactly what he was saying.

But she was under a spell.

And this wasn't logical Lois's night.

This night was for Lois the opera singer—the woman who'd had flowers hurled onto the stage for her, the woman who'd been cheered and told she had an amazing voice, who'd shaken hands with film stars. It belonged to the woman who'd seen the desire in Max's eyes and been kissed by him in a way she'd never known a kiss could be.

'That's fine by me.'

And there it was again. Undiluted desire flared in his eyes and she knew it was mirrored in her own.

Heart pounding, she walked to the door.

The last boundary.

He unlocked it, slotted the key card into place and soft wall lighting illuminated the hall. Kicking his shoes off and taking her hand, he led her down the corridor and into the lounge. A huge wall of windows revealed an expanse of the London city skyline, twinkling with lights from the towering buildings and the glittering river several floors below. But she didn't have time to drink it in because Max wasn't hanging around to look at it.

Standing before her, he lifted his hand to her cheek, his fingers once more softly trailing a line down her jawline to her chin, lifting it upwards, making her lips part and her eyes close in readiness as every one of her rational objections disappeared, erased by his touch.

'Lois…'

His voice was a light whisper, but heavy with desire. When his lips brushed hers their touch was soft and light, but then he pulled her to him, erasing any remaining distance between them, strong arms holding her. When he deepened his kiss she moaned, responding, raking her fingers through his hair, bringing him impossibly closer. She reached inside his dinner jacket, easing it from his shoulders, throwing it onto a nearby armchair. Her fingers were hungry to explore the shape of his broad shoulders, the strength in the muscles of his back, the warmth of his skin through his shirt.

He took his kisses to her throat and she arched her neck, drawing him down further, and as his lips found her collarbone he brought his fingers to her bare shoulders, then lower, tracing a line around her necklace and then curving over her breasts, sending fizzing darts of desire to the very place right between her thighs that ached for him the most.

His fingers found the zip at the back of her dress and he undid it. The heavy velvet fell from her shoulders and with a soft thud landed on the carpet, encircling her feet. He stopped kissing her only to stand and look at her, naked before him in the almost darkness except for a strapless bra and knickers and the gold, glittery heels. He groaned.

'You look sensational.'

The Lois she knew so well would have tried to cover herself—would have laughed off the compliment and, despite the only twinklings of light coming from the windows of distant buildings, would have been horrified that he was fully dressed while she stood almost naked before him.

But tonight's Lois was different. Tonight's Lois wanted Max. She knew the risks and was willing to take them. She'd deal with tomorrow when it came.

'Is there a bedroom?' she asked.

His eyes didn't leave hers as he took her hand. 'This way.'

She didn't notice that the bed was a four-poster…didn't notice the opulence of the fabric it was draped in or the richness of its colours, or the softness of the deep carpet. There was only Max, kissing her, crushing her to him, his hard erection pressed against her.

Her fingers found the buttons of his shirt and she began to undo them, not wanting even that fine fabric between them. Max wanted it there even less than she did, and ripped the shirt open himself, sending buttons in all directions. In another moment he'd unclasped her bra, and that champagne fizzing coursed through her as he cupped her breasts and dipped his head, running his tongue over one taut, peaked nipple and lightly squeezing the other, sending hot waves of pleasure to her very core.

He moaned as she undid the button on his trousers and unzipped him. His black satin boxers couldn't hide his huge erection and Lois knew her eyes had widened. He lifted her with ease and instinctively she wrapped her legs around his waist, gasping as his erection nudged her exactly where she wanted it to be.

Carrying her, kissing her neck, her breasts crushed against him, he laid her down on the plush bedding. She didn't want to wait another moment for him to be inside her. But he paused, reaching for his trousers, finding his wallet and a condom, tearing it open and rolling it on in one swift, practised movement. Then he was over her, his hard, toned body about to bear down.

'Max...'

It was as soft as a breath but loaded with impatient longing. His mouth met hers as he lowered himself towards her, not pausing, sinking into the wetness between her thighs, pushing into her, making her gasp and groan all at once.

Wrapping her thighs around him, she wanted to draw him deeper, but he knew what she wanted and he drove himself into her, finding the exact part of her that was screaming to be satisfied. He was all that existed. Nothing else mattered. She knew only the ever-swelling wave of desire endlessly cresting as he thrust into her with hungry greed.

She called out, almost surprised, when he brought her to the sweet, desperate edge of ecstasy, before sending her crashing over into the oblivion of orgasm only a moment before claiming his own pleasure with a final thrust, arching back, eyes closed, burying himself in her completely.

Neither of them spoke until their ragged breathing had begun to settle.

'Perfect,' he whispered, still breathless, lying on his back beside her.

'Mmm...' Her eyes were still closed. She was still savouring the sensations washing over her. Her body was relaxed, weightless, all tension gone, her skin tingling. The decision this new for-one-night-only version of Lois had made was a good one. If this wasn't right, what was?

Max rolled onto his side to face her and lifted himself on one elbow.

'It was a little fast and furious.'

Lois opened her eyes. He bit his lip in mock contrition, eyes twinkling mischievously. Dear Lord, he was handsome.

She smiled. 'Maybe a little.'

'I couldn't resist you a moment longer. We'll take it slower next time.'

He traced a finger lightly across her shoulder and down her arm, making her shiver.

He looked concerned. 'Are you chilly?'

'No, I'm okay.'

*Next time?*

Max stood to pull the bedding down, giving her a glorious view of his toned, strong, tanned, heavenly body.

'Get under the covers, stay warm.'

The for-one-night-only Lois who'd materialised this evening would have real Lois's gratitude for ever. Real Lois would never have been able to agree to this—would never have been able to stand almost naked before him, even in the dark. But she would always have wondered what she'd missed.

A large, gleaming copper bathtub sat at the foot of the bed. Max nodded towards it, a dark eyebrow raised. 'Seems a shame not to use it.'

*And he wanted her out from under the covers.*

He ran the water, tipping bath foam into the steam which rose from it, letting the bath fill as he lit the candles in hurricane jars on the table, giving the room a soft, warm glow.

Returning to the bath, he turned off the taps, swishing his hand around in the water.

'Coming in?'

Reaching for a throw, she wrapped it around herself before sliding out of bed. He took her hand as she stepped into the bath and cast the throw aside, lowering herself into the water.

Max stepped in and sat at the opposite end.

This hadn't been in the plan. Go in, get the job done and get out of Dodge asap. That had been the plan. No delays. No distractions. But he hadn't factored in meeting Lois.

He took a breath. The plan still held. He couldn't stay. He'd explained that to Lois earlier and she'd seemed okay with it. She wouldn't be here with him now if she wasn't, would she?

Lois lay with her eyes closed, her head resting on one of

the towels draped over the edge of the bath behind her. The water was warm…the vanilla scent like fresh-baked cookies. She looked completely relaxed, her breaths long and slow, her lips curved slightly upwards in a tranquil smile. The steam had settled onto her skin in tiny beads, some of which had run downwards over her neck and breasts and found their way back to the water. She still wore the emerald necklace; it rose and fell hypnotically.

The room was silent.

London would still be busy, even at this time of night, but for now they were the only people in the city. Alone, legs casually entwined beneath the warm water, peaceful, sharing this moment.

Inhaling a long breath, filling his lungs with the warm, steamy, cookie dough scent, he rested his head back and closed his eyes. It would have to end, but right now it was bliss.

'I could fall asleep lying here,' said Lois dreamily.

Max opened one eye, his stomach clenching again at the sight of her. She was so beautiful. And so damn sexy. Her breasts slowly rose and fell with her breathing, almost but not quite revealing the deep pink of her nipples through the bubbles. Clearly he'd had long enough to recover from their 'fast and furious' encounter on the bed—his reaction demonstrated that he was more than ready again.

'But that's probably not a wise move.' She opened her eyes, meeting his, and smiled. 'Can you pass me the soap?'

Max reached for the bar of soap in the dish beside him, dipped it into the water and created a lather in his hands. 'Allow me.'

Lois sat upright and held out her arm, which he took, soaping it before taking her other arm and doing the same. Kneeling before her, he soaped his hands again, and she lifted her chin as he caressed her throat and shoulders, spreading his fingers to encase her breasts, thumbs skimming over the taut nipples, hearing her gasp as he did so. She got to her knees, her waist clear of the water, and rivulets were running down her curves as she rose to allow his fingers to roam over her. She gasped again as they found a different spot from the one he'd found earlier, but one that was equally sensitive, judging by the way she arched towards him.

'Do that again,' she murmured, her eyes meeting his, full of unabashed, wanton desire.

He didn't need telling twice. And she *was* telling him, instructing him, almost daring him not to do as she demanded.

Letting his fingers be guided by the shape of her, he slipped them further down until they nudged her where he knew she ached for them. She gripped his shoulders and he felt her nails as he slipped inside her with his fingers. When they'd had sex earlier it had been the fast, frantic sex of two people who couldn't get close enough, fast enough, and although he'd felt her climax, he hadn't savoured it as he was going to savour it now. This time he wanted to give her the time she deserved. They had all night, and he wanted to draw out every sensual moment.

For it could only happen once.

Dipping his head, he took one of her nipples between his lips. She placed her hand on his head, keeping him there, but he wanted something else too. He lifted the plug from the bath to allow the water to drain away.

'I don't want this to end, Max.'

He lifted his head, taking her chin between finger and thumb, tilting her face to him. 'It's not ending yet, Lois.'

Her mouth was on his, her kiss sweet, luxurious, demanding. This woman was unbelievable. The Lois he knew from the ITU was a capable, knowledgeable professional. The Lois he'd seen on stage tonight had an amazing talent and could hold an audience rapt. But the Lois here, now, in this bedroom, was a glorious goddess—and he didn't know how long he could wait to be inside her again.

But wait he would. Because he wanted to give this woman

so much pleasure. He lowered himself, crouching on his knees. The water had drained away, leaving vanilla-scented bubbles at the bottom of the glowing, candlelit copper bath. He wanted to taste her, and when he did she moaned softly, raking her fingers through his hair, arching to meet him.

And he knew he had her. She said his name just before he took her over the edge, and he slipped his fingers inside her again to feel her pulse onto them, squeezing them as wave after wave of pleasure overtook her. He rose up to take her in his arms and she almost collapsed into them, pressing her lips to his.

He reached behind her for a towel, opened it and wrapped it around her.

'Let's go to bed,' he growled.

Lois lay on the bed, her breathing still heavy, watching Max as he gave himself a rough towelling down before joining her. Her eyes, despite herself, were drawn to his huge erection, which did nothing to help ease her rapid breathing or slow her heart rate.

She met his gaze. He was grinning.

'I did say it wasn't going to end just yet.'

But as he reached for the wallet he'd dropped onto the bedside table, his face dropped.

'I don't have another condom.'

'The famous Lothario that is Max Templeton only carries one condom around with him? You do surprise me.'

Trying to supress her grin was impossible.

He sat down on the edge of the bed. 'It's not like that, Lois. That's just the papers. Do you have one…?'

'No, sorry.'

'Damn it.'

'I'm sure you could get the concierge to procure some for you. A place like this will do whatever its top clients require, I imagine.'

He turned around to face her, the agony of his disappointment apparent in his eyes.

'I'm on the pill.'

She smiled as his expression changed to one of relief, quickly followed by the narrowing of his eyes.

'You big tease.'

She laughed, dodging as he poked her playfully in the ribs.

'The concierge!' he said, poking her a second time as she laughed all the more.

'I'm sure he's very discreet,' she replied, biting her lip, trying to stifle her amusement.

But suddenly, he looked serious.

'You're definitely on the pill?'

'Have been since my teens...dysmenorrhea...so yes, definitely.'

His face softened.

His eyes darkened.

Her breathing deepened.

Dear Lord, one look from him and she was putty in his hands.

He climbed onto the bed and her thighs parted instinctively as he knelt between them.

'You're so beautiful, Lois.'

She reached for him, pulling him down towards her. He'd satisfied her in a way she hadn't known she could be satisfied, but there was still an ache deep inside her which only he could quell.

Those hypnotic blue eyes...eyes she'd seen so many times before, but never quite like this, never filled with desire as they were now...were looking at her with such longing. She knew what his eyes were capable of. She'd seen others practically fall at his feet, say yes to things they hadn't really wanted to say yes to, stare at him awestruck, enchanted by their power.

But this was something else. He was looking at her as though she was the only woman in the world…as though she was the one he desired above all others…as though she was *everything*.

And then he took her…slowly, gently. Almost too gently. She wanted him badly, right now. But he'd promised her slow, hadn't he? And he was clearly going to keep his promise.

Time stopped as he eased into her and she didn't breathe, feeling every inch of him as he entered, oh, so slowly. But soon he filled her, and when he did he stopped, pulsing gently inside her, holding his breath for a moment, his eyes closed. Then he opened them and looked at her, holding her gaze as he began to move, building the pace, building the tension within her once more, increasing her need for him with every stroke until she shattered around him and called out, gripping him with her thighs and her hands as he found his own climax, thrusting into her, growling her name, closing his eyes tightly.

Breathing heavily, he lay beside her. Still flooded with powerful, shocking, perfect waves of pleasure, she didn't want to move. If this really was for one night only, she'd remember it for the rest of her life.

# CHAPTER NINE

FOR A MOMENT Lois didn't know where she was. She lay looking up at an unfamiliar ornate white plaster ceiling rose and
the crystal chandelier which hung from it. She was naked and
alone.

*Where was Max?*

The room was silent. He was probably in the bathroom. Was
he coming back to make love to her again?

She closed her eyes, remembering last night—the way he'd
looked at her, touched her, kissed her, sent her to the edge of
places she'd never been to before and on to the sweet, powerful ecstasy beyond.

She wasn't cold, but a shiver ran up her spine. That other
Lois had appeared from nowhere, conjured up by his persuasive eyes, taking control, doing things that normal, regular Lois
would never have dreamt of doing. She'd been naked before
him, had bathed with him, allowed him to explore every inch
of her. The dim, soft candlelight had empowered her, but even
so, normal Lois would have been way out of her comfort zone.

Sitting up, she looked round. The door to the en suite bathroom was open. He wasn't in there.

Reaching for the towel, she got up and wrapped it around
herself. It was still a little damp from last night.

*Last night... Dear Lord.*

'Max?'

She padded into the lounge, the deep carpet soft and luxurious underfoot. It was as they'd left it last night, but now mid-morning summer sunlight streamed through the huge windows and the Thames twinkled far below, busy with boats of all kinds.

She glanced around. Her dress lay on the floor, a heap of green crumpled velvet. Drawing the towel around herself tightly, she went out into the hall. Her case stood by the door but there was no sign of Max.

She walked back to the lounge and sank down into one of the armchairs, grabbing a cushion and hugging it to herself. Max had warned her he wasn't staying in London for long, and that had obviously been his way of saying he was offering a once-in-a-lifetime deal.

One night of passion.

For one night only.

He could at least have waited until she'd woken up, though… couldn't he?

A sudden loud buzzing at the door made her jump. She sat upright, putting the cushion to one side. Was it Max?

'Hello?' she called through the door.

'Breakfast, madam?'

*Breakfast?*

Clutching the towel tightly, she opened the door an inch to see a uniformed porter with a silver trolley laden with an array of dome-covered silver dishes.

'Would you like me to set it out in the dining room, madam?'

'Oh…erm…no, thank you.'

*She was practically naked.*

'I can manage, thanks.'

'Very well, madam, if you're sure. Oh, Mr Templeton requested fresh juice but didn't specify which kind, so Chef has sent up a selection.'

'Thank you.'

'Good day, madam. If you require anything else, you can call me directly on the iPad in the lounge.'

*Max had ordered breakfast?*

Perhaps that was his parting gift? His way of saying thank you and goodbye? Was that his usual MO?

She lifted the lids on some of the dishes: sliced fresh fruits, croissants, toast... And there was a pot of tea...and one cup and saucer.

*One.*

For a wild moment she'd thought he might have ordered breakfast for them both. But he'd ordered it for *her.*

*Thanks, Max, but I'm not hungry.*

Sinking back down into the armchair, she tucked her knees up in front of her, hugging them. Had he regretted last night so much that he'd had to get away so soon? She buried her face in her hands. Oh, God, how was she going to face him at work? She groaned.

Would anybody notice if she never turned up for work again? If she took a flight to South America and never came back? If she just hid here in this hotel suite for the rest of her life?

*He'd seen her naked.*

She hugged her knees more tightly and buried her face on top of them.

*What had she done?*

She'd never be able to walk back onto her unit again. Or at least not until Max had gone off to his new life in California and the coast was clear. She had a couple of days off work now, and was grateful that was how her shifts had fallen. Maybe her blushes would have subsided a little by then.

*Work.*

Was that where he was? Had he been called in to see Luke? She sat up suddenly hopeful.

*But why hadn't he said so?*

He could have woken her and she could have gone in too. Was Luke okay? Had something happened overnight?

She located her handbag, which she vaguely remembered dropping to the floor when Max had been unzipping her dress.

Rachel, the ward clerk, answered her call, and assured her that Luke was stable.

And Max hadn't been in.

He'd called earlier and spoken to his registrar for an update on all his patients, and then he had reminded them that he was on a day off and wouldn't be in until tomorrow unless he was needed.

Her heart sank. So there was no reason he'd needed to leave so early. No reason apart from the fact that he'd wanted to get out of there...away from her. Heat spread across her cheeks and the tiny light of hope she'd clung to was snuffed out.

So what was she supposed to do now?

Sliding under the duvet and staying there sounded like a good option.

*How stupid was she?*

To think that someone like Max would actually be interested in someone like her. What planet was she on? Men like him could have anyone they wanted, any time they wanted them—and she'd proved that last night, hadn't she?

There was no doubt he'd wanted her. She'd seen the desire in his eyes, felt it in his touch, his fingers, his lips. Heat rose through her, spreading, washing over her, making her skin burn and her insides flutter. It had been more than amazing. It had been unforgettable. One night only—but heavens, she'd remember it for ever.

She'd wanted it as much as he had. She'd known what she was getting into. Her eyes had been wide open. But now, despite the sunshine outside, the cold, harsh light of day had dawned and the reality of her foolishness faced her.

Had she held some naïve notion that he perhaps *liked* her? That maybe he would want to see her again other than at work?

No, of course not. That would have been silly.

So why did she feel so empty? So small? So worthless?

'Stop it,' she said aloud, sitting up straight. 'Stop feeling sorry for yourself.'

Throwing the cushion she'd been clasping aside, she stood and headed for the bathroom, letting her towel fall to the marble floor and standing under the huge rainfall shower as warm water cascaded over her.

This sort of thing happened all the time. There were one-night stands happening every night of the week. People gave themselves to each other on a purely physical and superficial basis as if it was going out of fashion—and if they all allowed embarrassment and humiliation to bother them, no one would ever achieve anything.

Reaching for the shampoo—a high-end brand she would never buy herself—she squeezed a generous amount into her palm, massaging it in vigorously. She was in the Royal suite of one of the most luxurious and expensive hotels in London, so why not make the most of it? Enjoy the breakfast Max had so generously sent as his *Thanks, but no thanks* parting gift. Lie on the four-poster bed and watch a good film, then tap the iPad to summon her personal porter to take her case and order her a taxi home.

Then all she had to do was figure out a way to work with Max Templeton for the next few weeks whilst simultaneously trying not to think about him at all.

It had been two long days since the show…since he'd seen her… since they'd spent the night together. The best night of his life— which had been followed by one of the most difficult mornings.

Meeting the health secretary in Parliament to discuss the screening programme's progress had been straightforward enough. Going to visit his mother hadn't. If he'd ever thought she'd already hurt him all she could, he'd been wrong.

*'The famous screening programme?'* she'd sneered, lighting a cigarette. *'You've been talking about that for years and nothing has happened yet.'*

*'It's a rigorous process,'* he'd replied. *'There's the medical research, the public health viability tests, the development of*

*IT support systems, the training of staff... Not to mention the hoops the health ministers make you jump through. But it's about to get off the ground. I thought you'd be pleased.'*

'*Hmm...*' She'd blown smoke from the side of her mouth as she'd looked down her nose at him. *'It's not going to help us, though, is it?'*

*'It'll help other families.'*

*'Too late for William, though. Much like you were when you should have—'*

She'd stopped mid-sentence, but he'd known how it ended. He'd heard it before.

*'The best thing you can do is make sure you don't have any children of your own—you'll pass the gene on and ruin another family.'*

Years and years of hard work, dismissed by her with a disdainful look and a few scornful words. Had he really expected her to find some solace in what his work had achieved? In the fact that he might help to prevent other sudden young cardiac deaths? He'd hoped rather than expected, perhaps. But it had been a vain hope, obviously.

Going back to the hotel to see if Lois was still there had also been a vain hope. She'd checked out by the time he'd done everything he'd needed to do and gone back. He didn't have her number and had no clue where she lived. Besides, seeing his mother had set every atom in his body on edge.

Why did she have to throw every single thing he did back at him?

Because he'd not done the right thing when it had really mattered. He'd cost her dearly. Because of him she'd lost her son, her husband and the life she'd expected to have.

And she'd blamed him.

And stopped loving him.

And she'd been right to.

He'd let William down. He'd killed his own father and he'd ruined her life. And his twelve-year-old self had realised very quickly that it didn't matter how many times or how hard he tried to win her love back. He had to get used to it. It was the new normal.

The only way he'd been able to deal with the new, cold, distant mother he had, had been to become the same as her. Close down. Shut his feelings away in a box in his head and padlock it. He'd thought he'd done that pretty well, but she still had the power to turn him into the twelve-year-old boy who'd seen his twin brother lying dead on the grass and been frozen with fear. The same boy who'd wept every night for too long, hoping that someone would tell him everything was going to be okay and that no one blamed him.

He approached the nurses' station. 'Morning.'

Everyone looked up and greeted him. Lois remained seemingly engrossed in the computer screen.

*She was annoyed with him.*

Not unsurprisingly. His meeting with the health secretary in Westminster had completely slipped his mind. He'd only remembered when he'd woken up the following morning, watched Lois sleeping beside him and recalled the events of the night before. Remembering how she'd looked on stage had led him to remembering why they'd been there—to raise funds for the screening programme. And that had led to him remembering his appointment with the Right Honourable Mark Wallingham at nine a.m.

He hadn't had the heart to wake her, so had decided to leave her sleeping.

That was what he should have done, wasn't it?

The right thing by not disturbing her?

Or had he taken the cowardly way out? Sneaking away at dawn so as not to have to face the difficult questions of the morning after. Not to have to risk seeing any possibility that she might feel anything emotional. He'd honed that skill to such a high level it was almost second nature.

Suddenly she was looking at him, emerald eyes challenging him to maintain his composure.

'I think we can discharge Luke Evans this morning. His white cell count is back to normal, obs are stable. If you can change his IV antibiotics to oral, I'll see if there's a bed on the ward.'

*He needed to speak to her...explain.*

'Shall we go and have a look at him?'

'Daisy will go with you.' She returned to the screen.

Daisy looked up. 'Sure. Ready now, Max?'

Lois really was annoyed with him.

'Yep, let's go. Sister, could I have a word with you afterwards?'

She stood up and straightened her uniform. 'I'm sorry, Max, I have a meeting.'

'Later, then?'

'You have a full day's clinic today,' she replied, glancing at him far too briefly.

He did. A long clinic. And an evening clinic he was doing to help with the long waiting lists. He wouldn't be done until way after her shift had finished.

She didn't want to speak to him...obviously. Perhaps it was for the best. When had he ever chased a woman the morning after? Never. So why the hell was he doing it now?

'I'd actually better get going,' he said. 'The first patients will be arriving as we speak.'

'Luke won't take you very long,' she replied over her shoulder as she stood up. 'He's much better.'

And she was gone, clutching a folder to her.

What had happened between them two nights ago had been a one-off. Possibly it should never have happened at all. But she was mad as hell with him and he needed to explain. What had happened wasn't going to happen again, but he owed her an explanation nevertheless.

# CHAPTER TEN

'CAN I ASK a quick question, Max?' said Tom.

'Of course.'

He was glad of the distraction. It had been a week since *that* night. A week to think about little else other than how amazing Lois had felt in his arms…how he'd made love to her and felt like the luckiest man alive…how he wanted to see that look in her eyes once more. The look she'd had as he'd kissed her, glittering with desire.

She'd barely looked at him at all since, and when she had it had been with a cool distance. It shouldn't have bothered him. But it did. Which concerned him.

'Alfie Martin,' said Tom. 'CVP has been teetering all day. It's down at two. BP ninety over forty. I think he's a bit dry.'

'Sounds it. I'll come and have a listen to his chest—just to make sure he's not overloaded and fluid's sitting in the wrong places. I don't want to risk any pressure on his graft.'

'Some help at bed four, please!'

Lois's tone told him the patient she was with took priority.

He strode over, threw back the curtain, glanced at the monitor, saw the figures and clocked the patient's deathly pallor.

Lois was turning up the IV fluid via the central line.

'Jay Vallini's patient: aortic arch aneurysm repair this morning, stable all day, but he's just dropped his BP and gone very tachy. Could be a leak.'

Max addressed Tom, who'd followed him over. 'Call the lab to bring up two units of blood. Asap.'

This was bad. The familiar dread filled him. This man's life was literally flowing out of him, and if he didn't act swiftly the patient was going to bleed out before their eyes. He checked himself. He knew what he was doing. He'd done it many times. This patient would receive the best of him—he'd do everything he could not to let him down.

*And try and do that without snapping at the staff for once.*

'I'll get the ultrasound.'

Lois still didn't look at him. She'd remained coolly professional all week. He should be grateful. He didn't want to get involved, and her reaction to what had happened between them told him that she didn't either. Perhaps it was her way of dealing with a one-night stand.

And he'd thought *he* was the master of *love-'em-and-leave-'em…*

'Need any help?' asked Daisy, peering in.

'No,' replied Max.

Daisy stood aside, allowing Lois to come back in with the scanner. Max reached for the trolley just as Lois pushed it alongside the bed. Their fingers touched and they both looked up at the same moment, their gazes clashing, something passing between them.

Something that pulled him in.

It was only a moment, but it was enough for him to know that he wanted more.

Before he knew it Lois was back in professional mode, as though nothing had happened. They'd connected again…and lost it. It had been only a second, but it had made him feel more alive than he had in a week.

'Substantial bleeding,' said Max, moving the probe, studying the image on the screen. 'He'll need to go back to Theatre.'

'I'll call CT,' said Lois, turning to leave.

'No time,' replied Max. 'The ultrasound has said enough.'

Tom appeared, holding two units of blood. 'Check it with me?'

Lois reached for a giving set and switched on the blood warmer.

'Get that in stat,' said Max. 'I'll ring Theatres.' He glanced through the patient's notes on the iPad, waiting for someone in Theatres to pick up. 'Ed? Hi—Max Templeton. I need to bring a patient to Theatre asap. Sixty-four-year-old chap; George Frost; aortic arch aneurysm repair from this morning. He's got a significant leak, so we'll need to open him up again. I'll be there in five and I'll be bringing the patient with me.'

But the response from Theatres wasn't what he wanted or expected to hear.

'There must be *someone*.' He glanced over to Lois and Tom, who were both staring at him, concerned. 'We'll be there in five minutes. Prep the theatre, get me a bypass machine and tell the staff I'll bring my own scrub nurse and anaesthetist.'

Lois stared at him. 'Problem?'

'The theatre staff are tied up with multiple patients from an RTC. Orthopaedics have taken up two theatres. We can use an empty theatre, but in terms of staff there's the on-call perfusionist and they can only spare a couple of runners.'

A frown creased her forehead. 'But you told them to get the theatre ready and that you'd get your own staff.'

'Toby will anaesthetise,' replied Max. 'I know he's not doing anything this evening. And you have theatre experience.'

Her mouth dropped.

'Lois, I know it's a big ask, but if we don't do this, we'll lose the patient.'

And he wasn't about to do that. He lost patients—of course he did. All surgeons did sometimes. It was never easy. Most surgeons dealt with it by reminding themselves that they'd done their best and could have done nothing more. But Max wasn't most surgeons. And to him, losing a patient was a personal blow—one he tried to avoid at all costs.

He turned to Tom. 'Your chap in bed three… I've got three minutes. Let's go.'

Lois glanced up as he left and the coolness of her gaze stung him. But he only had himself to blame for that. He'd set out the rules.

No promises.

There was no point in regretting that now.

It was what they both wanted.

Their time together had been limited to one amazing night.

It was meant to have been enough.

But it wasn't.

Gloved hands steepled in front of her, Lois stood at the theatre table, waiting. Toby was at the head of the table, dealing with the ventilator, monitoring the patient's vital signs and administering the blood which was just about keeping the patient from crashing. Deepa, the perfusionist, was checking the heart-lung bypass machine. The runners stood poised, ready to carry out whatever was asked of them during the surgery.

Max, who was once again pushing boundaries, strode in. She'd managed to avoid him pretty successfully for the last week, but now she was going to have to stand only a few inches from him for at least a few hours. But then it would be over and she could go back to pretending he didn't exist.

He took his place on the opposite side of the table. His scent was too familiar, and way too intoxicating, and her unruly heart began to thud hard in her chest.

*Damn him for doing that to her.*

'Ready?'

He glanced at Toby, who nodded.

'Bypass okay?'

Deepa gave a thumbs-up.

'Sister?'

His eyes met hers and heat rose within her as they took her

back to their night in the Savoy—to the last time she'd been this close to him.

'Ready.'

Pretending he didn't exist hadn't worked all week, if she was honest with herself, and it certainly wasn't working now.

'Scalpel.'

She placed a blade firmly into his outstretched palm.

'Music.'

Soothing classical music filled the room and Lois glanced around at everyone's bent heads. All of them were concentrating on the job at hand, Toby humming lightly. She placed the suction tubing, giving Max clear sight into the opened thorax. He held out his hand and she handed him retractors, clamps, artery forceps and cannulas without him having to ask.

'Ready for bypass in five. ACT okay?'

'ACT is fine,' replied Toby. 'But BP is in his boots and sats are down. He's lost a lot of circulating volume.'

'Cannulating,' said Max, taking the lines from Lois, who held them out ready.

Watching him, keeping careful track of the progress he was making, she ensured she was ready to pass the correct instrument at exactly the right moment. Every second counted—this patient was in a bad way. It was mesmerising, watching Max at work. His hands moved deftly and with precision. Even though he was under enormous pressure.

'Dividing the lines.'

He hadn't looked up since the surgery had begun. Head bent, moving swiftly, calling out instructions, he worked on his patient. A patient who, if Max hadn't been around when he had, and reacted as quickly as he had, and if he hadn't made a highly irregular request of her, might no longer be with them. It was still touch and go, but at least Max's actions were giving him a chance.

'Off and clamped,' said Deepa.

'Aorta connected,' he replied. 'Line test good?'

'Good swing and pressure,' said Deepa.

'Cannulating atrium...return losses,' replied Max. 'Ready for bypass?'

'All good.'

'On bypass,' said Max.

And then he looked up, meeting her gaze, making her heart kick against her ribs. He had one moment while the perfusionist made her checks. And he'd chosen to spend it looking at her. Dark-lashed, deep blue, his penetrating eyes looked up from over his mask, the weight of immense responsibility visible in them. The soft classical music still played and the ventilator clicked as Toby paused it. Monitors beeped. It was her and him. And despite the fact that he'd walked out on her, leaving her hurt and humiliated, she didn't want it to end.

'Bypass is good,' confirmed Deepa, breaking the spell.

And Max was gone. Back to his work. She could breathe again.

Max Templeton had cast some sort of spell over her, and if she had the time to think about it—which she didn't right now—she'd know he'd just made her want him now as much as she'd wanted him all along. And that was exactly what she'd wanted to avoid.

Jay Vallini appeared in the doorway. 'Want me to scrub, chief?'

Max didn't look up. 'I wouldn't mind. He's lost a lot of blood, and the aortic arch is so friable it's difficult to find anywhere suitable to graft.'

'I'm not too surprised it's leaked,' replied Jay, disappearing to the scrub room. 'His vessel disease is very advanced.'

'There's just no viable tissue,' replied Max.

Lois glanced at him. There was a hint of tightness in his voice.

'Pressures aren't great, guys,' said Toby, glancing up at them. 'Blood markers are showing AKI.'

'One hour on bypass,' said Deepa.

The pressure on Max was huge. This patient was deteriorating, and it didn't look as though they were heading in the right direction.

'It's not looking great, Max,' said Jay, now standing beside him and inspecting the patient's open thorax. 'There's nowhere else to graft.'

Max didn't look up. 'I'll find somewhere.'

'He lost most of his circulating volume before you got to him, Max,' said Toby. 'It was a pretty massive bleed. I'm not sure he's going to make it.'

Max said nothing. But Lois saw, beneath his mask, that his jaw had clenched.

'His sats aren't improving, even on bypass,' said Toby, 'and I'm giving him whole blood and packed red cells. I think we're losing.'

Max sucked in a deep breath, his mask drawn inwards as he did so. 'I just need to get the graft in place. Stay with me.'

Was he talking to the team or to the patient?

Suddenly the chest cavity filled with blood.

'Damn it,' said Max. 'Clamp.'

Lois passed him a clamp, then used the suction to try to clear the area so he could see.

This was bad.

'Cannula's gone,' said Jay.

Toby looked up. 'Sats dropping.'

'Clamp is on,' replied Max.

The bleeding stopped.

'Jay, you recannulate. I'll do the graft.'

Jay Vallini sighed. 'I think it's over, Max.'

But Max ignored him. 'I'm going to put the graft here. Cannula in, Jay?'

'In,' replied the older surgeon.

But he glanced at Lois, his eyes telling her he thought this was pointless. Her head told her he was probably right, but her heart told her to cling on to the same hope Max clearly had.

She glanced at him. His jaw was set, the tendons in his neck tight.

'Sats?' he demanded.

'Improving,' replied Toby.

'Good,' said Max.

For another hour they worked on the patient and steadily his vital signs improved, remaining stable when they took him off bypass.

Lois saw the change in Max. His shoulders relaxed and his jaw unclenched. He really cared, didn't he?

'I'll close up and get him to ITU, chief,' said Jay. 'You get home; you deserve it.'

'I'll just write up the op notes,' replied Max, moving away from the operating table and snapping off his gloves.

'Do that if you must,' replied Jay. 'But then you're officially off duty—I insist. I'm covering.'

'Thanks, Jay,' said Max.

Lois caught his eye as he left the theatre, squashing any thought that he might have looked at her on purpose for some reason.

No, he'd made his feelings very clear, hadn't he?

She was good for one night.

Nothing more.

Not even good enough for breakfast the next morning.

But she'd agreed to his terms and conditions, hadn't she? She'd been warned. And she only had herself to blame for how she was feeling now.

'Suture, please, Lois.'

She forced a smile as she handed Jay Vallini a suture. She still wanted Max Templeton—and it hurt like hell that he didn't want her back.

Theatre was quiet. The machines lay silent and redundant. The music had stopped. The lights were off.

Max was still writing up the op notes in the adjoining office and he'd probably be a while. From what Lois had seen, his notes were precise and exceptionally thorough. He might be the playboy the media described him as, but she couldn't deny that he really cared about his patients.

Finally off duty, Lois had gone to get changed when she'd realised that she'd left her pager on the table in Theatre. Now, dodging back into the darkened room, she picked it up.

She sensed Max before she turned around. It was as though the air suddenly contained electrified particles of him which reached her and, on touching her skin, ignited, making it tingle.

He stood in the doorway, an imposing, impressive silhouette, backlit by the light from the scrub room. Her breath caught in her throat and she stopped dead in her tracks.

'At last.'

He walked slowly towards her into the darkness, panther-like. Lois took a step backwards as he advanced.

'I've been trying to talk to you for days. You've been avoiding me.'

'Hardly.' She took another step backwards, bumping into the theatre table where they'd been standing earlier that evening. 'I've seen you nearly every day.'

'Yet you've still managed to make yourself scarce.'

She gripped the black padded table behind her to steady herself. 'I should get back.'

'You're off shift. I need to speak to you.'

Her heart hammered in her chest. She didn't want to speak to him.

*Did she?*

'I wanted to say I'm sorry.'

'There's nothing to say sorry for.'

*There was quite a list.*

'For not being there the other morning.'

'No need.'

It was better he hadn't been there. It would only have been awkward. He clearly regretted their night together.

'I'd forgotten I had an early meeting in Westminster that morning. I couldn't miss it and—'

'You could have woken me.'

*What? Where had that come from?*

She was glad he'd slunk off and ended their ill-judged tryst. But he'd had a meeting.

*He hadn't slunk off because he'd wanted to.*

'You looked so peaceful. I didn't have the heart.'

She glanced around sharply. 'Shh…someone might hear.'

'There's no one down here…and I've locked the door.'

*'What?'*

'You've been darting out of my way any time I've come anywhere near you. I had to do something.'

He looked at her, and she couldn't think of anything but how she wanted to be lost in his eyes, his arms.

*He'd had a meeting. He hadn't slunk away because he hadn't wanted to face her. She didn't need to feel humiliated. He hadn't meant to hurt her.*

'Why didn't you tell me?'

'I told you: I'd forgotten about the meeting and only remembered when I woke—'

'No,' she cut in. 'Why didn't you tell me afterwards?'

'I tried. You were avoiding me. I couldn't get near you. And every time I tried you apparently had to be at some meeting or other, or anywhere else I wasn't.'

'Have you heard of telephones?'

He sighed. 'I don't have your number—and before you say anything, I couldn't very well ask any of the staff for it, could I? How would that have looked?'

She lifted her chin. He was probably right. It would have looked odd to ask for her mobile number.

'Email?'

*'Email?'* He repeated the word as though it was the most ridiculous thing he'd ever heard. *'For the attention of Sister Newington. Apologies I was absent from bed the morning after*

*we slept together, but I had an appointment with the health
minister which had completely slipped my mind. See you on
the ward round.'* He folded his arms, resting his chin on his
fist. 'Hmm... I'm not sure that's great hospital email etiquette.'

'Oh, all right—point taken. But you could have tried harder.
I don't remember you trying to speak to me particularly.'

He spread his arms wide. 'Lois, I've tried everything. I sat
down beside you at lunch the other day and you leapt up, telling
me your break time was over. I waited for you after the Gold
Command meeting, but apparently you had to rush off. I even
went to the chapel to see if you were doing your choir practice.'

Lois rolled her eyes. 'Well, I won't ever be doing that again—
it got me into all kinds of trouble.'

'Lois...'

He took a step towards her and she gripped the theatre table
more tightly. His warm, musky scent filled her nostrils and she
was immediately transported back a week, to the opulence of
the Savoy and the very nearly perfect night they'd spent together—marred only because he'd disappeared the next morning, leaving her wondering why.

'I'm sorry I didn't try harder, but I've finally tracked you
down now and I want to apologise. I couldn't get out of the
meeting but I wish I could have stayed. Maybe I should have
woken you, but I didn't have the heart. I thought about leaving a note, but I didn't have time—and anyway, I'd intended
to be back before you checked out. But you'd gone by the time
I got there.'

'I stayed for hours! I had breakfast...watched a film. You
hardly *rushed* back.'

He sighed. 'I had a lot to do that morning and it took longer
than I'd expected. I'm sorry. I know how it must have looked.'

'It looked like you regretted it.' She met his gaze, determined
not to fall under the spell of his eyes.

He swallowed, appearing to struggle to decide which words

to speak, and when he did they were spoken with conviction, even though they were only a whisper.

'Far from it. Every moment of that night is etched in my memory.'

Her heart slammed into her ribs.

*Did he really mean that?*

'I'm not here for long, Lois, but while I *am* here I'd like to spend some time getting to know you. If you don't want to then just say, but I haven't been able to stop thinking about you since that night.'

*Same here.*

Her mind was whirling. She didn't want a relationship. She'd fought her instincts when Emilio had been making his advances. Not hard enough, as it turned out.

*And why had that been?*

Because, stupidly, she'd believed his lies. Emilio had appeared, fed her a few compliments and she'd decided to rebel against everything her mother had ever told her. And it had ended in her complete humiliation. Emilio had used her. Was she about to make the same mistake with Max?

But Max was looking at her with those *Take me now* eyes, bewitching her, enticing her to believe his words…

He lifted his hand, touching her chin, lifting it between thumb and forefinger. Heat flooded through her as she looked into his eyes…shooting through her and settling between her thighs, exactly where he'd touched her that night and sent waves of pleasure coursing through her.

She didn't want this.

*But she did.*

He held her gaze and her resolve weakened.

His voice was low and husky. 'I missed you that morning.'

*Dared she believe him? If she did, would she find out too late that it was a lie?*

'I wanted to wake up with you and make love with you again, with the sunshine streaming in through the windows.'

Then it was better that he *had* gone before she woke up—because he would have been disappointed. The only way she'd been able to get naked with him that night had been because she'd known the only light had come from a few flickering candles. The summer sunshine streaming in through the enormous windows in the morning would have been a complete dealbreaker.

'Well, you had a meeting, so…'

Tilting her chin, she took a breath, trying to ignore how his warm scent and the nearness of him gave her butterflies, which wouldn't listen to her when she silently begged them to stop dancing in her stomach.

This was Emilio all over again, and she wasn't falling for it.

'So that's why I'm here…that's why I've been trying to track you down for days and speak to you…why I've had to resort to locking the door to a theatre.'

'I can't actually believe you've done that. Isn't that entrapment, or something?'

He took a step back, his brow suddenly furrowed, and she immediately missed his proximity. Slipping his hand into his pocket, he produced a silver door key, offering it to her.

She looked down at it. She could easily take it from him, unlock the door and leave. She didn't want another T-shirt with *Lois is a gullible idiot* printed on it.

So why wasn't she reaching for the key?

Because, in spite of what she kept trying to tell herself, he wasn't like Emilio, was he? He *hadn't* used her. He'd given her plenty of opportunities to walk away that night—just as he was doing now. But she hadn't wanted to and she didn't want to now.

Besides, he wasn't exactly committing to spending the rest of his life with her, was he? This was a no-risk, once-in-a-lifetime chance to enjoy life, have some fun. No promises, no expectations, no danger of a broken heart. She was just creating some exciting memories to look back on one day. And proving her mother and Emilio wrong. She *was* attractive.

The *other* Lois was back. The risk-taking, daring, you-only-live-once Lois from the night of the show.

The very same Lois who'd slept with Max a week ago.

*And had the night of her life.*

'You've driven me crazy all week, Lois.' He was still standing back from her…cautious…watching. 'I needed to explain and I couldn't get near you.'

She searched his eyes for tell-tale signs that he was lying… and didn't see any. He took a step closer and she gripped the table, her nails digging into the thick black rubber.

'That day in the staff restaurant, when you ran off as soon as you saw me approaching…even though you'd left half your coffee behind… I so nearly came after you.'

She dropped her gaze so that she could take a breath.

He took a step.

There was only a breath of air between them now.

And that was too much.

'Lois?'

She looked up into piercing blue eyes and was instantly lost…immediately transported back to the hotel suite, when she'd stood before him and he'd slipped her velvet gown from her shoulders. Her skin prickled with fizzling champagne bubbles.

He paused, his eyes seeking and clearly finding her acquiescence.

And then he kissed her.

After the micro second it took her to return his kiss, he deepened it, then traced a line of kisses to her throat. This felt as right now as it had in the hotel over a week ago. And the reason she'd thought about little else since was right there, in his kiss. Heat blazed through her and her skin burned for his touch. Reaching up, she wove her arms around his neck, drawing him closer. He groaned and whispered her name as he lifted his head from her throat, trailing soft kisses back up her neck before his focus returned to her lips, now warm, swollen, and desperately wanting to taste more of him.

'Are you sure the door is locked?' she murmured.

'I wouldn't do *this* if I wasn't sure…raise your arms.'

And, taking the hem of her scrub top, he lifted it up, pulling it over her shoulders and head, letting it drop onto the table behind her.

He took a long breath as he looked at her, raw desire flaring in his eyes, orange flames blazing within the dark blue pools.

'You are so unbelievably gorgeous.'

And she felt it.

Hooking his fingers under the straps of her bra, he pulled them down before reaching around her back, unclasping it. The weight of the release of her breasts into his warm hands as he cupped them, his thumbs skimming her nipples as they peaked at his touch made her gasp.

'Max…'

His hands held her waist, his fingers slipping under the waistband of her scrub trousers, pushing them down until they fell around her ankles and she could step out of them. She pulled at his top, reaching up, her hands running the length of his hard, toned torso as she did so. He grasped it, taking it from her when she could reach no further, tearing it off over his head and throwing it behind her onto the table.

When he lifted her, she instinctively wrapped her legs around his waist, gasping as the hard evidence of his arousal nudged her. The theatre scrubs did nothing to restrain his desire, and the ache deep within her only intensified as, dipping his head, he took one nipple and brushed it agonisingly lightly with his tongue, making her arch backwards, face upturned to the ceiling. Her body pushed into his, wanting only to be closer. He turned his attention to the other nipple, and the sweet agony at the loss of his mouth on her was only momentary as he sucked. Her hand went to his head, fingers raking through his dark hair, bringing him closer, urging him on, needing more.

Pushing her knickers to one side, he skimmed his thumb over her, taking her breath. Her arms around his neck, she adjusted her position so that she was over him, in exactly the place she wanted to be. The need to have him inside her was almost more than was bearable.

'Hold on tight,' he whispered.

Her eyes widened and she held on around his neck, her thighs gripping his waist. Suddenly she remembered their motorbike ride dash across London, when he'd given her the same instruction.

'Because we're not going for a Sunday drive?' she said.

He grinned: a wide, sexy-as-hell smile which lit up his flaming blue eyes with an erotic wickedness.

'No, it's not going to be a Sunday drive, Lois.'

Letting go of her with one hand, he pushed his scrubs down before grasping her thighs again firmly.

'You sure?'

His voice was dark, throaty, heavy, his eyes brim-full of desire. His erection was poised—tantalising torture, ready for her agreement—and his ripped chest was expanding and falling with his heavy breathing, the muscled contours catching the dim light coming from the next room, making her want to touch them.

But she needed to hold on.

'I'm sure.'

The words left her lips, but barely had a chance to escape into the crackling air around them. Because no sooner had she said them than his lips were on hers, crushing them, silencing her and the soft moan that followed.

'Hold on,' he whispered again, his eyes glinting.

She held his gaze as he thrust inside her with a groan, closing her eyes only a moment after he closed his own as hot desire flooded through her. Then, exquisitely, he held still, just for a moment, allowing them to savour the feeling…the sweet bliss and the agony of wanting more all rolled into one. And then he began to move…slowly…his eyes locked onto hers.

As she arched back, taking him deeper, the look on his face in the dimly lit room, told her she'd just intensified his pleasure too, and he picked up the pace, his breathing deepening, his skin glistening with a sheen of sweat. The strong muscles of his chest and arms were taut, moving rhythmically like a beautiful machine, sending wave after relentless wave of pleasure flooding through her, filling her; warming her. He was sending her closer and closer to the edge with every stroke as he drove into her, building the sweet pleasure-pain tension deep inside her until she groaned his name, letting her head fall back as he took a nipple into his mouth.

She shattered around him, eyes squeezed shut, whispering his name. 'Max…'

'Don't let go.'

'No,' she managed. 'I won't.'

He slowed his rhythm, as if he wanted to savour his release a moment longer, but she knew the moment he allowed it as a deep, guttural groan left his lips. His head went back as he thrust one last time, and the light hit the curves of his chest as he arched, beaded and glistening with sweat, his breathing fast and ragged until he lost control over its rate and surrendered to the all-encompassing moment of oblivion.

She let out a satisfied sigh. She'd made a choice tonight. She was choosing to live a little.

And it felt amazing.

# CHAPTER ELEVEN

LOIS FOUND HIM in the chapel, sitting at the back, elbows on his knees, head in his hands.

She sat down on the bench beside him. 'You did everything you could, Max.'

He sat up, placing his own hand over hers where she'd rested it on his thigh. 'Obviously not everything. His daughter was devastated.'

'Everyone else had given up on him. You gave him a chance and an extra week of life he wouldn't have had. Don't beat yourself up.'

He withdrew his hand. 'I should have got that graft in more quickly.'

'Max, stop it. He was desperately ill. Even Jay Vallini said he'd been in two minds whether to operate in the first place. It's really sad, but you gave him a chance—it just didn't work out.'

'Because of me.' He stood, clearly wanting to leave.

'Where are you going?'

'Home.'

'Do you want me to come with you?'

She remained sitting, looking up at him, into those indigo eyes which couldn't hide his anguish. He cared deeply about his patients, and it had become more and more obvious the longer she spent with him. He tried to hide it, for some reason, and most people might not have noticed the little giveaway signs that revealed just how much his patients meant to him.

The way he touched their hand, arm or shoulder when he spoke to them…how he'd sit with relatives answering questions until they had no questions left…how he came in early to check every patient each morning and stayed late doing the same before going home, even after a busy clinic or theatre list.

'No.'

'But I put a chilli in the slow cooker this morning and you said you'd be my guinea pig and try it.'

He looked down at her and she gave him her best puppy dog eyes, complete with turned down mouth.

'You promised.'

He shouldn't be on his own tonight. Not when he was feeling the way he clearly was. In the last week they'd spent almost every evening together, either at his flat or hers, and tonight it was her turn to cook.

A soft, gentle smile curved his lips. 'I did promise that, come to think of it.'

Returning his smile, she stood. 'Come on, then.'

He still looked forlorn. Her instinct was to take him into her arms, but they'd both agreed to keep whatever it was that was happening between them outside working hours—well away from the all-seeing gossipmongers of the hospital and hidden from any potential press interest.

Anyway, she had the rest of the evening to try to lift his mood.

Lois had the most comfortable sofa he'd ever sat on. It was as large as a bed, strewn with brightly coloured throws and huge cushions, and you sank down into it as if it was a giant marshmallow. It would easily sleep a family of four.

He set the wine glasses and what remained of the bottle of wine they'd had with dinner on the coffee table. Lois lit the candles in the jars she had dotted about the room, then sank down beside him. Draping his arm around her shoulder, she nestled into him, sipping her wine.

This felt comfortable…right. He kissed the top of her head and she looked up, a soft smile on her lips. But he tensed when he saw she wore the same look she'd worn in the chapel earlier.

A look of concern.

For him.

And he didn't want to see that…not in anyone's eyes and especially not in hers.

'Do you want to talk?' asked Lois.

'Not really.'

*Not at all. Because that would involve bringing up subjects he really didn't want to talk about, wouldn't it? And if she knew the truth she might reject him, as everyone else had done.*

For some reason, it was more important than anything that she didn't do that.

'Actually, forget that,' she said. 'We *need* to talk.'

'We do?'

'Your patient. George Frost.'

'Oh.'

*Damn it.*

'You struggle with it, don't you?'

'With what?'

'Losing a patient?'

His breathing deepened.

*Don't go there, Lois.*

'A little.'

Not the fullest answer he'd ever given to a question, but it was more than he'd ever given anyone else.

'Because of what happened to your brother?'

He stiffened.

*Too close to the truth.*

'Probably.'

She sat up straight, his arm falling from her shoulders as she turned to face him. He watched the dancing flame from one of the candles, not wanting to see any hint of kindness in her eyes. Tiny wisps of dark smoke drifted up from the wick, swirling upwards before disappearing. He drained his wine glass.

'That wasn't your fault either.'

His stomach clenched. In his head he knew that as a twelve-year-old he couldn't have been expected to resuscitate his brother...not really. But his head wasn't in charge of how he felt. It had been *his* fault. He hadn't done anything to help when William had collapsed. He'd not only let William down—he'd ruined their family.

Afterwards, the family had never been the same again. His mother had barely been able to bring herself to look at him. His father had found comfort at the bottom of a bottle, and Max struggled to remember ever seeing him completely sober ever again. He'd died almost a year to the day after William. And Max's world had imploded for a second time.

If he told Lois all that—if he could even find the words to do so—she'd never look at him in the same way again, would she? She'd feel sorry for him...pity him. And he didn't want that. Which meant he really didn't want this conversation.

'I guess losing William just means that I don't want to lose anybody else, and that's why I find it difficult to lose a patient. Grief is hard, isn't it? I don't want to put anyone through that if I can help it. So, yes, I have a tendency to morph into a bit of a raging bull if I think one of my patients might die and, yes, I'll do anything to save them. I'm well aware that people around me sometimes think I'm an arrogant braggart at those times.'

'No-o-o!' said Lois, grinning. 'I've never heard anyone say that.'

He laughed. 'I'm sure you have.'

Lois pretended to think hard. 'No, not arrogant braggart... Maybe a pompous prat, or an egomaniac, or...'

'Okay, okay, you can stop. I get the gist.'

At least he'd managed to change the subject.

'Tell me about William.'

He stiffened and drew in a breath.

*Maybe he hadn't.*

But he could tell her a little.

'We were twins…best mates…did everything together. We were as thick as thieves most of the time, but we could argue and scrap like we'd been trained for it at others. We were close.'

'I'd have loved a brother or sister.'

'I only had him for twelve years.' He picked up his phone and scrolled, stopping at a photograph and holding it to show her. 'This is us.'

She glanced at him before looking at the photo and gasped when she saw it. 'You're exactly the same as each other! What a lovely photo.'

He managed a thin smile. 'That was taken a week before he died.'

A week before his world imploded.

She sighed and looked into his eyes. 'I'm so sorry, Max. I can't begin to imagine how hard that must have been. Were you there when it happened?'

He swallowed. 'We were in the garden, playing football. He just collapsed. He was running around one minute and gone the next…snuffed out like a candle…in a second.'

She closed her eyes for a long moment, opening them again and looking at him with such pity he could barely look back at her.

'Your parents must have been devastated. Their only comfort would have been in still having you.'

The bitter laugh left his lips before he realised. 'Not really, no.'

But he didn't want to give her the whole story—the complete account of how he'd let his brother and his family down and how his parents had never forgiven him. What if she felt the same? What if she blamed him too?

'My father died a year later, and I was shipped off to boarding school soon after. My mother barely spoke to me after that—other than to remind me never to have children myself.'

'But you don't have it, do you…the valve condition?'

'No. I was checked out almost straight away after William died. My echo was normal. But of course there's a genetic risk. I'd never have children…no way. I'd never want to put another family through that.'

'I see… I can't imagine what you all went through. It's awful your father died, and so sad your mother reacted in that way. Have you tried to build a relationship with her as an adult?'

He sighed. 'A few times. There's only so much rejection a person can take, though. I've given up trying now. It's too late.'

'Perhaps, because you look so alike, rather than seeing you as a comfort she was reminded of William and it hurt too much. Still, it's terrible she reacted that way.'

'In truth, it's one of the reasons I'm leaving for California. Living in the same city, I feel obliged to go and see her. But every time I do, I get told the same thing and I'm reminded that she'd prefer William to be there than me. I can't keep doing that—and quite honestly the sooner I leave this place, the better. Anyway, enough of this… I sound like I'm looking for pity—which I'm absolutely not. Drink?'

He wanted to end this conversation. Lois was too kind, and spilling everything out to her would be way too easy.

'Please,' she replied, shifting a little so he could reach the wine bottle.

'Let's change the subject,' he said.

She held her glass out and he took it and topped it up.

'Any news on the screening programme?'

He relaxed. 'Going to plan. The NHS trusts in the pilot have received their funding and are completely on board. The first scans will begin at the end of the month. Which reminds me—how do you fancy a weekend in Monte Carlo?'

'Seriously?' She took the glass from him.

He grinned. 'I've been asked to go and visit a patient I operated on six months ago. He was a Hollywood heartthrob in his day. He gave me a very handsome donation for the programme and he's on holiday in Monte Carlo…on his yacht, of course. He's wondering if I'd pop over to review him…all expenses paid.'

'You're kidding?'

He took a sip of wine. 'No, not kidding. And I want you to come with me.'

'When? I'll have to see when I'm on shift.'

He smiled. 'Lois, you're the only person in the entire world who, when offered an all-expenses-paid trip to stay on a luxury superyacht in Monte Carlo, would say she has to check her shifts first.'

She raised an eyebrow and grinned at him. 'Well, I do… So your wealthy Hollywood patient will have to wait until I'm free.'

Drawing her legs up onto the sofa, she nestled into his side as he planted a kiss on top of her head. He'd escaped the inquisition about what had happened with William…for now. But if they continued to get closer, as they had been, it would surely come up again, and he was pretty sure that Lois wouldn't let him get away with avoiding the topic a second time.

# CHAPTER TWELVE

ANCHORED JUST OFFSHORE, the yacht had a top deck that was a perfect vantage point to take in the stunning alpine vista. Belle Epoque and art deco architecture mingled with ultra-modern skyscrapers tapering towards the shoreline, nestling below a backdrop of rugged mountains. The harbour was crowded with watercraft: enormous cruise liners, yachts of all sizes, brightly coloured bobbing boats and RIBs. The sunlight on the blue of the Mediterranean made it shimmer with almost blinding brightness.

Lois marvelled at the view. Max lay beside her on a sun lounger, eyes closed, shades covering them, naked apart from swimming shorts, and glistening with the sun lotion she'd just more than enjoyed applying to his perfect body.

'Are you ogling me, Sister Newington?' he asked, without opening his eyes.

'Just checking I haven't missed a bit.'

She *had* been ogling him. Watching him and wondering how on earth she'd ended up here, being wined and dined by one of Hollywood's finest actors, on a superyacht, in one of the most exclusive resorts in the world.

And besides all that she got to sleep with the gorgeous man who lay beside her, looking like a Greek god who'd just competed at Olympia.

*If her mother could see her now...*

*'It won't last. He's just using you for what he can get and*

*you're giving it to him. Men want women they can show off in front of their friends, boast about, imagine other men being jealous over. They don't want a plump plain Jane.'*

She could almost hear her mother's voice, scornful, disapproving, contemptuous. But her mother wasn't here, was she?

Max sat up slowly and removed his shades. 'So it's okay if I check you out too, is it…? Just to make sure you haven't missed anywhere with your sunscreen?'

He grinned, and Lois pulled her sarong around her. She'd braved wearing a swimsuit—before they'd jetted off she had scouted round the shops to buy one that promised to hold her in all the right places, also finding a couple of matching sarongs for an extra layer of security.

'I was just going to get a drink,' she replied. 'Do you want one?'

'I want *you*,' said Max, standing, striding over, and straddling her lounger before planting a kiss on her lips. 'I'm not sure how I'm managing to keep my hands off you…lying there semi-naked, looking like a dream.'

She took his face in her hands, pulled him to her and kissed him back. 'Well, you'll have to try—because we're not exactly alone here, are we?'

The yacht had more staff than guests—which of course had its advantages, but meant that someone might appear offering food or drink at any moment.

'I'll save you for later, then. Fancy a swim?'

Her heart sank. The prospect of walking across the deck in front of Max in nothing but a swimsuit, even if it was one that promised to hold everything in, filled her with dread. He'd seen her naked many times in the last few weeks, since they'd embarked on their very secret affair, but only ever in lighting that had been low enough for her to feel comfortable. The bright morning sunshine of this glorious Mediterranean summer's day gave her nowhere to hide.

'I think I'll just stay here. You go.'

'Come on, it'll be nice. And besides…' He grinned and slipped the edge of her sarong from her shoulder. 'I want to see you properly in that sexy crimson swimsuit.'

Every part of her screamed *No!* and she shifted her position, pulling the sarong back into place. 'It's not sexy…it's just a swimsuit.'

'Everything on you is sexy. A bath towel…a onesie…your uniform.' He drew in an exaggerated breath and pretended to shiver. 'No one else wears that uniform like you do.'

'When are you going into the clinic to give Art his check-up?'

'Why are you changing the subject?'

'I've just remembered you're here to give Art his check-up, that's all.'

'After lunch. He's taking us to the casino this evening, as a thank-you. If I go for a dip, will you slather me in sunscreen again afterwards?'

'My pleasure,' she replied, picking up her book again. 'Enjoy.'

She watched over the top of her book as Max strode towards the pool. It was like watching an advert for male swimwear—except that she wasn't looking at a TV, he was right there in front of her. Bronzed, lean and beautifully muscled. He sat on the edge of the pool and dropped down into the blue water, his head disappearing before surfacing again, dark hair wet and blacker than ever.

'It's lovely, Lois. Come and dangle your feet if you don't fancy a swim.'

It was tempting.

And it wasn't.

'Maybe… I might just finish my chapter.'

He gave a thumbs-up and struck out, making his way across the pool with long strokes. The pool sparkled in the sunlight as his arms sliced through the water, scattering glittering crystals back onto the surface. It did look inviting.

*Would the crimson swimsuit do everything the persuasive sales assistant had promised? Hold her in? Smooth her out?*

There was only one way to find out. Anyway, Max had told her so often now how much he loved her figure she was almost beginning to believe it. *Almost.*

Clutching the sarong around her, she stood and walked quickly over to the pool, but a wave of nausea washed over her and she sat down on the side, closing her eyes until the accompanying dizziness passed. The midday heat here was something else.

Max smiled up at her and stood, smoothing his hair back from his forehead as he rose out of the water, skin glistening.

'You okay?' he asked, frowning. 'You look a bit pale.'

'I'm fine. I stood up a bit quickly, that's all. It's the heat.'

'Are you coming in? It'll cool you off.'

'I'm okay here, thanks. I'll watch.'

'Okay. Kiss me first.'

Lois pretended to look horrified, and pulled back as he moved in for a kiss. 'No, you're all wet.'

He grinned a mischievous, sexy grin, and she laughed as he moved closer, standing between her knees. He took her by the waist, pulling her towards him, planting a kiss on her oh, so ready for him lips.

She looked down at her costume. 'You've made me all wet.'

He looked down too, and bit his lip in mock contrition. 'Oh, dear. You may as well come in, then.'

She laughed. 'You're incorrigible.'

'I think you might have said that to me before.'

'It must be true, then.' She prodded him playfully on the shoulder, but he still had hold of her waist and she shrieked when he lifted her. 'Put me down!'

'You said it.'

He let go of her and she splashed down into the chest-deep water, letting out another shriek, her sarong floating up behind her.

'You…!'

'Now, now, Lois, let's not have any bad language on board this very posh yacht.'

Sweeping her hand through the water and upwards, she sent a cascade of glittering water over him, making him cover his face. Laughing, she did it again. But he responded in kind and drenched her. The sarong was soaking wet. There was absolutely no point in keeping it on.

Apart from the fact that it covered her *'voluptuous'* figure.

*Mutton dressed as lamb.*

No.

Stop.

They were words from the past. She didn't need to hear those words right now. Right now, she wanted this moment.

'God, you look gorgeous.'

He'd stopped scooping water and now stood a few feet away. An Adonis—just looking at her. No, not just looking. *Admiring.* The look in his eyes was one of admiration.

Butterflies.

Dancing butterflies.

Twirling, looping, fluttering.

There was no reason not to believe him. Shrugging the sarong from her shoulders, she let it fall into the water, her eyes not leaving his as she did so, watching him as he drew in a breath, pausing before moving through the water towards her and taking her in his arms. Drawing her in to him, he kissed the top of her head.

'You look so good I could devour you.'

She allowed him to pull her into his arms. Was she making the same mistakes she had with Emilio? Was the same old deep-seated need to be validated by someone else still lurking like a predator below the surface, ready to pounce? Even though she'd tried so hard to unmask it, understand it and overcome it?

He let go of her and stood back, looking into her eyes again, a frown creasing his forehead and concern etched on his face.

'You didn't hug me back. What's wrong?'

'Nothing. Go and enjoy your swim. I might get out and read a little more.'

'I don't want you to get out and read. I want to know why you suddenly changed.'

'I'm just not that keen on swimming, that's all.'

'Or on receiving compliments…especially about how you look?'

She stared back at him. He'd mentioned compliments before…that night after the show. But he'd never been specific about the sort of compliments she struggled with the most. He was right, though.

'Where does that come from, Lois?'

Her heart rate notched up. 'From looking in the mirror.'

She laughed. If she made light of it maybe he would too.

But his frown only deepened. 'Why would you say that?'

'Well, I'm not exactly a supermodel, Max, am I?'

She forced a laugh. *Keep it light.*

'Thank goodness. You're amazing as you are.'

'Voluptuous?'

She smiled, but could see immediately that Max wasn't convinced by it.

'That was a compliment,' he said.

'Well, *"voluptuous"* sounds much better than fat.'

Why could she suddenly feel the sting of tears? She turned away from him and began to wade towards the edge of the pool, but he reached for her arm and she was forced to turn back to look at him.

Deep blue eyes looked into her own. 'You're not fat.'

'No, I much prefer voluptuous—that's what I've called myself ever since you said it.'

*Don't cry, Lois.*

She tilted her chin. 'So, thanks for that.'

But somehow trying to smile again only brought her closer to tears.

His frown returned. 'Somebody has hurt you, Lois. Who? Tell me.'

His eyes searched hers…beautiful, earnest blue eyes, lulling her in as always.

Did she want to tell him?

She swallowed, staring down at her hands, swishing them on the surface of the water. For some reason she wanted to explain to him. It was because his eyes told her that he cared about her answer.

'She didn't mean it.'

'Who didn't?'

'My mother.'

*'What?'*

'I understand why…now. It took me a long time, but I realised that she just did it to keep me by her side…because she needed me.'

'What did she do?'

'I was her carer when I was growing up, and she was quite needy. I did everything for her—she never left the house.' Lois reached for her sarong, scooping it from the water, needing to hold on to something. 'She'd tell me I wasn't pretty…that I was overweight…and that no one would ever want me… But it's fine. I know why she did it. I'm fine with it now.'

Max stood with his hands on his head. His mouth had fallen open. 'Well, that explains a few things. Why didn't you say anything before?'

'Why would I? And what do you mean, it explains a few things?'

'You're uncomfortable whenever anyone compliments you—like you can't believe it. You're so capable and confident at work, and yet you can suddenly close down. Sometimes I only have to look at you a certain way, or tell you that you look beautiful, and your whole demeanour changes. Oh, Lois, I hate it that you went through that. I wish I could change it.'

'You have, Max. You've definitely helped. It's just a slower process than I'd imagined, that's all. But I'd never have worn this until I met you, for starters.'

She spread her arms wide, giving him her best *Ta-da!* pose.

He smiled. 'If I said you looked amazing, would you believe me?'

She drew in a breath. *Would she?* There was nothing but honesty in his face.

'No, don't answer that. It was unfair to put you on the spot like that. Hear this instead: Lois, you look amazing in that swimsuit. Stunning, gorgeous and sexy as hell. So, come here and give me that hug.'

She waded through the water towards him, a smile spreading slowly across her face as she watched his eyes darken in that way they did…the way he looked at her when he wanted her. He took her into his arms and she wound her own around him, pulling him closer, leaving him in no doubt that she was hugging him.

He dipped his head, nuzzling into her neck. 'You don't know what you do to me, Lois.'

But she did. She could feel it through the crimson fabric.

# CHAPTER THIRTEEN

'SHALL WE WALK up to the clinic rather than get the car?' asked
Max as they alighted from the tender in the harbour. 'We should
make the most of this gorgeous weather. It'll probably be raining back in London.'

The heat was so intense that she'd have been glad of a car,
really, but Max was right. In another few days they'd be back
in London. She was glad of the wide-brimmed straw hat the
woman at the swimwear shop had somehow persuaded her
to buy, and she pulled it low to shield her eyes as they wound
their way up through narrow streets towards the clinic for Art's
check-up.

Stopping beside a low wall, with a stunning view down
the cliffside and out to sea, Max stood behind Lois, his arms
around her waist. 'Beautiful, isn't it?'

She was glad he was holding on to her. Was it the heat or
the height that was making her feel light-headed? Maybe they
should get a car back…

'Gorgeous.'

He released his hold of her. 'I want a picture of you… Turn
around so I have both you and the view.'

And that was when everything went black.

In a haze, Lois felt the squeeze of a BP cuff on her arm and the
light pressure of a sats probe on her finger.

*Where was she?*

'BP's up to a hundred over sixty,' came an unfamiliar voice with a French accent.

'I need an ECG.'

Max's voice…steady but laced with concern. He was clearly addressing someone else. Unfamiliar fingers lifted her top and placed stickers on her chest. Her head felt heavy and nausea swept through her.

Unfamiliar faces swam into view. She must have fainted.

*It would be the heat.*

'Sharp scratch on your arm, Lois.'

A different voice. A blood sample.

*This was all very unnecessary.*

She'd just overheated, and was perhaps a little dehydrated. She tried to sit up, but suddenly Max came into view and he gently pressed her down.

'Lie down, Lois. You fainted, and we're just trying to find out why. You'll be fine, but stay lying down until your BP comes back up.'

'ECG, Doctor.'

One of the nurses handed him a sheet of printout paper.

Lois watched his face as he read it, the concern vanishing as he looked at her and smiled. 'It's fine. A little tachy, as expected, but otherwise normal.'

'BP one ten over seventy.'

'Feel as though you can sit up a little?' asked Max.

'Yes, please. I don't like being a patient.'

He held out his arm and she took it, pulling herself forward as one of the nurses levered the backrest out.

Max handed her a glass of water. 'Drink this—you're probably a bit dehydrated. I'm going to call Art and postpone his appointment until tomorrow—you need to rest.'

'There's no need to do that. I'm fine now.'

But Max had taken his phone out of his pocket and was already tapping the screen. 'I'm calling him and I'm going to get the car to take us back. Don't argue.'

She sipped at the cold water, embarrassed by the fuss, her

inbuilt loathing of being the centre of attention compelling her to want to run. But Max was clearly not letting her go anywhere until he was satisfied that she was okay.

And suddenly she realised why that felt so extraordinary. It was because it was new. No one had ever cared that much before.

Max had already changed into smart trousers and a shirt and was sitting out on the balcony of their cabin, looking across the pink-and-peach-streaked early-evening sky, thinking about earlier, when Lois had fainted, and what it had done to him.

His reaction had been instinctive, fuelled by the surge of adrenaline which had rushed through him, his mind racing, automatically fearing the worst…that she had an undiagnosed cardiac condition.

He'd carried her into the clinic, his heart banging against his ribs, where he'd barked out urgent orders to the staff, fear gripping him, his ambition to end his perceived reputation as arrogant forgotten.

It had been much more than his need to save every patient that had made him feel sick to his stomach for the few minutes it had taken him to realise her heart was fine.

Lois was much more than a patient.

Much more than a colleague.

And she'd become much more than a short-term, mutually agreed hook-up.

*How on earth had that happened?*

Because the most unlikely thing had happened, that was how.

He'd fallen in love.

*So now what was he supposed to do? Tell her? Did he even dare to hope that she felt the same? Would it make any difference to anything if she did?*

Her life was in London and his new life—his long-planned fresh start—was five thousand miles away. Only three more weeks before he left London. That had always been the plan.

Get the screening programme over the line and then wheel-spin out of there.

But as each day passed and his leaving date got closer his heart grew heavier.

'Can you do my zip?'

Turning to look back inside the cabin, he drew in a breath, taking her in. Wearing a black, sleeveless, knee-length cocktail dress, fitted at the waist and curving over her hips, she was elegance personified. A double string of pearls hung at her throat, drawing his eye down to where blonde curls lay on the generous curves of her breasts. His instinctive reaction didn't surprise him—he'd got used to Lois having that effect on him.

He left the balcony and walked over to her. 'You look gorgeous...far too good to waste on going to the casino... Let's stay here.'

Lois managed to dodge his kiss, laughing and pretending to look horrified. 'No, no, no. I've spent ages putting this face on—don't mess it up.'

He gave a fake groan and grinned at her. 'Here, I'd better do that zip, then.'

Running his finger down her spine, he zipped her up, planting a light kiss on her shoulder when he'd completed the task. He badly wanted to swing her round to face him and kiss her full on the lips, but she'd already slipped her heels on, picked up her clutch bag and shawl, and was heading for the door.

'Are you sure you feel well enough to go tonight?' he asked.

She grinned at him, and every promise he'd made to himself not to fall in love vanished.

'I'm fine. And anyway, according to you, I've got to lose my gambling virginity.'

'If you're sure you're okay?' he replied.

She never failed to surprise him—strong, sassy Lois.

'Here, you've forgotten your phone.' He picked her phone up from the table and handed it to her, glancing at the screen and frowning. 'You've got a missed call. It's a French number. Could be your blood test results.'

## CHAPTER FOURTEEN

'I CAN CHECK it later,' said Lois. 'The driver will be waiting, and the—'

'Check it first,' Max cut in. 'Please.'

'The most it's going to show is mild dehydration.'

'Let's just make sure. They've left a voicemail—it'll only take you a minute to listen to it.'

'Okay.'

Someone being so concerned about her was definitely still alien but oddly nice at the same time. She picked it up and dialled, listened to the voicemail.

And froze.

Hands shaking, she pressed Repeat and listened again, unable to take in the words.

*Tu es enceinte.*

You're pregnant.

She looked down at the phone as though it was something she didn't recognise.

*It didn't make sense. The test must be wrong.*

But her recent nausea, the light-headedness and the faint suddenly all made sense.

The phone fell out of her hands onto the sofa, where it landed with a soft thud.

Max's words were echoing in her head…

*'I'd never risk having children.'*

*'The sooner I leave this place the better.'*

She looked up into deep blue eyes, concerned…questioning, and her hand instinctively went to her belly.

'What is it?'

She hardly knew how to say the words. Didn't know if she could.

*She was pregnant.*

*He didn't want this.*

'Lois, what did they say?'

She swallowed, confusing, conflicting thoughts swirling around in her head, none of them making any coherent sense.

*He didn't want children.*

*She couldn't tell him.*

'Lois, for God's sake. What did they say?'

'I'm pregnant.'

It was a strangled whisper. She dropped her gaze, not wanting to see the undoubted horror in his eyes.

He didn't speak, but she could hear that his breathing had deepened, feel the sudden tension in the air between them.

'You said you were on the pill.'

His voice was barely audible, but there was an unmistakable accusatory tone in his words.

'I was… I am. I… Maybe I forgot to take it once.'

Their eyes met. Lois searched for reassurance.

*Take me in your arms. Tell me it's all going to be okay.*

But neither of them could find words. A thick, heavy silence hung between them, palpable, like a barrier keeping them apart.

Max sat down in an armchair, his elbows on his knees, head in his hands, covering his face, muffling his words. 'This can't be happening…'

But it was.

She looked down at her hand, which lay gently, tentatively on her belly, where Max's baby lay nestled inside her…tiny, innocent…and unwanted by him.

*When had it happened? Had she forgotten a pill?*

She must have. This was her fault. And Max clearly thought so too.

'I'm sorry, Max. You don't have to be a part of this if you don't want to.'

He looked at her for a long moment, as though a million thoughts were flashing through his mind all at once and he was unable to make sense of any of them, as though he didn't quite recognise her.

'Maybe they're wrong.'

He relaxed slightly, as though that was the conclusion that made the most sense to him and there was still hope that this wasn't real.

But it *was* real. Her recent nausea, her reaction to the heat, the faint earlier… It all made sense. Anyway, somehow she *felt* it. There hadn't been a mistake. She was pregnant.

But Max was tapping on his phone.

'What are you doing?' she asked.

'Calling the clinic.'

'There's no mistake, Max. Think about it.'

He stopped dialling, but continued to stare down at his phone.

'I've had nausea; I fainted this morning. It all adds up. I'm pregnant.'

'You can't be.' He stood up, hands on top of his head, turning around to face the balcony, looking away from her. 'You *can't* be.'

'The casino…'

'What?' He spun round, looking at her, incredulous.

'We're meeting Art at the casino.'

'I don't think that's happening tonight—not now. Do you?'

'You should let him know.'

He sighed, shaking his head and reaching for his phone. 'I'll text him. I don't want to speak to him. I'll tell him you're still feeling unwell.'

'I'm not "unwell", Max—I'm pregnant.'

'Stop saying that.' He slammed his phone down onto the table. 'How the hell did this happen?'

'Seriously?'

'It was a rhetorical question.'

He sighed again, and paced out onto the balcony, bracing his hands on the railing and staring out to sea.

*Was she supposed to feel entirely responsible for this? If he thought that, he wasn't being entirely fair.*

She followed him, but stopped in the doorway before stepping outside. Suddenly there was a wall between them. He didn't turn around.

'I'm sorry, Max. You obviously don't want this. And of course you don't have to be a part of it.'

He swung around and stared at her, frowning as though she'd said something he didn't understand.

'You think I won't accept my responsibilities? If you think that, Lois, you don't know me at all.'

*Perhaps it was sinking in.*

'I'm just letting you know that I understand this isn't in your plan. I don't want you to feel you have to change anything... your new job, for example.'

He laughed harshly. 'You think this changes nothing? Lois, this changes *everything*...you have no idea.'

Lois looked down at her hands, at the dark pink polish on her fingernails. Because of her job, she could rarely wear nail polish, but she'd gone to the salon and enjoyed choosing a colour for their holiday. She'd been excited about spending a week in the sunshine with Max...not knowing this was how it would end.

With him out on the balcony, a wall around him so thick that even a battering ram couldn't break it down, and her somehow unable to take the few steps that would take her to be beside him.

Suddenly, Max was a million miles away. Soon he'd be five

thousand miles away for real. When he left for his new life. The life he'd worked so hard for, for so long.

'I know it does, but we can manage. You can still go to California, if that's what you want to do.'

But she didn't want him to. She wanted him to stay with her and the baby.

'I've signed a contract in LA.'

And he didn't want to stay, did he? He was telling her loudly and clearly that he didn't want her. He was rejecting her. He'd told her right from the start that he wasn't staying—that he had other, better things to do— and she'd understood.

But that had been before she'd fallen in love with him. Before the baby. Did she expect him to change his mind now?

*She wasn't enough for him to stay.*

'And you can still go there.'

They were the hardest words for her to say, but she had to give him the freedom he'd yearned for…

*Because she'd stupidly fallen in love with him.*

'It would be a lawyer's dream if I reneged on my contract at this stage.' He turned back to face the ocean, leaning on the railing. 'Damn it.'

'You don't need to renege on it. You can still go.'

'You just don't get it, Lois.'

'Then tell me. Tell me what I don't get. Because we're being confronted with a situation which most people would find joyous, and you're turning it into some kind of disaster movie for no good reason.'

Max pressed his palms to his face and drew in a long, slow breath before he looked at her again, his eyes glittering. 'No good reason?'

His voice was low and so quiet that it sent a shiver down her spine.

'Of *course* there's good reason. What did I tell you about my having children?'

'That you didn't want them.'

'I *can't* have them,' he corrected. 'Can you remember why?'

'You don't need to speak to me as though I'm five years old, Max. Because of the genetic risk.'

'There's a tenfold increase in the chance of this baby having valve disease. *Tenfold*, Lois.'

'But there's screening now—the screening will pick it up if it's there. And it may not even be there.'

Max threw up his hands. 'Well, that's great, then! The baby will have aortic valve disease...but at least we'll know about it in advance. Cool!'

'Even if the test is positive—which it might not be—the surgery can be done before birth.'

'Again, Lois, you haven't thought this through.'

*Why was he so angry?*

'I understand why you have concerns, but you're overreacting. The screening programme you've worked on all these years—'

'Was never meant to be used to diagnose a child of *mine*.'

'Look, I know you've never wanted this, but the reality is that this baby is coming now; it's real. And I for one am glad you developed the screening programme, because it might just save our child's life.'

'You can't have the test until twenty weeks.'

'I know.'

'Which is...when? Well, we don't know, do we? However many weeks from now... That's weeks and weeks of worry.'

'I'm not worried.'

He stared at her as though she was mad. 'Well, you should be.'

'Why?'

'Because there's a significant risk, Lois.'

Max took a step closer, so that they were almost touching, and lowered his voice further. It was carefully controlled, like a warning.

'And if there is a valve defect? Who do you think will do the surgery I've pioneered?'

She looked up into his eyes. Eyes that had lost the look of admiration she'd begun to grow used to seeing...eyes that now blazed with torment and anguish.

And then it hit her. 'There's only you...'

'And I can't operate on my own child.'

His voice was cold as ice and her skin prickled. She stared back at him. Into eyes that had lured her so many times. Eyes that had been so full of desire that she'd begun to believe that her mother and Emilio had been wrong. Eyes that now looked at her as though she'd let him down...in the worst possible way.

'I see.' She lowered her gaze.

'So how can I feel "joyous" about this?'

'You've trained others.'

'I'm *training* others—there's a difference. The plan is that after the trial is finished I'm going to return for a few weeks to complete any surgery that's needed, and train up Jay and a few others while I'm doing it.'

She flinched at his anger. If ever she'd daydreamed about telling the man she loved that she was having his baby, it hadn't been this that she'd imagined as the scene that followed. Tears pricked her eyes but she swallowed them away. She was having a baby. And it looked as though she was the only one of them who felt any joy about that. She didn't want the tiny life growing inside her to somehow sense that it wasn't welcome. Max wasn't thinking clearly, and she didn't want to be around that.

'I'm going to get changed.'

Picking up her dropped phone and handbag, she walked back to the bedroom, took off her dress and sat on the bed. It was a shock to him. Hell, it was a shock to her. Perhaps, in the morning, after a good night's sleep, when the initial shock had settled, they'd be able to talk more easily.

She rested her head back onto the soft pillows, curling her

legs up. There was no point in crying over spilt milk—this was happening and they both had to get used to it.

'Still ticking?' said Art Beauchamp, as Max pulled the stethoscope from his ears.

'Definitely ticking. Echocardiogram next.'

Max hadn't come to bed last night. He must have slept on the sofa in the lounge. When Lois had woken, he'd already showered and dressed and was sitting out on the balcony in the morning sunshine, reading something on his phone. When he'd realised she was walking towards him, he'd stood and announced that he was going for a swim on deck.

There had been no chance of any kind of conversation on the tender to the harbour, or in the car up to the hilltop clinic, as Art had accompanied them and chatted away about his latest film project.

Lois picked up the ultrasound gel which had been warming. 'Ready, Art?'

It was a relief to be in the cool clinic, away from the blazing heat of outside, but the atmosphere between her and Max was even cooler than the air being pumped out by the air con.

Art made a show of bracing himself as Lois squeezed gel onto his chest. 'Let me have it, Nurse.'

She smiled as he grimaced. 'Not too bad, is it?'

'It can be darn cold if it isn't warmed properly,' the actor faux-complained. 'I'm sure it can't be good for your heart, making you jump like that. So, how long have you two been an item?'

Lois glanced at Max, but he was turned away from her, concentrating on the echo images of his patient's heart.

*Were they an item? If they had been, the news they'd had last night seemed to have changed things...drastically.*

'I met Lois when I started my stint at the hospital in London.'

*That was very diplomatic...and vague.*

'Three months or so, then,' said Art. 'A long time for you, Max. You're not going to settle down on us, are you?'

*What was this? Some kind of confirmed bachelors' club? Should she remind them that she was actually there?*

Max removed the probe. 'Your valve is looking good.'

*Nice save.*

'Wonderful,' said Art. 'Wires next? And what was your lovers' tiff about?'

'Yep, an ECG next,' replied Max, wiping off the gel with a tissue and ignoring Art's last comment. 'And then we'll get some bloods sent off to the lab and you're all done.'

'Funny, isn't it?' said Art conspiratorially to Lois as she attached the ECG leads. 'How a heart specialist has never been able to sort out his own heart. Perhaps you'll be the one to fix him.'

'Keep still, Art,' said Max. 'I need to be able to interpret the trace, and you moving around like that is making it look as though a spider has crawled all over it.'

Art grimaced at Lois. 'Someone's rattled his cage. We'll have a good night tonight, Lois, even if this one…' he nodded towards Max '…is still in a strop. What's your game? Blackjack? Roulette? Poker?'

*None of the above.*

'I'm a complete novice,' she told him.

Art's eyes glittered. 'Awesome. Well, don't worry. You have a couple of old timers to teach you everything we know.'

'We have to fly home this evening,' said Max, tearing the ECG paper from the machine and scrutinising it. 'Something's come up.'

Lois stared at him, then quickly remembered that Art was on the couch between them, no doubt watching her reaction.

'Oh, that explains the bad mood, then,' said Art. 'Well, you're welcome to take the Gulfstream back. Let me know what time and I'll get the pilot organised. Work, I assume? Well, it won't be long before you come to LA, my friend, and leave all this on-call business behind you. Life will be much better then.'

'Nothing untoward going on there,' said Max, placing the ECG trace on one side. 'Remnants of your previous heart attack, but nothing new. Thanks, the jet would be great, but we can easily take a commercial flight.'

'A clean bill of health, then?' said Art. 'And no, no. I won't have you flying commercial; take the jet.'

'You'll live to fight another day. Thanks—any time this evening would be good. Now bloods—just rest your arm on the side, please. Tourniquet?'

Lois handed him a tourniquet. He took it without looking at her, wrapping it around Art's arm and feeling for a vein. She handed him the tray with the syringe, needle and blood bottles.

'Thanks, Lois,' said Art pointedly, making Max look up at him.

He pressed his lips together, saying nothing.

Lois smiled at Art. He'd clearly noticed the tension between them, and for some reason he was taking her side. But when he found out—if he ever found out—that she'd just ruined his friend's life, he'd maybe change his mind.

Max pressed a cotton swab into the crook of Art's arm as he withdrew the needle. 'We should get the lab results in a day or two.'

'I appreciate it, Max.' Art stepped down from the couch. 'I'll get them to call you when the flight's arranged. Make the most of your last few hours of sunshine.'

Max busied himself labelling the blood bottles on the other side of the room and Art touched Lois's arm as he headed for the door.

'Ignore him; he'll come round. Whatever you've rowed about, he'd be a fool to let it come between you for long. Max might be many things, Lois, but he's no fool.'

And with a wink, he was gone.

Art was right. Max was no fool. She watched him handing

the labelled blood bottles to one of the clinic staff and give them instructions. This time yesterday she'd been the patient and he'd taken care of her. He'd taken great care of her. And it had been quite overwhelming. But now, less than twenty-four hours later, it was as though he couldn't bear to even look at her.

And he'd cut their holiday short. It was over.

Was he going to cut her loose too? Or was he just in shock? Perhaps Art was right there too. Maybe he'd come round.

But coming round to the idea of having a baby he most definitely didn't want was a pretty huge ask.

# CHAPTER FIFTEEN

MAX NUDGED THE volume up higher, knowing it wouldn't fully obliterate any of the thoughts that were swirling through his mind at a hundred miles an hour, but hoping it might dull some of them.

Picking up the first flatpack box, and not bothering to read the instructions, he began to attempt to construct it. Lois was taking the rest of her planned leave from work, so he hadn't seen her in the few days since they'd got back from Monte Carlo. She'd sent him a text to say she was booked in at Queen's Hospital for a scan the next day at three p.m., and he was welcome to attend.

Should he go?

Probably—he had a responsibility.

Did he want to go?

Hell, no.

He wanted to turn the clock back and for all this to never have happened.

*All* this?

Including Lois?

None of this had been in the plan, had it?

Screening programme.

California.

New life.

That was the plan.

The packing box refused to play ball, and in frustration he threw it to one side. 'Goddammit!'

He had two weeks left before his flight left for LA and he'd barely made a start on packing. He'd found other things to do instead. Like extra shifts at work…extra sessions at the gym; the extremely well attended leaving do the staff had arranged for him—although Lois hadn't been there. He could have had all the packing done by now if he'd put his mind to it. So what had stopped him? Was something deep in his subconscious mind telling him he didn't want to leave?

He'd almost told Lois he loved her, hadn't he? He'd not quite got so far as to allow the words that had formed on the tip of his tongue escape from his mouth, but it had been close.

And that must mean something.

He did love her.

He wanted nothing more than to be with her.

Right now.

But he'd hurt her. From twelve years old onwards, his life had been spent trying desperately to ensure that no other family's lives would be destroyed. He'd worked hard to become a cardiac surgeon, created the screening programme, developed the foetal surgical technique, saved every patient he could.

He'd done all right.

He could never have hoped to undo what had happened to William, but he'd generated something good from something so bad.

Until now.

Now, he'd messed up big-style. He'd vowed never to have children so that he wouldn't be the cause of even more pain. So that he didn't hurt anyone else.

But now he'd done just that. And the person he'd hurt was Lois…the woman he loved…the woman he should have protected…the woman whose life had been turned upside down because of him.

\* \* \*

Queen's Hospital was unfamiliar territory…which was exactly why Lois had chosen it for her maternity care. There were the same familiar smells as in every other hospital she'd ever been in, though. Cleaning fluid, disinfectant, the faint floral scent of the air freshener being pumped out at regular intervals from the devices on the wall.

She'd been to Reception, checked in, changed into a hospital gown and now sat waiting to be called, her clothes in a plastic bag on the floor beside her.

Max hadn't shown up.

Every time the door had opened her stomach had lurched, but every time it had been someone else who'd come in— excited, happy-looking couples, fathers-to-be with a protective arm around their partners. But no Max.

She'd hoped that over time he might have moved on from the initial shock and come to terms with the fact that he was going to be a father. He'd said he wouldn't shy away from his responsibility, but that could have meant anything. Maybe he meant he'd send money—not that she wanted it. He was obviously still planning to leave to go to his new job in California— she hadn't been able to bring herself to go to his leaving do and had insisted she work the shift on the unit to allow others to go.

Doing this alone was a daunting prospect, but an exciting one too. She wanted this baby. If Max didn't, she understood why. Having a child had never featured in his life plan. He'd worked all his life towards the moment when he could leave London and begin his new life. That moment had arrived for him. And neither she nor the baby were enough to make him want to stay.

What was wrong with her that once again she'd fallen for a man who was completely emotionally unavailable? Would staying in London to be with her and the baby be such a bad thing? Not if he loved her. If he loved her, he'd change his plans—it wouldn't be a big deal.

But he didn't.

So it was.

The problem was, she'd fallen for him…and she was hurting.

She could never have believed it was possible to hurt so much.

Crushing, aching, desperate pain.

And anger.

At herself for having fallen for him.

And, illogically, at Max for making her do so.

Max strode quickly towards the radiology department. He was late, but he'd had to review a transplant patient who appeared to have developed sepsis. He'd dealt with the patient, written up the treatment plan, had him admitted and then had run to his bike, roaring across London to get to Queen's.

He knew his registrar could have dealt with the case, but as usual he'd been unable to walk away without making sure his patient was stable. Anyway, the patients helped him to focus. They took his mind off Lois. The second he wasn't with a patient Lois was there, filling his senses.

*Lois.*

The woman he just couldn't get out of his mind.

No matter how hard he'd tried.

She'd tempted him to want things he'd ruthlessly taught himself not to want.

Happiness. Family. Love.

Falling in love with her had been too easy.

So easy he hadn't even seen it coming.

Which meant his defences—usually titanium grade—had been down.

Completely.

The coolness between them was killing him. It seemed to have been mutually agreed without them saying anything at all to each other. It had somehow just happened.

But it was for the best.

That was what he'd repeated to himself as he'd packed and got ready for his flight...as he'd tried to fall asleep at night... as he'd found himself pulling on his helmet and revving his bike, ready to go over to her place and tell her he loved her.

But he'd turned off the engine and gone back inside.

Because, although he desperately wanted to speak the words he'd never spoken to anyone else, he couldn't face her.

Because she'd tempt him all over again.

And he'd only hurt her.

*Again.*

He saw the sign: *Maternity Ultrasound Department.*

He swallowed. Suddenly, his feet were glued to the floor. What was he doing here? This was something he'd never wanted. Something that had never, ever been in his grand plan. But Lois was in there. The woman he loved. Going through this...because of him.

'You going in, love?'

He turned and saw a woman in a cleaner's uniform smiling up at him.

'Come with me. I'll show you where to go. First time, is it?'

'First time...? Yes,' he replied, still rooted to the spot.

'Aw, come on...don't be nervous. They might be able to tell you if it's a girl or a boy. It's amazing what they can tell these days.'

A girl or a boy. If that was the only question that needed answering he might be able to move his feet and go and do what he should be doing—being with Lois.

The woman held the door open for him, smiling kindly. 'Have you got a preference?'

'Pardon?'

'Boy or girl?'

'Oh, no...not really.'

'As long as it's healthy,' she said. 'That's all any of us want, isn't it?'

His chest tightened. 'Yes,' he managed. 'That's all we want.'

Somehow, his feet carried him to the waiting room.

She wasn't there.

He was too late.

'Can I help you?' asked the receptionist.

'Lois Newington. Her appointment was at three…am I too late?'

'Are you Dad?' The receptionist smiled at him kindly, but his stomach lurched at her words.

*Dad.*

A word he'd never thought would be associated with him.

He wanted to run.

He wanted to see Lois.

'Yes…'

'She's in room four. You're not too late. Georgie! Would you take this gentleman to room four, please?'

Heart hammering, he pushed the door open.

Lois was lying on a couch in the darkened room. The sonographer was poised, with the probe ready to scan, but paused as Max entered.

'Hello?' The sonographer looked at him.

'This is Dad,' said the nurse called Georgie, who stood in the doorway just behind him. She gave him a nudge. 'You can go and sit by Mum to watch the scan.'

'Thanks,' he replied as she left.

*That word again.*

'Hi,' said Lois.

'Hi.'

*Was this real?*

He pulled a chair over and sat down, staring at the as yet blank ultrasound monitor.

*What was he doing here?*

'You made it, then?' said Lois.

'Yes.'

'You okay?'

A pause. 'Yes,' he replied. 'You?'

'A little excited,' she replied.

She was smiling. Her eyes were bright, her cheeks flushed. She looked beautiful…radiant.

'Ready?' said the sonographer.

'Very,' replied Lois.

Max watched as the ultrasound probe made contact with Lois's abdomen. He looked up at her face…the face he loved… watching as she smiled when she saw her baby for the first time.

And then she frowned.

She gaped, her hand flying to her mouth.

*What? What was it? What had she seen?*

The heart valves wouldn't be visible at this stage.

His stomach lurched and he turned sharply to the screen, realising instantly why Lois had reacted with such shock.

'Well, you two seem to have worked it out for yourselves,' said the sonographer, smiling broadly. 'You're having twins!'

Joy and anguish collided—conflicting emotions crashing into each other. Horror. Fear. Wonder. There were so many questions he couldn't answer. So much instant and terrifying fear and anger that he didn't know where to begin.

He wanted to take her in his arms.

He wanted to close his eyes, open them again and for this not to be happening.

This was all his fault. He'd known he must not have children. He been warned to let the horror that had destroyed his family die out with him. He'd been told time and time again not to pass it on.

And now that was exactly what had happened.

History would repeat itself.

His worst nightmare.

No. It was even worse than that.

He'd done this to the woman he loved. He was the direct cause of a whole new nightmare that would affect even more lives.

*When would this ever stop?*

'Are they okay?' asked Lois.

'Everything's looking fine so far,' replied the sonographer.

'From what you can tell at twelve weeks,' said Max.

It would be another two months for the cardiac screening. Two...long...months. Of worry. Of wishing he wasn't the cause of it.

'Of course,' replied the sonographer. 'We'll get you booked in for your next scan before you leave today. But in the meantime you can relax, because everything looks fine...with both of them. Would you like a photo?'

'Please,' said Lois.

She was beaming...joy shining out from her.

'Here you go.' The sonographer handed a black-and-white image of the twins to Lois. 'Pop back through to the changing room, and when you're ready they'll book you in for your next appointment.'

She left the room, leaving them alone.

Lois was looking at him, and he saw her joy slowly evaporate.

'They're fine, Max.'

'You can't say that, Lois. We don't know that. It'll be another two months before we know that.'

'And there's no point in worrying over it until we do know,' she replied, sitting herself up and swinging her legs over the side of the couch. 'Why spend two whole months worrying about something that might never happen?'

'Because the statistics—'

'Are just statistics,' she replied, easing herself off the couch and slipping her feet into her shoes. 'I'm not going to waste time being worried. If there's a problem it'll be picked up and dealt with—in the meantime, I'm going to enjoy being pregnant.'

Brave Lois. His brave, sassy Lois.

The temptation to take her into his arms and allow the words that were suddenly on the tip of his tongue to be said was enormous.

*I love you.*

They were the words he should be saying right now. They were the words Lois deserved to be hearing.

And he couldn't say them.

Because Lois deserved so much, and he wasn't the one who could provide anywhere near what he wanted for her. How could he care for her when he couldn't even care for himself? How could he give her security and protection? And as for love... The only people he'd ever loved, he'd hurt. And the latest proof of that was standing right in front of him.

What Lois and the babies would be put through because of him was something he'd have given anything to avoid. But avoiding it would have meant he'd never have got to meet her at all. And the thought of that was physically painful.

# CHAPTER SIXTEEN

LOIS HAD NEVER seen anyone visibly pale the way Max had done when the twins had appeared on the screen. He'd just looked at her, his jaw tight, a vein at his temple pulsing hard. And, as much as she might have wanted him to, it had been clear he wasn't going to take her into his arms and tell her everything would be fine.

And that had hurt.

They'd gone their separate ways after the scan. She back home and Max back to work. She'd watched him leave, striding out towards the bike lockers without looking back.

Taking the scan photo out of her bag, she looked at it, a smile spreading across her face. She traced the outline of the babies' heads with her finger. She was going to have to do this alone. It was scary and exhilarating at the same time.

Now there were two babies, and only one of her. How was she ever going to manage all by herself?

She knew Max well enough to know that whether he wanted this or not he'd still feel responsible. And he'd want to do the right thing. What he thought the right thing was, she didn't know. But it clearly wasn't staying in London. Whatever it was that they'd had together had gone. It had been nothing more than a summer fling.

Had she repeated what had happened with Emilio? Stupidly allowed herself to fall for empty compliments and be swept away by the charms of a charismatic, emotionally disconnected man?

It was too easy to think that. Thinking that would reduce Max to the same level as Emilio, and that just wasn't the case. Max had meant what he'd said. He'd single-handedly slayed the dragon that her mother's words had created and that had been with her ever since she'd said them. Max had taught her to truly embrace her curves, to genuinely appreciate herself for who she was—to free herself from the chains of her past and believe in her own worth.

And she loved him for that. She always would. Even though he hadn't loved her enough to want to stay and make it work between them.

Placing the photo on the coffee table, she sat down on the sofa. He hadn't left yet but she missed him already. Glancing around the room, she took in the familiar objects…shelves full of books, knick-knacks from her travels. Candles, cushions, throws and rugs scattered around. It was her sanctuary—a cornucopia of the things she treasured. And it had felt complete with Max there. As if he'd been the final addition it had needed…the final treasure.

Before he'd arrived at St Martin's she'd expected an arrogant, egotistical surgeon—and she'd thought she'd witnessed that on day one, when they'd met. But little by little she'd begun to see chinks in his armour…clues to the man underneath the cool titanium plating he seemed to wear, and to the deeply caring nature that he chose to hide.

And the reason why he hid behind the impenetrable wall he'd built around himself was clear—he'd learnt to close his emotions down because the people he'd loved most in the world had closed down on him just when he'd needed them most. He could easily have given up—flunked school, never done anything with his life—and who could have blamed him? But he hadn't done that. He'd chosen a much more difficult path to walk. He'd tried to create something good out of something terrible.

Training to become a cardiac surgeon was tough, but he'd done it—even without his parents to support him. And now he'd come through again, with the screening programme. Max Templeton had been through hell and had responded by being more successful than most people ever got to be. And even though he still wore his armour, there were small fissures that, if she looked hard enough, she could peer through. And what she'd seen had made her want him even more.

But he was leaving. And although knowing that had been her safety net when she'd allowed him into her life, what she'd seen since then had made her realise that, actually, she really wanted more time with him.

In challenging, life-threatening situations on the ITU, when he showed what some might see as over-confidence, snappiness and even egotism on his part, she saw what was really going on in his head... He was simply concentrating. Giving everything he had to save his patient and remembering what happened with William.

But Max had made it clear from the start that he was going to a new life in California. He'd set out the boundaries of their... *What had it been?* An affair? A liaison? A summer fling? And finding out she was having his babies hadn't changed that. She wasn't enough for him. But that wasn't news...she'd known that from the start.

There was a knock at the door.

# CHAPTER SEVENTEEN

'MAX!'

'Can I come in?'

She opened the door wider and stood back. 'Of course.'

He kicked off his shoes and walked through to the lounge.

'Would you like a coffee?'

'I'm not staying.'

She lowered her eyes and his stomach clenched—it was just a tiny hint that once more he'd hurt her.

'Okay. Well, have a seat anyway.'

He sank into the sofa and she sat down beside him with her feet curled up beside her in the way she always did. Candles flickered in their little glass jars. Everything was as it had always been. Like a home. Only one thing was different.

There was a new photo.

Black and white.

On the coffee table.

Propped up in front of a pile of books.

Their twin babies.

*Please be okay. Don't let me have cursed you.*

'You okay, Max?'

'We should talk.'

'Okay…'

But his carefully rehearsed words had disappeared without trace—had abandoned him just when he needed them.

The decision he'd come to had been easy to make. He was

going to be a father and he had to face that…even though everything about it terrified him. What good could he be to any of them? He'd already hurt Lois and given the babies a heart condition that meant they'd need surgery even before they were born and would need monitoring and treatment for their entire lives.

He'd done enough damage, and now he needed to do whatever it took to put that right.

'It's my last shift tomorrow,' he said.

'Yes, I know. I'm not on shift so I won't see you.'

'I just wanted to see you before I go…to let you know what I propose.'

'Right.'

Her eyes searched his. She was waiting for him to say more.

'I'll come back for the twenty-week scan, so that I can supervise the screening and the surgery—even though I can't actually do it myself.'

'You don't need to do that.'

'I'm not going to shirk my responsibility, Lois. You know the risks you're facing, and I'm the one who's best placed to oversee things.'

'You're still talking as though the twins have the condition. They might be fine.'

'I'm glad you think that. But, as I've told you, the statistics show—'

She stood up, her eyes flashing with anger. 'Stop! I refuse to worry about something that may never happen. You don't need to come back to London once you've left. I don't need you to. It's more than obvious that you don't want anything to do with me or the twins…so just go. I absolutely refuse to allow you to come back here out of some sort of misplaced sense of responsibility. You feel guilty, Max, and that's crazy—this took both of us. I don't want you to come back just because you feel guilty.'

'You have no idea what I feel.'

His voice was low. Guilt was only one of the myriad emotions that had been keeping him awake at night. Try adding remorse, shame, anger and fear—that would be a little nearer to the mark.

Her eyes glittered. 'So tell me,' she said. 'I'd love to know, Max... You're such a closed book, I really have no idea. Why is the fact that we're going to be parents so bad? Why do you have to be so damn negative about this?'

'William died because of me.'

*Why was he telling her this?*

This wasn't part of the speech he'd so carefully prepared.

She took a step back, away from him. 'What do you mean? Of course he didn't. He had a heart condition.'

'He collapsed in front of me...and I didn't do anything.'

'You were twelve years old, Max. You couldn't have done anything.'

'I could have called an ambulance...started CPR. But I didn't. I froze...did nothing.' He plunged the knife deeper into his heart. 'I did nothing to help my brother.'

Lois stared at him as though he'd confessed to murder. He might as well have done.

And then her face and her voice softened. 'You were a child, Max. It wasn't your fault.'

He rubbed the back of his neck. 'I didn't save him.'

And he couldn't look at her. Because he could hear pity in her voice and he didn't want to see it in her face. He didn't deserve it...didn't want it. He focussed on the candle on the table, which flickered its orange glow onto the photo of the twins.

'Would you expect a twelve-year-old today to save someone if they had a cardiac arrest?'

Of course he wouldn't.

He shook his head. 'That's not the point.'

'But it is, Max. It's exactly the point.'

Her voice was soft, full of concern, empathy and understanding. But he didn't want any of those things. He deserved to pay for his mistake.

'It's a completely unrealistic and totally unfair expectation that you've put on your twelve-year-old self.'

*William would be alive today if he'd done the right thing— done something—protected him. He didn't deserve forgiveness. He'd pay for his failings that day for the rest of his life. And rightly so.*

'You don't need to spend the rest of your life trying to put right what happened, Max. You were a young child. You're entirely blameless.'

The orange flame from the candle flickered more strongly, as though a breath of air had passed over it.

No one had ever said that to him before. At the time, everyone had been so wrapped up in the horror of what had happened no had stopped to wonder if he felt guilt as much as he felt grief. Until now. Until Lois. But still he couldn't look at her.

'This is why you've reacted to the pregnancy like this, isn't it? Max, when William collapsed you couldn't possibly have known what had happened or what to do. You didn't do anything wrong or bad. You found yourself, through no fault of your own, in a situation which most adults and even many medical professionals would find extremely difficult. You didn't do anything wrong. You're a good person.'

His throat constricted and his mother's scornful face and disparaging words came back to him.

Anger welled up inside him and he couldn't hide it when he spoke. 'I'm *not* a good person, Lois. William was my twin. I should have been there for him and I wasn't. I ruined everything.'

'No, you didn't. It was a tragedy, but it wasn't of your making.'

He laughed…a harsh, sneering laugh. 'Try telling my mother that.'

'She doesn't blame you.'

And then he saw her expression change from one that showed

she was sure about the truth of her words into one of confusion and then horror as she looked into his eyes.

*'Does she?'*

Everything had been padlocked securely away in a vault in his head for over two decades. All the grief, the pain, the guilt. Now suddenly the padlock had snapped open, and the demons inside the vault streamed out as his mother's words ricocheted in his mind and fired like bullets from his mouth…

*'"Why didn't you do something, Max? What were you thinking…? Nothing? You've destroyed us. Your father died of a broken heart because of you. Don't ever have children of your own and destroy another family. You have to make sure this gene dies out with you."'*

His voice cracked on the final words and he glanced at Lois.

'Don't feel sorry for me, Lois. I hear what you're saying, but she's right. I vowed then that I'd make damn sure I never did this to another family…and now that's exactly what's happened. So how the hell can I be happy about it?'

She didn't need to speak. Her face told him what she was thinking. She was horrified. And so she should be. But better she knew what he was —knew that there was something so inherently wrong with him that even his own mother hated him. He dropped his gaze. He'd seen all he needed to.

'Max.'

Her voice was soft, gentle, but his fists clenched in response. He didn't want her pity.

'She's wrong.'

She took a step towards him, placed her hands on top of his fists and he looked at them. His knuckles were white.

'Look at me.'

But he could only gaze ahead, over her shoulder, at the candle in the little votive jar, its flame dancing happily as if nothing had happened…as if he hadn't just fired decades worth of hurt at her and finally ended everything they'd had. They'd had a summer of bliss together and he'd fired a missile at it.

Lois lifted his chin, forcing him to look at her. There was no pity in her eyes. Just truth, honesty and genuineness. And the tension that had clenched every part of him began to release its grip and melt away.

'William will always be with you, but you have to let go of the guilt.'

He shook his head. 'It'll never leave me. Maybe you're right, and my mother shouldn't really blame me... I don't know. But she's right that it is my responsibility to make sure I don't curse another child with the gene that could kill them and destroy those they leave behind.'

'William wouldn't want you to live with this burden on your shoulders.'

'It's been there for so long now that it's just part of who I am.'

'You can change. Let me help you to do that. Can I hold you?'

She looked uncertain, and he wondered if she realised just how she'd challenged him. He wanted nothing more than to be held by her. He wanted to be able to allow her to soothe his twelve-year-old self, who'd never been soothed by anyone. She got him. She understood. And he was grateful to her. In love with her. But he wasn't ready to forgive himself. In fact, he was even less likely to forgive himself now. Because now he was responsible for wrecking even more lives.

'I should get back.'

'To work? It's eight p.m.'

'I need to check on a patient with sepsis.'

He knew she wouldn't be able to argue with that. Even if she wanted him to stay, she'd have to let him go for a patient.

'Oh, okay. Will you come back after?'

'No.'

She nodded and took a step back. 'When is your flight?'

'Thursday.'

Two days. One more shift.

'Okay.'

He took her in for what might well be the last time as his heart broke in two...as he clenched his fists against speaking those three words... The three words that he'd both wanted and not wanted to say all summer. Even if he couldn't love her in the way she deserved, he should tell her he had done, in his own way, this summer. He'd fallen in love for the first and last time...with her. She should know that.

He got up from the sofa—the sofa big enough to fit a family of four.

*Tell her.*

But his mouth was dry. He walked out through the kitchen, clenching his fists harder, his nails digging into his palms.

*Last chance, Templeton. Now or never.*

He reached the hall and slipped his shoes on.

She was standing behind him. He wanted to hold her.

But he'd done enough damage.

She deserved to know that she'd been more than a summer romance. She was having his babies.

'I did love you, Lois.'

And before he could register her reaction, he opened the door and walked out into the street...out of her life.

# CHAPTER EIGHTEEN

THE NURSES' STATION was decked out in good luck balloons and there was a huge cake in the office with a golden film award on the top, and lettering which said *Good Luck in Hollywood!*

The staff had certainly pulled out all the stops, but the only genuine smile Max had managed all morning had been when he'd reviewed Harry Weston and seen that his patient had turned the corner after his sepsis diagnosis. It looked as though he was going to make a full recovery.

He'd smiled plenty, of course—how could he not when the staff had made such an effort for his send-off? But the smiles hadn't been because he was excited and looking forward to leaving London and starting his new life in California.

Today was supposed to feel good.

Tomorrow, when he boarded the plane, was meant to be the happiest day of his life so far.

But today didn't feel good.

And tomorrow wasn't going to be the happiest of his life.

Why?

Why, when this was what he'd worked his whole life for, dreamt about, wished would happen sooner?

He looked up at the bouquets of balloons bobbing on their ribbons and smiled at Daisy as she walked past the nurses' station.

Because he'd made the biggest mistake of his life...and there was a pretty high benchmark already.

*What have you done, Max? You've walked away from the only woman you've ever loved.*

Idiot.

The story of his life.

'You coming to cut the cake, chief?' Jay was beaming at him. 'And I think they're expecting a little farewell speech.'

'I'm just checking some results.'

'Your transplant chap?' Jay sat down beside him at the desk as he scrolled through his patient's latest bloods.

'Yeah, white cell count is much better. Looks like he'll be okay.'

'Excellent,' said Jay. 'Come on, then. Let's go and get your swansong done whilst we've got both the early and the late shift here together.'

'I'll pop in in a bit,' he replied, still scrolling.

'Not putting it off, are you?' asked Jay. 'Are you having second thoughts about leaving us? Because if you are, you know there'll always be a place for you here.'

'Thanks, Jay; that's kind.'

'It's not kind,' the older surgeon replied. 'You're an excellent surgeon, Max—any hospital would welcome you with open arms. I just hope that California appreciates you. I know working over there has been your goal for a long time, and even though it'll be very different, and will take some getting used to, there comes a time in life when you have to do what's right for you—make that leap of faith, take a risk and do what will make you happy.'

Max looked up from the screen. Being with Lois made him happy. Looking into her eyes, holding her, having fun with her. This summer had been the happiest time in his life since...

'So, if you've thought it all through, and you're doing what's right for you,' continued Jay, 'then you have to go in search of what will make you happy.'

Lois made him happy.

So why was he about to throw all that away? Why couldn't he be happy about this pregnancy as Lois was?

*Why was that so hard?*

Suddenly everything seemed clear. How had he not seen it before? Lois was where his happiness lay. It wasn't in California.

*What had he done?*

Yes, he was terrified that the babies might have the same heart condition William had had. Yes, he was devastated that he was the cause of all this worrying and waiting, and the tests and possible treatment for Lois and the twins. And no, maybe he wasn't good enough for her—maybe he wasn't capable of bringing her the happiness she deserved. But everything was a risk. Life was a risk. And sometimes you had to take a risk to grow, to learn, to achieve something worth having.

And Lois was worth taking a risk for. She was worth risking everything for.

It might be way too late, but suddenly he knew what he needed to do.

He logged out of the computer and stood up. 'I need you to cover for me.'

'What? There's a party waiting for you.'

'I'll come back later,' said Max, sliding his stethoscope from around his neck and pushing it into his pocket. 'I need to do something first. Cover for me, Jay…please?'

'Of course,' said Jay. 'I'm only catching up on paperwork this afternoon, anyway, so take as long as you need.'

'You're a star,' replied Max, clapping him on the shoulder as he handed his bleep over to him.

His happiness lay with Lois…and the babies. Yes, there were risks involved, but if taking them gave him even half a chance at spending the rest of his life with Lois they were worth taking.

All he had to do now was tell her, hope she'd forgive him, and hope that she'd be prepared to take a risk on him too.

# CHAPTER NINETEEN

LOIS LAY ON her mat amongst twenty other mums-to-be, who were at various stages in their pregnancies, listening to the yoga teacher's soothing but instructive voice telling them the importance of box breathing.

'In for four…hold for four…'

Lois held her breath, and had counted to seven before she opened her eyes to check if the suddenly silent yoga instructor was still there.

She was, but she was staring towards the door at the back of the room and blinking as though she couldn't understand what she was seeing.

Lois turned her head as everyone else did.

And gasped.

At the same moment everyone else did.

Max.

He stood there in the doorway.

Large as life and as devastatingly handsome as ever.

*What was he doing here?*

And how had he known she was here? The only person she'd told was Natalie. She'd confided everything to her friend yesterday, telling her not to say anything to anyone.

Ever since the first night they'd slept together she and Max had made sure that no one knew of their affair. She hadn't wanted to be in the papers, labelled as the latest notch on his bedpost, and Max had wanted to make sure that any publicity was focussed only on the screening programme rather than his personal life.

'Can I help you?' The yoga teacher had flushed a deep pink. 'Are you looking for someone?'

'I'm looking for Lois.'

There were more gasps. Deep blue laser-like eyes looked at her, and those pesky butterflies flew into action in her stomach.

Max didn't move.

'I've come to tell her that I love her. And that I'm sorry for being so stupid. And that, if she'll have me after everything, I want to stay here to be with her and the twins. Not because of some inbuilt sense of duty...but because I want to. More than anything.'

Lois sensed without seeing them that all eyes were suddenly focussed on her. He loved her. He'd said the same when he'd come to her flat after the scan. But he'd said it so quickly and then he'd left—and he'd said it in the past tense. But this was now. He was saying it now. He wanted her and he wanted the babies.

She rose to her feet.

The room was silent.

Max stood watching her, his eyes never leaving hers as she walked towards him.

She hadn't been just a summer romance.

He hadn't been rejecting her.

He'd been scared because he'd hurt her and he'd just needed more time to realise what he wanted.

To make his choice.

And he'd chosen her.

She picked up her pace and walked towards him, almost running the last few yards as he opened his arms and she flew into them. There were cheers, whistles and clapping and his arms closed in around her, pulling her in towards him.

'I think we just went public, Max.'

'I think it's about time we did. There's a leaving party going on at the unit right now. If you're sure about this, we could go there…tell everyone the good news.'

'Good news?'

'May I?' He held his hand over her belly.

She smiled, grasping his hand and guiding it, her smile widening as he touched her and looked at her, admiration in his eyes.

'Yes, good news, Lois. The best news. I've loved you for a longer time than I realised and I already love these two. What more could I ever have asked for?'

'I love you too, Max.' She turned back to the class. 'I may just duck out a little early, if that's okay? See you all next week?'

There was a chorus of 'Bye!' and 'See you next week!' And Max took her by the hand, holding the door open for her and letting it close quietly behind them.

'How did you find me?' she asked.

'Long story.' He grimaced. 'I tried the flat, but of course you weren't there. I called you, but there was no answer. So I rang Toby and asked for Natalie's number, spoke to her and she told me. Don't blame her—I was very insistent.'

Lois laughed. 'I won't blame her. Can we talk before we go into work?'

'Of course; let's sit here.'

There was a shady bench under a tree whose leaves were just showing the first signs of autumn, glowing orange in the early-afternoon sunlight.

'So what changed your mind?' asked Lois, sitting down and placing her gym bag on the seat beside her.

'It wasn't sudden, if I really think about it. It had been happening slowly…ever since I met you. The thought of California and the new job lost its sparkle…bit by bit. The more I got to know you, the less I wanted to leave.'

'But you seemed so determined to go…even yesterday.'

'I couldn't bear it that I'd hurt you.'

'You didn't.'

'I also couldn't bear it that I might never see you again. So I had a dilemma.'

'In what way?'

'I could run away, so that I didn't have to see what I was putting you through. Or I could spend the rest of my life regretting that and wondering if we could have been happy together.'

'You're not putting me through anything I don't want to go through, Max. I'm *glad* we met. I'm *glad* we had an amazing summer together.' She placed her hand over her belly. 'And I'm glad we're going to be parents to these two.'

'And are you glad I came to find you and made you the centre of attention just then? Or, since the show, have you realised that you *should* be the centre of attention? That you deserve to be?'

A woman walked past with her dog and did a double-take when she saw Max.

'I guess I'll have to get used to a bit of attention if I'm with you.'

'There are a few other risks in being with me.' He placed his hands over hers on her lap and looked deeply into her eyes. 'I can't offer any guarantee of a roses-round-the-door future.'

'Well, that makes us a good match…because neither can I. But what we *can* guarantee each other right now is that we love each other—and that's a pretty good starting point, if you ask me.'

# CHAPTER TWENTY

LOIS TRIED DESPERATELY to slow her heart rate as the ultrasound probe made contact with her ever-growing belly. Max squeezed her hand and gave her a reassuring smile. But she knew that he was more nervous than she was. He'd tried to hide his fears over the two months they'd needed to wait to have the screening scan, but she knew he felt responsible for their shared nervousness.

Increasingly, over the last couple of weeks as the appointment had approached, he'd not slept well, and she'd awoken a few times at night and found him pacing around downstairs, wide awake. He'd tried to tell her that he was concerned about a patient, and she'd allowed him to think that she believed him. But, although he cared deeply about his patients, she knew what the real cause of his sleeplessness was. He was worried about the twins…and about her.

If either or both of the twins had the heart condition, she knew how he'd react. He'd be devastated. But she'd be there for him and they'd all get through it…whatever happened.

Jay Vallini stood to one side of the cardiac radiologist, watching the screen intently. The older consultant had given strict instructions. Today, Max was not a cardiac surgeon. Today he was a father, and he was there to support Lois. So Max had done as he'd been told and was now holding her hand rather than making a diagnosis.

Jay had been right when he'd assured Max that if he wanted to stay on as a consultant at St Martin's he'd be welcomed with open arms. Max had managed to get out of his contract in LA, and had signed a full-time contract at the hospital. And he really had been warmly welcomed as a permanent member of staff.

Their relationship had been warmly welcomed too. One or two of the staff had said they'd sensed there was something between them. And Tom had hugged her and said he wished he'd put money on it because he'd 'just known'.

In a few moments they'd have the answer to the question that had so nearly been the cause of their break-up. Max's realisation that his love for her far outweighed his fears and his guilt over what might or might not happen with the twins' health, and the fact that he was willing to risk telling her he loved her, was what had saved them.

The pressure of Max's grip on her hand increased. She looked at him and he managed a smile...managed not to divert his gaze from her and go into doctor mode and scrutinise the screen. He was trusting the two consultants who were doing that for them. And he was being there for her.

She steadied her breathing.

'Would you like to hear twin number one's heartbeat?' said Jay.

'Please,' replied Max, still looking at her. His jaw was tight, but somehow he was managing a small smile...for her.

And there it was. The first heartbeat...fast but regular.

'Twin number one is fine,' said the radiologist, still staring at the screen.

*De-dum...de-dum...de-dum.*

He moved the probe to twin number two and the sound faded before being picked up again.

Lois held her breath and closed her eyes.

*Please be okay.*

There was a long minute while the radiologist took measurements.

*De-dum...de-dum...de-dum.*

'And so is twin two. They're both fine—no heart issues whatsoever.'

Lois opened her eyes. Max had let his head fall back, and his eyes were closed. But when he opened them and looked at her his eyes shone with a fusion of relief, gratitude and the release of weeks of bottled-up dread and fear.

She smiled at him. He cared so much…about all of them. 'They're okay, Max.'

He nodded slowly.

'We're going to nip out and give you two a few moments,' said Jay.

'Thank you…both of you,' said Max, his voice thick with emotion.

'So your mother was wrong, Max. You didn't need to vow never to have children. You have two healthy children right here.'

'And *your* mother was wrong, too,' he replied, smiling at her. 'You're the most perfect, beautiful, gorgeous woman in the world, and you're going to be an amazing mum…and wife… if you'll have me.'

'Wife?'

'I know this isn't the most romantic proposal in the world… maybe I'll have to whisk you away somewhere more special and repeat it another time to make up for it… But I love you, Lois Newington. Completely. I want to build a life with you and raise our family together. Will you marry me?'

He hadn't let go of her hand even for one second throughout the whole procedure and he still held it now. And she knew that she could trust him never to let it go…*ever*.

'You don't need to whisk me away somewhere more special, Max. Where could be more perfect than the place where we found out we're having two healthy twins? Yes, of course I'll marry you.'

And as she lifted her arms, and he bent towards her to take her into his own, she took a long, deep, contented breath, drawing him in, knowing that she'd be able to do that for the rest of her life.

# EPILOGUE

EVEN AT ONLY eighteen months old, the twins were proper water babies. Lois laughed as she placed a tray of drinks down on the table by the outdoor pool, watching them splashing around with Max in the sunshine.

Moving to the countryside had been a joint decision. Max continued to practise in London, but they had a huge house and an enormous garden for their growing family to live in. And with baby number three on the way, it was proving to be a good move.

'Come on in,' called Max, dodging as the twins, with delighted squeals, threw the beach ball at him in turn.

Lois slipped the sarong from her shoulders and kicked off her flip-flops. The blue swimsuit didn't hold her in all the right places, because she was four months pregnant and no swimsuit would. But it didn't matter. Max loved her just as she was. And she knew that because he told her every day. And if he didn't tell her, he showed it. In all sorts of ways.

'Mummy, throw ball!' called William, batting the brightly coloured ball with his chubby little hand.

Max waded over to her where she sat on the edge of the pool, dangling her legs in the water. 'Coming in?'

'I might just sit here and watch.'

She loved watching Max with the children. It only strengthened the knowledge that she'd done the right thing that day when he'd come back to tell her he loved her…loved her so much that he'd been prepared to hurt himself to protect her.

'Mummy, in pool,' said Isabel, kicking her legs ferociously to propel her and her inflatable ring towards her.

'Mummy's coming in.' Max took her by the waist, lifting her into the water as she laughed. 'Let's get her all wet, kids.'

William and Isabel squealed with laughter as they splashed her, laughing even more as Lois made unsuccessful attempts to shield herself from the watery onslaught.

'My hair!'

But Lois knew there was no point in trying to object. It would just make all three of them scream even louder with laughter and try even harder to soak her completely. But she didn't mind. Max had turned her world upside down and given her a life she'd never even dared to dream of…a family she couldn't have loved more if she tried.

'Your hair is perfect, Mrs Templeton.' Holding her to him, he kissed her. 'And even if it wasn't, I'd still fancy you like crazy.'

Somehow the twins had managed to manoeuvre themselves in their inflatable rings so that there was one on either side of them, trying to elbow their way between them.

'Mummy! Dada!'

They both laughed.

'Well, just remember where fancying me like crazy got you last time,' said Lois, glancing down at William and Isabel and grinning.

'It got me a life more perfect than I could ever have imagined and I wouldn't change a thing. I love you, Mrs Templeton.'

'Love you t—'

But Lois couldn't finish her sentence, because suddenly the twins, moving as one, as though having planned it with some sort of twin telepathy, splashed her with such a volume of water that her words were swallowed with a mouthful of pool water.

Squeals of delight told her that her shocked expression must be hilarious, and joining in with their laughter was impossible not to do.

'Oops…' said Max, grinning, his dark hair even darker for being wet and his blue eyes sparkling with joy.

She scooped up a handful of water and it flew in a glittering arc, cascading over all four of them in sparkling, sunlit droplets. Over her family. Her whole world.

\* \* \* \* \*

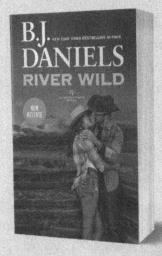

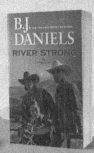

# Subscribe and fall in love with a Mills & Boon series today!

You'll be among the first to read stories delivered to your door monthly and enjoy great savings.

WE SIMPLY LOVE ROMANCE

# MILLS & BOON

## JOIN US

## Sign up to our newsletter to stay up to date with...

- Exclusive member discount codes
- Competitions
- New release book information
- All the latest news on your favourite authors

> ### Plus...
> get $10 off your first order.
> *What's not to love?*

Sign up at **millsandboon.com.au/newsletter**